RUNAWAY BRIDES
The
Cowboy's
Honor

AMY SANDAS

sourcebooks
casablanca

Copyright © 2019 by Amy Sandas
Cover and internal design © 2019 by Sourcebooks, Inc.
Cover art by Gregg Gulbronson

Sourcebooks and the colophon are registered trademarks of
Sourcebooks, Inc.

Published by Sourcebooks Casablanca, an imprint of Sourcebooks,
Inc.
P.O. Box 4410, Naperville, Illinois 60567-4410
(630) 961-3900
Fax: (630) 961-2168
sourcebooks.com

Printed and bound in Canada.
MBP 10 9 8 7 6 5 4 3 2 1

This one is for Halcyon, my wild child. Joyful, silly, full of adventure and courage. Thank you for always reminding me to laugh, dance, and take time for cuddling. Love you.

ONE

Emmanuel Church
Boston, Massachusetts
June 14, 1882

COURTNEY ADAMS STOOD PERFECTLY STILL IN FRONT of the full-length, gilded mirror while her mother adjusted the pearls around her neck. The other attendants had already gone to find their places, so it was just the two of them in the private preparation room.

"Mother…"

Beverly Adams shifted her attention from the pearls to the lace detail on Courtney's bodice.

"Mother…" Courtney tried again, just a bit louder this time but certainly not loud enough to bring her mother's censure. A lady had to control her tongue and speak in modulated tones at all times. Even if she was feeling intense emotions.

Especially if she was feeling intense emotions.

She knew she was supposed to smile and accept whatever came next, but she simply couldn't contain the questions and concerns buzzing through her any-more. And she was running out of time.

"Mother, how did you know Father was the man you should marry?"

Mrs. Adams glanced up, allowing a frown to tug only briefly at her elegant brows before she smoothed her expression back into one of placid dignity. "What a ridiculous question, Courtney," she replied, then stepped around behind her daughter to smooth out a few wrinkles that threatened to ruin the elegant fall of Courtney's gown.

Courtney should have expected the response, but she didn't think it was a ridiculous question at all. Surely, it was natural for a bride to have a few misgiv-ings on her wedding day.

She watched her mother's movements in the mirror. Mrs. Adams was not an emotionally demon-strative person, but Courtney hoped that maybe on this day—the day of her wedding—her mother might have some words of wisdom or encouragement.

But she had now focused her attention on Courtney's hair with a fleeting press of her narrow mouth. It was the only indication of her displeasure and could be easily missed by the casual observer. But Courtney had had twenty-one years to become familiar with the expression, and she had no need to question the cause.

Courtney's pure white gown showed off her lively green gaze and red hair to dramatic effect. Beverly Adams valued subtlety in all things. Unfortunately, subtlety was not something Courtney had ever been able to accomplish—not in her appearance or in her often-exuberant personality.

She tried again. "How can I be sure I will be happy with Geoffrey?"

For a moment, it seemed her mother was going to ignore the question, but then she stopped fussing with Courtney's appearance and lifted her hazel gaze to the mirror.

"You could not hope for a better match than Geoffrey Cabot. He is young and charming. He is also dedicated to charitable work and is active as a community leader. Your union has been arranged since your childhood and will strengthen bonds and increase the fortunes of both of our families."

Courtney was well aware of all those things. "But what about happiness? What about passion?" she asked, finally giving voice to her true concerns.

"Such things have no place in this discussion or any other," Mrs. Adams replied in a tone that was both dismissive and coldly admonishing. "Respect and consideration are the true hallmarks of a successful marriage."

The words were familiar to Courtney. Her mother had been preaching such maxims since she'd come of age. Not long ago, she would have been comforted by the reminder. Having been betrothed to Geoffrey nearly all her life, she knew her future husband to be a compassionate man who never failed to offer a lovely compliment or two at every encounter.

Not many young women were lucky enough to marry a man they could honestly call a friend.

So why did she feel such a heavy press of dread in her chest? Why did she feel as though she were being forced down a path she no longer wanted to travel?

"Alexandra found passion in her marriage, and I have never known her to be happier."

"Do not mention her name to me." Her mother's voice was low and frigid. "Alexandra Brighton disgraced her family and ruined her good name when she ran off. You will not use her as an example for *any* behavior, do you hear me?"

There were so many things Courtney wanted to say. Alexandra was one of her very best friends, and just last summer, she'd run away from a perfectly acceptable fiancé in favor of adventure and romance with a bounty hunter in Montana. Courtney thought what Alexandra had done was the bravest thing she'd ever heard of. But her mother would never think so.

This had been a pointless endeavor. Trying to talk to Beverly Adams about anything beyond familial obligation would never get her daughter the reassurances she so desperately needed.

Courtney shifted her gaze back to her own reflection. "Of course, Mother," she replied.

"Good. Now, no more nonsense."

After a thorough sweeping glance, her mother gave a brief nod and provided a final bit of instruction. "Keep to a sedate pace and maintain your posture. Eyes forward. No smiling."

As motherly words of support went, they left much to be desired. But Courtney should have known better than to expect more.

"Yes, Mother."

Her mother turned and walked away. With a near-silent click of the door, Courtney was left alone for the first time that day.

In less than twenty minutes, she would be walking down the long aisle of her family's church toward a man she had been betrothed to since she was two and he a young boy of eight.

There might not be a grand love between them, but such emotions rarely existed in the unions among their social set.

Expecting any more—*wishing* for more—was not done.

Except...that's exactly what Courtney *had* been doing.

At their last encounter, she'd even gathered the courage to ask Geoffrey why he'd never tried to kiss her.

He'd laughed. Not a great guffaw, which would have been far beneath his dignity, but a soft chuckle, as though her inquiry was all part of some private joke they shared between them. He had patted her hand and given her a gentle look as he said, "Such demonstrations are not for us, are they?"

She had smiled back, but his words had haunted her ever since.

What did he mean, such things were not for them? She had asked for a kiss. Was that so odd a thing for a young woman to request of her future husband?

She had spent her whole life preparing for this day, feeling nothing but gratitude for being fortunate enough to have such a young, handsome, and charming gentleman as her fiancé. Yet now that the day had come—she was finally marrying Geoffrey and starting on a new phase of her life—she felt...dissatisfied.

A knock on the door startled her from her

troublesome musings. Courtney swept across the room in a rustle of silk and satin, grateful for the distraction.

A young errand boy stood outside.

"Hello," Courtney said, greeting him with a smile. "May I help you?"

"I, ah…" the boy stammered, his eyes wide as he blushed a deep red.

He was quite young, and Courtney suspected he was not accustomed to whatever task he'd been given. She noticed that he clutched two letters, one in each hand. She gave a nod of encouragement. "Are you here to deliver a note?"

"What? Oh, yes, miss." The boy looked at the two letters, his gaze flying from one to the other and back again. Then he thrust one of them forward. "Here. This one is for you. I was instructed to wait until you were alone."

Courtney smiled again as she took the letter he extended. Before she could offer him a token in thanks, he sped away.

The handwriting on the sealed note was Geoffrey's. It had been addressed simply to *My Beloved*.

A spark of warmth flickered inside her. He had never called her that before. That he would be so thoughtful as to send her a note in the last moments before they were to wed made Courtney feel instantly guilty for the seeds of dissatisfaction she had allowed to grow.

See, she thought as she tore open the seal. *He loves you after all.*

She didn't dare sit down to read the message. Not after her mother had smoothed every detail of her gown into perfection. So she took to strolling sedately back and forth across the room as she eagerly read Geoffrey's last words to her before their wedding.

My Dearest Beloved, he began, and Courtney couldn't contain the warm flush of pleasure at the effusive greeting. Perhaps he had just been waiting for this day to declare his more amorous feelings.

It is with a heavy heart that I prepare for my wedding day, knowing it takes me that much farther away from a life of happiness with you. I can barely stand the thought of vowing my everlasting devotion to another woman when you are all I have and ever will desire.

Courtney's heart seemed to stop beating as her breath caught mid-inhale.

The letter had not been meant for her at all. The note must have been delivered to her by mistake. She immediately wanted to stop reading. The words were too personal, too intimate. Her possession of them felt like a violation of the deepest privacy. But she couldn't put the letter down, couldn't look away from Geoffrey's distinctive script swirling over sentiments he had never—and doubtless would never—express to her.

Despite the circumstances that will make me a husband to another, I will always and forever belong only to you. You are the light in my heart, the fire in my soul. I hate that we must continue to hide this love. Though I wish it could be different, I can only assure you with every devoted breath I take that our

*love will not weaken during the hours we are apart.
It will only flourish in secret until those rare and
beautiful times when we can be in each other's arms.*

*Loving you endlessly,
Geoffrey*

Courtney stared at the letter until the words blurred, rereading it over and over to assure herself she wasn't imagining what she saw. There was no way around it.

Her fiancé's dedication to his secret lover was undeniable—his love and passion laid out in black ink upon pure white paper.

Oh my God, she had been so *stupid*.

Here she had been trying to convince herself that it was simply Geoffrey's nature to behave so conservatively. She had been desperate to believe deeper emotion might eventually grow between them...once they became more comfortable with each other as husband and wife.

The letter made it painfully clear how foolish she was to harbor such hopes.

He was already passionately in love with someone else. And he had no intention of bringing that relationship to an end. Not now, on the day of their wedding. Not ever.

Courtney's marriage to Geoffrey would never be more than her mother had intended it to be—an advantageous union between two powerful families.

An icy sensation spread through her veins, her hands going numb.

For a second, she wished she hadn't read the letter. She wished she could be standing before her mirror, still in possession of a thin thread of hope that something like love might develop between her and the man she was to marry.

But she *had* read it. The words were burned into her mind. There was no erasing them.

What on earth was she supposed to do now?

As soon as she thought the question, she heard her mother's voice in her head. *Nothing. You do nothing beyond what is expected of you. Destroy the letter. It does not change a thing.*

It changes everything! Courtney mentally shouted in response.

She turned back to the full-length mirror.

The young lady in the reflection wore an elaborate gown ordered straight from New York City. An all-white configuration of satin, brocade, velvet, and lace. Layered and draped in artful display around a figure so stiffly corseted there simply was no allowance for bad posture, despite her mother's constant concern. Two strands of pearls encircled her throat, and more were clasped around her wrist. Pearl drop earrings swung delicately from her ears.

Her hair, only a slightly more subdued shade of red than it had been in her youth, was perfectly coiffed atop her head with the popular orange blossoms adorning the piled curls. Her veil was a waterfall of tulle falling to the floor behind her. And her expression was set in the calm, placid lines she had been trained to present despite whatever might be running through her thoughts or ravaging her heart. Nothing was more uncouth than an honest display of emotion, after all.

The mirror offered up the perfect image of the hopeful bride.

But inside...disillusionment rolled through Courtney like a crushing wave.

The truth of what her life would look like as Mrs. Geoffrey Cabot had suddenly become crystal clear.

According to all the criteria set by her mother and society, there was no denying it was an excellent match. The wealth and privilege she would continue to be afforded as Mrs. Cabot was more than many people could ever dream of having. And there was still the promise of respect and consideration.

It should be enough.

But it wasn't. She *wanted* love. She wanted passion and adventure and excitement.

Love, happiness, and all her dreams come true.

Things she would never have with her husband.

Could she accept such a future?

Did she have a choice?

Did she have a choice?

Her eyes widened in the reflection. Her lips parted as she drew in her first true breath since reading Geoffrey's misdirected note.

She had a choice.

Alexandra's flight from Boston and the resulting broken betrothal to a man of immense fortune and prestige had been the greatest scandal of last year. People had speculated about it for months, but eventually life had gone on.

And Alexandra was now enjoying a grand and

passionate love with the man she was meant to be with. She had run away and had claimed her happily-ever-after.

What if Courtney did the same?

Her gaze darted to the casement windows lining the wall of her room.

Running away was not something she had ever thought to consider, but in that moment, it seemed like her only option for true happiness—if she was brave enough to claim it.

Everyone would think her mad. Her mother would never forgive her. But if she settled for anything less than *everything* she wanted, she might never forgive herself.

I have a choice.

With a burst of unnatural energy, Courtney pulled her veil from its pinned moorings and tossed it to the floor. Then she dashed to the window, released the latch, and swung the casement wide. Thank God she was on the ground floor and a drop of only ten feet or so greeted her when she leaned through the window and looked down. She could manage that.

She did not have to marry Geoffrey. She did not have to commit herself to life with a man who would never truly want her.

She did not have to end up like her mother. Passionless, resigned, stiff and unfeeling.

Sitting on the ledge of the windowsill, Courtney tucked her legs through the opening, sweeping her many layers of satin and lace over the edge until they draped toward the green lawn below. She closed her eyes for a moment, taking a deep breath. Then with an odd little laugh and no further thought, Courtney braced her hands on each side of her hips.

And pushed off.

TWO

Open range near Lawton Ranch
Montana Territory
June 25, 1882

"SHIT."

Dean Lawton swept his Stetson off his head and smacked it against his thigh. It was only morning, but the sun's rays were already hot enough to cause perspiration to soak into the collar of his shirt and bead across his brow.

It wasn't the heat of the summer sun that had his blood boiling, however.

He had been heading home after spending the last couple weeks out on the range. He rarely got away from his office and all the responsibilities that kept him close to the ranch, but the long days of riding had been exactly what he'd needed to clear his head after a big fight with his brother over mail-order brides, of all things. He'd been reluctant to come in, but tomorrow was his monthly trip to town for supplies and news.

He'd still been a few hours out from the homestead

when he'd come upon what could only be described as a scene of senseless slaughter.

Nearly a half dozen cattle killed and left to rot on the open prairie.

Dean scanned the devastation, one hand clenched into a fist.

Cattle rustling was not uncommon. It was an expected risk when herds were allowed to roam freely over thousands of acres with only a distinct brand declaring what ranch they belonged to. But rustling was done for profit. The stolen cattle were taken and rebranded so they could quickly be sold at market before their loss was noted.

This was different.

The murderous destruction Dean was looking at churned his stomach. It served absolutely no purpose. And it wasn't the first time. Worse yet, if his suspicions about who was responsible were correct, it likely wouldn't be the last.

Dean swung down from his horse to walk among the carcasses, surveying the violence up close. He didn't expect to find any of the animals alive, but he felt the need to check every one anyway. Maybe he'd finally find some evidence—some solid proof— and he'd know for sure whether his suspicions were correct.

Please, God, let me be wrong.

His men were all beginning to wonder what Dean intended to do to stop the killings. And perhaps more importantly, why he hadn't done anything yet.

He shoved his fingers through his hair and squinted against the sun as he looked out over the open range.

Always decisive on matters regarding the ranch, Dean knew his hesitation was sure to make his men speculate. As boss, he couldn't afford to lose their confidence or respect. But the matter of the slaughtered cattle was not something for which he had a ready solution. Especially not if Anne's family really was behind it all.

Sick with anger over the senseless killing, Dean turned away from the violent scene. He'd have to get some men out here to see to the carcasses. Leaving them would risk the spread of disease and discord—neither of which he could afford right now. He'd lost too much of his livestock already. And his lack of forthrightness in dealing with the matter had put the confidence of his men at risk.

Setting his hat firmly back on his head, he mounted his horse and rode hard the rest of the way home, whatever peace he'd managed to find out on the open range long gone.

∞

The next morning, as Dean hitched up the wagon for the ride into town, the thundering hoofbeats of an approaching rider had him looking up to see his brother heading toward him.

The last time he and Randall had been face-to-face, they'd nearly come to blows—something that hadn't happened since they were kids. Time to himself had gotten Dean past his anger, but he'd been on edge since finding the dead cattle. If his brother knew what was good for him, he'd avoid any mention of brides.

Dean finished hitching the wagon just as Randall drew his horse to a stop alongside him.

The younger man tipped his Stetson back with his thumb as he leaned forward and gave Dean a wide grin. "Still mad at me?"

"What do you want, Randall?" Dean asked as he checked the girth on each of the horses.

His brother sighed. "Pilar said I needed to apologize for butting my nose into your business. I know I got your dander up with my little suggestion, but you had to know it was made with good intentions."

"I don't need your good intentions. I need you to mind your own damn business."

"You *are* still mad."

Dean scowled before turning away to jump up into the front of the wagon. He wasn't mad, but if Randall kept it up, he'd likely get there.

"Shit, Dean. You can't go on like this forever, you know."

"Like what?"

"All ornery and serious. You need a little happiness in your life."

"I'm happy enough."

"Bullshit."

Dean gave his brother a hard look. He knew where Randall was coming from, and deep down he appreciated it, but dammit—he didn't need him interfering. Dean had his own way of doing things. He *liked* his way of doing things.

"I still think it's a good idea," Randall insisted.

"It's a terrible idea."

"Getting married changed my life for the better."

"My life is fine the way it is," Dean countered. "You should know the last thing I'd ever do is order some fancy Eastern woman out of a catalog like she was some spare part for a plow. What were you thinking?"

"Well, it's not like there are a whole lot of women around here to choose from," Randall argued. "I'm lucky I found Pilar down in Texas."

"I don't. Want. A wife," Dean said with a growl of frustration as he flicked the reins to start the wagon in motion. "And I'm not gonna keep having this same damned argument."

Randall looked like he wanted to push the issue, but shockingly, he didn't.

As Dean drove away, Randall called out from behind him. "Oh, hey! I almost forgot. Can you pick up a special package for me at the post office? You'll know it when you see it.'"

Dean gave a nod but didn't bother looking back. Instead, he kept his gaze focused down the long dirt drive that took him to the main road into town. Long prairie grass waved gently alongside him and the scent of wildflowers drifted on the summer breeze, but Dean was too irritated to take much notice of the land he'd loved all his life.

It was long past time for Randall to give up on the crazy idea that Dean needed a wife.

He had Lawton Ranch. It was his responsibility to ensure that his granddad's legacy remained as prosperous going into the future as it had been in the decades before Dean took over. With the issue of the slaughtered cattle requiring resolution, Dean had more than enough to deal with right now.

THREE

A LITTLE GIRL WITH TWO MESSY BRAIDS TIED WITH yellow ribbon leaned toward her mother to whisper loudly, "But why is she dressed like that?"

The mother cast a weak smile of apology in Courtney's direction as she leaned toward her daughter to whisper in a much lower voice. Her words still managed to carry quite well in the confined space of the stagecoach despite the constant rumble of the wheels over the road. "I don't know, but I do know it isn't polite to talk about people."

Courtney maintained an imperturbable expression and turned her attention to the dust-covered window. The child's question was innocent enough, but Courtney had already gone through all the curious stares and probing questions she wished to endure from her fellow passengers.

Yes, she was wearing a bridal gown. *No*, she did not have any luggage or any personal belongings at all. *Obviously*, she was running away. *And no*, she wasn't sure she had made the right decision.

At least the child tried to whisper. Some of the others had been much bolder.

"I think she needs a bath," the girl added in the same loud whisper.

Courtney resisted the frown tugging at her brows. Perhaps the child wasn't so mannered after all.

Though she wasn't wrong.

Courtney had never been so dirty in her life. Not to mention tired and sore from being tossed about as the stagecoach raced over the dusty plains from one stop to the next. She hadn't had a good meal in far too long. And she was desperately trying to hold off the uncertainty that had been threatening to overwhelm her in recent days.

The adventure and excitement of being on her own had sustained her quite well in the beginning. She had thought herself quite clever when she'd located a jeweler's shop on her way to the train station in Boston and exchanged her pearls for cash. With her optimism high, she'd soon been settled in a private car as the train rattled away from the Eastern Seaboard toward new lands and a new life.

But the more time she'd spent alone, staring out the window at scenery that passed far too quickly to appreciate, the harder it had been to hold back her doubts. Hoping to distract herself, she'd managed to acquire what she needed to write a couple letters.

The first was to her parents, apologizing for the distress her abrupt departure had likely caused them. She doubted any explanation she could provide regarding her decision to flee her own wedding would be enough to make up for what she had done, but she wanted them to at least know she was all right.

Her second letter was to Geoffrey.

She hadn't realized that she still clutched his own letter tightly in her fist until she'd gone some distance from the church. And then she'd taken the first opportunity to discard the love note.

In the end, she decided to be completely honest with her former fiancé. Geoffrey had been a friend to her once, after all. She explained the misdirected note and declared her desire for something more in a marriage and in her life.

Giving words to her feeling had been a liberating experience.

But it had only kept the creeping doubts at bay for a short while.

Courtney had always been so assured of her place in the world. She had never lacked for friends, activities, or opportunities to show everyone how charming and witty and gracious she could be. Without all of that— without the trappings of a world she had rejected— what did she have to offer?

These thoughts of uncertainty and self-doubt were her only companions during the long, solitary days in her private train car. Yet she almost preferred them to the curious stares and constant questions she'd received once she'd transferred to the stagecoach for the remainder of her journey.

The man beside her shifted position yet again. He'd been doing that consistently since he'd gotten on the coach two stops back. An older man near forty, dressed in a brown suit and bowler hat, and with slightly bulging pale eyes, he'd introduced himself as Mr. Martin. If she'd known what a brief nod of acknowledgment would trigger in the man, Courtney would have made sure to avoid even that.

He'd started out in the seat across from her and had proceeded to make himself a nuisance all day, asking questions and giving her leering glances. He'd even changed seats at the last stop to sit right beside her. With the coach filled to capacity, there was nowhere for her to go. She was already pressed up against the side of the vehicle.

He shifted again, and the hand he had been resting on his knee just *happened* to graze Courtney's thigh.

She was already sitting ramrod straight, thanks to her constricting corset, but somehow she managed to stiffen even more at the contact. It was on the tip of her tongue to loudly and succinctly berate the man for his forward behavior. But the desire to avoid a scene was too deeply ingrained in her and everything he did was so subtle, he could easily claim it an accident and her response an overreaction.

He did it again. This time, his upper arm pressed briefly to the side of her breast.

She was going to go mad.

Before the heat of her temper rose any higher, the coach rolled to a jostling stop. Almost immediately, the doors opened.

"Everyone off," the driver called from outside.

There were a few annoyed glances and some low-muttered grumbling from the other passengers, but they started disembarking all the same.

"Have we arrived in Helena?" Courtney asked hopefully, but the others were too busy gathering their things and making their way from the coach to respond.

"Allow me to assist you, ma'am." The smell of cheap cigars and sweat assailed her nostrils as Mr. Martin leaned indecently close to speak directly into her ear.

Courtney grasped the edge of the door and hoisted herself forward. "I'm quite all right," she replied as she stepped—or stumbled, rather—from the stagecoach to the dusty street. Giving an impatient sweep of her arm to gather the trailing skirts of what had once been a pristine white wedding gown, she stepped up onto a wooden boardwalk. While the other passengers collected their belongings, Courtney, who had no possessions to worry about, glanced around.

The town they had arrived in consisted of only one street. A dirty, dusty street with a row of buildings running along each side and houses scattered beyond. From the way Alexandra had described it in her letters, Courtney had expected Helena to be…bigger. It was late morning, and a good number of townspeople were out and about in the summer sunshine. A few of them had stopped to watch the travelers disembark from the stage and were now staring unabashedly in Courtney's direction.

It took every bit of self-control not to roll her eyes. Goodness, had no one ever seen a wedding gown before?

As the driver of the stage hoisted a bag onto the boardwalk beside her, Courtney asked, "Excuse me, but have we reached Helena already?"

Without glancing up, he said, "No, ma'am. This is White Sulfur Springs."

"What? But I bought a ticket to Helena."

The driver shrugged. "Last stop," he said, then

turned back to the coach to take another bag being handed down from the top of the vehicle.

Courtney was left standing there in uncertainty.

She regretted yet again not being more frugal with her limited funds. She was down to her last few dollars, and now it seemed she might be stranded in this little town. Panic started to rise in her chest, but she refused to allow her emotions to get the better of her. There had to be something she could do.

She'd sent a telegram from Billings before getting on the stagecoach, notifying Alexandra of her expected arrival in Helena. Although Alexandra and her husband preferred to travel about, exploring the territories they both loved, her friend had mentioned in her last letter that she intended to be at her father's home near Helena for an extended visit over the summer.

Now that she wasn't going to make it that far by stage, Courtney needed to let her friend know where she was. Maybe Alexandra would be able to send someone to come fetch her.

Doing her best to ignore her personal irritation and physical discomfort after so many days of travel, Courtney took another look around.

She noted signs declaring a dentist's office, a general store, a saloon…but nothing indicating a telegraph office.

Then she saw the post office.

Perfect. She'd send a letter to Alexandra. It would take a few days to get to her, but it was better than nothing. Hopefully, she had enough money for a hotel room and a few meals to get her through until her friend came for her.

Clasping her hands together to hide the dirt

smudges on her elbow-length white gloves, Courtney tipped her chin up and walked confidently toward the post office. Fully aware that her trailing skirts were passing over the rough wooden boards, she told herself it didn't matter. She had tried for a while to keep the gown as immaculate as it had been when she'd set out, but the effort simply grew tiring in its futility.

Stepping into the post office, Courtney resisted the urge to sneeze. Dust from the street hovered in the stifling air. A counter ran through the center of the room, separating the shelves of postal packages and letters in the back from customers entering at the front. Courtney approached the harried-looking man behind the counter with a faint smile.

"Good afternoon. I would like to post a letter, please."

"The rates are over there," the man replied as he gestured toward a sign hung on the wall without even bothering to look up.

"I am afraid I must write the letter first," Courtney said. "Do you perhaps have some paper and ink I may use?"

The man looked up then. His eyes went curiously large, and he immediately straightened to full height, which happened to be a few inches shorter than Courtney.

She'd gotten that same look of incredulous surprise so many times over the last weeks that it really shouldn't have bothered her any longer. But it did. Keeping her expression placid, she forced a sedate smile.

The clerk blushed. "Ah…well, ah, let me see here." He started to scurry around behind the counter. "We don't usually keep such things on hand, but, ah…yes!

Here we are." He withdrew a small scrap of paper and a lead pencil nub and slid both across the counter.

"Thank you. It shall only take a moment."

She scribbled out a quick note, telling Alexandra that the stage would not be reaching Helena after all and that she was stranded in White Sulfur Springs, and could her friend please send someone as quickly as possible to fetch her? She didn't intend for the letter to sound desperate and impatient, but there was no hope for it. She *was* desperate and impatient. After folding the sheet, she carefully addressed the outside and set the letter in the bin initially indicated by the clerk.

"Two cents, please."

Discreetly withdrawing the proper coins from where she had them tucked into her glove, Courtney paid the postage fee.

"Is there a hotel in town where I might procure a room for a few days?"

"Miss Mabel has a boardinghouse down the road, though I don't know for sure if she's got any open rooms."

Courtney smiled her thanks to the postal clerk, already envisioning a quaint but comfortable room with clean sheets on the bed. Maybe even a hot, tasty meal. She had given up on finding food that was near the same quality she was accustomed to, but she would settle for edible and filling right now. She couldn't very well expect a rugged town in the Western Territories to provide the same levels of comfort as a big city back East. She had left Boston in search of a new life. It was time to embrace all of what that meant.

As she stepped onto the boardwalk, blinking against

the bright summer sunlight, Courtney didn't realize she had stepped right into someone's path until it was too late.

And of course, it had to be Mr. Martin.

What should have been just a very brief bumping of elbows and shoulders became much more when he took swift advantage of the encounter by wrapping his arms around her in an exaggerated and unnecessary attempt at steadying her.

Courtney immediately put her hands up to try to shove him away, but her efforts were ineffectual. He was intent on holding her close.

"It's my lovely traveling companion," he exclaimed. His face was so close that she could feel the heat of his breath on her cheek. "What a pleasure to run into you again so soon."

"I would thank you to release me, sir."

"Not yet, sweetheart. I never did get your name."

"And you never will. Now let me go," Courtney stated more forcefully. Her stomach turned in distress as she glanced around to see if there was anyone who might come to her aid.

"Let the lady go."

Despite their low timbre, the words were spoken from behind her in such a hard and forceful tone that Mr. Martin's grip around her waist loosened as though on command. She did not waste time in giving a solid push against his chest and wrenching free. She quickly backed away from Mr. Martin's grabby reach, which brought her closer to her unknown rescuer.

Turning to acknowledge the man who had come to her aid, all she saw was the expanse of a broad male chest covered by a faded blue cotton shirt. The scents of horse and leather and sunbaked earth filled her nostrils. Distracted and still a little distressed, she felt her foot catch in the twisted length of her skirts on her next step, and she started to stumble. Warm, rough, capable hands grasped her arms as the stranger held her secure until she regained her balance. A low sound escaped the man's throat as his hands dropped away.

"My apologies," he muttered as he stepped back from her. The velvety texture of his voice soothed and flustered at the same time.

Courtney took a deep breath, trying to regain her composure after the discomfiting experience of being handled so familiarly first by Mr. Martin and then by the tall stranger. She wasn't used to such treatment… but while Mr. Martin's *assistance* had caused only irritation, this stranger certainly deserved her thanks. She corrected her posture and made sure her expression was perfectly neutral before she lifted her chin, prepared to utter a swift expression of gratitude.

The words never made it past her lips.

In fact, everything—her train of thought, her breath, time itself—just *stopped*.

The man stood a few inches taller than her and wore a wide-brimmed cowboy hat that blocked the sun, giving her an unimpeded look at one of the most handsome faces she had ever seen.

His skin was bronzed from exposure to the sun, and a hint of sandy-brown beard shadowed a hard jawline and square chin. Though his mouth was pressed into a firm line, it didn't disguise the masculine beauty of his arched lips beneath a well-shaped nose and strong cheekbones. His features were put together in a way that was rugged yet undeniably attractive.

But his eyes—pale blue like a summer sky brushed with wispy clouds—were what had given her the intense little shock of awareness. It was like being woken up from a hazy dream. Everything just suddenly become more vivid, more…awake. His gaze held a hint of impatience as he looked down at her from beneath a furrowed brow.

While she stood dumbfounded, he swept his stunning gaze over her person.

His hard expression tensed even more as he took in the sight of her elaborate wedding gown before finally returning to her face. Only now, instead of impatience, she saw the glimmer of something more in his eyes.

She had to consciously tell herself not to react to the way he eyed her so openly. Keeping her expression calm and unruffled under this man's intense regard was not an easy task, especially now that she was dealing with strange little sparks that had ignited beneath her skin everywhere his gaze had fallen.

She was accustomed to inciting admiration in the gentlemen of her circles—she had been told she was beautiful often enough throughout her life to believe it was so. But she could not say she had ever inspired the flash of irritation she noted in his eyes when he finished his perusal.

He sent a focused glare toward the post office behind her before looking down at her once again. "You've gotta be kidding me," he muttered, his smooth-textured voice a strange contradiction to his harsh visage.

He was scowling. At *her*.

The tingling sparks of attraction coalesced into a ball of indignant fire that seared a path through her center. Her balance and composure now restored, she tipped her head and mimicked a tone her mother most often used when she was discussing fortune hunters and social climbers. "I beg your pardon."

"As do I," Mr. Martin stated in irritation.

Courtney had completely forgotten he was there.

Why *was* he still there, anyway?

"The lady and I were having a little chat," the odious man continued. "There is no reason for you to butt in."

The cowboy kept his focus on Courtney. "You wanna continue your chat with him?" he asked with a jerk of his head.

"I do not," Courtney replied without hesitation, and the cowboy gave Mr. Martin a dark look.

"You heard her."

There was only a brief pause before Mr. Martin gratefully took himself away. Courtney released a subtle breath of relief. She would have again attempted to offer her thanks, but something in the stranger's manner stopped her.

His expression had turned suspicious now that it was just the two of them standing there on the boardwalk. "Tell me you're not one of those Eastern brides."

She could not believe she had briefly thought his voice was soothing. There was nothing in his tone but a harsh, abrasive command.

Courtney did not respond well to commands. "I do not have to tell you a thing," she replied, her tone as sharp as his. "You are a complete stranger to me."

He was not deterred in the slightest. In fact, his cool eyes became even more direct and intense. "That's a wedding dress."

She met his gaze, refusing to be cowed by his rudeness. "It is."

"And you just got to town?"

"I did."

"From where?"

"Boston." Courtney wasn't sure why he was asking so many questions. She was even less sure why she was answering them.

"I knew it," he snarled beneath his breath. "Randall's gone and done it this time."

The derision in his tone put her on the defensive, but his comment simply confused her. Best to retreat—nothing good would come of this.

"I do believe this conversation has run its course. Although I appreciate your assistance just now, I should be on my way. If you'll excuse me." Courtney made as if to step past him, but he essentially blocked the boardwalk and clearly wasn't budging.

If asked whether Courtney Adams was prone to disagreeable displays, anyone of her acquaintance back home would have offered endless protestations to the contrary. Courtney was known for being consistently bright, effervescent, joyful, and pleasant. She charmed people with her smile and set them at ease with her light and amusing banter—when she wasn't following her mother's instructions to be placidly polite.

No one knew that, in contrast to all her outward pleasantries, she possessed a fierce temper that she often had to work diligently to prevent from rearing its head.

This was one of those times.

The muscles of his jaw bunched and released as he lowered his chin a fraction, causing the brim of his hat to shadow his face. "Why are you here?"

Courtney bristled. "I came west to start a new life," she answered in a tone that dared him to challenge her further.

He gave a short grunt that she didn't even bother to interpret.

His body—lean and muscled, dressed in cotton and denim—was taut with what she could only identify as extreme aggravation. His features were tense, and his eyes were hard. She was equally tense, though it was from a sense of disorientation that she did not appreciate. Nor did she particularly appreciate it when he swept those eyes over her once again. Slowly this time, taking in every detail—from her torn and dusty hem to her soiled full-length gloves to her less-than-elegantly coiffed hair—before coming back to meet her gaze.

His stark assessment left her stunned. She'd felt the coldness of his startling gaze, and she'd felt his disdain. She had never been treated with such disrespect, and the burning fire of her temper flared hot within her.

"Now, if you do not mind stepping aside," she continued in a sharp tone, "I must be on my way."

"You've got somewhere to go?"

Courtney glanced down the road in the direction of the boardinghouse. "Of course. I just need to wait for my escort to arrive."

He huffed an angry sigh. "That'd be me."

Courtney had to concentrate intently to keep her eyebrows from shooting upward in shock as she stared at the man still blocking her path. His shirtsleeves were rolled up to his elbows, and the muscles of his forearms were dramatically defined by the way his arms were crossed over his chest. She had no idea what to say.

"Pardon me?"

"I've been sent to fetch you." He said the words as though they contained a bitter taste, and he wished not to keep them in his mouth any longer than he had to.

"You?" she asked, her eyes widening.

Alexandra must have known the coach would not make it all the way to Helena and arranged for this man to see her the rest of the way. She *had* traveled this route before, Courtney reminded herself.

The cowboy—who still hadn't bothered to offer his name—glanced across the street, and his scowl darkened. Courtney followed his gaze to see that Mr. Martin stood on the opposite boardwalk staring at them with an angry, almost jealous look on his face. A trickle of unease teased the back of her neck.

"Look, none of this was my idea, and I ain't happy about it. But you're my responsibility now, so you'll have to come with me until I figure this mess out."

The man's rudeness was unparalleled. Courtney could not imagine why Alexandra would have sent this ill-mannered cowboy to pick her up, but if he was here to see her to Helena, she supposed she should be grateful. At least she would not have to sit in this dusty town any longer than necessary. This challenging journey would soon be over. The thought had her brightening considerably.

She straightened her spine and even managed a smile as she replied. "I wish you would have indicated that sooner. I would be happy to go with you. Unless, of course, you haven't quite finished interrogating me," she added with a lifted brow.

Rather than being chastised, however, he pinned her with a hard look. "You're gonna have to lose that high-and-mighty attitude of yours quickly enough out here. No one's gonna stand for it long."

Her temperature rose a couple degrees as she squared off and sent a hard look right back at him. "But I suppose I am expected to endure *your* overwhelming rudeness?"

"You'll have to endure a helluva lot more than that, princess. A woman like you, out here…" He didn't bother finishing the thought, as though the rest of what he'd say should be obvious. "If you weren't ready for the challenge, you shouldn't have signed up for it. You may as well head right back to where you came from."

Courtney had nearly had enough. It took every bit of her mother's training to keep her from stepping up to the man and giving him a true piece of her mind. Instead, she spoke in even tones. "I can't go back," she said. "But I assure you I will manage just fine."

For a second, it seemed he might refuse. With a hard gaze, he glanced around them, as though assessing whether he could just leave her there.

He wouldn't, of course. Alexandra wouldn't have sent him if she didn't trust him to do his job. Perhaps it was just his nature to be rude and contrary.

After a moment, his expression changed. The lines of irritation bracketing his mouth and weighing on his brow slowly shifted into a reflection of cold determination.

Courtney had no idea what he was thinking. She just wished it would get them off the boardwalk. From the corner of her eye, she could see that they were drawing the attention of passersby. Public scenes were not acceptable. Nor was the fact that she could feel tiny rivulets of sweat running down the back of her neck and beading on her brow. Any longer out here under the direct sun, and her skin would start to pinken.

"Fine," he said, the word clipped and cold. "I don't see any choice now. But you're gonna regret it."

"I shall be the one to determine any regret I may or may not feel. Now lead the way, Mr...." She trailed off, expecting him to supply his name.

He didn't.

Instead, he turned on his heel and started walking away, leaving Courtney with no choice but to follow.

A more uncouth, ill-mannered, infuriating man she had never met.

She managed to catch up to him and maintain her pace beside him, but just barely. The narrow shape of her gown and the weight of the gathered skirts trailing behind her made the swift pace he set difficult. But Courtney was not about to ask him to slow down. The quicker they got to Alexandra, the sooner she would be free of his company.

After passing by several storefronts, he suddenly turned to cross the street. "This way," he muttered.

Stepping from the boardwalk, he turned back and took her elbow to assist her to the street. It was a common courtesy she would have expected from any gentleman of her prior acquaintance. Yet coming from this man, the simple gesture held an unexpected feeling of significance, despite the scowl he flashed in her direction as he did it. Courtney accepted the warm grip of his hand but couldn't dismiss the way it made her insides seize with an odd, instinctive disquiet or the way his light-blue eyes made her breath catch despite his less-than-amiable expression.

She expected him to release her once she stepped to the street, but he kept his large hand in place as they continued to the other side. She noted more openly curious glances from people they passed, and she kept her posture straight and proud while the cowboy ignored them outright.

"Where are we going?" she asked as they stepped up onto the opposite boardwalk and continued walking in long strides.

"To the judge."

"The judge? Why?"

He kept his hand at her elbow as he tossed her a swift sideways glance. "Now that you're here, you're my responsibility." His tone made it quite clear how he felt about that fact. "If I want to keep you safe, well, it's best to make it official. It's what you came here for, isn't it?"

Courtney hid her confusion and the sudden flash of doubt that burst through her.

What *had* she come here for?

To start anew. To discover what she was capable of. To find out if there was more to life than following the well-laid plans of her family and society.

To be independent.

If she wished to accomplish any of those, she had to be brave.

Fearless, perhaps.

From the moment she'd leapt from that church window, she'd accepted that her life would never be the same. She did not *want* it to be the same. Her experiences since leaving Boston had already shown her how little she knew of the world. There was so much to see beyond the privileged, tightly knit society in which she'd lived.

Not lived. Existed. There had been no risk and few decisions that had not been made for her, either by her parents or by the simple dictates of strict social expectation.

She was in a new world out here in Montana Territory. She needed to remember that.

If this cowboy, whom Alexandra had obviously trusted enough to send for her, said they needed to stop to see the judge, then perhaps that is what she needed to do. She was not about to embarrass herself by revealing her ignorance. Her reluctant escort was already irritated enough—she did not want to give him any more reason to eye her with derision.

Maybe they registered newcomers to the area or something. It was not likely to be anything dastardly if the Honorable Judge John Wilkerson was involved, she figured as she noted the name painted on the window of the small wooden building they approached.

Entering the office, her erstwhile escort brought her right up to the clerk who sat at a tall desk in the corner. "We're here for one of those civil proceedings."

The clerk's gaze widened comically as he took in Courtney's elaborate white gown and noted the way the light-eyed man's hand was still wrapped around her arm.

As though just realizing he still held her, the cowboy quickly released her elbow. The clerk gave a slow nod and turned to enter the back room, leaving them alone in the small foyer.

The cowboy turned toward her, and Courtney again found herself stunned by his gaze. In the dim light of the small room, without the blazing reflection of the sun, his eyes seemed even more intense. With a hint of surprise, she noted the tiny fan of lines at the corners of his eyes. Oddly, rather than detracting from his appearance, the detail made him even more striking.

For a second, it seemed as though he might say something, but then the clerk peeked his head back through the door to give them a wave. "This way, please."

Hiding her confusion and internal disquiet behind an imperturbable facade, Courtney preceded the cowboy into the back office. Whatever they were there for, they might as well get it over with so they could be on their way.

The judge was seated behind a large, scarred desk with papers scattered haphazardly across the surface and a thick cigar smoking in a dish on the corner near his elbow. He was a man in his sixties at least, with white hair that fell straight to his shoulders, an iron-gray beard, and small, dark, deep-set eyes. He eyed them both with an intimidating scowl that didn't seem to affect her companion in the least.

The man beside her walked right up to the desk and said with impatience, "Let's get this done quick."

The judge slid a glance at Courtney, where she stood three steps behind the grumpy cowboy.

"The lady is willing?"

"Look at her."

The judge took in her appearance in another sweeping glance. "You're prepared to see this through?" he asked her.

"Of course," she replied in clipped tones. She was getting tired of repeatedly having to answer that particular inquiry. She wouldn't be here if she wasn't ready for a new life.

The judge gave a grunting nod, then rang a bell set to the side of his desk. The clerk from out front immediately appeared at the door.

"Fetch Mary and come back down here."

The further the scene progressed, the more confused Courtney became. The sense of being off-balance had not left her from the moment she collided with Mr. Martin outside the post office and had only gotten worse the longer she was in the cowboy's company. Looking to the judge for some clarity, she straightened her posture and regulated her voice into one of calm inquiry. "Your Honor, I am rather unfamiliar with these particular proceedings. Might I ask what we are waiting on?"

The white-haired man replied gruffly. "A wedding needs witnesses."

A wedding? What? Why would they need *her* to witness a wedding?

She swung a questioning gaze to the cowboy, but

he stood still and stiff beside her, staring straight ahead. She was not going to gain any clarity from him.

Courtney pressed her fingertips to the spot between her eyebrows where a fine little headache was starting to spark behind her eyes.

She just wanted to reach Alexandra. Why on earth had they stepped in on someone's wedding?

Within only a few minutes, the clerk returned with a young woman dressed in a flowered cotton dress covered by a blue apron. Her fair hair was pulled back in a simple knot at her nape, and her hands appeared to be covered in a fine layer of flour. When the woman caught sight of the cowboy, her eyes widened in shock. Her gaze swung to Courtney, and she gave a shy little smile before she approached the judge's desk.

The judge had called her Mary, and as the young woman's gaze slid covertly to the slim clerk, a pretty pink blush warmed her cheeks. The clerk came to stand beside Mary, giving her a sweet sideways smile before he too faced the judge and waited.

And Courtney finally understood.

She was here to be a witness for the union of this young couple. Though why the cowboy felt he had to drag her here to participate was beyond her. Surely, there was someone else in this town who was willing.

Courtney almost smiled at the silent little courtship occurring between the young couple. They were both all shy glances and sweet smiles. And so young.

Maybe that was the reason a stranger had to be called upon to witness the rites. Maybe their families were against the union.

The two were obviously smitten and old enough to decide their futures for themselves. If they wished to be married, Courtney believed they should be given every opportunity to find their happiness with each other.

"All right then. Sign here." The judge pushed a document across the desk toward the cowboy, who immediately took up the pen and scrawled a hasty signature.

When he stepped away, the judge nodded toward Courtney. "Now you. On this line, here."

The judge was clearly anxious to see the task finished. The cowboy stepped to the side, his attention focused hard on her in a way that had the muscles along her spine tightening. She glanced to the young woman and then to the clerk, who were both so distracted by each other they barely acknowledged the proceedings.

She stepped forward to glance down at the document, noting the scrolled heading stating *Montana Territory, Meagher County, Certificate of Lawful Union*.

"Just sign it, and we'll be on our way," the cowboy said, his tone low and annoyed.

Courtney shot him a stern look. His impatience was extremely irritating, but if the soon-to-be-married couple was not concerned with his attitude, then she could endure it. Courtney leaned forward to sign her name where the judge indicated, directly below the cowboy's scrawl. As soon as she lifted the pen, the judge slid the document toward Mary and the clerk. They each stepped forward and signed their names.

"It's done," the judge declared. "I will have this submitted to the registry."

That was it?

Without another word, the cowboy turned and

gestured for Courtney to precede him from the room. What an odd and shockingly brief ceremony—if it could even be called that.

Stepping back outside, Courtney lifted a hand to shield her face from the sun. "That was not very romantic," she said now that they were out of earshot of the newlyweds.

The cowboy slid her a dark glance as he turned and started walking. She had no choice but to fall into step beside him.

"You expected romance when you decided to come out here?"

She'd had just about enough of his snide tone. "Of course not," she snapped. She hadn't really expected anything, to be honest. Just something…different.

"Good," he replied just as curtly. "'Cause I might as well break it to you now—you're not gonna get it. The marriage isn't gonna last."

His blatant pessimism was irritating.

Considering the state of her own disastrous non-marriage, she wasn't exactly trusting of the idea that happily-ever-after truly existed, but at least she was willing to hope it might. She thought the young couple was rather cute and obviously quite taken with each other. Despite their youth, there was no reason to think they wouldn't make it and have a very happy life together.

"That is a terribly cynical assumption."

"Not an assumption. Fact. You'd better get used to the idea."

She would have loved to argue the point, but he abruptly turned toward a wagon hitched to two horses

waiting on the street. Stopping beside it, he gave a jerk
of his head. "Hop up."

Courtney cast a disdainful glance at the rough
wooden conveyance loaded up in the back with a
variety of crates and sacks. There were no cushions on
the bench seat and no cover from the sun. "I am not
riding in that."

His lifted his brows. "You've got another option,
princess?"

Of course not. She just hated having to acknowledge it to this arrogant, disrespectful cowboy.

"Didn't think so. Now, hop up."

Why Alexandra had chosen to send this bad-
tempered, rough-handed man to fetch her was beyond
Courtney's comprehension.

Or perhaps all the men out here were like this?

Grasping fistfuls of satin and brocade in her hands,
she lifted her foot toward the step board on the side
of the wagon. But her skirts were too narrow to allow
the maneuver. Before she could attempt an alternative
method of ascending to the upper seat of the wagon,
the man gave a grunt of annoyance. Then he gripped
her waist and hoisted her off the ground.

Courtney's gasp was half surprise, half outrage.

His familiar manner was as stunning as his bad
attitude.

Needing a moment to catch her breath after the
unexpected assistance, Courtney settled herself stiffly
on the rough wooden plank that passed for a seat
while the man—she still had no idea what his name
was—walked around and jumped up to take his place
beside her.

"A bit of a warning would have been polite," she chastised as she straightened her skirts.

He did not bother to reply, just lifted the reins and issued a low sound from his throat that had the horses starting off down the road.

"How far is the drive to—"

"Look," he interrupted without taking his gaze off the road ahead. "I'm not much for chitchat, and if I were, I sure as hell ain't in the mood for it today."

Courtney gaped with wide eyes—though really, how she could be surprised by further evidence of his rudeness after the way this man had been behaving was beyond her. She was not about to satisfy him with any sort of response or waste any more time expecting anything from him but abject insolence. Turning her gaze forward, she decided to ignore him altogether.

She hoped Helena was not too far away.

FOUR

DEAN LAWTON HAD NEVER BEEN SO BURNING MAD IN all his life.

His brother had gone too damn far.

Dean should have known something was up that morning. There had been an odd tone in Randall's voice when he'd mentioned the *special package* waiting at the post office. But Dean had blown it off. Randall was easily excitable and often got worked up over inconsequential things.

This, however, was anything but inconsequential.

His brother had actually brought one of those brides from the brochure all the way to Montana.

Randall had a tendency to be impulsive and reckless, but this was just plain crazy.

If his brother thought bringing the woman here—dressed up in all that bridal fluff, with her fiery-red hair and those tilted green eyes of hers—was going to change Dean's mind about the whole idea, he was about to find out just how wrong that assumption was.

Dean had married the woman all right. But only to make sure she had the benefit of his lawful protection while he figured out how to clean up the mess his brother had made.

Dean hated to admit that when he'd realized who the woman was and why she was in White Sulfur Springs, he'd been sorely tempted to just turn and walk away. But a quick look around had proven how vulnerable a lady as green as she was would be on her own.

He couldn't bring himself to just leave her. And the only way to ensure no one would bother her was to make it very clear that she was under his protection.

Temporarily.

Once he got her back to the ranch and Randall saw how totally unsuited she was to being a rancher's wife, his brother would have to see how stupid the idea had been in the first place.

Sometimes, the only way to get his brother to see reason was to force it down his throat. He'd get Randall to admit he was wrong and promise he wouldn't ever interfere in Dean's life again. By then, Dean would have figured out how to help to woman return to wherever she came from, or he'd arrange for her be transferred into someone else's care—someone of her choosing, preferably in another town. Then it would just be a matter of having their hasty civil union annulled, and his responsibility to the woman would be at an end.

The fancy lady beside him probably wouldn't be happy about getting an annulment. She hadn't seemed to believe him when he'd told her the marriage wasn't going to last. Dean got the sense she wasn't one to easily accept disappointment.

He almost felt guilty about that. But he told himself she must've accepted the possibility things wouldn't work out when she'd signed up to become a bride to a total stranger.

He purposely didn't think about what reasons the redheaded woman might have had for coming west to find a husband. It was none of his damn business.

Though he did wonder why she wasn't already wed to some fancy man back east. Despite her vivid hair and uppity manner, she was young and passably pretty, with a nice enough figure—at least she seemed that way from what he could tell with all the extra fripperies and layers of her gown.

Her fluffy white skirts filled the entire front of the wagon and flowed over his boots. Without even having to look at her, he could tell that she was sitting as stiff as a board, with her spine ridiculously straight and her hand grasped tight to the edge of the wagon as though she were scared she'd get bounced out of the thing. Her other hand was often lifted to shield her face from the sun as she took casual glances at the land they passed through.

She'd remained silent after they'd left town, but she didn't need to say anything for Dean to be fully aware of her presence. From the moment she'd turned toward him on the boardwalk, he hadn't been able to shake that awareness.

He knew it for what it was.

That didn't mean he welcomed it.

He'd just have to ignore how his body got all tight when she turned her eyes on him and how touching her had sent shocks of white lightning chasing across his nerves. She'd only be around a short while. Surely, he could endure his unexpected attraction for that long.

The drive to the Lawton Ranch took more than an hour, and that whole time the woman said absolutely nothing, just continued to sit stiff and straight beside him. But as he turned the wagon onto the long drive that wound through stretches of bunchgrasses and sagebrush as it made its way to the house Dean's grandfather had built nearly forty years before, Dean noticed the woman leaning forward a bit in her seat, as though she were eager for her first glimpse of the house she believed would be her new home.

He tightened his hands on the reins as he thought of his brother's reckless decision to bring the woman out here with a promise that couldn't be fulfilled. Randall must have been drunk at the time, or stupid in love, as the man had been most days since bringing Pilar home as his bride after a cattle drive to Texas two years ago.

Ever since Randall and Pilar had moved into the new house his brother built, Randall had been stuck on the thought that Dean needed what he had.

He didn't.

He had Lawton Ranch.

The homestead was nestled in a wide, rugged valley between rolling pine-topped hills. As it came into view, pride and ambition flared in Dean's chest. Dean's granddad had chosen the spot because of the sheltering stretch of ponderosa pines that spread to the north, the river that twisted and turned along the southern edge of the property, and the thousands of acres of free range extending in all directions.

This was what mattered.

Built from nothing by Augie Lawton, the ranch had grown into a prosperous enterprise under the old man's stern and roughened hand. Now that it was Dean's to manage, he intended to follow his granddad's example and honor his memory by breeding the best cattle in the territory. It's what he'd been raised to do.

The main house had been built in two stories, with a wide front porch. Painted a cheery yellow with white trim, it was showing the need for a fresh coat. Dean made a mental note to have that project seen to before the summer was through. The barn, set back behind the house, was of weathered natural wood, as were the bunkhouses and the storage sheds that sat on the other side of the large fenced-in riding arena.

As they neared, Dean noticed a loose pole on the hitching rail in front of one of the bunkhouses that would need to be fixed.

He recalled the summer when he'd been assigned the task of replacing and rebuilding all the fencing on the homestead. It had taken him months to see the job done, working from sunup to sundown. He had been only ten years old but still remembered his granddad's firm pat on the back when the job had finally been finished—just before the old man told him to go on and muck out the horse stalls.

Dean had learned a valuable lesson that summer. There was always something that needed doing on a ranch like this, and there was no time for self-congratulation. Ranching was hard work. All day, every day.

With Augie's death five years ago, the property had been passed on to Dean and Randall. No one had been surprised that Dean had received the controlling percentage. He'd been trained by Augie from the time he was seven years old to take over as boss when the time came. Lawton Ranch was Dean's responsibility, and it was one he took very seriously.

Despite Randall's insistence otherwise, Dean did not need the responsibilities of a wife added to everything else right now. Especially not some fancy Eastern lady who wouldn't know the first thing about ranch living. A woman like the one beside him could only cause unnecessary distraction.

"Is it always so quiet? Where is everyone?"

Dean tensed at the woman's questions as he brought the wagon to a stop in front of the house. The clear and precise way she talked brought up vague memories of how his mother had sounded. He hadn't thought of her in a good long while. He preferred it that way.

"Working," he stated without bothering to glance in her direction.

"Is Alexandra in the house?"

Now he did send her swift look. *Who?*

Before he could voice the question, a rider came thundering up on horseback. Dirt stirred in the yard as Randall pulled up alongside the wagon and hopped to the ground before his horse completely stopped.

Dean stepped down from the wagon as his brother tossed a wide grin at the woman still seated in the buckboard.

"Well, who have we here? My brother heads off to town for supplies and comes back with a beautiful woman. How come I never get so lucky?"

"Because Pilar would kill you," Dean grumbled.

Was Randall really going to pretend he had no idea who this woman was, with her fancy bridal gown and Eastern airs? Maybe he should have punched his brother in the nose like he'd wanted to when he'd brought that damn brochure home those weeks ago.

"Besides, you should know," Dean said as he went to the back of the wagon to start unloading the things that would be needed in the house. "You brought her here."

Randall gave him an uneven, squinty look of confusion, while the Eastern woman frowned. The frown made the outer corners of her eyes tilt up even more, and the jut of her chin brought Dean's eyes to the purse of her lips. They were awfully pretty lips.

He quickly looked away as he hefted a crate filled with canned goods in his arms and walked up alongside the wagon to set it on the porch.

"What are you talking about?" Randall asked, automatically walking to the back of the wagon to grab the next crate before following Dean's path to the porch.

As Augie's successor, Dean had received firsthand instruction on every aspect of how the ranch worked. Randall, younger than Dean by three years, had learned by following his older brother around and imitating his actions—at least until he'd get bored and wander off, leaving the rest of the work to Dean.

"Don't pretend you don't know," Dean said as he passed his brother on his way back for another crate.

"Sorry, Brother," Randall replied with a grin. "I've got no idea what you're talking about."

His brother's perpetual good nature was too much

for Dean today. He slammed the last crate onto the porch and rounded on Randall. "The bride from out east. From the pamphlet you showed me."

Randall stopped beside the wagon with a sack of flour hefted over his shoulder. His expression of confusion deepened, then twisted into a look of shock as he looked up at the woman who still sat in the wagon, her gaze darting swiftly from one of them to the other as though she couldn't quite make out what they were saying.

Randall's gaze slid back to Dean as he asked in a tone thick with incredulity, "You sent for one of them Eastern women?"

"Just a moment," she said.

"*I* didn't. *You* did."

Dean and the woman in the wagon both spoke at the same time, but Randall didn't seem to hear either of them. He shook his head in amazement. "I can't believe it. It's about damn time, but I never woulda thought you'd actually go for the idea. I'll be damned. When's the wedding?" he asked with another grin.

Dean crossed his arms over his chest. "You missed it. Judge Wilkerson married us in town. Meet my new bride."

"*What?*"

This time, it was the woman and Randall who spoke in unison.

"That is quite enough. I am not going to listen to another word of nonsense from the two of you." Her words dropped fast and sharp as she suddenly rose to her feet. Grasping her voluminous skirts in both hands, she lifted a foot over the sideboard as she started to disembark from the wagon by herself. "I do not know what kind of twisted farce you two seem intent upon playing out, but it is far from amusing and I have had more than enough of it."

As she shifted her weight to the lower step, the wagon rolled a bit. She swayed to compensate for the change in balance and tried to bring her other foot around to a more secure position, but her skirts got in the way, and in a twisting flurry of white, she started to tumble.

Dean made it to her just in time to grasp her around the waist and bring her safely down to the ground. It didn't take much effort. Despite the layers of material floating about her legs and the stiff corset encasing her waist, she was surprisingly light and, once her feet were free from her skirts, rather graceful as he set her down in front of him.

She wasted no time thanking him for saving her from a face full of dirt as she shrugged off his hands with a fierce glare of indignation that sparkled little gold flames in the depths of her green eyes. Stepping away from him and Randall, she swept her skirts out of her way and lifted her chin to pin them both with a stern glare.

"I demand that you bring me to Alexandra immediately."

Dean scowled. That was the second time she'd said that name. "Who the hell is Alexandra?"

She took a slow breath and brought her hands up to smooth the material of her dress where Dean's hands had grasped her middle. Her jaw was tight and her tone stiff as she replied, "My friend, Alexandra

Kincaid. The one who sent you to pick me up in town." Her eyes met his intently—insistently.

A chill ran down Dean's spine.

"I'm afraid we don't know any Alexandra Kincaid. This here is the Lawton Ranch," Randall replied, still smiling, though a wary look had entered his blue gaze.

Dean stood still and silent as he watched the woman's reaction. Her eyes darted wildly around before returning to him. Distrust, shot through with anger and confusion, flashed in her gaze, though she managed to keep her expression amazingly neutral. "If Alexandra did not send you, then who are you and why did you bring me here?"

Dean could feel Randall staring at him from where he stood beside the wagon still holding that damn sack of flour. His brother's silence only solidified Dean's terrible suspicion. "Why did you come to Montana?" he asked, his body already tensing in anticipation of her reply.

She narrowed her gaze. "I already told you."

"Why are you dressed in a wedding gown?" he pressed, feeling the back of his neck getting hot.

She stiffened sharply. "That is none of your business."

An icy chill cut through his unnatural sweat as he acknowledged that he might've made a terrible mistake. He was very rarely wrong about anything, but as the truth started to sink in, he realized this mistake was worse than any he'd ever made. Remorse burned heavy in his gut as he thought over everything she'd said and realized that not once had she admitted to being a mail-order bride. He'd just taken one look at her and assumed.

Shit.

Refusing to glance toward Randall, Dean kept his gaze pinned on the proud and angry woman.

"What exactly is going on here?" she asked. Her tone was sharp but controlled, while her eyes held a barely banked golden fire.

Dean took a long, fortifying breath. "You recall that little meeting in front of the judge?"

"You mean the one you dragged me to without the courtesy of an explanation—no, without any courtesy *at all*?"

Dean lowered his chin. "Do you know what that was about?"

She planted her hands on her hips. "I am not an idiot. We stood in as witnesses for that young couple's marriage."

Aw, hell.

Dean forcefully released the tension in his jaw enough to respond with one word. "Nope."

She stiffened. Her eyes grew big and dark. "Of course we did."

"Holy shit," Randall hissed.

Dean tossed a silencing look at his brother. "Shut up, Randall." Looking back at the redhead, he felt a sickening twist in his gut.

She shook her head in a decisive rejection. "No. I do not accept this. The two of you have obviously lost your minds. Those young people in town were clearly smitten with each other. Of course it was their marriage." Her eyes found his and she insisted with calm command, "You are mistaken."

Dean felt her hard gaze like a fist to the gut. All he

could do was give a negative shake of his head and watch as her subtle, hopeful expression dropped away to be replaced by a sudden storm of furious outrage. The show of temper came on so swiftly that he nearly took a step back. He didn't. But only because he figured he was due the blast she was about to deliver.

"How dare you...*marry me*? You married me! We are married. Husband and wife. Oh God, this cannot be happening." She stepped up to him and jabbed a finger toward his chest. Though she was not close enough to touch him, Dean could feel the fury radiating off her in waves. She was a slim woman and tall, though still a few inches shorter than Dean's six foot two, and she was a sight to behold in her righteous indignation. "You listen to me, Mr...."

"Lawton," Randall offered helpfully when her words stumbled to a halt. "Dean Lawton."

Dean was going to kill his brother.

The woman didn't even flick a glance at Randall. "I did not run away from one wedding only to be strong-armed into another. You will fix this, and you will fix it now."

Dean took a slow breath, taking some time before answering, hoping it would give her temper a chance to ease. Then he replied in as even a tone as he could muster. "I can't. Not tonight," he added when she immediately opened her mouth to protest. "By the time we get back to town, the judge will be home, and he does not take house calls. We'll go back first thing in the morning to get an annulment. That's what I meant to do eventually anyway."

She sucked in a swift breath at the last, her

expression shifting into one of shock. "That is what you meant to do anyway? An annulment, you mean? Is *that* what you meant when you said the marriage wouldn't last?"

"Uh-oh," Randall muttered as he took a giant step back.

Dean's hands fisted as his sides. Why the hell was Randall still hanging around? For the show, obviously.

"You married me with the full intention of some-day dissolving the marriage?"

Dean figured silence was his best response to that question, considering the bright pink that had entered her cheeks with the revelation. Damn, but the woman had a temper.

"I have never in my life met a man who was so dishonorable.. You are despicable," she said with a harsh narrowing of her gaze. She drew in a slow breath and closed her eyes for just a moment. When she opened them again, her expression had shifted to one of calm dignity. And just like that, her temper was back under wraps. The only remaining evidence of her wrath were the licks of golden flames in her eyes. "I am finished with this conversation," she stated with astonishing control. "Be ready to take me back to town first thing in the morning, Mr. Lawton."

With those final words on the subject, she swept up her skirts with one graceful arc of her arm and strode proudly up the porch steps and into the house, allowing the door to slam shut behind her.

FIVE

"Why are you still standing there?" Dean bit out between clenched teeth.

Randall finally carried the sack of flour to the porch and dropped it on top of one of the crates. "Helping," he said with a grin.

"If you value your life, you'll get yourself gone real quick," Dean warned. He could see the laughter about to burst from his brother's chest. The man took nothing seriously.

Randall gestured toward the wagon. "Did you manage to pick up my package? I'd understand, I suppose, if the task got lost in all the excitement of your nuptials."

"Randall."

"Sure do wish I could have been there," Randall continued in a remorseful tone. "Family should be present for such an auspicious event."

"*Randall.*"

His brother chose to ignore the warning tone in Dean's voice, though he did start sidestepping toward his horse. "I'm sure you made a handsome groom."

His grin was downright irritating. "An ornery one, but handsome."

"Dang it, Randall. *Get!*"

"I'm gone," his brother replied with one last laugh and a leap into his saddle. Dean watched his brother ride away. Mainly because he didn't know what else to do. Then he remembered the wagon still half-full of supplies that needed to be taken to the barn.

Grateful for the task, he jumped into the driver's seat and drove around the house to the barn beyond, silently fuming over everything that had happened over the past few hours.

He'd made a mistake. A big one. Huge, to be honest.

Dean didn't often make mistakes. He made choices and decisions all the time. Some turned out well, some not so well, but those were simply the consequences to having more than one option. He always made the best of any outcome he received.

He honestly couldn't remember the last time he'd made a true error.

The woman inside the house deserved an apology. And an explanation.

Well, as good a one as he could manage without coming off as a complete jackass.

Truth to tell, he *was* a jackass.

He'd completely lost his head when he'd seen her there, stepping out of the post office in that white gown, all ruffled and laced and fancy. She had been so obviously out of place on that dusty boardwalk, looking exactly like the images of those women in the pamphlet Randall had brought home several weeks ago. *Ladies of the East willing to travel to the Western Territories for promise of a husband.*

Randall had thought one of those ladies would be the perfect solution to Dean's problem—never mind the fact that Dean didn't *have* a problem.

Dean had been stunned by the sight of her. Stunned by the thought that his brother would go ahead and bring one of those brides to town without consulting him. Whether Dean wanted her or not, she'd become his responsibility the moment she'd stepped from the stagecoach, and in his frustration, he'd acted without fully thinking things through.

He stopped the rise of his panic by reminding himself that he'd be taking her back to town first thing in the morning to have the little civil union annulled. It would be like the whole thing had never happened.

Except for the woman's righteous fury over having been manhandled into a marriage she didn't want. Even if she had come to Montana expecting marriage, she was dead right about the fact that Dean's actions had not been honorable. He had behaved as despicably as she'd accused.

His only excuse was that he'd lost his head. It was not something he did often.

Reckless behavior ran in the Lawton bloodline. His granddad Augie Lawton was well known for his hot-headed bluster and damn-the-consequences attitude, and Dean's dad had been as impulsive and wild as they come. More so even than Randall.

Dean had always believed those family traits had skipped over him. But today had proven otherwise.

The woman had been right on another score as well. He'd have to make this right.

But first, he had to finish unloading the wagon. And he really should go fix that hitching rail. And hadn't the boys mentioned something about a warped floorboard in the bunkhouse? He should probably check it out before it got worse. Then he'd go talk to…his wife.

Shit. He didn't even know her name.

Courtney stood alone in the center of what appeared to be a small parlor. She'd been standing there a good fifteen minutes and was still fuming. She had never before experienced such a complete unleashing of emotion. Had never had reason to give such a scathing speech to anyone.

In all honesty, it had felt wonderful. The release of tension was noticeable almost immediately. She was still furious, but at least the anger wasn't all pent up inside her like a volcano desperate to erupt.

If her parents knew she had let loose with such a display of temper and lack of self-control, they would have expired on the spot. Such things were simply not done. In addition to wealth and influence, her family was dedicated to the strict cultivation of dignity, virtue, and restraint in all things.

Though she felt a little better after her tirade, it was an uneasy feeling. She was not accustomed to behaving in such a liberated manner. It was confusing and exciting and more than a little scary.

But this was what she had chosen. *This*, over a life of buttoned-up boredom, of passionless companionship.

It had been the right choice. Right?

Courtney nearly groaned. She needed to get to Alexandra.

Seeing her old friend was the only thing that made sense in her flight from Boston. Though Alexandra had been raised in the West, she had spent several years being groomed by her aunt in Boston. Alexandra would understand in an instant what Courtney had been going through since she'd made the decision to jump out that window.

Those men outside—Dean Lawton and the other one, Randall, who hadn't been able to stop grinning during the whole disastrous revelation—were strangers.

They were also quite possibly completely insane.

What kind of mess had she landed herself in?

Her fury threatened to slide into despair with that thought, but she held it in place.

This was not part of the plan, and it was assuredly not her fault. She thought she had been helping a young couple get married. Of course, the cowboy's rough demeanor had caused some wariness, but how was she to know his manner was anything out of the ordinary?

Alexandra had told her more than once that the men who carved out their lives in the Western Territories were very different from the gentlemen in Boston. Courtney had simply had no point of reference to imagine just how different they were. The other man, Randall, looked a lot like his brother, with the same lean height, sandy-brown hair, and light eyes, though his features were less angular and his expressions far less fierce. But he too behaved very differently from the gentlemen back home, with his loose-limbed movements and overt, friendly demeanor.

Taking a heavy breath, Courtney strode toward the wide window overlooking the front of the house. The wagon was no longer outside. She had been so wrapped up in her righteous anger that she hadn't even heard it being driven away. Both men were gone as well.

In fact, everything was eerily still.

Having lived in Boston all her life, she was accustomed to the constant motion and clamor of bustling city life. She leaned closer to the window and swept her gaze as far as she could in all directions. An expanding stretch of green dotted with clusters of shrubs and rocks and trees extended beyond the small yard and the long dirt road they had come down.

Aside from the house, barn, and other outbuildings, she was surrounded by nothing but nature.

Courtney turned back to the interior of the house.

It was small, though certainly larger than the other shack-like structures she had seen in the distance along the drive from town. At least there was a parlor. She wandered out into the entryway and noted the staircase that led up to the second floor, where she assumed the bedrooms were located. Continuing down the hall, she headed back toward what she hoped would be a kitchen. Surely, there had to be a servant about somewhere. The kitchen seemed a logical place to start looking for someone who might assist her in finding her bearings.

Not to mention she was absolutely starving. The last meal she'd had was early that morning. Bitter coffee and some bread with jam. She would give anything for some glazed ham or baked fish smothered in creamy lemon sauce with a steaming baked potato.

Her stomach grumbled at the thought.

After passing a rather impressive dining room holding a long wooden table and matching chairs that would easily seat a large family, she stepped into the kitchen.

It was a cheery room painted in white and yellow with a sturdy wooden counter running along one wall beneath a row of windows. There was a large iron stove to one side, and opposite that was another smaller table, painted white, with two chairs set up beside a back door.

The room was neat and tidy with no evidence that anyone was about.

At this time, back home, the kitchens would have been flooded with staff beginning preparations for the evening meal. Then again, the meals back home were likely a bit more elaborate than what she'd find here.

As she stood there, uncertain of her next move, the back door opened and a woman swept in carrying a basket on her hip and two loaves of bread tucked under her arm. Dressed in a bright-colored skirt and red blouse, the woman was short of stature and rounded in a matronly way. She had warm, brown skin and her hair—ink-black with strands of gray liberally threaded through—was pulled back into a long braid down her back.

Noticing Courtney standing there, the woman,

who appeared in her midfifties, startled and made a sound somewhere between a harsh gasp and a smothered shriek. Dark-brown eyes widened as she pressed the bread loaves to her ample chest. "Ay, dios mío."

She clearly hadn't expected to see someone standing in her kitchen.

Courtney's smile came naturally as she spoke. "Good evening, how do you do? I am sorry. I did not mean to startle you."

The older woman continued to stare at her with big eyes that roamed swiftly over Courtney's appearance—from her slipping coiffure to the fine lace details of her dress's bodice and down over the draped layers of satin and brocade with touches of velvet that made up her bridal skirts. By the time the woman's brown eyes met Courtney's again, a wide smile had spread across her lips. She bustled forward quickly to set her burdens on the table, muttering under her breath as she did so.

Courtney had always been fascinated by foreign cultures and had loved learning new languages. She was actually rather good at them and could speak fluent French and Italian. She also knew a smattering of Russian and possessed enough Portuguese to manage a basic conversation. Unfortunately, she knew very little Spanish. In truth, she knew only enough to recognize by its similarity to Portuguese that it was the language the woman was speaking as she approached with her now-empty arms spread wide to take Courtney into a welcoming embrace.

Courtney was shocked as the stranger wrapped her up in a hug, still speaking in rapid Spanish and smiling brightly. The physical contact was unexpected. She could not recall the last time she had been embraced in such a way, or by whom.

Drawing back, the woman grasped Courtney's face gently in her hands and met her stunned gaze. She seemed to have asked a question, though Courtney had no idea what it might have been. For a brief moment, it felt like she might be able to interpret some of the words, but just when she thought she grasped something recognizable, the language took a turn and she lost all comprehension. "I am sorry. I do not speak Spanish."

The woman laughed, and her eyes sparkled with amusement as she shook her head and gave Courtney's cheek a little pat before she turned back to the table to begin unloading the basket.

Courtney watched, listening for any words she might recognize, as the woman continued her one-sided conversation. She thought she caught the word for *hungry*, which made sense since the woman was throwing together a large plate of food. And possibly the word for *chief*, though that did not seem to make sense at all.

Finally, the woman turned back to Courtney and gestured for her to come forward and sit at the table, where she had set the plate holding a generous portion of bread topped with thin-sliced beef and crumbles of white cheese. Despite its simplicity, the meal looked amazing and smelled even better. The beef seemed to have been seasoned with something Courtney couldn't quite identify but was anxious to taste.

While Courtney filled her empty stomach, the cheerful woman continued to bounce around the kitchen with limitless energy. Occasionally speaking in Spanish with a smile or curious look tossed in Courtney's direction, she readied food for the evening meal. Much of what she pulled from her basket appeared to have been prepared elsewhere and just needed to be warmed, while other items were quickly thrown together with what was available in the kitchen as the woman loaded the stovetop with pots and pans.

Just as Courtney finished the food on her plate, feeling wonderfully satisfied by the savory meal, the woman rushed forward to sweep the dirty dishes away. Then she returned and grasped Courtney's hands to urge her to her feet.

"Por favor, ven conmigo," she said with a series of nods.

Courtney understood the woman wanted to take her somewhere. Satiated and relaxed by the delicious meal, she followed the woman a short way down the hall to another small room. It was a bathing room, complete with an enormous porcelain tub that had a curved headrest on one end and a water pump and spout on the other.

Just the idea of a bath made Courtney's skin tingle with anticipation. It had been days since she'd last had a proper washing. She glanced at the woman with wide, hopeful eyes and received a grin and a nod.

"Sí, puede bañarse."

As Courtney debated whether she could take the risk of completely disrobing in the house of a man who had married her against her will, the woman pumped the handle of the spout until clear water began flowing into the tub. She looked over her shoulder at Courtney and waved her free hand to indicate Courtney's gown. "Desvístete."

Courtney looked down at the dress she'd been wearing since leaving Boston with only one washing in between at a small laundry outside the train station in Billings. Then she looked to the tub longingly before glancing back at the door. "I, ah…" She didn't feel like she was in any particular danger, but the impropriety of stripping down and bathing in the house of a stranger was not easy to overcome.

Then again, the stranger—What was his name? Dean. Dean Lawton—was her husband. Which made this *her* house. Surely, there was no impropriety in bathing in her own home.

Without any further debate, Courtney carefully removed her gloves, making sure her money stayed safely tucked inside before she reached around to start tugging at the tiny buttons running down her back. Her new friend swiftly stepped around behind her and brushed her fingers aside.

The older woman made short work of releasing the gown, then held it for Courtney to step out of. She made *tsking* sounds of dismay as she tried to shake out some of the deep-set wrinkles and brush off the trail dust. Seeing the futility of the effort, she draped the gown over a long bench set in the corner of the room, then turned back to assist Courtney with her many layered petticoats, bustle bump, and corset.

Courtney could not understand what the woman was saying as she peeled away one layer after another, but there was obvious humor in her voice as she

addressed the contraptions worn to create the silhouette preferred by Boston's elite.

Once Courtney was down to her chemise and
drawers, the woman swept from the room, making
sure to draw the door gently closed behind her.

Courtney eyed the tub. It had been half-filled with
water from the spout, and although she suspected the
water would be quite cold, the bath looked infinitely
inviting. After setting her gloves on the bench beside
her gown, she began the task of removing the many
dozen pins holding her hip-length hair in the thick
chignon she'd managed to create.

From the day she'd stopped wearing her hair free
down her back as a girl, a maid trained in creating the
most current and stylish coiffures had managed the
daily task. Courtney had been quite proud of herself
for figuring out how to keep her hair contained once
it had started falling from her bridal coiffure. Luckily,
the original elaborate style had come with a grand
supply of pins, so Courtney was able to get the unruly
tresses twisted and tucked enough that the pins had
done the rest.

A gentle knock at the door made Courtney jump.
She heard the woman's familiar voice a moment
before she opened the door again, carrying a large pot
of steaming water. After pouring it into the tub, she
left and returned two more times with more water,
turning the cold water into a warm, luxurious bath.

Bustling around with quick, efficient movements,
the older woman withdrew a large square of cloth
from a cupboard, then a dish of soap, setting them
both on the stool that stood beside the tub.

Turning to Courtney again, she smiled and nodded as she gestured to the tub. "Señora, báñese, por favor."

"Thank you. Gracias," Courtney replied, trying to recall the very little Spanish she knew. "Ah… ¿Cómo se llama?"

Though Courtney's accent was probably deplorable, the woman's grin widened at her attempt.

"Me llamo Jimena."

"Jimena. That is beautiful. My name is Courtney. Me llamo Courtney."

Jimena repeated the name, then gave a smile and a shake of her head as she spoke too rapidly for Courtney to make anything out, although she again thought she heard the word for *chief*.

Backing out of the room, Jimena seemed to instruct Courtney to shout if she required assistance.

After the door closed and Courtney was left alone again, she did not to waste a moment in slipping off her underclothes and getting into the water. She had no idea where the cowboy had gone and no idea when he'd be back. She did not want to be naked and vulnerable in a bathtub—even one as long and deep as this one—when he did.

Sinking into the warm water, she sighed as it lapped at her chin and completely covered her everywhere else. It was heaven. After allowing herself only a few minutes to close her eyes and relax, she sat up and reached for the cake of soap. Bringing it to her nose, she inhaled the delightful scent of orange with a hint of spearmint.

The bath did not nearly approach the degree of luxury she was accustomed to back home, but at that moment, Courtney couldn't imagine anything more decadent.

SIX

It wasn't until after Courtney got out of the tub and used the large cloth to squeeze the excess water from her hair before wrapping it around her body that she realized all her clothes were gone. Her custom-made wedding gown, her shoes and stockings, every item of underclothing. Even her gloves.

A rush of panic seized her.

She couldn't recall seeing Jimena taking anything from the room. But then, Courtney had been so desperate for the bath, she hadn't noticed much beyond the inviting water.

Surely, the kind woman did not intend to just leave Courtney stranded in the bathing room with nothing to wear. Securing the towel beneath her arms and tucking the end in at her chest, Courtney took a seat on the bench and finger-combed through her hair, keeping a cautious eye on the door.

After a while, she heard a noise in the hall and rose to her feet. Jimena gave a quick little rap on the door and called out a greeting before peeking her head in.

Seeing that Courtney was out of the bath, Jimena

swept into the room, carrying a brightly colored skirt-and-blouse combination similar to what the older woman wore herself.

"Where are my gown and all of my other things?" Courtney asked, then repeated the phrase in Portuguese for good measure as she gestured toward the bench where her clothes had been.

Jimena appeared to understand the question well enough as she replied in Spanish, finishing her explanation by dramatically holding her nose.

Courtney lifted her chin, trying not to blush in embarrassment. "You try traveling across the country with nothing more than the clothes on your back," she replied in a low mutter.

Setting the clothing on the bench Courtney had just risen from, the older woman shook out a simply made but pristine combination of camisole and drawers. Jimena continued speaking in rapid-fire Spanish as she held out the cotton garment for Courtney to step into the leg holes.

From what she could grasp of the few familiar words, the clothing belonged to Jimena's daughter. The skirt's hem hovered a couple inches from the ground on Courtney's tall form. It was a vivid blue trimmed with a green ruffle and embroidered with multicolored threads in a flowery design. The blouse was of light, white cotton and was also colorfully embroidered, this time across the shoulders and chest. Once the blouse was tucked into the skirt, Jimena wrapped a yellow sash around and around Courtney's waist and tucked the ends securely in the folds to keep it all secure.

It was unlike any outfit she had ever worn, but the bright colors were cheerful, the materials were soft and clean, and the skirt swirled in a way that almost made Courtney want to spin in place like a girl. Jimena motioned for Courtney to take a seat on the bench. She combed through Courtney's long tresses, then braided the length into a single plait down her back.

Finally done, the older woman urged Courtney to stand while she took a good look at her work. Smiling widely, she reached up to gently pat Courtney's cheeks in a motherly fashion. The open and friendly gesture made Courtney distinctly uncomfortable, but she smiled back at the woman.

She was shocked to feel the prick of tears in her eyes. "Thank you. I am not sure why you have decided to be so nice to me, but I appreciate the kindness."

Jimena gave a quick reply before she ushered Courtney from the bathroom and back out to the parlor, where a tray of refreshments had been set on a small table in front of the sofa.

Courtney took a seat as Jimena poured a glass of cool lemonade. The older woman's eyes suddenly widened as she handed Courtney the glass. "Dios mío, casi se me olvide." She reached into a deep pocket of her skirt and withdrew something that she handed to Courtney.

It was a cotton handkerchief wrapped securely around Courtney's money.

"Gracias, Jimena," Courtney murmured as she curled her fingers around the precious riches. The meager coins had come to represent her tentative grasp on an independent future. They were all she had of value in the world and represented the only way she was likely to get away from this place and continue to Alexandra's.

Jimena gave one last smile as she clasped her hands together in an almost prayerlike gesture. The words she said were terribly earnest in tone, but before Courtney could try to understand their meaning, the woman turned and bustled from the room.

Leaving Courtney alone once more in the quaint little parlor.

The sudden absence of Jimena's energetic amiability left Courtney feeling an abrupt wave of weariness and doubt as she looked around at the unfamiliar surroundings.

She would never have expected her adventures to bring her to this strange home in the middle of Montana cattle country. She had never seen as much open land as she'd noted on their drive from town. Raw wilderness extended in all directions, broken up by nothing more than a few tiny homesteads and grazing cattle or sheep in the distance. The Lawton Ranch was by far the largest home she'd seen in the territory.

Tomorrow, if Dean Lawton was to be believed, she would be on her own again. She would have to find somewhere to stay in town while she waited for Alexandra to reply to her letter, unless she managed to find another way to continue on her journey.

For the first time, Courtney wondered what she would do once she actually made it to Helena. She could only stay with Alexandra's family as an uninvited guest for so long. If she intended to remain out here, she would need to find a way to replenish her funds, to rent a room, perhaps. To live.

A heavy sigh escaped from her chest before she could stop it. It was all so overwhelming when she stopped to consider what she had done. Overwhelming and terrifying.

She forced herself to look on the bright side. Optimism was her only friend at the moment.

At least she wasn't still on the dreadful stagecoach. And she was certainly significantly closer to Alexandra than she was to Boston…and Geoffrey.

Over the many days since leaving, the stab of his betrayal had eased to a deep ache made up of regret, embarrassment, and a strange sort of empty sadness.

Such emotions were so foreign to Courtney that she honestly had no idea what to do with them. She had always felt completely self-assured. Her place in the world—or, more accurately, in Boston—was one of an elevated social status where she was adored for her charming and friendly manner, her somewhat impulsive energy, and her loyalty to those deserving her friendship. She had never had cause to feel regret, but she did now in how naively she had believed in a future that had been so laughably out of reach.

Since reading her fiancé's misdirected letter, she had struggled to maintain her trust in the idealistic belief that even the most difficult situations worked out all right in the end. Every time the journey became challenging, she'd had to remind herself it was exactly what she'd wanted. She had wanted to test herself, to have an adventure, to discover what it was to be truly independent.

Closing her eyes, she rested her head back against the high sofa cushion.

Well, she had certainly been tested.

Was it truly possible that she and the cowboy had been married?

She knew it was. The civil ceremony had been short and odd, but nothing suggested it hadn't been legal.

Only until tomorrow, she reminded herself when panic started to tighten her chest. Until then, she remained an uneasy guest in the home of a stranger. A stranger who had rather underhandedly taken her before a judge and married her.

He'd *married* her! Why on earth had he done that?

As though thinking of the man had summoned him, the front door of the house opened on slightly squeaky hinges. Booted steps sounded on the wooden floor in a long, determined stride that approached the parlor.

Courtney had already adjusted her position to sit at the edge of the sofa with her legs pressed together from her thighs to her instep beneath the brightly colored skirt. Her spine was straight and immovable, despite the lack of a corset. She had angled her head to train a steady, imperious gaze at the man the moment he came through the door.

She knew it would be him.

But she had no idea the sight of him would send her insides into such a flurry of activity.

It had to be her righteous fury that shortened her breath as her stomach executed a wild spinning free fall. It was her indignation that had her clenching her teeth against the urge to lick suddenly dry lips.

He stopped right there in the doorway. Not stepping into the parlor to join her, yet not passing by either.

His light eyes found her and, after only the most abbreviated glance at her altered appearance, locked upon her face.

Oh, how she wished she was dressed in her usual finery with her hair elaborately coiffed and her most elegant jewels around her neck and dripping from her ears. She would employ every trick she'd ever learned, every nuance she'd ever observed amongst her acquaintances, to demonstrate who she was, where she came from, and just how big a mistake he'd made in forcing her into such a situation.

But she was on her own, having cut ties to all those social trappings.

They stared at each other in silence while Courtney couldn't help but notice how very different he was from the men she was accustomed to. It wasn't just his rugged, casual attire, though she marveled at the way his slightly faded denim pants formed to his long legs. And the cotton shirt he wore did nothing to conceal the lean strength of his torso, his wide shoulders, or his taut, muscled arms. It was more than the dusty leather gloves on his hands or the sturdy belt encircling his hips or the wide-brimmed hat that he still wore despite having stepped indoors.

It was in his expression. There was a confrontational sort of self-assurance in the hard lines of his jaw, nose, and brow. The slight hollowness of his cheeks and the firm press of his lips suggested he was not a man to mince words or offer platitudes. And his eyes—those light, piercing eyes of his—were filled with bold, unwavering confidence.

Their mutual staring began to feel uncomfortable,

but Courtney was not about to speak first. Not that she didn't have a lot to say—far more than the man was likely prepared to hear—but she was not going to offer the common courtesy of communication until he provided her with a much-needed apology.

After a few more extended breaths, the cowboy gave a short, irritated sigh and lowered his gaze as he removed his worn and dirty gloves. Gathering them in one hand, he smacked them once against his thigh, sending dust up into the air, where it floated down to what had been a nicely cleaned floor, before he tucked both gloves into his belt. "I don't want a wife."

Courtney blinked.

Those were not the first words she had expected to hear from him.

I am sorry.

I have made a dreadful mistake.

Will you please forgive my rash and reckless behavior?

All would have been fine and proper choices.

This—this declaration uttered in such a curt, irrevocable tone—instantly got under her skin.

Though fury burned through her blood, she was determined not to repeat her earlier tirade—as liberating as it had been—and did not alter her expression in any way. When she replied, despite the sparks of temper glowing fierce within her, her tone was as flat and emotionless as the one her mother perpetually maintained. "Is it common around here for men to force innocent, unsuspecting women into marriages they themselves do not want?"

He swept his hat off his head and tossed it onto a table set against the wall, almost disrupting a vase of flowers. He shoved his hand back through sandy-brown hair that had fallen over his forehead. "You were in a wedding dress, for God's sake."

She rounded on that point. There was no way she would allow him to turn this back on her. "That is another thing. What if I *had* been a woman seeking to become a bride? You married me thinking that to be the case, and yet you never intended to honor the union." His features tensed, but he did not reply. "No matter how you look at it, your behavior was reprehensible."

Clearly, he was not accustomed to having his actions questioned or criticized. Frustration flashed in his gaze, but he did not try to defend himself.

Because he knew she was right?

Courtney rose to her feet, no longer able to contain the seething energy running through her body. Carefully leveling her tone, she said, "Did it never occur to you that I might have been *fleeing* a wedding, not running toward one? I assure you, Mr. Lawton, I did not jump through a window, betray my family's trust, sell my grandmother's pearls, and ride thousands of miles on a train and then a dusty coach to marry a rude and reckless cowboy. I was trying to *avoid* becoming a bride. Thank you so very much for so effectively ruining my efforts."

His expression darkened during her outburst, but his eyes never left her face. There was something in the way he looked at her that tripped over nerves already frazzled beyond belief. When he spoke, his words were low, almost soothing. "It'll be taken care of tomorrow."

The confidence in his statement and the steady

focus of his gaze had her feeling suddenly as if she had just blown the situation out of proportion. But her temper had risen too high to accept that as she completely gave up on maintaining an even tone to unleash her anger and frustration in a far more satisfying way.

"Indeed," she declared sharply. "Until then, I would like to make something quite clear. Though I seem to have no choice but to stay in this house until morning, I will not consent to your presence as well. You may take yourself off to wherever else you'd like to go, but you will not remain with me."

She realized fleetingly that she should feel some shame for speaking her mind so freely, but it felt too wonderful, and frankly, he deserved it. She had only a moment to indulge in her satisfaction at having put him in his place when he left his position in the doorway and started toward her with slow, long strides.

Courtney refused to retreat, though every nerve in her body sparked to life at his approach. Instead, she lifted her chin and allowed all her righteous indignation to shine in her eyes.

The cowboy stopped just short of towering over her, and his proximity—the earthy male scent of him, combined with the strength of his presence within the confines of the small parlor—had a rather distinctive effect on her. She experienced an instant rise in body temperature that brought an unwelcome rush of warmth to her cheeks while her belly tensed with unexpected trepidation.

Looking into her eyes, he replied in that low and soothing voice, "Now it's my turn to make something clear. You can make all the demands you want, princess, but I take orders from no one. Tomorrow, we'll go to town and dissolve this marriage as I said we would. But I will sleep in my own damn bed. If that doesn't meet with your approval, you are welcome to make use of the barn."

Courtney gasped. Her eyes narrowed as she met his stern gaze. "You are no gentleman."

His mouth tilted into something not quite a smile. Even knowing it was not an expression of humor or pleasure, Courtney found herself momentarily fascinated by the way the movement softened his hard-lined mouth and added intriguing curves where they hadn't been.

"I never claimed to be."

"Tomorrow will not come soon enough," she breathed.

Something flickered in his gaze. "Yeah, well…" he said in a roughened tone. "At least for tonight, you'll have to endure my limited hospitality. Be ready at dawn."

Then he turned and strode from the room, leaving Courtney gaping after him.

As his booted steps retreated down the hallway, she released a heavy puff of breath and dropped back onto the sofa. Fanning herself with one hand, she lifted her lemonade with the other. The heat of her anger still boiled beneath her skin.

How had he managed to get the last word?

It was his sort-of, almost smile. She had allowed it to distract her at the moment when she should have been the most on guard.

That would not happen again.

SEVEN

DEAN STORMED DOWN THE HALLWAY WITH LONG strides.

Damn. He still hadn't gotten the woman's name.

It didn't matter. She'd be long gone after tomorrow.

He'd already decided to help her get the rest of the way to meet up with her friend. Though he was sorely tempted to change his mind after that scene in the parlor, he'd see the task done. He figured he owed it to her, even though she made it damn hard to feel bad for her.

Jesus! He had never seen a woman with such an all-fired temper. Even when she was talking slow and keeping her voice real even, he could see the fire blazing in her eyes.

He'd been a bit surprised at first to see her dressed as she was. Jimena must have gotten some of Pilar's clothes for the woman to borrow. Wearing the bright skirt and loose blouse, with her fiery hair drawn back in a simple braid, she presented a very different picture than she had earlier, when she'd been encased in her many-layered and stiffly corseted bridal getup.

She almost looked pretty.

No. That was a lie.

She wasn't pretty. She was beautiful. Just not in the way he typically admired. With that dramatic hair contrasting with her fair complexion, the tilt of her striking eyes, and the lushness of her coral-colored lips, she was a sight to be sure. It was her attitude he detested.

And that couldn't be softened by a change of clothes.

She'd sat and stared at him with the same prim and self-important bearing he recognized from the faint recollections he had of his mother. This woman and Roseanne Lawton were cut from the same cloth. Spoiled, pampered, selfish, and ill-prepared for when life got tough.

He shook his head to clear away any more thoughts on the woman. Or his mother.

The rich scents of supper simmering in the kitchen spurred an ache of hunger in his belly. He needed to bathe and dress before dinner. Jimena did not suffer dirt and dust at the table.

As Dean saw it, the best thing that had come from his brother's rash, impulsive decision to marry Pilar on that drive down to Texas was that her mother had traveled up to Montana with them. For a household that had seen only men for the last two decades, having a woman around who loved to cook was a damned blessing. It was a good thing there was always so much work to do around the ranch, or Dean would have gotten fat from the delicious meals Jimena dished up.

He stepped into the bathing room and was instantly hit by the steamy scent of mint and citrus.

The idea of that tall, slim redhead stripping down naked in this room not long ago had Dean's shoulders drawing up as his stomach muscles tensed. A flashing image of her pale skin slathered with soap bubbles and nothing else shot through his brain, causing an instant reaction below the belt. Everything in his body tightened up.

He kicked the door shut behind him, then strode forward to pump fresh water into the tub. A cold bath would do him good.

~∞~

His bride managed to avoid him for the rest of the night, staying upstairs in the bedroom she'd claimed down the hall from his own. He wasn't so lucky with his brother and his family. Though Randall and Pilar had a fine working kitchen in their house beyond the eastern horse pasture, they'd decided, along with Jimena, to intrude upon Dean's quiet dinner.

It didn't matter that they took four or five suppers a week together and that Jimena had clearly planned for such a big meal to be shared. It was obvious they had all gathered at his table for one reason only.

Curiosity.

Well, they'd be sorely disappointed. Dean was not in the mood to share the slightest bit of information with any of them.

Randall, of course, couldn't keep his busy mouth shut. "So, how's the little woman settling in?"

Dean ignored him as he stuffed a mouthful of food past his teeth.

"Jimena says she's a real lady. Sweet and polite."

Dean coughed at that, nearly choking on his tamale.

"Are you sure you wanna take her back before the judge tomorrow? I could take over on the ranch for a while so you could have a bit of a honeymoon."

Dean didn't reply right away. It was not the first time Randall had asked for more to do. Though Dean loved his brother—even when he irritated him—he struggled with the idea of passing on any more responsibilities to the younger man. First of all, it'd take precious time he didn't have to teach Randall what Dean had absorbed on a daily basis from the age of seven. Not to mention his brother's attention didn't often stay on one task for long, and Dean worried that Randall's desire to be more involved in running the place wouldn't last.

There had been a time when Dean was young that he had envied his brother's freedom. While Dean had been practically roped to his granddad's side, learning every aspect of running a cattle ranch the size of the Lawton spread, Randall had been free to run wild. And that's exactly what he'd done.

Of course, as he got older, Randall had learned to buckle down when necessary. He drove the cattle to market each year, rode out with the cowboys during branding season, and managed to complete any other small task that was sent his way. He just had too much of their dad in him.

Dean couldn't risk giving his brother more responsibility if there was any chance Randall wouldn't follow through.

"You're the foreman," Dean finally replied. "There's more than enough for you to do."

Randall set his fork down and leaned forward over the table. "The boys don't need me to babysit them. They all know what to do. I'm barely necessary. Maybe, if I helped you out with more of the administration tasks, you'd be freed up to handle that other problem."

Dean tensed. He really did not need to be reminded of the issue with the slaughtered cattle just now. He had already told Randall and the other cowboys not to bother the women with information on the violent acts. He did not want them getting spooked.

He met Randall's open expression with a hard look. It took only a moment for Randall to realize his slip, and he lowered his gaze back to his food.

Dean hoped that would be the end of it, but he should have known better.

"So, what exactly do you intend to do about your new bride?" Pilar's soft-spoken question was accented with Spanish. She had known a good amount of English when she'd met Randall, but they had been teaching each other their respective languages from the moment they met so she had become quite proficient.

His brother—not so much, yet.

In the short time the petite Texas woman had been married to Randall, Dean had come to see how she was a perfect balance to his brother. While Randall was impulsive and took nothing seriously, Pilar was thoughtful and patient.

Her question reignited Dean's shame in having acted so rashly in marrying the redhead on sight. He met Pilar's dark-brown eyes. He hated himself for the silence that followed her words, but he couldn't bring himself to admit his error in judgment.

"See!" Randall shouted with a grin and a dramatic gesture of his fork. "It's like I told you. For the first time in Dean Lawton's perfectly structured life, he doesn't know what the hell he's doing."

Dean swung his gaze back to his brother as his chest tightened. "Not the first time."

Knowing exactly what Dean was referring to, Randall replied in a lower but no less insistent tone, "Maybe this marriage is an unexpected blessing. I think this woman could be good for you."

"Did you even see the woman? She's used to a far finer life than what we have here. Trust me, the lady wants nothing more than to move on. You'd best get anything else out of your head right now," Dean said, bringing an end to the discussion. Rising from his chair, he looked at Jimena. "Thank you for the wonderful meal."

Before anyone else could say anything in response, he left the dining room, taking his dirty dishes with him to the kitchen. Then left the house altogether. He kept walking until he reached the barn. Stepping into the familiar hazy shadows, he made his way down the center aisle between the stalls as every now and then a horse nickered or huffed in greeting. At the far end of the barn was his office. Aside from the open range, which he so rarely got to visit these days, this was his last true place of refuge.

He was sick and tired of his brother's interference. He knew Randall meant well, but Dean was content with how things were. He'd once imagined a different future, but with that no longer possible, he had no desire to start yearning for anything else.

He lit a lantern that hung from a nail on the wall and sat at his desk to pull out one of the ranch's financial ledgers.

When he got too wound up in his thoughts, going through the books always settled him down. Decades worth of ranch business were captured in the many ledgers that had been started by his grand-dad when he'd first decided to raise cattle nearly thirty years ago. Almost everything in those books was noted in his granddad's neat and even hand: the price of feed for the horses, lumber, tack, and other equipment; cattle prices; even the price of sheep for a short stint when Augie Lawton had considered diversifying his herd.

In only one of those books was there a section filled out by Dean's father. It spanned just a couple years prior to his unexpected death. Matthew Lawton's handwriting was a far cry from his father's regulated script. Bold and slanted, it was nearly unreadable. But Dean had learned how to make it out easily enough.

Then everything returned to Augie's hand. The old man didn't give up the ledgers again until his fingers became too weak to grip the pencil. Only then did he allow Dean to take over the task. That was more than five years ago now.

It stunned him how quickly time passed when its pages could be flipped through with a flick of a finger.

Dean reached the pages that spanned the spring of '79. The information was faithfully recorded. No detail was missed. There was no shocking rise or fall in the prices, no significant change in the numbers plugged into those pages.

It didn't tell the whole story.

Regret flowed dark and heavy through Dean at the sight of those even rows of descriptions and currency listings that he himself had entered. Perfect rows. Even script. Just as Augie had taught him. Just as the ranch deserved.

Dean slammed the book shut and stood in a rush that scraped his chair back over the wooden floor. The sound was jarring after the steady silence that had been interrupted only by the sound of turning pages.

He stalked over to a narrow cabinet in the corner and took out a bottle of bourbon and a glass, bringing both back to the desk. As he poured the liquor, he couldn't help but think of the woman sleeping in his house right now. The house he'd remodeled for nearly two years to ready the place for a different woman who would never come to live there.

Lifting his glass, he tipped the whole of its contents down his throat.

EIGHT

COURTNEY WOKE THE NEXT MORNING IN A FRIGHTFUL mood.

Despite her utter exhaustion and the fact that her bed had been far more comfortable than other accommodations she'd experienced since leaving Boston, she had barely slept a wink.

She would have thought nighttime in such a secluded, isolated area would have been silent. It was far from it. The quiet had been punctuated by the hooting calls of night-hunting owls, the incessant rustle of crickets, and the distant sound of horses in the barn. Sounds that had Courtney's eyes popping open every time she heard something new and unexpected.

But it was not just the unfamiliar sounds that had kept her alert through the night.

The bedroom itself was lovely, if she were honest with herself, containing a large brass bed covered in what appeared to be a hand-stitched quilt made of various patterns in pale green, yellow, and peach.

But the door had no lock.

Courtney had shoved a little white-painted wooden

chair under the handle, hoping it would keep any unwanted visitors at bay. Not that she truly expected anyone to intrude upon her privacy, but just the thought of being in the house alone with that man had her insides spinning into a mini-riot.

The night before, with her hunger still satisfied from the meal Jimena had provided for her before her bath, Courtney had been content to stay in the little bedroom while the others ate downstairs. From her window, which overlooked the barn and the pasture beyond, she had seen the brother drive up in a wagon just as the sun was setting. Seated beside him was a young woman dressed in a way similar to Jimena, with thick black hair in a braid that was wound around her head like a crown. The beautiful woman, likely Jimena's daughter, was very obviously with child, which explained the sedate pace of the wagon.

Though it had grown dark by the time supper ended, there was enough moonlight to see the couple leaving again, accompanied by Jimena. Courtney was disturbed by the older woman's departure. Having Jimena nearby had been the only thing to help ease some of her discomfort.

As she had sat watching the others drive away, she'd heard the sound of booted steps making their way up the stairs. The steps stopped some way down the hall, followed by the distinct sound of a door opening and closing again.

Courtney had spent her entire life surrounded by servants and family and friends. Yet she found herself alone in a house with a strange and bad-tempered man, in the middle of the Montana plains, with no lock on her door. She had never felt more vulnerable.

To say she spent a night filled with anxiety and uncertainty would have been an understatement.

When the waking sun started to shift the darkness into lovely shades of gold and she came to another realization—her windows faced the east—she gave up on sleeping altogether. With a heavy sigh, she rose from the comfortable bed, still wearing the borrowed blouse and skirt. A small wooden bench sat before the windows, and Courtney took a seat. Bringing her feet up, she tucked her skirts around her legs and wrapped her arms around her bent knees. She turned her gaze out the window, over the barn and pastureland, as the sun slowly crept over the horizon.

Courtney had always been a city girl. She loved the hustle and excitement, the culture and society of Boston, and she always enjoyed her family's annual shopping trip to New York City. But she couldn't deny that the scene spreading beyond her window was beautiful—in a quaint, pastoral sort of way.

The sleepy yet elegant stretch of dawn first gilded the tips of a small copse of trees that spread to the north, then lit across the roof of the barn before finally spreading through the morning mist to glisten across the endless expanse of grass and reflect on the surface of a river that wound casually through the southern stretch of her view.

Horses grazed in the distant pasture, and she thought she could see the gable of a little house over a gentle rise in the landscape. She wondered if that was where the brother and Jimena's daughter had their home.

Courtney wasn't sure how long she sat there as the sun brightened the strange and unfamiliar world around her, but at some point during her quiet observance of morning's arrival, the ugly mood she had woken up with shifted into a sense of hope. Soon, the odd events of yesterday would be resolved and she would be on her own again, independent and free to take another step in her new life. Her current circumstances were nothing more than a momentary setback, a brief bump in the road that spread before her.

As her usual optimism settled back into place, she noted the cheerful appearance of Jimena, in another brightly colored skirt and blouse, coming over the rise, driving the little wagon.

Courtney released a breath, feeling some relief in having the other woman nearby again.

Her relief was short-lived, however, as at nearly the same moment, a door opened down the hall and booted steps sounded on the wooden floor. Courtney tensed, half expecting the cowboy to come to her door.

He didn't, and her heart rate slowly returned to normal as she heard his steps receding down the stairs and then out the front door.

He would be taking her back to town today. Back to the judge to have the marriage certificate torn into a thousand pieces. She was still stunned by the idea that a man would simply marry a woman right off the train, even if he didn't intend to stay married to her. That *she* was the bride was even harder to fathom. It just didn't seem real. And it wasn't really. Soon it would be just a distant memory. One that she and Alexandra would laugh about once she reached Helena.

A soft knock on the door brought her out of her uneasy reverie and to her feet.

It was Jimena, carrying her wedding gown and all the layers of her underclothes, cleaned and pressed. She must have stayed up half the night laundering the fine clothing.

The shorter woman swept into the bedroom and began laying the items out on the bed, a litany of Spanish flowing from her lips. Jimena, apparently, was a morning person.

Thankfully, Courtney was not expected to respond to the woman's one-sided conversation. After she removed her borrowed clothes, Jimena tossed under-garments over Courtney's head and expertly cinched her back into her corset, then buttoned up the long row of buttons on the back of her gown, which amazingly was not nearly as badly ruined as Courtney had expected.

Once Courtney was dressed, Jimena nudged her toward the chair and stepped behind her to unravel the braid that had gotten messy during the night. Courtney tried to tell the woman a few times during the process that she could manage to do a few things for herself, but Jimena waved off her words with a smile and continued at the task.

Courtney wondered if the kind woman was aware of the strange circumstances that had brought Courtney here. The prior evening in the kitchen, she had gotten the sense that the woman believed her to be a true bride. Did Jimena now understand the truth?

Embarrassment burned in Courtney's cheeks, which managed to spark a bit of her temper. She had nothing to be embarrassed about, except maybe that she hadn't realized a stranger might marry her off the street. It was Dean Lawton who had behaved dishonorably.

But she highly doubted that the man had any experience with such a vulnerable emotion as embarrassment.

"Terminé. Estás preciosa." Jimena stepped back and clapped her hands. "Mira," she said as she turned Courtney toward an oval mirror on the wall.

Courtney stiffened.

The white gown looked nearly as good as new, and her hair had been beautifully dressed in a thick chignon at the back of her head. The coiffure was accented with braids and twists rather than flowers, but even without any of her grandmother's pearls, the effect was startling.

She looked like a bride. Again.

"¿No te gusta?"

Courtney turned quickly to Jimena. "It's beautiful," she assured the older woman with a smile, though she doubted she sounded very convincing. "You have managed a miracle. Gracias."

Jimena nodded and smiled then gestured toward the door. "El jefe estará esperando."

El jefe.

Jimena had used that phrase yesterday as well. Courtney realized it more likely translated to *boss* rather than *chief* as she had first believed. Jimena was obviously referring to Lawton.

He was probably as impatient as she was to see this marriage annulled.

And she was going to have to make the long drive back to town with the insufferable man. She closed her eyes for a moment, recalling the derision and arrogance in his fine-honed features, the light of annoyance in his eyes.

She could not wait to be free of him.

Now back in her fine clothes, she felt a return of her usual confidence. Lifting her head and drawing as deep a breath as the corset would allow, she left the corner bedroom and walked at a sedate pace down the stairs. Before Courtney stepped outside, Jimena, who had followed her to the front door, stopped her to give her a quick but warm embrace.

Though awkward with such an emotional display, Courtney appreciated the gesture nonetheless, and she smiled as she thanked the woman again.

Then she turned and stepped out onto the covered porch.

The wagon was pulled up in front of the house, and Dean Lawton stood beside it with his thumbs hooked through the belt loops of his denims and his cowboy hat tipped low over his eyes to block the swiftly rising sun. Despite the casual way he leaned back against the wagon with his legs crossed at the ankles, his impatience rolled off him in waves.

Courtney paused before descending from the porch, forcing him to lift his chin to look up at her. When he did, she stiffened at the sudden swirling sensation inside her.

The man looked terribly handsome in the light of a fresh morning, despite the way his eyes crinkled at the corners when he squinted against the sun's slanted rays.

Or maybe because of it.

He cast a brief but sweeping glance at the return of her wedding gown before the corner of his mouth tilted in a way that had nothing to do with amusement and he gave a curt nod toward the wagon. "Let's get this over with."

"Gladly," Courtney replied, then descended the three steps to the ground and approached the wagon. She paused to grasp her skirts in one hand, but when she looked for Dean to offer a hand to assist her up into the wagon, he wasn't beside her.

A second later, he grasped her waist from behind and lifted her from the ground until her feet made contact with the step board on the side of the wagon.

Goodness! Courtney barely caught her breath before he released her to take long strides around the wagon to the other side, where he leapt up to take the driver's seat.

As the wagon jostled and swayed, Courtney quickly took her seat, grasping the side of the wagon to keep her balance.

With a flick of reins and a low murmured word, he set the horses and wagon in motion.

The drive into town was horrendous.

No conversation.

No pleasantries.

All Courtney could do was watch the scenery pass by. It was beautiful, but she couldn't enjoy it when she was more uncomfortable than she had ever been in her life. Mainly because she could feel the tension in the man seated beside her. The cowboy was like a tightly wound spool of wire that at any second could burst into spinning.

She kept waiting for him to say something—anything, really—but he never did.

And she certainly wasn't about to.

It wasn't until they reached the edge of town that he finally spoke. "After seeing Judge Wilkerson, I'll get you a room at the boardinghouse and ask around town for anyone heading in the direction you're going. There's likely to be someone around willing to get you the rest of the way to your destination."

Courtney looked askance at the man beside her. His tone was stiff, and his words had a sense of reluctance about them. Like he regretted having to do even that much for her.

"No, thank you. I will manage on my own," she replied.

He slid a glance in her direction. She saw the doubt in his eyes and clenched her teeth with irritation. "If you say so," he said.

Drawing the wagon to a stop in front of the judge's office, he wasted no time jumping to the ground and coming around to her side, where he stopped and reached for her waist again.

Why on earth couldn't he just offer his hand like a gentleman?

Her breath caught as she flew from the wagon to the ground. She grasped his shoulders to steady herself against the swiftness of the maneuver.

Likely noticing her imbalance, he kept his hands on her for a couple moments after her feet hit the ground, making her breath catch for an entirely different reason.

Standing there between the wagon and his tall, lean,

male body, Courtney experienced a rush of heat that blasted from her toes up through her center to her face. His large hands were wrapped almost completely around her waist, his strong thumbs pressing firmly to her belly while his broad shoulders were close enough to block her view of anything else, leaving only him. On her swiftly drawn breath, she detected the scent of fresh hay and warm male as her gaze found the pulse thrumming at the side of his throat.

Her mouth going dry, she tipped her head back to look at his face. His expression was all hard lines and enticing shadows, except for his eyes. Even topped by the slash of his heavy brows, his eyes held a silvery light. He was an odd mixture of impatience and pride, mystery and enticement, especially when he looked at her as he was now.

Did he ever smile? A real, genuine smile?

She blinked.

She shouldn't care. She *didn't* care.

His handsomeness was stirring her brain. She could certainly appreciate an attractive man. It didn't change the fact that she also thought him insufferably ill-mannered.

She dropped her hands from his shoulders, and he stepped back, releasing her. "You do not need to do that every time," she chided stiffly. "Offering your hand is perfectly acceptable and would see the job done just as well."

"With all that flounce and fluff?" he asked with a dubious glance at the draped layers of her gown and the extended train of her skirt. "I doubt it. You'd be more likely to end up with a mouth full of dirt."

Then he turned away and started toward the judge's office, leaving Courtney to follow behind him.

She gave a huff. No manners at all.

Sweeping her "flounce and fluff" out of her way, she followed him with as much dignity as she could manage, since she'd finally noticed that several people in town had stopped to watch her and the cowboy's odd confrontation.

She could only hope no one knew their purpose for getting to town so early.

They stepped into the small office building to find the same gangly, young clerk sitting at the desk in the front room. "Judge Wilkerson in yet?" Lawton asked without preamble.

The clerk glanced curiously at Courtney as she stepped around from behind Lawton to stand at his side. She made sure at least five inches separated them, but she was not about to cower behind his shoulder. She wanted to see this done as much as he did.

"Uh, he came in just a bit ago. I'll see if he's free."

They waited in silence as the clerk sidled out from behind his desk to disappear into the room beyond. A minute later, the young man returned and gave a gesture for them to follow. "He's on a tight schedule today, so it'll need to be quick."

"It won't take a minute," Dean said as he once again led the way into the judge's chamber.

Exactly as yesterday, the judge sat at his large desk behind stacks of paperwork. He looked up at their entrance, showing only mild curiosity at their return.

"Mr. Lawton, Mrs. Lawton," he said in a gravelly drawl. "What can I do for you today?"

Courtney nearly flinched at being addressed in such a way. The term made this marriage seem that much more real, as ridiculous as it was, and momentarily threw her into a panic that stole her voice.

Dean was not similarly affected. "We need an annulment."

The judge stilled. Bushy brows dropped dramatically over his eyes, and his thin lips pressed into a harsh line. His sharp gaze jumped back and forth between them, taking in their appearance and their manner, which was clearly one of discomfort and impatience. Then he released a breath that was somewhere between a sigh and cough as he leaned back in his chair.

Meeting Dean's eyes, he said, "No."

Courtney was stunned by the denial. Of course, the judge would grant an annulment. He couldn't just refuse, could he?

Her attention flew from the judge to the man beside her. Her husband appeared more irritated than stunned as he took a step forward, his body tall and tense. "What do you mean *no*?"

"I mean, Mr. Lawton, that I will not grant you an annulment. You came in here yesterday all fired up and demanded a civil union. I performed that union. You then took your bride home. Why the hell would I allow an annulment the very next day?"

The rising frustration in the man beside her was almost palpable.

Courtney felt only a growing sense of disbelief. What kind of place was this where a man married a stranger off the street and a judge could refuse to do his civic duty?

"We didn't suit." The words were low and forced through gritted teeth.

"You can't know that after less than one day."

"Excuse me...Judge Wilkerson, is it?" Courtney asked as she also stepped forward to once again stand beside the man who was currently her husband. She needed to do something to end this farce. "I am afraid this situation was actually a bit of a misunderstanding." She smiled and gestured toward her *husband* as she continued. "We both made some erroneous assumptions yesterday that led to the union of which you speak. We are simply here today to rectify that situation. We should not have married in the first place."

The judge sat quietly as she spoke. When she finished, he reached for a small case set at the edge of his desk and withdrew a thick cigar. Bringing it to his nose, he took a long sniff before meeting her gaze across his desk.

"Whatever they were, the circumstances that brought you here yesterday don't change the current situation. You two are married. Husband and wife. And I will not tear that union asunder on a whim. We have far too few weddings in these parts—too few women—to take such a thing lightly."

"But, Your Honor—" Courtney began before her argument was cut short by the judge rising to his feet.

"I will give you one month. One month to discover if you might suit after all. Take your bride home, Lawton. If you still do not want each other after four weeks' time, come back and I will dissolve the union."

"Judge—" Dean started.

"That's my final word," the judge stated sharply. "Now go. I must prepare for my next meeting."

"Your Honor—" Courtney tried again, but Dean grasped her firmly by the elbow. When she looked up at him, he gave a short jerk of his head. He led her from the room with long strides, past the clerk and out onto the boardwalk. Courtney practically had to run to keep up with him and finally managed to free herself from his grip once they reached the street.

"Hold on just one moment, Mr. Lawton," she said as she spun around to face him. "Tell me he did not mean what he just said."

Dean stood there with his eyes narrowed and his jaw tight. His words were hard and heavy. "He meant it."

"That cannot possibly be ethical. Or lawful."

"Ethics don't matter. And Wilkerson *is* the law. If he says four weeks, then that's what it is."

"Well, we have to change his mind. We have to explain. We have to go back in there," she finished as she started to step around him and march right back into the judge's office.

She was brought up short again by Dean's hand around her arm, gentle but firm. "It won't do any good. Any more arguing on our part is likely to extend the duration."

"Would you stop doing that!" she shouted as she shook off his hand. Her breath was getting tight. She pressed her hand to her sternum and tried to breathe deeply—a difficult task with her cinched corset. "I will not," she stated in a fierce whisper. "Stay married. To you."

"We've got no choice," he replied, his voice low but still tight with his own angry resistance.

Courtney shook her head in denial. "I do not accept that," she stated emphatically.

"You have to," he countered.

"There must be a way."

His expression darkened to one of frustration. "Wilkerson ain't one to be circumvented."

"It is ludicrous."

He nodded his agreement.

Knowing he didn't want this any more than she did, she found his acceptance infuriating. The hopelessness of the situation was like a weight pressing her into the earth. Her instinct was to push back, to fight it. "I do not want to be your wife."

He stepped toward her again, the look on his face dark, his tone harsh when he spoke. "I sure as hell don't want to be your husband. But for four weeks, that's what we are, so get over it."

Courtney's chest heaved as anger replaced her quiet panic. "You did this. You and your heavy-handed, thoughtless actions. I came out here to finally feel free, to make my own choices in the world. And now I am trapped in this situation with you due to no fault of my own. By no *choice* of my own. I will not just *get over it.*"

"Then you'd better start planning for the next four weeks to be a living hell."

Her eyes widened. "Is that a threat?"

"It's whatever you make it, princess. I've gotta go pick something up at the post office, and then we're heading back to the ranch. I'm not gonna waste any more of my day arguing with you about something that can't be changed."

He didn't bother waiting for her to respond. He just turned and walked away, leaving Courtney standing there with at least a half dozen people staring at her from the boardwalks and doorways nearby.

Lawton didn't seem bothered by all the attention they'd garnered, if he'd even noticed it, but Courtney was far too ingrained with the desire to avoid scenes and scandal at all costs. The little audience made her flush bright with embarrassment. Straightening her posture, she lifted her chin as she swept her gaze over all of those still staring at her.

One by one, they glanced away.

Grateful to no longer have anyone witnessing her growing uncertainty, she almost allowed her shoulders to drop a little. But then her gaze lit on a decoratively painted sign across the street. Her breath caught as she was hit with a delightful burst of inspiration.

With a half smile forming on her lips, she grasped her extra-long skirts in both hands and started across the dirt street to a quaint little corner shop with large windows displaying ready-made dresses and bonnets.

It was about time she had something to wear other than this cursed wedding gown. And her *dear husband* was going to foot the bill.

NINE

It took Dean more than an hour to find her. And by then, his frustration was high.

When he retrieved the package his brother had actually sent him to pick up from the post office, he understood what his brother had meant about Dean knowing it when he saw it. The postmaster opened the crate so Dean could verify the delivery. Inside was a baby cradle in a similar design to the one their mother had used for them.

He'd carried the heavy crate back to the wagon, only to find that his bride had not heeded his instruction. She was nowhere about.

First, Dean went to the boardinghouse, thinking she'd head there in an attempt to set some distance between them. That wasn't an option for them, however. Judge Wilkerson stated she was to go back to the ranch with Dean. If he found out she had gotten a room in town instead, the old man was likely to extend their marriage by another week. It was the kind of man he was.

Dean cursed himself, as he had about a thousand

times since yesterday. The consequences of his rash and misguided decision just continued to multiply.

When Mabel at the boardinghouse told him she hadn't caught a single glimpse of a redheaded woman in a wedding gown, he strode down the street to the restaurant. Maybe she had stepped inside for a bite to eat. They had left the house without breakfast. It would have been a reasonable assumption to think the woman might be hungry.

She wasn't there either. And hadn't been seen.

After leaving the restaurant, Dean stood on the boardwalk and scanned up and down the main road through town. He was sorely tempted to forget about the woman and just head over to the saloon for a much-needed drink. But that would only delay things, and he had to get back to the ranch. This was the second day now that he'd had to leave his responsibilities to come to town.

He might have caused this blasted situation, but he'd be damned if he'd allow it to be stretched out any longer than absolutely necessary. The woman was going to have to learn that if she wanted to make it through the next four weeks as painlessly as possible, she'd have to stop being so damned contrary and just do things his way.

And right now, all he wanted to do was get out of town and return to the ranch.

Where the hell did she go?

He checked the bank, the church, the general store, and the dentist's office.

Hot, tired, and frustrated, it wasn't until he circled back around toward the wagon that he caught sight of the dressmaker's shop.

THE COWBOY'S HONOR   107

The shop had opened a couple of months ago, and he couldn't imagine it had gotten much business, with so few women in the area. But today there happened to be one more.

Sure enough, when he ducked in through the doors and heard the chatter of female voices coming from the back of the store, he recognized the cultured tones of his bride. He gingerly made his way past a little sitting area arranged with curved and cushioned chairs upholstered in a pale-pink shade. A crystal vase holding full-blown roses stood on a slim-legged table, and the shop was filled with the flowers' scent. As he sidestepped past elegant displays of ribbons and lace samples, the phrase "a bull in a china shop" came to mind. He'd never felt so large and physically awkward.

But he forged on.

Stacks of cloth bolts in various colors, patterns, and fabrics covered two long worktables near the back of the store. A familiar pile of white froth had been tossed onto a nearby chair.

Beyond that stood a folding privacy screen that effectively concealed the only other two occupants in the shop—his wayward bride and, presumably, the dressmaker.

"Here is another one I've almost finished," the dressmaker said. "I can alter it to your measurements easily enough. It would make a wonderful day dress. Very pretty, but practical enough for life on a ranch."

Hit with the realization that his bride was dressing and undressing just beyond that flimsy screen, Dean came to a sudden stop. The muscles in his thighs tensed as unwelcome heat shot through his insides.

He ground his back teeth and chased away the unwelcome physical reaction.

She was just a woman. One with a fiery temper and an uppity attitude who happened to be stuck in his life for the next four weeks. Nothing more.

"It is pretty," his wife replied softly. There was a note of reluctance in her voice. Likely, she was fighting her disgust over the plainer fashions worn by the women of these parts. She wasn't going to find anything with near the elegance of the creation she'd shown up wearing.

His bout of lust back under control, Dean crossed his arms over his chest and leaned his shoulder against the post beside him. He didn't relish having to wait for the woman in this den of femininity, but he wasn't about to let her out of his sight again until the ink was dry on the annulment paperwork.

"I'll take this one as well," she stated after another minute.

"As you wish, Mrs. Lawton. I will have it delivered with the rest of your order as soon as it's properly altered. And you're sure it's all to be billed to the Lawton Ranch?"

The sound of fabric sliding over skin reached Dean as the dress was removed.

"Indeed. As I said, it's my husband's wedding gift to me. I can't very well be expected to manage as a proper Western wife if all I have to wear is my wedding gown."

The smugness in her voice was not lost on Dean, and he clenched his teeth against refuting her claim. He'd had enough of making a fool of himself today. If she wanted to charge a few frocks to the ranch, so be it. If it'd assure her cooperation, it was worth the cost.

"But don't you want to keep it at least? It's so lovely that it could become a family heirloom."

"No." The reply was swift and flat. "The gown has no value to me. You may resell it or take it apart and refashion it into something else. Whatever you wish."

"Thank you, Mrs. Lawton. It is rare to be in possession of something so fine. I have a hundred ideas for it already."

"You are more than welcome. I suppose I will wear that blue one there, since it is finished and fits me near enough. The rest should be ready in a few days?"

"Yes, Mrs. Lawton. I'll have the dresses and the undergarments you requested delivered to the ranch as soon as they are ready. I'll work day and night."

There was a further rustle of fabric and shifting movement as his wife finished dressing. When the dressmaker stepped to the screen and started to pull it back again, her attention was directed toward her customer, so she did not see Dean standing only a few steps away.

"Thank you, Mrs. Lawton. I've only been in town for a couple months, but I will admit I was starting to despair of having any real customers. I was honestly considering returning to St. Louis when you walked in this morning."

"My pleasure. You have done me a great service today, Mrs. Grainer. I am sure the ladies about town will soon realize what lovely dresses you offer, and your shop will become quite popular. Give it time."

"I hope you're right," the woman replied as she

turned around and jumped a clear foot as she caught sight of Dean. "Oh my word," she gasped.

"What is it?" Vivid green eyes in a fair face framed by slightly mussed red hair peeked around the edge of the screen. Her lively, curious expression shifted instantly into tight annoyance. "Oh, it is my husband. I can see how his harsh visage could cause a fright."

"Hello, *Wife*," Dean replied. "Doing a little shopping?"

She smiled then. Brightly and beautifully. The change made her lips curve in an attractive bow and brought a sparkle to her eyes. It was the light of mischief, but it affected Dean all the same as the tension tightened his muscles and that unwanted desire returned with a vengeance.

"Why, yes I am," she answered cheerfully as she stepped out from behind the screen. "I was certain you wouldn't want your wife to go on with nothing to wear."

He lowered his chin, breaking eye contact.

The sudden picture flashing through his head of her having nothing to wear did not help his current state one bit. To combat it, he intentionally noted that she was wearing a dress in robin's-egg blue with draping skirts and a plain, fitted bodice. The dress was a far cry from her wedding gown in terms of fanciness, but it was still more elaborate than what most women in the area would be wearing.

"I will just get this order finished up. Would you like me to start a line of credit, Mr. Lawton?" the dressmaker asked.

After an awkward moment passed while he didn't

answer, his wife spoke up. "That would be lovely, Mrs. Grainer. Thank you."

Mrs. Grainer stepped away, leaving the two of them alone.

Dean's gaze fell to her feet, peeking from beneath the flounced ruffles decorating the hem of her new dress. "New shoes as well," he muttered.

She lifted her skirt a couple inches and turned her foot this way and that to show off the serviceable brown leather short boots. "I couldn't very well be expected to continue wearing my slippers."

Dean didn't like the way the little glimpse of her slim ankles made his stomach clench. "And you're putting it on the ranch's credit." His words were low and graveled.

"I am," she replied defiantly, bringing his attention back to her pert face. "I figured it was the least you could do since you haven't even deigned to offer an apology for your actions yesterday."

Dean clenched his teeth. She wasn't wrong.

He should apologize. He knew it.

But it was a helluva lot easier to just pay the damn dress bill.

"Did it occur to you that I might not have the money to spend on a new wardrobe?"

Her eyes widened. Obviously, it hadn't. "No, actually. Umm…do you have the funds?"

His reply was stiff. "It's a little late for concern, but yes, I do."

"Then all is well," she replied with a ready smile.

He realized with some surprise that her cheerfulness was not put on. She was smiling in earnest.

"What the hell put you in such a happy mood?" he asked.

She gave a little shrug. "Shopping always has a way of turning the worst days brighter. Don't you think?"

"No."

"Well, that's too bad for you. I have decided not to dwell on what cannot be changed. If I am to be stranded here, I am going to make the most of it. In four weeks' time, the marriage will be as if it had never existed, and I will continue on my way as planned. I came out west for an adventure, and that is what I am going to have. It might as well start now." Her eyes tipped up at the outer corners as she met his hard stare. "You may remain harsh and angry over the unfortunate circumstances we find ourselves in. I honestly expect nothing less from you. I, however, have decided to get over it."

Dean nearly choked in reaction to that last quip. She'd done it on purpose—taken his words and twisted them inside out to suit her new approach to the situation. Her about-face was irritating and impressive at the same time.

But mostly irritating.

"Time to go," he said curtly. "There's work to be done yet today."

"I'm ready. I just need to grab my bonnet."

Great. A bonnet too.

He turned—resisting the twist of amusement that threatened his lips—and started from the shop, feeling more than hearing her as she rushed to follow close behind him. As soon as they stepped into the sunshine, she came up alongside him despite his ground-eating stride. He had to admit to a small dose of admiration for her clever bit of revenge. From the periphery of his vision, he saw her place a straw bonnet on her head and tie the ribbons beneath her chin, covering the vivid red of her hair and shading her creamy skin.

She'd probably throw a fit if the sun started to bring out some freckles.

Though, in thinking about it, the damned things would likely only make her more attractive.

Stopping at the wagon, Dean turned and grasped her about her trim waist. His stomach clenched as he realized she no longer wore the stiff, unnatural corset. Under his hands was nothing but warm, soft woman.

Before he could lift her, she leaned away from him and pressed her hands against his shoulders in an attempt to hold him at bay. "You do not have to lift me up every time," she stated firmly. "Now that I do not have the confining skirts of my bridal gown, I am sure I can manage just fine with the offer of your hand."

He paused. His eyes slid over her features, and he noted again how pretty she was, especially since she wasn't glowering at him as intensely as she usually did. Her eyes were smart and direct beneath the elegant line of her russet-colored eyebrows. Her cheeks were high and held a faint rosy hue, while her nose was straight and narrow, and her lips… Their natural coral-pink color made him hold his breath. He wasn't sure he'd ever seen lips that color before. And surely he'd never seen a mouth that curved in such a way, with pert arching lines and a lush dip at the bottom.

When he didn't speak and didn't move to let her

go, she tipped her head curiously and lifted one brow by the tiniest degree. The shift in her expression fanned the inner discomfort he'd been feeling since he'd run into this woman.

He replied in a tone rougher than it should have been, "This is quicker." And he swung her up into the wagon, ignoring how the sudden widening of her eyes at the maneuver sent a streak of satisfaction—and something else—shooting through him.

TEN

WHEN COURTNEY ADAMS SET HER MIND TO SOME-
thing, she didn't often fail. She enjoyed facing chal-
lenges head-on with unwavering faith that things
would turn out as they were meant to.

Of course, it was rare for anything not to go in her
favor. Her father had once told her she had been born
under a charmed star.

So, despite the extremely odd and distressing news
that she had been married without her consent and
the fact that she was now stuck in this rural area
of Montana—who knew how many miles from
Helena—she had decided to stop dwelling on what
had gone wrong and start enjoying what was right.

One, she was well out of Boston.

Two, she was not married to Geoffrey and living in
complete ignorance about his love affair with another.

Three, aside from the little issue of being the
momentary bride of a gruff yet stupidly attractive
stranger, she was entirely on her own, which led to…

Four, her adventure had begun.

She was going to spend the next four weeks on a

real working cattle ranch. How much more adventurous could a pampered lady from the east expect to get?

And, of course, she knew she was pampered. She knew the man sitting beside her on the uncomfortable wooden seat saw her as the spoiled little heiress she was. He probably also thought she was a frightful shrew after the fit she'd thrown the day before.

But she didn't particularly care what he thought of her.

She had come west to test herself, to push herself to new limits of experience and previously unexplored levels of independence, and to discover if she was worthy of more than to be the arranged bride of a man who possessed all the characteristics of a perfect husband but reserved his love and passion for someone else.

Love and passion.

If she was to be honest with herself—and Courtney always tried to be at least that—beyond independence and self-confidence, perhaps she was hoping she might find something like that for herself.

She had to admit that Alexandra's escapade the year before and her letters detailing her new life had inspired Courtney more than she'd been willing to acknowledge.

She feared, however, that the kind of connection her friend had found with her bounty-hunter husband was not for everyone. Courtney couldn't think of a single other person of her acquaintance who had the same.

So true love and passion were probably a long shot. Adventure was still a worthy goal.

"I'm sorry for what happened yesterday."

Courtney startled at the roughly muttered words. She'd assumed their drive would be made in silence, as the previous two trips had been. But then the meaning of his words sank in and she turned to face him.

"You're sorry for what happened?" she repeated, slightly incredulous.

Aside from a quick and subtle flick of his gaze to the side, he kept his focus trained on the road ahead. It took a few moments to realize that was all he was going to say. *That* was the extent of his apology.

After waiting so long for it, Courtney had built up the moment of his contrition in her mind. The reality did not come close to what she'd envisioned. She couldn't even say she'd heard any honest regret in his tone.

She suspected his pride kept him from saying more. But she had a touch of pride herself.

"Oh," she exclaimed with a good dose of drama, "you must be referencing the fact that you dragged me before a judge and married me against my will."

"I didn't know it was against your will," he grumbled.

"A simple question, such as *Do you want to marry me?* would have cleared that up rather nicely."

"You showed up in town wearing a wedding dress."

The way the muscles of his jaw clenched when he spoke was fascinating.

"We have already gone over that. More than once," Courtney replied, trying not to get irritated. "It is no excuse for the way you treated me."

He took a deep breath. "I know. I just said I'm sorry."

"Well. That must have been extremely difficult for you, but I find it a little difficult to simply forgive such high-handed, careless behavior," she finished primly as she turned to face forward.

She would forgive him eventually, of course. She was not good at holding a grudge. But she figured she deserved to see a little groveling first.

That, and she suspected her refusal would trigger a rather heated response, and she'd decided she liked it when he got all gruff and irritated. It was far better than extended silence.

Muttering something incoherent, he gave an expert flick of the driving reins, and the wagon drew up to a swift and sudden stop right there in the middle of the dirt road.

Courtney glanced about, wondering what had caused the abrupt halt.

But she could see nothing to suggest a need for the maneuver. Just the long stretch of the rutted dirt road ahead and behind them, and the endless raw countryside all around. They weren't near any other homesteads at the moment, and there was certainly no other traffic. She might have suspected a wild creature of some sort had gotten in their way, but there was nothing.

Then the man beside her—her husband—turned in his seat and swept his hat off his head to smack it hard against his thigh.

"I apologized. You're gonna accept, then we're gonna move on. Got it?"

The flash of ire in his gaze and the way his features became all tense and hard sparked an answering response inside her. A brilliant flare of heat threatened her recently reestablished good humor, but she resisted its lure. As much as she may have enjoyed it, she really should not lose her temper again.

"No," she replied in a tone of forced lightness, "I

do not. Frankly, an apology means nothing if it isn't sincere. And I find myself doubting yours, especially as I still have absolutely no idea why you did what you did." She smiled. "If you'd care to enlighten me, perhaps I will reconsider."

His gaze narrowed, causing fine lines to fan out from the corners of his eyes. It was odd how those lines made him appear more human somehow, more vulnerable.

Then he spoke and ruined it. "It's none of your damn business."

Courtney stiffened at his language and the heavy-handed tone, but she continued to meet his gaze as she rested her hands calmly in her lap. "I disagree. Since it landed me in the position of being your *wife* for the next four weeks, it most certainly is my business." She lifted a brow, figuring she would give him a little nudge. "I gather it has something to do with your brother...Randall, is it?"

He smacked his hat against his thigh once again and glanced skyward, as though wishing for a heavy dose of patience to be delivered from the heavens. Then he put his hat back on his head and slid her a sideways glance. "You're not gonna let this go, are you?"

Another practiced smile. "I'm afraid not."

The lines across his forehead deepened. He really did not want to do this.

Courtney smiled wider.

He took a heavy breath, then shifted his gaze to look out over the horses, which had started to graze on some grass at the side of the road.

"My brother got it into his head that I need a wife." He paused, and Courtney held her tongue, fighting the urge to ask why. "A few weeks ago, he brought home one of those pamphlets for Eastern brides seeking husbands in the Western Territories. I told him to go to hell, and he said something to the effect of that if I didn't have any interest in finding a bride, maybe he'd do it for me."

Courtney gasped. "He wouldn't have!"

"I didn't think so either." He glanced at her from the corner of his eye. "Then I saw you."

"And your first thought was that your brother had brought me here to marry you?" She could not manage to keep the incredulity from her voice.

He muttered a few incoherent words beneath his breath as he swept his hat off again. Apparently, it was something he did when he was particularly agitated.

"Women like you aren't common around here. The last time a fine-stepping Eastern lady passed through these parts was more than twenty years ago. Before I headed to town yesterday, Randall asked me to pick up something special at the post office."

"I was at the post office," she said, starting to see how he might have jumped to a certain conclusion.

He eyed her directly. "Wearing a wedding gown."

He was really stuck on that point.

But maybe she could understand his assumption. "Still, you could have asked me who I was and why I was there. And you certainly didn't have to take me straight to the judge and marry me, *especially* since you didn't even intend to honor the union."

He lowered his chin a notch while still holding her gaze. "I know." His voice was hard and curt. "But at the time, it seemed like the best way to keep you safe from unwanted attention while I figured out what to do with you."

Courtney's eyes widened in astonishment. "You married me to protect me?"

"These parts can be dangerous for a woman alone. Since I thought you were brought here on account of me, I figured you were my responsibility."

It took a moment for that idea to sink in, and when it did, a rush of warmth accompanied it. But Courtney wasn't quite ready to accept the explanation as it was. "Surely, marriage was not the only solution to the situation."

He muttered a curse under his breath. "Probably not, but I was frustrated about Randall going behind my back. I wasn't thinking straight."

"You were not thinking much at all, in my opinion."

The muscles in his jaw ticked. "I didn't ask for your opinion."

"Well, now you have it. I imagine you will be getting quite a bit more of my opinion over the next four weeks, so you should probably get used to it."

"Now, hold up," he said, his spine going stiff and straight. His features darkened with tension, and his light eyes met hers, hard and direct. The hard shift in his manner caused a wary thrill to chase along her nerves. The broad width of his shoulders was intimidating when so close, and for a moment, Courtney had to resist the urge to shrink away.

She was *not* a shrinker.

She didn't think his rough, commanding attitude was intended to frighten or bully. It seemed more that he was just accustomed to his orders being followed. This man was *not* like the gentlemen back home. He was not bound by the social parameters of behavior she was accustomed to maneuvering around to get her way.

This man lived by different rules. Rules she was not privy to, though she suspected she was about to learn a few of them.

"We're gonna get something settled right here and now," he continued. "We might be married on paper until Judge Wilkerson rips that certificate to pieces, but you are not my wife. I am not your husband. This was a mistake…one I've apologized for once and won't again," he added when she opened her mouth to interrupt.

Courtney pressed her lips together. She could bide her time for the chance to respond.

"You'll have a room in my house," he continued in that sharp tone, "and a seat at my table. But I do not need to hear your opinions or thoughts or anything else you might have to share."

Her eyes narrowed as the blood in her veins grew hot. But still, she held her tongue.

"I have a ranch to run. You need anything, you go to Jimena. Otherwise, you keep to yourself. Got it?"

Courtney took a steady breath, then smiled slowly, though her heart beat fast and heavy with the desire to bash the man over the head. She had never in her life been spoken to in such a manner, and she wasn't about to allow it now. Not from this uncouth, ill-tempered cowboy.

"Again…no, I do not *get it*," she stated firmly. "I

have no intention of getting in your way or interfering with your ranch, Mr. Lawton. However, I will not be shoved into a corner so you can do your best to forget I exist. I've just liberated myself from a gilded cage, and I have no plan to accept more of the same from you. I'm here to start living my life in full, and I will do it on my terms."

He stared at her. His lean, muscled body was unmoving and only inches away. His icy gaze flashed, while his mouth pressed into a firm, frustrated line.

She stared back, soaking in the heightened energy that seemed to bounce between them. Something about going toe-to-toe with this man made her feel so thoroughly...alive. She was not about to let him intimidate her with his harsh, masculine irritation. And she absolutely refused to think about how, in the oddest way, when he was all intense and annoyed, his handsomeness became that much more obvious. It was because of the hard angles and shadowed hollows of his face, those intriguing lines at the corner of his eyes, and the harsh shape of his mouth that looked well-suited for smiles and laughter if the man would just lighten up a bit.

No. She wasn't going to think about that at all.

"Lest you forget," she continued in a lowered tone, "*you* dragged me into this mess of a marriage, so you are going to have to deal with me. As I am. Opinions and all."

His brows lowered, and somehow, the shift actually softened his expression. Not by much, but enough for Courtney to notice. Then one corner of his mouth tilted upward. She wouldn't have called it a smile exactly, but it seemed to be something rather close to it.

"How could I possibly forget when you keep reminding me every chance you get?" His tone was rueful.

Almost amused.

Courtney's insides fluttered wildly, nearly distracting her from her purpose. She would not let the suggestion of his smile ruin another good argument. Keeping her internal reaction under wraps, she lifted her brow in a subtle question, intentionally challenging him to dispute her. "I simply want to make sure we understand each other, Mr. Lawton."

He narrowed his gaze in a hard squint for several long moments, then gave a rough clearing of his throat. "It's gonna be a long four weeks," he muttered as he shoved his hat back on his head and picked up the reins to start the wagon moving again.

And the point for that round went to Courtney.

ELEVEN

THE SUN WAS GETTING HIGH BY THE TIME THEY reached the ranch, and Dean still had a lot of work to do that day. He hoped Randall had at least gotten the horses moved to the western pasture as he'd asked.

He should probably ride out there to check.

His mind on other things, Dean drove the wagon around to the barn as he would have any other day. He didn't realize his mistake until he stepped to the ground and saw the crate in the bed of the wagon that he still needed to bring over to Randall and Pilar's place. "Aw, hell."

"What is it?"

Dean hopped back up into the driver's seat. "I forgot to take care of Randall's package. I'll bring you 'round to the house first."

"Can I go with you?"

He glanced at her. "Why?"

The look in her eyes suggested the answer should have been obvious. "Since I'm to be living here for a while, I may as well get properly introduced to your family, don't you think?" She tilted her head, and a hint of challenge entered her tone with the next words. "Or were you hoping to keep them in the dark about our circumstances? I can understand if you're reluctant to admit what your reckless behavior has wrought. I'd be ashamed as well."

Dean didn't bother with a reply as he flicked the reins and started off toward the narrow dirt road that led to Randall's.

He wasn't proud of what he'd done yesterday, but he sure as hell wasn't ashamed of anything. Marrying the woman had been a huge mistake, but how could he have known she wasn't who he thought she was? How could he have known Wilkerson wouldn't grant an annulment?

Shit. He was making excuses for himself, and he knew it.

He shouldn't have acted so rashly in the first place. Shouldn't have married someone when he'd had zero intention of honoring the commitment. It didn't matter that there were no vows spoken, no promises to care for and protect and honor and obey. All of that had been implied in the act. And Dean hadn't intended any of it.

There was no honor in what he'd done.

He didn't like knowing it was true and hated having to admit it to her even more. Still, the least she could have done was accept his apology.

But of course not. The woman was intent upon being contrary.

The drive around the horse pasture was not long, but by the time he drew the wagon up to Randall's house, Dean was tense and impatient, something he had been a lot since coming into contact with the Eastern lady. He expected his brother to be out on the range, but Pilar and Jimena were likely to be home. Jimena, of course, had already encountered his bride, but Pilar had not.

And Pilar had a way of subtly telling a person exactly what she thought without having to say a whole lot. And lately, she had not been inclined to hold anything back.

This was not going to be a pleasant visit.

Pulling the brake handle on the wagon, Dean hopped to the ground once again. With his gaze lowered, he made his way around to the other side. Then he tipped his head back to see his bride standing on the running board, her hand extended oh so elegantly as she waited for him to offer his own.

Some stubborn element inside him refused to acknowledge her none-too-subtle gesture. Doing exactly what he knew she was trying to avoid, he grasped her swiftly about her narrow middle and swung her to the ground. He was ridiculously pleased by her soft little grunt of exasperation at the abrupt maneuver.

Once her feet were on the ground, he didn't release her. Not right away. He stood there, his hands wrapped around her waist, her hands still tightly grasping his biceps, until she tipped her head back to look up at him.

There it was—that fierce little flash in her gaze and the haughty irritation she so carefully concealed beneath a flat expression, followed by the tiniest parting of her lips as her breath came just a bit faster.

As soon as he saw it, he realized it was exactly what he'd been after by ignoring her hand. He also recalled too late what her fiery nature did to him as his body heated up in all the right places.

He couldn't let her go. He didn't want to. In fact, against all rational reason, right then, he wanted to pull her closer. He wanted to feel the heat of her irritation through the new dress she wore. He wanted to know how far he'd have to lower his head to meet her mouth with his.

What the hell?

No, he didn't.

He dropped his hands from her body and stepped back, catching a glimpse of something strange flickering in her eyes before he turned toward the house to see Pilar already stepping onto the little front porch.

The house Randall built for his bride—per his oddly stubborn insistence, without Dean's help—was small and quaint and perfect for a budding family. Or a blooming family, as the case was.

Pilar was a petite young woman with large eyes the color of rich chocolate and thick black hair. She had a round, sweet face, a wide mouth prone to laughter or a curt word when appropriate, and a belly that was currently very big with the impending birth of their first child.

From the day Randall had returned from Texas with his unexpected bride, Pilar and her mother had started making subtle changes to the Lawton Ranch with their feminine influence.

Augie Lawton had spent thousands of hours ensuring that Dean understood the vital elements of running a successful cattle spread. Deviations from his instructions were met with swift and firm discipline.

When his granddad passed on, Dean honored Augie's memory and his legacy by running the ranch in the way his granddad taught him.

Pilar and Jimena's arrival had brought more than a few changes.

Having been so accustomed to the ways things were run by Augie Lawton, Dean had struggled with the effect the women had on the place. But he saw how happy his brother was with Pilar, and although he'd have a hard time admitting it out loud, Dean came to appreciate having an extended family around.

Pilar paused at the edge of the porch, drying her hands with a towel. "Hola, cuñado," she said with a smile and a nod toward Dean before shifting her gaze to the woman standing beside him.

"Hi there, Pilar," Dean replied. "Randall out on the range?"

"Of course." Her answer was uttered with a slight hint of humor as though she recognized his discomfort. There was a long pause before she turned a smile on the woman beside him. "Hello and welcome," she said.

"Ah, right," Dean said, glancing to the woman next to him. She stood with a pleasant expression on her face, eyes and lips tilted upward in a gentle smile.

Why the hell had he never seen that sweet expression before?

"This is Pilar, Randall's wife. You met her mother, Jimena Molinaro Garcia, yesterday."

"Yes, she was very kind," Courtney said, stepping

forward. "I believe I must thank you for lending me your clothes yesterday."

"Please, it was nothing at all. I am glad I could help." Pilar turned her dark eyes to Dean and tilted her head expectantly.

He froze, understanding exactly what they were waiting on. He took his hat off and pushed a hand back through his hair, stalling. "This is, ah… I'm sure Randall already told you what happened. She's gonna be staying a few weeks until we can get the matter taken care of."

Both women watched him stutter through the introduction. Pilar grew increasingly amused while his bride's eyes narrowed dangerously.

"You have no idea what my name is, do you?" she asked pertly.

He frowned. "I would, if you'd ever mentioned it."

"I would have mentioned it if you had asked me for it." She propped her hands on her slim hips, getting more disgruntled by the second.

"I didn't figure you'd be around long enough for it to matter."

"Well, now we know that's not the case."

They stared at each other. Tense, combative, and way too close.

Manners demanded he introduce her properly, and to do that, he needed to know her name. But something about the woman just made him want to aggravate her, so he didn't ask the obvious question. "Yep," he said with tight smile and a tip of his head. "For now, at least, you're Mrs. Lawton."

The direction of her gaze dropped briefly from

his eyes to his mouth, and when it did, he thought he detected something curious in her expression. But then it was gone as she cleared her throat and pinned him with a hot little glare. "Don't call me that. We may be married, but as you declared earlier, I am not your wife. Soon, this will all be just a bad memory."

"Suit yourself, princess," Dean said, slapping his hat back on his head. The fire in the woman was really something. He wondered how hot she'd burn if she were truly furious…or stirred by a different sort of passion altogether. "I just came by to drop this off." He reached into the back of the wagon and lifted the package he'd picked up from the post office. "Where do you want it?"

"In the house, please," Pilar answered, stepping aside to let him pass by.

Dean set the crate down inside the doorway, then headed back to the wagon. The two women stood in awkward silence as he leapt up into the driver's seat. "I've got work to do before sundown, so I'll leave you two to get acquainted."

Then with a flick of the reins, he drove off with a heavy sigh of relief. He was being a coward by leaving the woman with Pilar, but he figured she'd be better off there with company than sitting alone in his house all day.

He was doing her a favor, really.

He just wasn't too sure she'd see it that way.

Courtney fumed as she watched her temporary husband ride away, unceremoniously dumping her off in his sister-in-law's hands.

Point to Lawton.

Realizing she had no choice but to make the most of her current situation, she turned back to Pilar and offered a weak smile. "I am sorry."

"Lo siento."

They both spoke at once, then laughed.

"There is no excuse for such behavior," Courtney offered first.

"No, I cannot imagine what came over him. Dean is not usually so…" Pilar trailed off as she searched for the right word.

"Rude," Courtney offered. "Obstinate. Domineering."

Pilar laughed again, the sound smooth and deep. "No, no. He can be all those things, though my husband says it was not always this way. I think I was going to say he is not usually so uncertain."

Now that was not a word Courtney would have applied to the swaggering cowboy.

"Please, come inside," Pilar said with a welcoming gesture. "The heat of the day will be on us shortly. Would you like refreshment? A drink or something to eat?"

Courtney hesitated. "I don't wish to be a burden to you."

"Not at all. Family is never a burden."

"Thank you. That is very kind. I haven't eaten yet today, so to be honest, I am really quite hungry. My name is Courtney Adams, by the way."

"Hola, Courtney, welcome to my home," Pilar replied with a wide smile, and she motioned for Courtney to follow her into the house. "Come, my mother is baking some bread, but we can have something fixed to eat in a couple minutes. Then we will enjoy some cool lemonade and chat about the rude manners of men."

Courtney laughed. "That sounds like a perfect way to spend the afternoon," she replied sincerely.

"And you can explain to me how you came to be married to el jefe. Randall told me, but I can hardly believe what he said."

Courtney gave a small shake of her head, thinking of the man who'd just driven away. "I'm not sure I can explain it properly myself."

"Did he really take you before Judge Wilkerson minutes after meeting you?"

"He did, though I had no idea at the time that we were being married."

The other woman shook her head as they entered the house. The front room was an open area with a fireplace, a large sofa, and comfortable chairs, but they continued on to the kitchen, where Jimena greeted them with a wide smile.

"Please have a seat," Pilar said with a gesture toward the kitchen table before she turned to her mother and said something in Spanish. Jimena replied with a ready nod and started gathering food to set on the table while Pilar poured some lemonade from a metal pitcher on the counter. She brought a glass to Courtney and took a seat beside her.

"I just cannot imagine Dean doing such a thing.

He does nothing without thinking it through. He is very…deliberate, I think is the word. The actions you describe sound more like something my own husband would do."

Jimena said something that had Pilar laughing as a pretty rosy tone colored her cheeks. "Es verdad," she replied to her mother before directing her next comment to Courtney. "When Randall decided he wanted to marry me, he didn't hesitate in his court-ship. But I was reluctant to trust the interest of such a handsome, reckless vaquero," she explained. "For all I knew, he proposed to women all the time. I resisted for many days, until he came to our house to speak with my mother."

Jimena laughed quietly as she ground dried corn in a wide wooden bowl. It was becoming clear that although Jimena did not speak English, she could understand it well enough. Looking over her shoulder at her daughter she said, "Un hombre obstinado, enfermo de amor."

"He was very determined," Pilar agreed, another pretty blush warming her skin. Turning back to Courtney, she explained, "He had somehow learned enough Spanish to ask my mother for her blessing of his courtship. I decided he might be a worthy man after all. I was not wrong."

Though Courtney could well imagine wide-smiling Randall going so far in his efforts to win Pilar's affec-tion, she could not see his ill-tempered brother doing anything similar.

"Well, I am afraid my situation is quite different. Unfortunately, the judge will not grant an annulment for another four weeks. He insists we get to know each other before ending the hasty marriage."

Pilar's expression was sympathetic. "That does sound like something Judge Wilkerson would do." She reached out and gave Courtney's hand an encouraging pat. "Please let us know if there in any way we can make your stay more enjoyable. I can well recall my first months on the ranch. There was a lot to get used to."

Courtney smiled her gratitude, but it was hard for her to imagine there being anything at all enjoyable about having to spend the next four weeks in the company of the irritable boss of Lawton Ranch.

No matter how nice he might be to look at.

TWELVE

It was nearing sundown when Dean looked up from the fence he was repairing to see Randall riding in on the dappled gray mustang he'd had since he was fifteen. His brother had named the poor horse Lucy despite the fact he was a gelding. It had always been Randall's way to be unexpected and ridiculous.

A handful of ranch hands had ridden in just ahead of Randall. For the most part, the men spent weeks at a time camping under the stars and eating from the chuck wagon that traveled with them, but whenever any of them were near enough to make use of the bunkhouse, they didn't resist the opportunity to enjoy Jimena's cooking.

Aside from his brother, who was foreman, Dean had nearly twenty-five hands working Lawton ranch. It was the most the ranch had ever had. After Augie's death, Dean had dedicated himself to making the ranch prosper, and his work had paid off.

After securing his gelding by the water trough, Randall walked up to Dean with tense shoulders and a hard glint in his eyes. "I found four more near Freeman's Rock."

Dean swallowed an expletive. He didn't want his brother to know how much the loss bothered him. Instead, he gave a short nod and turned to rest his forearms on top of the fence, sending his gaze eastward. Randall's house stood past the pasture, and beyond that, where the river straightened out and began to flow faster, the land opened up to a few hundred thousand acres of free range.

"Something's gotta be done." Randall's voice was heavy with frustration.

"I'll handle it."

"How?"

"I said I'll see to it, and I will."

"Dammit, Dean, this ranch is partly mine. Granddad may have given you a ruling share and made you the boss, but almost half of those cattle are mine. We can deal with this problem together. There's gotta be a way to find out who's behind it."

If his brother didn't have any idea who might be perpetrating the crimes, Dean preferred to keep it that way. Randall was likely to go off half-cocked, without any proof. Unfortunately, proof had been damned near impossible to come by. The killings were totally random, with no rhyme or reason behind when or where they occurred. And Dean was not about to go accusing anyone without solid evidence against them.

"Maybe the MacDonnells know something," Randall suggested as he came up beside him to rest his arms on the fence in a replica of Dean's stance.

Dean glanced sharply at his brother. "Why would you say that?"

Randall shrugged. "Maybe the same thing is happening to their stock. We could work together."

Dean didn't reply.

"You can't avoid them forever," Randall said.

"I don't intend to."

"I could ride over there tomorrow and have a talk with Horatio. See if he knows anything or if he's heard of any others in these parts describing the same incidents."

"No."

Randall pushed off from the fence in frustration. "Dammit, Dean. Let me do something. I can do more for this ranch than act like a glorified hand."

Dean understood his brother's irritation. He did. But now wasn't the time to be taking risks.

"I get it, all right? I'll think about giving you some more responsibilities. But I will *not* have you riding off to the MacDonnell's place on this matter. Got it?"

The two men squared off for a long moment. Both intense and stubborn. But Randall would back down eventually. Dean was still boss.

Suddenly, his younger brother's expression shifted into one of shock as his eyes grew wide and his mouth dropped open. "Shit! You think *they're* responsible for the killings, don't you?"

Aw, hell.

Dean had known Randall would come to that realization eventually. His brother was impulsive and wild, but he wasn't stupid. Dean had just hoped to be able to resolve the issue first.

"But that's crazy," Randall stated emphatically "The MacDonnells would never do such a thing."

Dean shook his head. No point hiding his thoughts now. "I don't want to believe it either. But think back to when the first killing happened." He waited to see the flicker of acknowledgment in his brother's eyes. "Right. The day of Anne's funeral. And the next?"

Randall looked confused at that one, so Dean provided the answer. "The day that should have been her twenty-second birthday."

"Shit!" Randall hissed as he shook his head. "I can't believe it."

"All the incidents since those first two have been random, but near enough to the MacDonnell homestead that someone could have ridden out, killed the cattle, and gone home without much effort."

"But why?"

Dean didn't want to answer that. He didn't want to believe Anne's family, lifelong friends of the Lawtons, would have turned on them in such a way. But grief could do terrible things to people.

"We don't know for sure it's them," Dean explained instead. "It's just a suspicion at this point. I can't do anything without solid proof. I *won't*," he stated firmly, looking his still-stunned brother hard in the eye. "And you won't either. Got it?"

Randall nodded readily. "Yeah. I got it."

Dean gave a nod of his own. "Now, why don't you head home? I imagine Pilar's been waiting for you."

"Sure," Randall replied, though his movements were reluctant as he turned to his gelding. Just before hoisting himself up into his saddle, he looked back. "I'm sorry, Dean. I never woulda thought…"

"Don't worry about it. I'll handle it. Get on home."

After his brother left, Dean stayed out by the arena until the sun gave up its last rays of light over the horizon. He loved the ranch. It was the kind of love that had formed in his bones, passed down through generations.

And someone was threatening it.

He didn't want to believe Anne's family had anything to do with the senseless slaughter. Ranchers themselves, the MacDonnells understood the value of livestock as more than what it brought at auction. The cattle were the ranch, the soul, the lifeblood.

An attack on Lawton cattle was a direct attack on Dean.

He bristled with the urge to fight back. To strike in anger and frustration and grief.

But he needed proof. He needed to be convinced unequivocally that the MacDonnells were behind the killings. Until then, his hands were tied and he hated it.

As stars blinked to life in the sky above, he slowly approached the house, gearing himself up for another confrontation he didn't want to have. Through the window of his office at the back of the barn, he'd seen his red-haired wife return to the main house a few hours ago with Jimena.

Since arriving at the Lawton Ranch with Pilar, Jimena had insisted on cooking for Dean whenever he would allow it. It had taken him a while to accept her frequent presence in his house, since there hadn't been a female at Lawton Ranch since his mother left nearly twenty years before. But Pilar explained how much her mother loved to be in the kitchen. It gave Jimena joy to cook for her family, and Dean was now family. Apparently, so were the ranch hands she fed whenever any of them were in from the range. Dean employed a camp cook, and Augie had made sure Dean and Randall both knew how to fix their own food in the kitchen as well as out on the range, but their skills just couldn't compete with Jimena's culinary talent. It hadn't taken long for Dean to get used to the various appetizing smells that would greet him when he returned to the house at the end of the day.

Eventually, he and Jimena had settled on a compromise of sorts. She would come over to cook on nights when the family gathered at the big house for the evening meal and whenever there were men in the bunkhouse. It was much easier to prepare big meals for the ranch hands from Dean's kitchen than from her own. Any other night, Dean managed on his own.

Though Randall and Pilar were not expected to join him tonight, Jimena was likely preparing something for his men.

And there was also his bride to contend with.

After the discussion with Randall, Dean was really not in the mood for another argument, which he definitely expected to have after the way he'd deserted her earlier. He certainly hadn't planned to dump her off in such a manner. He just hadn't been prepared to face both women staring at him like he was some jackass for not knowing his own wife's name.

He'd have to swallow his pride and ask her. He couldn't go on much longer without knowing, and at this point, he was pretty damn sure she wasn't going to offer it to him freely.

Jimena was standing at the stove when he entered the house through the kitchen. She gave him a swift look over her shoulder, but that was all it took for him to realize she had sided with his bride. The disappointment and animosity in her dark, flashing gaze made that fact clear as day, even without the sudden litany of Spanish that flowed from her lips like a blast. He didn't understand a word of it, but there was no doubt she felt he was at fault in regard to the situation with his new bride.

He was. He just didn't feel like hearing it right then.

Sweeping his hat off his head, he stood stiffly in the middle of the kitchen for about two minutes, enduring the woman's tirade before he interrupted.

"Enough, Jimena. I get it, but this is between me and the woman." He crossed the kitchen. "I'm gonna wash up for dinner."

After taking a quick bath, Dean headed first to the parlor. He was surprised to find it empty, half expecting to find his bride waiting in ambush to give him a piece of her mind. He paced the room a few times, then decided he'd be better off waiting on the porch, where at least he could enjoy some fresh air.

He stepped outside and walked forward to brace his hands on the railing. The night was only slightly cooler than the day had been, suggesting they were in for a hot summer this year. Crickets were making themselves known, and a quiet scuffing came from the barn.

It was a beautiful night. The sounds and scents soothed his riotous mood.

They always had.

When he'd been young—shortly after his mother left—he'd often get to feeling all pent up, as if emotion might explode from his chest. Augie would bring him out here on those nights to just sit in silence and listen. And Dean would realize that no matter what was going wrong in his life, if he had the ranch, he was doing all right.

He'd left his hat off after his bath, and he shoved both hands back through his still-damp hair as he gazed skyward. Tonight, he was badly in need of some of that peace and confidence. He filled his lungs with the night air, releasing it all on a heavy exhale.

A familiar creaking sounded behind him. Turning in place, he came up short at the sight of his bride sitting in Augie's old rocking chair in the corner of the porch.

Everything inside him pressed outward for a sharp second.

He wasn't likely to find peace tonight.

THIRTEEN

THE MOON AND STARS WERE BRIGHT ENOUGH ON THE clear night for Dean to see that his bride was watching him, with her hands resting peacefully on the armrests of the chair and her spine straight against the back.

When the silence between them reached an awkward length, she finally gave a slow nod in his direction. "Good evening, Mr. Lawton."

Dean tipped his head. "Evenin'."

Another dragging pause, then she sighed. The sound was part exasperation, part resignation. "How was your day?" she asked politely.

"Fine," he answered automatically. It took him another minute under her steady gaze to realize she expected some reciprocation. For some reason, this woman's presence chased away all the manners he'd ever been taught, not to mention most of his good sense. "And yours?"

Her smile was unexpected. "Quite lovely, actually. Pilar and Jimena have been very welcoming."

Though her smile looked nothing but sincere—and

far too pretty—Dean heard the censure in her words. He decided it best not to respond beyond a low sound of acknowledgment.

More silence.

Then the lady stood. Her skirts made a soft swish when the fabric slid against her legs as she approached. It was just a few steps, bringing her to the railing beside him. He tensed as she stopped with her hands linked in front of her. The breeze stirred some loose curls that lay against her check and neck and sent a whiff of something sweet on the air to his nose.

His stomach tightened, and his stance tensed under her regard.

"Mr. Lawton, though there is no reason for you to be so gruff toward me and every reason for me to be quite put out by the situation in which you so unconscionably placed me, I have chosen to accept your rather reluctant apology and forgive the circumstances that brought me here." Her tone was reasonable and matter-of-fact despite the challenging words. When she paused, she lowered her chin modestly. The adjustment should have made her look demure, but it managed to do the opposite. As she looked up at him from beneath the sweep of her lashes, there was an expression of determination on her pert features. "But I *am* here, Mr. Lawton. Since I do not relish the idea of having to endure your ill humor for the next four weeks, I suggest you find a way to accept it."

He hated having to say it, but she was right. He wasn't even sure why he tended to be so rude to her. He wasn't usually that way.

Then again, maybe he was, and she was the only

person who'd bothered to call him on it. "I shouldn't have shoved you before the judge like I did."

She lifted one brow in an elegant arch. "No, you shouldn't have."

"I lost my head," Dean continued. "It doesn't happen often, and I didn't handle it well."

There was a hint of naughtiness in the way her smile tilted. "I might have experienced something similar. I shall endeavor not to lose my temper so willfully again."

He felt a tug of disappointment at the thought but didn't want to delve too deeply into what he found so appealing about her fiery little outburst.

"Perhaps we'll survive this marriage after all," he suggested.

"I do hope so," she replied with a heartfelt sigh. "My new life has barely just begun."

Optimism and excitement were evident in her voice. The sound had a singular effect on him, making him wonder when he'd last felt such uplifting expectation.

He turned to face her more fully and noted how her forehead was just about level with his chin. If she tipped her head back—as she did then—to look him in the eye, it really wouldn't take much effort to reach her mouth with his.

Shit. He needed to stop doing that. There was gonna be absolutely no kissing of this woman.

Dean cleared his throat and held out his hand. "My name is Dean Lawton, but you can call me Dean."

Her russet brow arched higher, and an interesting curl formed at one corner of her mouth. "Such pretty manners," she replied.

"My granddad made sure I had 'em, even if I don't always use 'em," Dean replied with a lopsided half smile.

She didn't take his peace offering right away. In fact, she grew quite still as her gaze dropped to his mouth. She'd done that earlier, and even as his belly tightened with how his body interpreted her interest, he wondered what it was about his mouth that drew her attention.

And then she told him. "I like your smile, Mr. Lawton."

Dean tensed, and the smile slipped away. For all her reserve, the woman hadn't been lying when she'd said she intended to share her opinions freely. She'd thrown him off yet again. It wasn't as though he was accustomed to getting pretty compliments from the ranch hands. He had no idea what a proper response might be.

Apparently, she did not require one. With a wide smile of her own, she lifted her hand to take his. The moment their palms met—hers soft and warm, his callused and rough—and his fingers curved around hers, something strange and electrifying passed between them. He could see she felt it too because her gaze flickered and her smile faltered for a split second before she recovered herself to reply. "My name is Courtney. Courtney Adams." She gave a soft laugh. "Or at least it was up until yesterday."

There was a honeyed tone to her voice that hadn't been there before. It flowed through Dean's blood and angled straight to his groin. Though he had a wild urge to slide his fingers up over her wrist to tug her in a bit closer, he released her instead.

"As long as you stay clear of ranch business, we should get on just fine," he said.

As he intended, his curt words had her expression sliding back into one of calm imperturbability. All the honey was gone from her voice when she replied, "Then we shall be fine indeed." Clasping her hands in front of her again, she tilted her head to the side. "May I ask you a personal question, Mr. Lawton?"

He wanted to say no. But he found himself giving a short nod anyway.

"You have indicated more than once that you have no wish for a bride. Why exactly are you so opposed to marriage?"

He should've known that was coming.

He took a moment to note the way she looked up at him, her fingers linked between them, her head tilted back and slightly to the side as she studied his face. Those eyes, all direct and softly questioning.

After a moment of his continued silence, her lashes swept over her gaze as she glanced down. "I shouldn't have pried."

"Maybe not," Dean replied, his voice sounding rough to his ears, "but I reckon you deserve to know anyway."

Her gaze rose to his again, her elegant brows lifting just a touch as she waited for him to continue.

With a sigh, he shoved his fingers back through his hair before turning to brace his hands on the porch railing. "I was engaged once." He felt her surprise at his admission in the way her body subtly tensed beside him. He shouldn't have been able to feel so small a change, but he did. "Anne grew up at the neighboring ranch, and I'd known her just about all my life."

Since Dean's time had been most often spent at Augie's side, for many years he had barely taken any notice of the little girl running around in baggy breeches with two long, brown braids trailing down her back. It wasn't until Dean was around eighteen that he first wondered what it might be like to kiss the pretty neighbor girl.

But Anne, who'd ridden her father's ranch like one of the hands since she was fourteen, had neither the time nor inclination for romantic gestures.

Of course, we'll marry, she'd reply with her wide grin the few times Dean broached the idea with her, as though it was a foregone conclusion. And it had been. A marriage between them would link their families' ranches and increase the prosperity of both. It made perfect sense. *But not yet*, she'd add.

And Dean had been content to wait. When they were both ready, they'd settle down together, and there would be no one else for him from that moment on.

But that moment never came.

Dean took a steadying breath and sent his focus out past the bunkhouse and the land beyond as he continued, "When my granddad died more than five years ago, this whole place became my responsibility. I'd been raised to take over the ranch, and Granddad made sure I knew what that meant. It was a lot of work: getting my footing as the boss, keeping Randall in line and making sure he did his part, ensuring the ranch remained prosperous and became even more so."

"I'd say you've managed quite well," she said softly.

He shrugged. "It's all that's been expected of me since my dad died…" Dean almost mentioned his mother leaving but stopped himself. That was likely to open a whole other round of questions he had no desire to delve into.

"Anyway, the ranch took all my time and attention for a while. It was a couple more years before Anne and I got around to deciding on a wedding day." He took a shallow breath. "She died less than a week before we were to be married. She was the best horse-woman I've ever known, yet she was thrown from her horse in a freak accident that took her life."

Courtney took a step toward him and murmured gently, "I'm so sorry."

Dean turned his head to look down at her. The compassion in her deep, green eyes made his muscles tense in rejection. His gaze shifted to where she had rested her slim hand on his upper arm in an offer of comfort. Then he watched as she slowly lowered it to her side.

He didn't want her sympathy. The sentiment con-flicted with the guilt he'd been wrestling with these last three years.

Anne had ridden over to talk to him. She'd hinted the day before that she had something important to discuss in private. But something came up, and ranch business took precedence over everything else, so he'd been in town that day and missed her visit. It wasn't until after she'd been found that he discovered the note she'd left him. The emotional, tearstained note that called off the wedding. It seemed that while Dean had been busy taking charge of the ranch, she'd fallen in love with another man. And though she hated the idea of hurting Dean, she had to follow her heart.

She chose someone else.

Her note didn't name the other man, and no one came forward after her death.

Not that it mattered at that point. Anne was already gone.

Had she been upset when she hadn't found Dean at home? Had emotional distraction caused her accident?

If he'd been home, they could have talked it out. He'd have understood. He'd have released her from the engagement. She was his friend, after all. He'd have wanted her to be happy.

But he hadn't been home, even though he'd said he would be. And she had ridden off to her death.

He'd never forgive himself for that.

"You loved her very much."

Dean stiffened at the softly spoken words. The truth came out before he could stop it. "Not enough."

He'd loved Anne; of course he had. But he knew when he read her letter that he hadn't loved her in the way a man should love the woman he intended to marry. She'd wanted that kind of love, and she'd deserved to have it.

If Dean hadn't been so focused on managing the ranch, he might have seen it sooner. If he'd found more time to spend with Anne, courting her, something more could've developed between them. Or at least, he might have noticed when her emotions strayed.

But he'd made a commitment to honor his grand-dad's legacy. Lawton Ranch was his responsibility.

And now he had a responsibility to honor Anne's memory as well.

Feeling the steady, quiet presence of the woman

beside him, he drew a heavy breath and let it out as he straightened up and turned toward her.

She was closer than he expected, and her fresh female scent swept into his nostrils with his next inhale. He recognized it from the soap he used every day, but it was different on her somehow.

Hunger kicked to life inside him. He stomped it down.

"I've got no time for a wife," he said a little gruffer than he intended. "Running this ranch is my main priority, and it takes all I got."

If he couldn't be a proper husband and give a wife the attention and affection she deserved, he wouldn't take on that role.

He wasn't sure his explanation made any sense. He'd never before had to clarify his feeling on the subject, and her expression was impossible to read as she looked up at him. He started to wonder if maybe he shouldn't have been so forthcoming.

But then she smiled.

It was just a gentle curve of her mouth: almost sad, but still beautiful. "Well, I'd be the first to admit that I know nothing about managing a cattle ranch, but it's my opinion that you are doing a fine job of it."

Her words were not what he'd expected, but they somehow managed to shake off the melancholia that had fallen over him. He gave a short grunt and replied, "Another opinion?"

Her lips twisted into a smirk. "I warned you I had a few."

"I just didn't expect to be graced with them so frequently."

With her mouth resisting the pull of a smile, she narrowed her gaze and tipped her head to the side in that way she had. "Are you teasing me, Mr. Lawton?"

He shouldn't be.

"I might be."

"An earnest apology and now this?" she asked. "Be careful, I might just start to like you."

Dean fought against the lure of laughter in her eyes and how her playful tone made him want to respond in kind. "I'm sure I'll change your mind on that soon enough."

The honey was back in her voice as it flowed out in a warm laugh.

His hunger rose up again as well, in a fierce, deep rush. He tightened the reins on his unwanted physical reaction. It could only lead to no good. Clearing his throat, he grasped for a quick change in topic. "Once our association is resolved, I'll help you get to your friend's place."

Her laugh had settled into a small smile that remained in place as she replied, "That is kind of you, but I already sent her a letter letting her know I was here—well, in town, anyway. She might even arrive before our four weeks are up. I can't imagine how I am going to explain this…odd situation to her."

"Blame it on me and my bad manners."

"Oh, I most certainly will," she replied with a pert little nod. "You can count on that."

She sure had a way with that sass of hers. As he resisted a smile, her attention fell to his mouth again.

Desire seared through him.

He took a step back. "I expect dinner will be ready soon," he said. "We should head inside."

"Of course."

He held the door open for her to pass through into the house. She kept her chin angled down as she walked past him, and his gaze fell to the graceful line of her nape, where fine red curls brushed against smooth skin. The sight struck Dean acutely. Such a softly feminine detail.

In the same instant, he was hit with another whiff of her scent. His senses already heightened, he noted how the orange of his soap was sweeter—warmer—on her skin. And the spearmint, when mixed with her natural female scent, hit just the right note to go angling straight through him.

He inhaled deep through his nose, trying to breathe in more of her.

The sound drew her attention, and he caught a flash of green as she glanced at him from the corner of her eyes a split second before she passed by and entered the house.

It took all Dean had to maintain control over the desire running like a wild mustang through his blood.

FOURTEEN

COURTNEY WAS STILL REELING FROM THE CONVERSA-
tion on the front porch as she took a seat at the dinner
table. She shouldn't have pried into such a personal
matter. He might be her husband, but Dean Lawton
was a stranger.

His response to her inquiry had not been at all what
she expected. Courtney sensed there was more to the
story than what he had been willing to admit.

Behind that serious and focused facade, the cowboy
was an enigma of condensed thought and carefully
contained emotion. Even his lean, muscled body con-
veyed a steady brand of self-control. But something
had become clear to Courtney while he recounted the
story of his former fiancée and her untimely death: the
man possessed depths he did not wish others to see.

With her thoughts still consumed by what Dean
had told her, she took a little while to realize it was
just the two of them for supper. Jimena had made a
couple trips back and forth to the kitchen to bring out
the food, but then had not reappeared.

"Will the others be joining us?" she asked.

Dean's light gaze met hers from across the table. "Not tonight. They only come by a few nights a week. Otherwise, I eat alone."

"Oh." She wasn't sure what else to say. She couldn't imagine spending the majority of one's evening meals without some form of company. But she guessed the man across the table actually preferred it that way.

Luckily, he didn't seem to expect any further response from her, as he turned his attention to the meal. Supper continued in awkward silence, another odd experience for Courtney. One of the first things a young lady mastered at finishing school was how to maintain the flow of dinner conversation in a way that was neither intrusive nor forced. It was the duty of an accomplished hostess to ensure guests remained engaged and amused by a variety of topics and delightful anecdotes.

All that kept the current dinner interesting were the unexpected moments when her untethered gaze accidentally met his over the table. Then, for a brief, flashing second, his striking eyes would penetrate the dull quiet that hovered over the table to spear her with intense self-awareness.

It was during one of these fleeting meetings of gazes that Courtney noticed wariness in his eyes and realized he had no idea how to handle her presence in his home and in his life.

Of course, she already knew he didn't want her there, but more than that, it seemed he was honestly thrown off by her.

She was pleased to discover she was not the only one feeling so deeply awkward in this unexpected situation. She had to suppress a grin at that. At least she was skilled at concealing her internal discomfort. This man did not appear to be quite so good at hiding his distress. Or perhaps *annoyance* was a better word. She could read it in the subtle lines that marred his forehead and in the way the outer corners of his mouth tugged downward.

As the meal eventually came to its inevitable conclusion, Courtney gave up on her efforts to avoid staring at him. Honestly, there wasn't much else to look at, aside from her food, and though it had been delicious, she had seen enough of it already.

Lawton had just placed his knife and fork across his plate and used his napkin to wipe his mouth before leaning back in his chair, obviously well satisfied. Still sitting stiff and straight at the edge of her seat, Courtney found his relaxed masculinity fascinating to observe.

The man knew how to lounge, and he made the casual posture look shockingly attractive.

Here in his home out on the Montana plains, he was not ruled by any social expectations other than those he chose to adopt. If he had wanted to, he could have eaten his entire meal with his fingers, and who would have stopped him or railed at him for it?

And now that he had enjoyed his fill, he leaned back with his feet braced wide. One large hand was splayed on the surface of his denim-clad thigh, while the forearm of his right hand rested on the table. His shirtsleeves were rolled partway to his elbows, and the collar of his shirt was undone.

Even in that frightfully relaxed pose, he was clearly

the king of his domain, *the boss*. He did not have to
flaunt his position of authority with unnecessary airs.
It was simply who he was. The nature of his role in
life came from what he did—day in and day out—to
make the ranch a success.

As someone who was currently wondering just what
she had to offer the world, Courtney found his innate
and unquestionable sense of self infinitely impressive.

She lifted her attention toward his face, wondering
if he were still as annoyed as he had been earlier.

To her instant mortification, she realized that while
she had been studying his posture, he had been watching her.

She fought a swift blush of embarrassment, but the
warmth rose to her cheeks anyway. Since she had
already been caught, there was no point in pretending
she hadn't been curiously assessing him, so she met his
gaze straight on.

His expression was…closed.

But not entirely emotionless.

She did not detect any of the frustration she
expected, and strain was no longer so deeply set in his
features, but there was a weightiness in his stare. His
light eyes were directly focused on her, and the effect
was disconcerting. Again, she got the sense that he was
trying to figure her out in much the same way she was
trying to understand him.

Then Courtney noticed something different about
his mouth. It was in the way the corners held a slight
suggestion of resistance while the wide and subtle
arches of his upper lip looked…almost sensual within
the shadow of stubble that spread across the lower

portion of his face. And his bottom lip… Courtney had a sudden urge to trace its shape with her fingertip, to discover if it was as soft and firm as it looked.

Her pulse began to race through her veins, and her breath shortened as though she had just sprinted down the upstairs hall in her home in Boston. The warmth in her cheeks expanded across her chest to her belly and *lower*, where an odd, deep ache expanded.

While she analyzed and wondered at the strange physical reaction, his expression slowly shifted. His eyes narrowed, and he lowered his chin just a bit while tension spread along his jaw. She could actually see his muscles bunching as he clenched his teeth. A new intensity was revealed in his gaze. It was dark and personal, and he appeared to be doing everything he could to contain it, but she caught a fleeting glimpse of it anyway.

And it resonated with everything she was feeling and more.

Goodness.

Thankfully, Jimena chose that moment to come back into the dining room, full of smiles and bright, curious glances. Courtney was starting to believe the older woman might have pinned a few hopes on this temporary marriage.

As Jimena started to clear away the serving platters still on the table, Dean rose to his feet and gathered up his dishes and anything else in reach.

Jimena started to admonish him, but he shook his head. "I've told you before, Jimena, that you don't have to clean up after me. I'm more than capable of bringing my dishes back to the kitchen."

Courtney swiftly stood as well. She had already realized that Jimena was not exactly the ranch's housekeeper or cook. She was a member of the family who gave of her time because she wanted to. Which meant Courtney would have to try to do more for herself while she was here or risk unintentionally insulting the kind woman.

Gathering her own dishes, Courtney followed them into the kitchen. The sink was already filled with water for washing. Jimena began taking care of the leftover food while Lawton returned to the dining room to fetch the rest. Courtney looked at the sink dubiously. She would have stepped in to help, but she honestly had no idea where to start.

Jimena noticed her expression and gave a laugh. She patted Courtney's hand with a shake of her head just as Dean returned with the last of the table settings. Then they were both physically shooed from the kitchen.

Back home, everyone would retire to the parlor after supper to play games or music, or just to talk about the latest local news or social events. At more formal affairs, the ladies would gather separately from the men, allowing the gentlemen to enjoy an after-dinner drink and a smoke before they reconvened for more socializing.

Here, in this little house, with Lawton following a few steps behind her, Courtney was unsure what was expected. Being uncertain was a totally new experience for her—an experience she'd had at least a dozen times already in the last few days. She suspected this new way of being was not going to go away anytime soon.

She entered the parlor to find the room lit with the soft glow of an oil lamp set before the window, casting an interesting dance of shadows across the pale-blue walls.

Courtney wandered to a bookcase that spanned the wall across from the window, wondering what reading might be found on a cattle ranch in Montana. As her fingers trailed over titles that ranged from manuals on agriculture and animal husbandry to a slim volume of poetry by Walt Whitman, she was fully aware of Lawton crossing the room behind her.

She'd half expected him to abandon her immediately after supper. She did not fool herself into thinking he had any intention of entertaining her for the rest of the evening. He was more likely to simply continue with his regular habits, doing his best to pretend he did not have an unwelcome houseguest.

Perhaps she should excuse herself and head up to her room. Being in her own solitary company, though decidedly dull, would not be nearly as awkward and strained as being in the same room with this man.

Awkwardness—another thing Courtney had never experienced before but had gotten a large taste of in the last couple days.

"Want a drink?"

His question startled her, though he'd spoken in a low and even tone. Courtney looked over her shoulder at him, a bit surprised by the invitation. She'd honestly expected him to ignore her.

He stood at a table set in the corner near the window, a small glass of amber-colored liquor already in his hand.

She was about to decline his offer, but then she realized it had likely been an afterthought on his part—and a reluctant one, judging by the tension in his stance and the taut line of his jaw.

If she had to hazard a guess, she'd say he was feeling as awkward as she was.

Her spirits lightened at once. "I would love a drink. Do you have any sherry?"

"Nope."

"Claret? Or a cordial of some sort?"

He glanced down at the table, which held a single crystal decanter and glasses that matched the one in his hand, and gave a slow shake of his head. "Your choice is bourbon or bourbon."

He expected her to refuse. He *wanted* her to refuse.

Bourbon.

She had never touched a drop of hard liquor in her life. Young ladies in her circle rarely imbibed alcohol, and even watered-down wine was served only in strict moderation. Courtney had snuck a sip of her father's port when she was fifteen and had been surprised by the potency of it.

She suspected bourbon would be significantly stronger.

With a shrug and a light smile, she replied, "Why not? I've started my adventure, after all. I may as well give it a try."

He hesitated just a beat before he turned and poured little more than a splash into another glass. Courtney crossed the room, reaching him just as he turned to offer her the drink. There was a flicker of something in his eyes that sparked a response in the center of her chest. She wanted to prove something to him, though she couldn't imagine why and she didn't know exactly what.

As she took the glass from his hand, her fingers slid against his for just a moment. The brief, almost caressing contact sent a rush of awareness through her, making her skin tingle. She lowered her chin. The last thing she wanted was for him to realize how he affected her.

Lifting the glass to her mouth, she immediately detected the alcoholic fumes. A second later, the amber liquid slid smoothly past her lips to burn a trail down her throat. She tried to hold in a cough, but it burst forth with a sputtering gasp as her eyes started to tear up.

Despite her distress, she didn't miss the telltale tug at the corner of Lawton's mouth before he said, "I should've warned you to start with a sip."

"Yes," Courtney gasped, pressing a hand to her chest in an attempt to stop the fiery burn. "A warning would have been nice. Goodness, how does anyone manage to enjoy this?"

"It's an acquired taste, I suppose," he replied as he lifted his own glass for a long, slow swallow.

Courtney did not miss the hint of triumph in his tone and wondered if this hadn't been some sort of test. *Let's see how tough the little Eastern lady is.*

Well, toughness came in all forms, and Courtney was not about to concede this point to him just yet.

She took another sip.

FIFTEEN

Every muscle in Dean's body tensed as he watched her lift the glass for a second sip. The woman was damned stubborn. And her lips were ridiculously pretty pursed around the edge of his mother's crystal.

Get ahold of yourself, Dean.

This time, she took an easy, measured sip. He watched, more than a little fascinated by the way she seemed to swirl the bourbon around with her tongue for a moment before allowing it to slip down her throat. No big gasps or tearing eyes this time. With a small breathy *hmm*, she lifted the glass, allowing the light of the lamp to shine through the amber liquid. Then she brought the crystal to her mouth again and took another slow taste. This one she savored, closing her eyes as though reveling in the warmth of the potent spirit spreading through her limbs.

Dean's body hardened nearly to the point of pain. He figured he'd never seen anything as erotic as this fancy city lady enjoying her first glass of Kentucky bourbon. His muscles burned and his stomach tightened with a deep achy feeling that angled straight to his groin.

Slamming down the rest of his own drink, he turned away before she opened her eyes and noticed his physical reaction. He crossed to the big front window. Instead of giving him a distracting view of the yard outside, the glass simply reflected the room back at him. His gaze followed her slim form as she turned to stroll back to the bookcase, taking her bourbon with her.

She glanced over her shoulder at him once. The swift and feminine little glance had his body going crazy all over again.

"Walt Whitman," she noted in a light tone. "Do you enjoy his verse?"

"I don't know," he replied, still watching her in the reflection. Half of the books were Augie's and dealt with ranching. The other half had been chosen by Dean's mother.

Courtney had paused and half turned back toward him, waiting for further explanation. "I don't have much time for reading," he added.

"Right," she replied softly as she turned fully around to look at him where he stood with his back to her across the room. She held a slim volume in her hand. "Do you enjoy spending time alone?"

The question came out of nowhere. "Do I like being alone?" he repeated, wondering why she'd ask such a thing.

When she simply nodded, he realized she knew he was watching her in the window's reflection. He probably should have felt shamed for observing her in such a way, but he didn't. She had taken the time to study him earlier at the table, and though she'd blushed prettily when she'd gotten caught, she hadn't apologized for her bold curiosity.

He wouldn't either. To be honest, he probably liked the feel of her eyes on him way too much.

"I suppose so," he answered honestly.

She took another sip of bourbon, standing there in her blue dress with the book in one hand and her gaze on his back. Then she walked forward to place her empty glass on the sideboard before she continued across the room to his side.

Though he kept his gaze directed forward, Dean felt her nearness down to his bones.

"I wonder if I would enjoy being alone."

The intimate nature of her hushed voice affected him in inappropriate ways. He shifted his stance and accidentally brushed her shoulder. He told himself he imagined the sound of her swift inhale and spoke quickly to cover up his own internal disquiet at the contact.

"Haven't you ever been alone before?"

"Not in any significant way," she replied. Then she smiled and gave a small gesture with her hand. "I mean, of course, I am alone when I go to sleep at night and other brief times, but I cannot say I have ever been completely on my own for any extended period. When I was young, I was always with my nurse or other servants. And of course my mother felt a near-obsessive need to monitor my behavior. At school, I always had my friends, and after, there were constant social events."

"Sounds awful."

She smiled at his reply. "I enjoy being around people. But I do wonder…" She glanced down for just a moment before lifting her chin quickly to look into his reflection again. "I wonder who I would be if I were on my own. Independent and free to make my own choices. Choices not based on my mother's expectations or for appearances' sake, but based on my own personal desires. What would I do?"

"What do you wanna do?"

She shrugged. "I have no idea. But I certainly hope to find out."

The breadth of her optimism was bewildering. Dean had always viewed life through a practical lens. He had been taught to weigh every option carefully and to make decisions based on the best probable outcome. He sure as hell didn't do anything based on hope.

Yet this woman had left the only life she'd ever known with nothing more than a reverent *hope* of finding something better.

"So, tell me," she said in a lighter tone as she broke her gaze from the reflection and turned toward him. "What do you enjoy about being alone?"

Dean knew it would be rude to continue facing the window, but he wasn't sure he could handle her direct gaze just then. The moment already felt too intimate.

He gave a shake of his head. "I never thought about it."

But now that he *was* thinking about it, he realized his answer wasn't too far off from what she'd said.

When he was alone, he didn't have to live up

to anyone else's expectations. He didn't have to be Augie's chosen successor, or the responsible brother, or the boss.

"Humor me, please," she urged. "If you had a whole day to yourself, what would you do with it?"

There was something in her voice—a quiet, seeking desperation—that made him reluctant to disappoint her. "I suppose I'd take a long ride out to some quiet, solitary spot where I could listen to wind across the prairie and not think about what work wasn't getting done."

"Sounds lovely," she murmured softly.

He looked down at her. She stood with her face tipped upward and her eyes closed, as though she were imagining what he described.

And then suddenly, he was imagining it too, but now she was with him in the vision. Riding beside him, smiling into the sun. Smiling at him.

No.

He took a step back, harshly clearing his throat.

Her eyes flew open, and he was caught by her vivid gaze. He froze in place. A shock of need that was both physical and...something else...rushed through him.

What the hell was she doing to him? She'd only been there a day, and she was already throwing his ordered existence off track. He didn't need to be daydreaming about long rides through the countryside with this woman. His focus needed to stay on ranch business and the problem with the slaughtered cattle.

A slight frown tugged at her brows. The shift in her expression did not detract from her prettiness. Rather, it brought further emphasis to the intensity of her eyes, her fine cheekbones, and the sexy curve of her mouth.

He needed to walk away, but something kept him there, waiting for what she would say next.

"With all the time you spend on your own," she asked quietly, "do you ever get lonely?"

An odd feeling arced through him. "I've got no time for loneliness."

She smiled at that. A sweet, sad little smile. But her voice, when she replied, was filled with that confounding optimism. "I suppose I had better find something to keep me busy then."

Dean's chest squeezed tight before releasing on a slow and heavy breath that helped him regain some lost control. "As long as it doesn't—"

"Interfere with ranch business," she completed for him, her smile never wavering. "Of course."

The corners of his mouth itched to smile. Definite sass. "I just wanna be sure we understand each other," he countered, combatting his reluctant humor with a flat tone.

"Oh, I wouldn't go so far as to say *that*, Mr. Lawton," she replied, an impish gleam in her eyes, "though I do believe we have potential."

A blast of warmth spread through him. The conversation had definitely gotten off track, and because he suddenly realized how much he was enjoying it, he decided it was time to end it. "Well," he said with a nod as he took another step back, "you have a good night."

Her eyes widened with surprise. "You are retiring? So early?"

"My day starts with the dawn," he answered. "Make use of the parlor as you'd like. I imagine I'll see you around supper tomorrow."

She watched his retreat with a steady gaze. "Good night, Mr. Lawton."

As common as they were, the softly uttered words shouldn't have had any particular effect on him, but they did.

He turned and strode from the room. His reactions to her were becoming a problem. The way his body kept responding to the slightest triggers was not something he'd ever experienced before. Not even when he'd been young and randy. His sexual appetites had always been something easily managed.

Anne had certainly never inspired anything close to what he felt when in the presence of the Eastern woman.

But then, Anne had been different. She'd always been different. And Dean's feelings for her had never really centered on the physical.

Dean looked around his bedroom. The one he'd been given as a kid. It was a simple space. The narrow bed he'd grown up in had been replaced with a much larger one, but otherwise, the room hadn't changed much over the years. He'd planned on moving to the larger bedroom, which had once been Augie's, after his marriage.

That room had now been claimed by his new guest.

Just the thought of her seemed to conjure her up as he heard the soft tread of her steps on the stairs. His body tensed again as he fought off the return of his acute physical awareness.

Did he imagine her steps slowing as she passed his door?

What cause would she have to hesitate?

Dean started stripping off his clothes. He needed to stop worrying about the woman and what she did.

She'd be here for four weeks, and then she'd be gone. As long as she stayed out of his way, all would be fine.

That should have been the end of it.

But something still kept him awake that night, just lying in bed staring at the ceiling.

A disquiet had lodged in his chest much like the redhead was now lodged in his home. He could declare nothing changed all he wanted, but it wouldn't make it true.

The moment he'd bumped into that woman outside the post office, something had been altered inside him. He'd felt it when he'd looked into her green eyes and noticed the soft wisps of hair curling at her temples and against her cheeks and slim neck. Not to mention when he'd gotten a good look at her wedding gown. In that moment, Dean's life had gotten kicked off track.

And what did he do?

He'd gone and lost his head and married the woman.

If Augie were still alive, he'd either beat the tar out of his grandson for his stupidity or laugh his ass off. Probably both.

He'd sure made a mess of things. All he could do now was minimize the damage and keep his bride from interfering in his life any more than she had already with her dress buying and bourbon tasting and pretty smiles and sassy tone.

Most importantly, he had to keep himself from doing anything else stupid.

He rolled over onto his stomach and punched the pillow into shape.

If only he could just keep the woman out of his head long enough to get some goddamned sleep.

SIXTEEN

THE NEXT MORNING, THE SUN WAS BARELY BREAKING over the horizon when Courtney heard the door down the hall open, followed by bootsteps making their way down the stairs.

The man certainly hadn't been lying when he'd said his day started at dawn.

Though that did nothing to explain why she had been waking up so early since she'd arrived at the Lawton Ranch. At least she had slept better last night. Sliding from the bed, she wandered to the window and looked out to see Lawton crossing the yard toward the barn, his long strides eating up the dew-wet ground.

He did everything in the same purposeful, almost impatient way. He was clearly devoted to the ranch, and of course, the cattle operation likely needed a great deal of attention. She just wondered if maybe he was little too dedicated. She had not imagined that thread of longing in his voice when he had spoken of spending the day alone, away from his many responsibilities. She had heard the weariness in his voice, though if she had mentioned it, he would have denied its presence.

She considered the possibility that he wasn't even aware of it.

As he disappeared into the barn, Courtney wondered if he would still have left the house first thing in the morning if theirs were a true marriage. Would he have abandoned a real wife, leaving her to spend her days alone and, quite frankly, bored?

Or would he have taken the time to acclimate his bride to her new life? Would they have woken up together to enjoy breakfast in the sunny kitchen? Would he have stayed up after dinner to tell her stories of his childhood? Surely, they would have gone to bed together—in the same bedroom.

Weeks ago, when Courtney had still been stirring up fantasies in her mind of what married life might be like, she had often wondered whether she and Geoffrey would share a bed on a regular basis. Considering the very platonic kisses they'd shared during their engagement, it had been difficult for her to imagine Geoffrey engaging in a passionate physical relationship.

Of course, now she knew that he was very passionate indeed, if some of the more explicit passages of his letter were to be taken at face value. It just wasn't something he had ever felt driven to explore with her.

Would Dean Lawton be the type of man to take his bride to bed every night?

The thought made Courtney fidget on the window bench, her skin flushing from head to toe.

During his reluctant apology, he'd claimed that he rarely lost control.

She could believe that. If she ignored his impulsive

behavior when they'd first met, his manner had been quite stern and taciturn. Still, despite his apparent control, Courtney suspected he had a whirlwind of a storm inside him, wrapped tight and primed for release. He might be adept at containing the intensity, but Courtney had caught more than a few glimpses of a deeper breadth of emotion he hadn't been able to hide.

With a true bride—a woman he trusted and desired above all others—would he still feel the need to hold back when it came to love and passion?

Courtney wrapped her arms tightly around her bent knees as heat infused her body.

She really shouldn't be wondering what Dean might be like if he felt comfortable releasing all the passion inside him. But goodness! She suspected it would be glorious.

The sigh that escaped from her lips was deep and long, coming up from the aching hollow at the center of her body. It was followed unceremoniously by a growl from her stomach.

Time for more practical and sustainable matters—breakfast.

Just as she had the thought, Jimena's little wagon crested the hill on the road from Randall and Pilar's.

Rising to her feet, Courtney decided to join the older woman in the kitchen. She might not have anything to do on this Montana ranch, but at least she had someone who seemed to appreciate a little company.

After dressing quickly and twisting her hair into a simple bun at the back of her head, she made it to the kitchen just as Jimena was lighting the big iron stove.

As anticipated, she was greeted with Jimena's wide smile. "Buenos días, señora. ¿Estás aquí para ayudarme a cocinar?"

"Buenos días, Jimena," Courtney replied. She really should consider asking Pilar to teach her some Spanish. By Jimena's intonation, she suspected she'd asked her a question, but she had no idea what it was.

The older woman shook her head and crossed the room to take an apron off a hook. Returning to Courtney, she said, "Tómalo. Ponte esto. Una esposa verdadera debe saber cómo cocinar."

"Cocinar?" Courtney repeated as Jimena slipped the apron over her head and spun her around to tie the strings behind her back. "Oh. You want me to help you cook. I am sorry, Jimena. I have never cooked a thing in my life. I will probably just get in your way and ruin everything I touch."

"Sí, sí sé," Jimena replied with another joyful smile as she patted Courtney's cheek, then turned back to the stove. "Vámonos."

Courtney stood still for a moment. Cooking had never been anything she'd considered attempting. She'd grown up with family chefs and a city full of wonderful restaurants. She'd never even set foot in the kitchen back home, let alone thought to put her hands to the work of fixing a meal.

But it was not as though she had any other plans for the day.

She wanted an adventure, right? And independence. Well, being able to cook her own food felt like a pretty independent thing to do.

Taking a breath that lifted her shoulders, she

looked to the older woman with a wry smile. "All right, Jimena. You will likely regret this, but where do I start?"

Jimena waved her forward, and Courtney took another few steps in her adventure.

Not much later, delicious smells filled the small kitchen.

Jimena appeared to realize rather quickly that Courtney's experience with such things was extremely deficient, and she did not let her near the stove other than to observe. She did, however, instruct Courtney on how to scramble the eggs for omelets, dice onions and peppers into small pieces, and roll out the dough for biscuits.

The dough was tricky at first, but Jimena hovered over her shoulder, directing her in the proper motions until she got it right.

The resulting meal was simple enough but filled Courtney with the distinct pride of accomplishment. Though she realized she had been nothing more than an assistant, it was the first meal she'd ever had a hand in preparing, and she was anxious to try it.

Before she could sit at the table, however, Jimena handed her a large tray containing two covered plates. Nodding toward the door, she said, "Llevale esto al jefe. Un hombre siempre es más feliz cuando es bien servido."

"Al jefe? You want me to take this to Mr. Lawton?"

"Sí," Jimena replied with a wave of her hand.

Courtney looked with longing at the plate that had been set on the table. She would have to hurry if she wanted to get back before her own food cooled. Adjusting her grip on the tray, she went out the back door and made her way across the yard to the barn.

She hoped he was still in there somewhere, though she had no idea where he'd find a place to eat. She couldn't exactly imagine him sitting down on a bale of hay in an empty horse stall.

Then again, maybe she could.

The tray was getting heavy so she picked up her pace a bit. She hadn't seen what Jimena had dished up since it was covered by a linen napkin to keep it warm, but it seemed like a lot of weight for one man's breakfast.

She made it to the barn, but not without a few stumbles in her new boots that nearly sent the tray and everything on it flying into the dirt.

The barn was cool and dimly lit. It took Courtney several steps down the center aisle before her eyes adjusted from the bright morning light outside. The place was oddly quiet, and she guessed that any horses not in use were probably out to pasture. She did hear a quiet bleating that might have been a sheep, but with her arms quickly tiring, she passed on the idea of investigating what had made the sound.

Peering ahead to the end of the long aisle, she saw no evidence of Lawton. Even the hayloft overhead was still and silent. Her arms starting to tense and shake from the effort of carrying the large tray, Courtney continued forward in measured strides.

Maybe he wasn't there. She paused to adjust her grip on the tray. "Mr. Lawton."

Hearing nothing, she called out significantly louder, "Mr. Lawton, I have your breakfast."

"Back here."

She hadn't expected a response, but that was definitely Lawton's voice. For some reason, the sound of it—even coming from the far end of the barn—caused a little twist in her belly. It wasn't an altogether unpleasant sensation and, for a ridiculous moment, felt an awful lot like anticipation.

SEVENTEEN

Dean did not want to see her that morning.

Not after the wicked thoughts that had kept him up all night. The simple sound of her voice, melodic and feminine, managed to stir his blood even as the obviously cultured, eastern intonation of her words sparked his irritation.

His body might be dying to have hers underneath him, but Dean still wanted her gone.

A cattle ranch was no place for a woman like her. His own mother had proven as much when she'd taken off for Chicago within days of his father's funeral, leaving behind two small sons. Ranch life had been too hard for a city-bred lady raised with all the comforts a wealthy family could provide.

His temporary bride was cut from the same fine and elegant cloth.

He probably should have gotten his annoyance under wraps before she reached his office, but he'd been so focused on making sure his body didn't reveal his physical reaction to her that he'd forgotten to conceal his bad mood. That being the case, he was pretty sure he knew why she came to an abrupt stop just inside the open door to his office, her robin's-egg-blue dress and her fiery-red hair creating bright splashes of color in the midst of the barn's dim brown hues.

As her gaze swept over his tense features, her eyes widened for a fraction of a second. Something akin to disappointment flickered in their green depths before she shifted her attention to a swift scan of the room.

His office was nothing special. Just a desk, some bookshelves, a table, and a couple chairs. It took only a moment for her to take it all in before her gaze returned to him, her expression blankly serene once again.

"I apologize for disturbing you, Mr. Lawton," she said. "If you would just show me where to set this down, I will leave you alone."

Even when performing the humble task of bringing him his breakfast, the woman managed to sound fine and proper. Why the hell did she even bother to carry his breakfast all the way out here? Usually, he made it back to the house later in the morning to eat whatever Jimena left for him in the kitchen.

He rose to his feet and stepped around from behind his desk. "I'll take it."

Noting how much was piled on the tray, a prickle of suspicion inched down his neck.

What was Jimena up to?

Though her posture remained stiff, a little sigh of relief lifted Courtney's chest as he took the burden from her hands. "Enjoy your breakfast, Mr. Lawton."

"You're not expecting me to eat both these meals," he said as he set the tray on the small table beneath the only window in the room and started to uncover the plates.

"What?"

Dean looked up to where she stood in the doorway. She had already turned to leave and now looked back over her shoulder. The twist of thick red hair at the back of her head allowed soft tendrils to curl at her nape and against her temples as a slight furrow above her brow shadowed her gaze.

"There's enough for two people here. It looks like Jimena expected you to eat with me."

Courtney's eyes widened as she glanced at the food. "Oh. I can take my meal back to the house, if you would rather enjoy your breakfast alone," she suggested, lifting her gaze back to meet his.

She had just given him an easy out. All he had to do was nod and say he'd only grab a few bites while he continued to work. Instead, he found himself saying, "You can stay."

Her surprise was evident and made him feel like an ass. "Are you sure?"

Nope. Not sure at all. But it was too late now. "If I send you back to the house, Jimena'll likely come out here and smack me upside the head."

Her lips twitched, then curled into a true smile. He was startled to notice that one of the arches on her upper lip lifted just a touch higher than the other. It was just a tiny imperfection—barely worth noticing— but it made Dean feel as though he'd been kicked in the gut.

"Well, that's not exactly incentive to stay," she replied slowly.

Dean narrowed his gaze in an exaggerated glower. "As much as I'm sure you'd like to see me bashed with an iron pan, I prefer my skull whole. Come sit."

Her movements were reluctant as she approached the rickety, old table. Dean accepted responsibility for that, realizing he hadn't made any effort to make her feel welcome despite the tentative truce they'd called. He'd never shared a meal with anyone in his office before—heck, he'd never eaten a meal in his office before—and figured there was only one reason Jimena felt he had to now.

He'd have to see about setting the woman straight on whatever she thought might be going on between him and his temporary bride. It was bad enough having to deal with Randall's constant interference; he didn't intend to suffer any matchmaking attempts from Jimena.

He set a plate of food in front of each chair and waited for his breakfast companion to be properly seated before he took his own seat. They ate in silence for a while, the atmosphere charged with an awkward awareness. He didn't have to stare across the table to know she sat with stick-straight posture and used her knife and fork with elegant grace. He'd noticed the same last night and had to forcefully keep himself from watching the beautiful way her hands moved while executing the mundane task.

His more relaxed manners were probably appalling in her eyes.

If Jimena was hoping something might develop between the two of them, he didn't see how breakfast in his dusty, hay-smelling office in the back of a barn was conducive to that. The woman across the table couldn't have appeared any more uncomfortable.

As host, it was Dean's duty to ease the tension in the room, but he wasn't particularly inclined toward light conversation. After a while, however, the silence seemed to just make things worse.

"I suppose you're used to finer fare," he finally said.

She looked at him with a brief start of surprise, clearly not expecting an attempt at conversation. Then she glanced down at her plate before meeting his gaze again. The green of her eyes was striking compared to the dark-brown tones of their surroundings.

Her lips tilted in a smile. "I'll admit that during my days of travel, I'd despaired of ever again having a satisfying meal. Train fare and quick stage stops leave much to be desired, I'm afraid. You are not wrong in thinking I've likely been spoiled by the culinary offerings available in Boston. Back home, there are fine-dining restaurants that specialize in various cuisines from all over the world." She paused to gesture toward the food on her plate. "But I would argue that Jimena's cooking could rival the best of them."

Dean was surprised by her praise when he'd expected the opposite. "She'd probably love to know that."

"I'll be sure to tell her," Courtney replied, her smile widening. "I'm looking forward to the new dishes she will introduce me to. There is something exciting about trying new foods and experiencing new flavors. I used to dream of traveling abroad, going from country to country, sampling their best culinary offerings."

"Did you?"

She looked up at him, surprised by his question. "Did I what?"

"Go to any of those places."

"No. It was simply a child's fancy. The farthest I've ever gone is to New York City."

He gave her a pointed look. "I'd say the farthest you've gone is Montana Territory."

Her expression brightened with a flash of amusement. "Right again. My experiences so far have certainly lent themselves to a sense of being in a completely different country. The new food, unusually vast landscapes"—she met his gaze with an impish curl to her lips—"strange marriage customs."

A half smile tugged at his mouth. Her humor was difficult to resist. "We are a land of few women. We gotta do something to keep them around." He immediately thought of his mother. "Though even marriage ain't enough to stop some women from leaving."

"What do you mean?"

"Nothing."

"Oh, I doubt that very much."

They stared at each other. He could see the curiosity burning in her eyes as she patiently waited him out. He shouldn't have brought up his mother. He rarely did. That wasn't to say he didn't think of her on occasion, but not nearly as much as he had since this woman stumbled into his life.

"Who left?" she asked after a bit.

He figured there was no reason not to say. It wasn't a secret. "My mother. Twenty years ago now."

Her eyes widened. "You must have been very young."

"I was seven. Randall was four."

"Why did she leave?"

Dean shrugged. "After my dad died, she couldn't find enough reason to stay. From all accounts, she'd loved him, but she'd hated it out here. She was used to a finer lifestyle in Chicago and went back to it as soon as she could."

"She left you and your brother behind? Why on earth did she not take you both with her?"

Dean looked down at his plate. "I'm pretty sure my granddad had something to do with that. With my dad gone, he needed someone brought up to take over the ranch."

"But she was your mother. Your place was with her."

He shrugged. "Maybe, but we didn't want to leave. Or at least I didn't. This was the only home I'd ever known."

"Even so," Courtney argued. "It should have been your mother's decision whether you stayed here or went with her."

Dean looked up. "It was."

He hated the awareness and pity that slid into her eyes. His mother had made her choice. It no longer affected him. He didn't regret one day of growing up on the ranch. His mother had written to them often in the beginning, describing her life in Chicago, promising to bring them to town for a visit. And Augie had made sure they replied to every letter. But the letters grew less frequent over the years and eventually stopped altogether. It had been nearly ten years since he'd heard from her. He rarely felt the loss.

Shaking himself from his thoughts, he realized the woman across from him was still watching him intently. He got the sense she was trying to see something inside him. He didn't like it.

"So, why'd you run away from your wedding?"

It was the first thing that came to mind as a change in topic, and he didn't realize until the words were spoken how abrupt the inquiry was.

Her eyes narrowed briefly. A clear indication that she saw his avoidance tactic for what it was. Then she set her fork down and folded her hands on her lap under the table. "It was nothing, really."

She obviously didn't want to answer, but Dean figured a response was only fair. She'd drawn something out of him he hadn't wanted to share, so now it was her turn. Besides, it was time he learned a little more about the woman who temporarily shared his name.

"Nothing. Really?" Dean's skepticism was thick in his voice. "Something had to make a woman jump on a train and head west without taking a minute to pack any personal items or figure out where she was going."

Her chin lifted a notch. "I knew where I was going."

"Right. To your friend. And where is she exactly?"

"Helena." Her tone had gone flat and defensive in the face of his questioning.

"Which is still another few days west of here." He could see by the widening of her eyes that she hadn't realized how far she was from her intended destination. He'd best know now if he was gonna have some crazed fiancé chasing her down. "What made you run?"

He admired the pride and self-possession she displayed then. Nothing changed in her posture or demeanor, but he sensed a shift in her, a disturbance originating from deep within.

"I discovered that the gentleman I was going to marry loved another," she replied.

Dean hadn't expected that. "He broke off the engagement at the last minute?"

"Not quite. According to the letter that was accidentally delivered to my room, he fully intended to go forward with the wedding while vowing rather passionately to his...lover that they would continue on in secret."

Dean sat back in his chair and gave a small shake of his head. At least Anne had chosen to end her engagement to him once she realized her heart belonged to another man.

He studied the woman seated across from him, the way she gave nothing away in her expression or tone. "He broke your heart."

Something flitted through her gaze. Then she sighed and her spine softened on her exhale. "No. No, he didn't. We were promised to each other as children. It was an advantageous match for both our families. I expected friendship and respect in my marriage. Deeper emotions do not generally come into play in such arrangements."

"But you'd hoped they would."

Her lashes fluttered as though she was tempted to glance away, but she held his gaze instead. She seemed reluctant to acknowledge that she might have wanted more out of her marriage than what was expected.

And why shouldn't she? Happiness was hard enough to come by.

Then she tilted her head in the thoughtful way she had. "I thought about it quite a bit those first few days on the train," she replied. "Though I initially felt quite devastated, it was mainly due to disillusionment and hurt pride, I suppose. It bothered me that I had been so naive. I certainly do not believe he planned for any of it to happen. He wouldn't have intentionally wanted to hurt me. I imagine it is the way of things when love is involved." The way she said that suggested she had never been in love herself. The wistfulness in her voice and the sad curve of her lips bothered Dean. "I can hardly fault Geoffrey for falling in love," she added softly.

His next words came out harsher than he intended. "If he loved someone else, why would he go through with the wedding?"

"His family had made a commitment. He couldn't just walk away from it."

"You did."

She took a deep breath and lifted her brows. "And my family has likely been greatly shamed by the scandal I caused. My behavior was unforgivably selfish."

Dean leaned forward to rest his forearms on the table. "Seems to me being a little selfish might be necessary every now and then."

Her eyes darkened. "Perhaps. My family may never forgive me. Boston society will certainly shun me, should I ever return."

"You plan on going back?"

Something pulled tight through his center at the almost expectant look in her eyes when she answered softly, "I don't know."

ᴇEIGHTEEN

* ⚜ *

Lᴀᴛᴇʀ ᴛʜᴀᴛ ᴅᴀʏ, Cᴏᴜʀᴛɴᴇʏ ᴡᴀᴛᴄʜᴇᴅ ғʀᴏᴍ ᴛʜᴇ front porch of the house as Dean rode westward from the homestead. The horse he rode was loaded with a couple saddlebags and other supplies. Courtney didn't take much note of that detail when she admired the overall picture he made atop his horse as they galloped into the distance, but it did come to mind later, when the hour grew late and he didn't return.

He didn't return the next day or the next or the next.

Apparently, this was not a surprise to anyone but Courtney, and though she was curious, she didn't dare to ask when he might return. And she certainly didn't dare to analyze why she felt abandoned by the action.

Instead, she set her mind to figuring out what she could do to stay busy.

Considering Dean's warning not to interfere with the workings of the ranch and the fact that she wasn't quite sure what that encompassed, there wasn't much to do.

Each morning, she woke before dawn to watch the sunrise from her bedroom window before joining

Jimena in the kitchen for what she quickly came to see as her morning cooking lessons. After breakfast, Courtney would spend a few quiet hours at the house by herself. It was a singular experience for her. She had never had much cause to spend extended periods of time in her own company. There had always been someone about when she was growing up, and then there had been endless social engagements or events to attend.

With no one around to dictate how she should spend her time, she began by choosing a book from the collection in the parlor to read on the porch. The first book she read was a selection of stories about the adventures of Lewis and Clark, the great explorers who attempted to chart the vast landscape of the American West. She found the descriptions riveting. Of course she had heard of the two men and knew of their efforts, but to read firsthand accounts of the trials and dangers they had faced in their explorations was truly eye-opening and, at times, rather terrifying.

After that, she needed something a bit less harrowing to read and picked up a slim manual on fly-fishing. It certainly was less harrowing, but not exactly riveting.

She then moved on to the poetry of Walt Whitman. *Leaves of Grass* was a bit of a revelation to her. The language was honest and shockingly sensual, quite unlike the poetry she'd been forced to read at finishing school. It inspired her to spend more time outdoors. She suddenly wanted to see the world as Whitman did and breathe in the beauty of the untamed wilderness. Montana seemed the perfect setting for such an exploration.

Her first little jaunt took her to the shores of the river, where she sat and listened to the music of the water. On another day, she followed the flow of the river for a little way until she caught a view of the open prairie that seemed to stretch forever. And one day she went east along the narrow dirt road to Pilar's house.

The other woman was outside when Courtney arrived, hanging freshly washed linens on a line to dry in the summer sun.

"Hola," Pilar greeted with a wide smile.

Courtney smiled back. Though she missed Alexandra and Evie, she was infinitely grateful to have Pilar and Jimena. If not for the two women, Courtney wouldn't have known what to do with herself on the Montana ranch, especially now that Dean had gone off to who knew where.

"Good afternoon," she replied, crossing the grass to the other woman's side.

Pilar bent forward to draw another clean white sheet from the basket at her feet. The awkwardness of her movement and the tension in her face had Courtney stepping forward.

"How can I help?"

Pilar flashed her a look that Courtney couldn't quite read. "You do not need to help me. I am sure there are other things you'd rather be doing on such a lovely day."

Courtney tipped her lips into a rueful smile. "Actually, no, there aren't. I've been quite bored these last few days. I'm almost desperate for something to keep me occupied. Besides, I could use the company."

Pilar nodded as she snapped the sheet with a vigor that had it floating up on the breeze before she lifted it to the line. "Ah, I imagine the big house can get pretty lonely."

"Indeed." Courtney sighed. "But I am dedicated to learning how to live a more independent life." She stepped up beside Pilar and smiled at the shorter woman. "I may as well start with learning how to hang laundry. As long as you don't mind, that is."

Pilar smiled. "I don't mind at all. Having someone to talk with always makes chores go so much faster."

"Is your mother not at home?" Courtney asked as she reached to pull a handful of crisp white linen from the basket.

"She's inside. Mama would much rather be in the kitchen than out in the sun."

"And your husband?" Courtney asked as she tried to shake out the damp and heavy sheet as she had seen Pilar do. It was heavier and more cumbersome than she'd expected from watching how deftly Pilar had handled the last one.

"He's been gone a few days now, though I expect him back soon. Randall knows I have no intention of birthing this baby without him at my side through the entire event."

Courtney managed to toss the sheet up over the line, but then had to spend some time straightening it and smoothing out the many wrinkles. "Did he and Dean ride out together?"

"Sí. It is not something they do very often," Pilar answered as she moved down the line. "El jefe is more often at his desk than on a horse."

Courtney recalled what he had said to her about having the freedom to ride out for the simple pleasure of it rather than for some reason relating to the ranch. The thought of him being in that small office room at the back of the barn, surrounded by dust and hay and dry ledgers, day in and day out…it bothered her. He seemed a man built for fresh air and open spaces and physical freedom.

But then, she didn't know him well.

After they finished hanging the laundry, the women retired to Pilar's front porch, where Jimena soon joined them with cool drinks. They sat shaded from the hottest part of the day. Pilar translated while Jimena reminisced about her childhood in Puebla, her life during the Mexican-American War, and the difficult years that followed. Though the older woman's history was at times colored with violence and intense struggle, Jimena described her family's perseverance and their dedication to seeing each other through with an optimism and internal strength that Courtney couldn't help but admire.

Pilar and Jimena both represented the independence and capability Courtney wished to cultivate in herself.

Before she returned to the house with a promise to return again soon, Pilar showed her the cradle Randall had ordered from New York. It was filled with carefully folded handmade quilts and soft knit blankets. Set beside the cradle was a basket half-filled with tiny articles of clothing.

"Did you sew all of these yourself?" Courtney asked, crouching to run her fingers over the laced edge of a yellow smock.

"Sí. Mama made the blankets, but I have been sewing the clothes."

"They are lovely."

"Gracias," Pilar replied. Then she sighed. "There is still much to do, and I fear time is running short."

"Let me help you." Courtney rose back to her feet to meet the tired gaze of her new friend.

"I couldn't ask this of you," Pilar argued, obviously uncomfortable with the offer.

"You didn't ask. I offered, and I truly wish to help." Courtney flashed a rueful smile. "I enjoyed learning needlework when I was young, and I do have some skill."

Courtney wasn't sure why she felt such an urgent need to be a part of what Pilar and Jimena were doing—making a home, preparing for a beautiful future. Maybe she was just excited to finally find something she knew she could do that would be of some benefit to those around her.

"All right," Pilar agreed with a heavy sigh as she ran her hand over the quilt. "I would be grateful for the help, but I insist on repaying you somehow."

Courtney grinned. "Perhaps you could teach me to speak Spanish."

Pilar gave her a side-eyed look. "If you are anything like Randall as a student, this may not be a fair trade. And I shall not have the freedom to give you a punch in the arm when your mind wanders."

Courtney laughed. "I promise to be an exemplary student."

Pilar's smile was teasing. "We'll see."

Over the next several days, a new routine emerged.

The morning cooking lessons continued, followed

by a little reading or a relaxing wander down to the river. Then Courtney would head over to Pilar's, where she would spend an enjoyable few hours sewing clothes for the baby while learning Spanish. In the evenings, Courtney and Jimena would return to the main house for another lesson in the kitchen.

Pilar said she was astonished by how quickly Courtney was able to grasp the Spanish language. Though Courtney had always possessed an affinity for languages, the immersive nature of conversing with Jimena strictly in the new language while they prepared meals helped a great deal.

Occasionally, small groups of men would come in from the range to stay in the bunkhouse for a night or two. Jimena made sure to cook something hot and savory for them, ringing a bell outside the back door to let the men know when the food was ready.

At first, the ranch hands looked at Courtney cautiously and curiously, giving her a respectful nod and muttering a greeting. When she took the time to ask their names and engage in a little light conversation with them, they softened up a bit, though they were all very careful to keep a respectful tone. Clearly, they had somehow been advised of her status as the boss's wife.

She noted the camaraderie of the ranch hands from a distance. It was enlightening to see how freely they joked and laughed and how readily they got their hands dirty when there was work to be done. Alexandra had been right when she'd said that men of the West were unlike the gentlemen Courtney was accustomed to, yet she understood she was only getting a glimpse of what these rough-and-ready men endured in their lives as cowboys.

It deepened her appreciation for what Dean was responsible for at Lawton Ranch. It wasn't just cattle. He was preserving a livelihood for all these men and so many others working too far out on the range to make it back to the bunkhouse.

In the evenings, after supper was cleaned up and Jimena had returned home, Courtney would often sit out on the porch for a while, listening to the approach of night and the distinct sounds that came with it. The odd noises that had kept her awake through her first night on the ranch had become a soothing melody that eased her mind after a long day. She felt practically content in those moments and started to believe she might actually succeed in this dream of western independence.

Though it was only temporary, she felt as if she had found her place on this sprawling cattle ranch. And if she could manage such a thing here, maybe she could do the same somewhere else.

The thought was encouraging, though a nugget of uncertainty remained within her. And it had everything to do with the man who was her husband.

Eventually, if she sat in the symphony of soothing night sounds long enough, she'd find herself wondering when Dean would return.

Perhaps he intended to stay away the entire four weeks of their marriage.

She could see him doing that.

But she hoped he wouldn't.

Then she got angry with herself for caring where

the man was and what he did. Lawton certainly wasn't
likely to return the courtesy.

∽∾∽

The sun was already above the horizon by the time
Courtney rose one morning more than a week after
Dean had left the homestead. Pilar and Jimena had
come to the main house for supper the night before.
All three women had been in the kitchen preparing a
traditional Tejano chili for themselves and the cowboys currently staying in the bunkhouse.

Courtney had discovered that she loved the many
spices and savory flavors Jimena used in her more
traditional dishes. And the chili was proving to be one
of her favorites.

After the meal, the women had stayed around the
table far later than they should have, talking of food
and babies and so much else. By the time Courtney
saw the two women off in their little wagon, she had
only enough time for a quick bath before seeking her
bed. Due to the late hour, she slept past dawn for the
first time since arriving at Lawton Ranch.

The house was quiet and still that morning as she
went about getting dressed. Jimena was likely to arrive
soon, and Courtney was looking forward to spending
another couple hours in the kitchen with the cheerful,
expressive woman. Now that she understood more
and more of what the woman said, she was discovering
Jimena possessed a bawdy sense of humor wrapped
within her beaming smiles.

Intending to twist her hair up into the simple bun

she most often favored these days, she looked around in confusion when she could not find her hairpins. Then she recalled leaving them on the stool beside the bathtub.

She had been so tired the night before that she hadn't even bothered to braid her damp hair before bed. This morning, it was a frightful mess of tangles.

Drawing her long hair over her shoulder, she went downstairs. Sun poured in through the east-facing windows, brightening the house. She loved the little house in the morning. It always felt like it filled right up with promises of a beautiful day.

Going straight to the bathing room to fetch her pins, she opened the door and came to a jolting stop.

Dean Lawton was home.

The air left her body in a sudden whoosh as tingling heat flew from her toes to the top of her head and back down again, making her feel as though she was in sudden free fall.

Because the man was standing right there in the bathing room. Naked.

Well, not totally naked. He still wore his hat.

In a flashing instant, Courtney was hit with the hard impression of his very finely sculpted male physique. The length of his back revealed an array of captivating muscles that defined his broad shoulders, ran down each side of his spine, and wrapped his ribs. And below were beautifully firm, curved buttocks and long, strong legs covered by golden hair.

Courtney had less than an instant to absorb the breath-stealing sight, because at the sound of her entrance, he swung around in surprise, providing her with another blast of visual perfection.

More golden hair sprinkled across a ridiculously toned chest, and then his hard, rippled stomach caught her gaze. But only for a moment, because what came next was too fascinating to miss.

As her attention dropped wide-eyed to that particularly male part of his anatomy, he reached up to swipe the hat off his head, bringing it in front of his groin to block her view.

Courtney couldn't move. A voice in her head was shouting for her to retreat, to back away and close the door, but it came from too far away and was far too easily ignored. She had never seen a man standing in all of his full naked glory before, and the sight of Dean in such a state—the visceral effect of it—had her locked in place.

As though fully aware of her state, he casually cleared his throat to gain her attention. Or rather, to draw her attention up to his face where his expression was tense and unreadable.

"Oh my God," she sputtered, feeling as though her tongue might never work properly again as her face went up in flames. "I'm sorry. I didn't know you had returned."

"I got back last night but spent the night in the barn."

Courtney blinked in surprise. "What? Why did you sleep in the barn?"

"I didn't sleep. Nettie was giving birth to her kids."

She wasn't sure if her confusion was due to his words or the fact that her mind seemed to have been wiped clean of coherent thought. "Excuse me?"

"Goats," he replied, one corner of his mouth tilting

upward in a way that had Courtney's belly fluttering. Was he amused? "Two goats were born last night."

She tipped her head. Was that supposed to explain something? She didn't even know the ranch had goats. Being a function of the ranch, the barn seemed to clearly fall into the category of interference, and after that time she'd brought out his breakfast, she'd never gone back. "And you were there?"

"Nettie was having trouble with her labor when I checked on her last night. I stayed to make sure everything went all right."

"And did it? Go all right?"

"Yep," he answered with a nod. "It was a tough night, but they're all doing fine."

"Oh. Good." Silence stretched as she couldn't help but glance at his body again. She noted the sweat coating his skin in a fine sheen and how the muscles in his abdomen tensed as her gaze passed over them, making her own belly tighten in response.

He gave another none-too-subtle clearing of his throat.

Courtney swiftly redirected her gaze to his face, her cheeks burning up again. Judging by the smile he seemed to be trying to hide, he was definitely amused by her distraction. It was humiliating to be caught so blatantly admiring his body, but she much preferred his amusement over anger or annoyance.

"I'll bring you around later to see them."

"See who?"

He lowered his chin for a moment, hiding his face, and when he looked up again, the laughter was clear in his eyes. "The kids."

"Oh, of course." What on earth was wrong with her? "Really? You would take me to see them?"

"Sure."

"That sounds lovely, but wouldn't you rather go to bed?"

Her question made him visibly stiffen. Sudden tension claimed his body from head to toe, drawing her gaze again. The change made his muscles that much more taut and interesting. She met his eyes in question, and what she saw there had her losing her train of thought.

Where there had been clear amusement just a moment before, now there was heat. Deep, heavy heat.

Dean knew she hadn't meant that they should go to bed *together*, but it didn't stop him from suddenly picturing just that. With her hair a river of fire falling over her shoulder to her waist in thick, unruly waves and her gaze all soft and disoriented, it was not a big challenge to envision her stretched out on his bed, gazing up at him with raw passion.

He should have booted her out of the bathing room as soon as he saw her standing there, but he'd been too stunned at first—by her interruption and then by the sensual interest in her gaze—to do anything. It had taken all his concentration to keep from revealing just how intensely that interest had sparked his own.

And then, she'd just started up a conversation as though it were the most common thing in the world.

Standing there, totally bared to her curious gaze while they discussed the events of the prior night, he found it impossible not to find the situation humorous. Surely, she'd realize the impropriety any second and beat a hasty retreat.

But she didn't.

She didn't even seem to be aware of how often her attention strayed from his face to travel over his body. And keeping his hat firmly in front of his sudden and painful erection, he made damn sure she didn't realize just how much that affected him.

"You've been awake all night," she added when he didn't reply. "Surely, you would like to get some rest."

Rest. Right. That's what he needed.

"Later today then," he said, hearing the tension in his voice.

"Wonderful." The brightness of her smile was as beautiful as anything he'd ever seen.

Dean waited while a few long moments passed. If she continued to stand there like that, looking all sweet and curious, he was gonna end up doing something he couldn't take back—like step forward and kiss the girl.

With a shake of his head, he shoved that dangerous notion aside. "Mind if I wash up now?" he asked.

Her eyes widened, and her mouth dropped open. The pink in her cheeks darkened attractively as she glanced once again at his nakedness. "Of course," she replied, her voice a low mutter as she brought her gaze back to meet his. "By all means. I'm so sorry to interrupt."

There was something provocative and mysterious in

those eyes of hers. Something that had Dean clenching his teeth to keep his feet rooted to the floor.

Why the hell didn't she leave?

"Do you plan to watch?" The degree of his present physical restraint had him practically growling the words.

"Oh my God," she gasped as she shook her head, sending ripples of fire down the length of her hair. "No. Sorry. Oh my God." Embarrassment brightened her cheeks, and for a second, Dean thought he saw something intriguing tugging at her lips even as she cast a last wistful glance over his body. She finally backed from the room, but before she drew the door shut, she charged back in and headed straight for Dean.

Every muscle in his body seized tight as she came up in front of him. A feeling like triumph flared inside him, but then she suddenly dipped to the side and reached for something on the stool beside him. Straightening again, she held up her hand, clutched around nearly a dozen hairpins. Her mouth opened and her eyes widened as she seemed momentarily stunned by their sudden proximity.

He understood the feeling. He was a bit stunned himself. It was all he could to do to hold his breath to keep from smelling her, wanting her, taking her.

"My pins," she breathed.

A strange and quiet sound rumbled in Dean's throat. It was all he could manage at that moment, but it spurred her into movement. She spun around again and fled the room. The door slammed shut behind her, causing a small framed painting to fall off the wall. "Sorry," she shouted from the other side of the door.

Dean chuckled as he tossed his hat onto the bench and turned to step into the cooling tub, but it was a strained sound. Settling back against the slanted side, he sank down until his head was submerged.

Unfortunately, a thorough thirty-minute washing did nothing to scrub away the persistent desire to have his redheaded wife join him in the soapy bath.

⁂NINETEEN

AFTER HIS BATH, DEAN WENT TO BED AND DIDN'T RISE again until well into the afternoon. He hated sleeping so much of the day away, but after the grueling week spent riding to the various slaughter sights with Randall in hope of finding some clues to the perpetrators, and then the anxious night he'd spent in the barn with Nettie as she struggled to birth the two kids, he'd been dead on his feet.

There was also the fact that he'd been feeling the strain of his anticipated reunion with his wife from the moment he and Randall had turned their horses toward home. He'd ridden out in the first place because he felt a need to get away from her. Something about her presence—her sassy little smile, her quiet, searching stares, her unsettling scent—shook him clear down to the toes of his boots.

It'd helped to get away. At least the thought of her was more distant, less immediate. And he'd had his concern over the slaughtered cattle directing his focus elsewhere. Unfortunately, he and Randall discovered nothing they weren't already aware of. Nothing to help clarify who was responsible. The culprit was careful, that was for sure.

Dean's first thought as he awoke was that he'd promised Courtney he'd take her to see the newborn goats.

Just the thought of spending time with her had his body and mind going into direct and immediate opposition. But he'd made a promise, and there had been no mistaking the excitement on her face when he'd suggested the outing.

After fixing up a quick bite to eat in the kitchen, he headed out to find his wife.

It was strange how it was easier to call her *wife* than to call her by her first name. Using *Courtney* felt too intimate when they still barely knew each other, and the term *wife* was—at least in regard to this situation—abstract and temporary.

He checked everywhere around the house, but the woman was nowhere to be found. He checked the barn, thinking maybe she'd decided to visit the goats on her own, but she wasn't there either. He returned to the house, considering the possibility he might have missed her there, but found no indication she had been there since morning.

What the hell?

He was reminded of when he'd had to search all over town for the woman, only to find her in the dress shop. Considering they had plans, he would have thought she'd stick around, yet here he was, chasing her down again.

Surely, she wouldn't have gone far from the house. The range was wide open and no place for a city lady to go wandering by herself. Montana's plains were not like a quaint city park where she could just go off on a pleasurable afternoon. She could encounter any number of dangers, including wild animals or stampedes. Not to mention, she could easily get lost out on the plains.

Then the image of the slaughtered cattle came to mind and, along with it, the acknowledgment that the most recent incident had not occurred very far from the house. He didn't think she was in any explicit danger. The attacks had all been on his cattle.

But they were escalating.

Icy fear slid down his spine. His wife—with her wide smiles and friendly manner—would make far too easy a target. Would the culprit go so far as to harm another person?

Dean headed back to the barn with long strides.

After saddling his horse, he rode out at a swift lope, then realized the one place he hadn't thought to look, though he should have. He redirected his mount along the narrow dirt lane to his brother's house, whispering a short prayer under his breath.

He saw them just as he topped the hill.

The three women sat together on his brother's front porch. They looked as calm and leisurely as on a Sunday afternoon.

Unfortunately, as his fear dispersed, his frustration intensified.

His wife—the crosswind that never seemed willing to do what she was supposed to—sat with a glass of lemonade in one hand, while the other hand was raised to block the late-day sun from her eyes. She wore a new dress the color of spring grass with a darker-green trim. Her order from town must have been delivered while he'd been gone.

"Hola, Dean," Pilar said first in greeting as he brought his horse to a stop in front of the porch. "Courtney said Nettie's kids were born last night."

"Yep," he replied without glancing away from his wife, his tone barely in check. "I thought you wanted to see 'em." She tipped her head as she regarded his tense manner. That she didn't feel the need to answer immediately only had him getting more irritated. He continued, "Either you want to see them or you don't."

"I want to see them, but if it is too much trouble for you, Mr. Lawton, I can certainly take myself to the barn without your escort."

"'Too much trouble' is spending time searching all over for someone who should be sticking close by."

Her eyebrows lifted. "You said I was not to interfere with ranch business. You never said I was to be confined to the house. I didn't know how long you would be sleeping. Was I supposed to sit outside your bedroom door to await your leisure?"

Her voice was as cool as a cucumber, setting Dean's temper into stark contrast.

He was making an ass of himself. Again.

His fear and the anger that followed were not appropriate to the situation, but he couldn't seem to get them reined in, not when he still had visions of those cattle in his mind and the knowledge of just how dangerous the open range could be.

Swiping his hat from his head, he hit it against his thigh and shoved his other hand back through his hair to get it off his forehead before he roughly replaced the hat.

The woman just stared back at him with those calmly narrowed eyes.

Jimena and Pilar quietly rose to their feet and went inside. He barely noticed them leaving. He was too busy trying to get his temper back to an even keel. This was the second time he'd lost his head due to this woman. It was not something he wanted to keep repeating. But there was just something about her that got him riled up.

In more ways than one.

He owed her an explanation. And probably an apology.

"The open range is not like domestic farmland or a city park. It's wild and free, and any number of dangers can be found out there. It's not a place for someone to go wandering about without proper precaution and knowledge of the area."

"I am not an idiot, Mr. Lawton." Though her tone was level and her expression neutral, he detected something beneath her outward layer of calm. Something turbulent building in those deep, green eyes.

He braced himself for one of her wonderful displays of temper, looking forward to the prospect despite himself.

But she held it in, limiting herself to a sharp and steady stare.

"You still want to see the kids?" he finally asked when it seemed she had more control of herself than he did at the moment.

She nodded. "I do."

"Come on then."

Dean watched as she rose from her chair and started toward him. The breeze lifted the loose curls away from her face, and as she came closer, he saw that her skin held a golden hue he hadn't noticed that morning, and a cluster of fresh freckles sprinkled across her nose and the crest of her cheeks. She had been spending some time in the sun while he'd been gone.

"You don't mind walking back?" she asked in a steady tone.

"You can ride with me."

She glanced at the horse, then back to him. "I'm not sure…"

Rather than get into an argument over the simple matter, Dean grasped her waist and lifted her up onto the saddle.

Her gasp sounded in his ears as he put his foot in the stirrup and swung a leg around behind her. "Hold on." He wrapped one arm around her waist and kicked the horse into a trot. The jarring motion managed to jostle her into a more comfortable position as she grasped onto the saddle horn to steady herself.

As they continued down the lane, Dean wondered if maybe walking the horse back wouldn't have been a better idea. The woman was too warm, too well-contoured to his own body. He could feel every inch of where her thighs covered his, her hips pressed to his groin, and the slim line of her back came up against his chest. Fiery licks of her hair flew against his face and throat in the wind, and if he lowered his head just so, his mouth would find the side of her neck.

Dean clenched his teeth and squeezed his thighs, urging his mount to a faster gait.

At least she'd decided to be quiet.

It only took a few minutes to get back, and Dean rode straight to the barn. He dismounted first, then lifted his hands up to help Courtney to the ground. She sat there atop the tall buckskin, gripping the saddle horn with two hands.

When she didn't shift or make any move to accept his assistance, Dean tipped his hat back on his head to give her a questioning look. "You plan on staying up there the rest of the day just to avoid having my hands on you?"

"What?" Her head turned, and she looked down at him with round eyes. "No. I, ah…I'm not sure I can let go."

"Why not?"

She just stared back at him without answering. Her cheeks were pale enough to cause those brand-new freckles to stand out, and her lips were drawn in a straight line. Stepping closer, Dean noted how dark her eyes were, dark and scared.

Shit.

"Haven't you ever ridden before?"

She gave a small shake of her head, then stiffened when that tiny movement shifted her balance in the saddle.

He was an utter ass.

He never would have ridden at the speed he had if he'd known she'd never been on a horse before. Dean planted his hands against the saddle on each side of her hips.

"Look at me, princess," he said when he noticed her attention had shifted to the ground below her.

"It is quite high, isn't it?" Though her tone was almost conversational, he could see by the white-knuckle grip she had on the saddle horn that she was still frozen with fear from the reckless ride. She'd probably been hanging on for dear life from the second he'd tossed her up there.

"Not too high," Dean replied, dropping his voice to a soothing lull. "Just look at me. See, I'm right here, standing next to you. All you gotta do is let go of the saddle, turn toward me, and drop down. I'll catch you, I swear."

She was silent for a minute while she seemed to be contemplating the situation. "I understand I am not in danger, I do, but my body doesn't seem to want to cooperate."

Aw, to hell with it.

Dean stepped forward until his chest pressed against the full length of her leg. She was sitting partially facing forward with the other leg bent and lifted toward the front of the saddle. He placed his hands on her hips and gently but insistently turned her until she was sitting sideways. As he did so, the horse adjusted his weight, shifting his stance just enough to throw her off-balance.

She gasped. Releasing the saddle horn with one hand, she reached to her other side and gripped hard to the back edge of the saddle.

"I've got you," Dean assured her. Once the horse settled again, he slid his hands up to grip her hips. "Now, I want you to let go and reach for my shoulders. Then it's just another second and you'll be on your feet. Can you do that?"

Her eyes fell closed. "I feel like an idiot," she whispered.

Dean's mouth cocked up at the corner. "No. That'd be me. I never shoulda tossed you up there and taken off like I did. Anyone who'd never been on a horse before would have been scared outta their wits. I'm surprised you weren't screaming your head off."

A scowl settled over her features, and pink entered her cheeks. The expression of proud indignation was far preferable to the previous panic. "I have more self-control than that."

"I'm aware," Dean replied. "Ready? I'll have a hold on you the whole time. Just use me as support."

She carefully and slowly released her grip on the saddle, then leaned forward just enough to place her hands firmly on his shoulders. In the next second, he lifted and drew her toward him, allowing her body to feel his, to recognize its solid strength and firm foundation. The moment her feet touched the ground, she released a heavy breath. The warm air from her parted lips gusted across his throat.

Then, to his surprise, she gave a shaky little laugh as she tipped her head back. They were still pressed together from chest to knee. Her hands were on his shoulders, and his arms were doubled around her waist. The color had returned to her face, and her eyes had retrieved their golden sparks. The self-deprecating smile curving her lips drew his focus while the feel of her in his embrace fired his blood.

He wanted to kiss her so damned bad.

He wanted to know what that smile felt like against his mouth. He wanted to tease the curled corners of her lips with his tongue. He wanted to learn the taste of her while he discovered just how to make her sigh.

"That wasn't too hard," she said in a relieved tone.

Dean had to disagree with that. It was hard all right. Very hard.

He couldn't speak, and he sure as hell couldn't seem to let her go.

She'd have to do it.

But she didn't pull away. She stared back at him, with her expression going all soft and questioning, her lips parting, and her fingers pressing into the muscles of his shoulders. When her gaze fell to his mouth, Dean was finally released from the moment.

He couldn't kiss her.

While she lived at the ranch and temporarily shared his name, she was his responsibility. He would be an even bigger jackass than he'd already proven himself to be if he took advantage of her like that.

Even though it looked as if she wouldn't mind a bit.

Even though he wanted to taste her so badly he ached from head to toe.

He had more honor than that...didn't he?

He abruptly dropped his arms from around her, stepped back, and turned away. "The goats are this way."

He started walking, figuring she'd follow if she wasn't too disturbed by what almost happened—that is, if she even realized how close he'd been to claiming her mouth with his.

If she ran off for the house instead, he'd completely understand.

TWENTY

Courtney watched Dean walk away, her insides in a ridiculous jumble and her thoughts all mixed up. What on earth had just happened?

Nothing.

Nothing had happened.

But for a moment, it had seemed as if Lawton was going to kiss her. His eyes had gotten so intense and focused when he'd looked at her mouth. His jaw had tensed and his arms had tightened around her, sending delicious little thrills racing through her from head to toe.

She'd wanted that kiss. So badly that she imagined she could taste it. Taste him.

What would it feel like? Free and unfettered, like the summer wind? Or magical, like a starry Montana sky: bigger than life, bright, and wonderful? Standing there in his arms for what had seemed like a pause in eternity, she'd practically ached to find out.

Then he had just turned and walked away.

Shaken from the harrowing ride she'd endured, followed by the internal upheaval she'd experienced in Dean's arms, Courtney took a moment to steady herself—at least on the outside. Straightening her spine, lifting her chin, and calming her features, she took a long breath, then started after him.

She wasn't going to miss out on seeing newborn goats just because she suddenly felt as if she didn't know up from down.

He was taking long strides around the back of the horse barn but at a slow enough pace that Courtney was able to catch up relatively quickly and without undue effort. By the time she fell in step beside him, she knew she appeared completely composed and fully recovered from her bout of fear, even if a riot still played about inside her.

They continued beyond the barn to a large fenced-in pen containing a small three-walled shelter tucked beneath a cluster of trees. The spacious pen contained mounds of hay bales and a collection of wooden crates stacked at various heights. Having always taken a different route around the homestead on her way to Pilar's, Courtney hadn't even known the pen was there.

As they neared, she saw a goat standing atop the stacked crates. He was a caramel-brown color with large white markings, and he stared at their approach with intent round eyes. As soon as Dean stepped up to the gate, the goat jumped to the ground and came forward, bleating noisily.

Courtney had never been in the presence of a goat before. She was surprised by the animal's abrupt movements, but Dean just reached out and gave a little scratch between its long, curved horns as he urged the goat aside so he could fully open the gate and enter the pen.

Then he turned back to look at Courtney.

Whatever had been shining so intently from his gaze earlier was now firmly banked behind his typically serious expression. "You coming in?"

Courtney glanced at the goat standing next to Dean and eyeing her intently. "I thought I heard once that goats have a tendency to charge at people."

"If they're agitated." Dean lifted his brows. "Do you intend to agitate old Jeb here?"

"No, not intentionally," she replied warily.

"Come on. Jeb will never forgive you if you don't give him some attention before going to meet the kids."

Stepping through the gate, she cautiously closed and latched it behind her. The caramel-brown goat came up to her and rubbed his head against her thigh. She tentatively placed her hand on his head, noting the coarse texture of his hair beneath her fingers. He gave a playful series of nods until she started scratching as she had seen Dean do.

"His name is Jeb?" she asked, warming to the insistent creature with his big, gold-colored eyes.

"Yep. He's our buck. He needs to stay separate from the nan and kids, so we've got him out here. Once the little ones are big enough to use the pen, we'll move Jeb over to Randall's place."

"Would he harm them?"

"No. But his purpose is breeding, so unless we want more kids, he'll be kept at a distance. You ready to head to the barn?"

Courtney nodded. She followed Dean from the pen with Jeb close at her heels, eager for more attention.

"Stay back, you ornery goat," Dean muttered in a tone that was more affectionate than anything else as he held the buck back with one hand so he could securely latch the gate with the other. "If you behave yourself, I'm sure the pretty lady will be back to say hello another day."

Courtney's insides gave a funny twist. Did Dean even realize he'd just called her pretty? She fought against the rise of warmth to her cheeks as she followed him into the barn via a side entrance. She'd never before been so strongly affected by such a simple compliment. Likely because she'd never heard one so sincere.

"Nettie and her kids, both females, are in a horse stall for now. In a few days, I'll take them out to the pen."

Nettie was a beautiful animal of pale gray and white. She lay curled up in a soft bed of hay in the corner of a large stall while two spindly-legged little things wobbled about nearby. Courtney smiled at the sight of the two kids. One was pure white while the other was white with just a few small caramel-colored markings on her face and one large one on her side. They were delightful, with their knobby knees, fuzzy coats, and oversize ears. Though Nettie stayed resting, the two little ones immediately came stumbling forward, their curiosity overcoming any instinct for wariness.

Courtney dropped to her knees in the hay as they approached. The white one took a tumble but hopped back to her feet to meet her sister at Courtney's side. They both started licking her hands and tried climbing into her lap, bumping against each other in their excitement and all the while making fierce little noises that went straight to her heart.

Courtney was in love.

"Oh my goodness." She laughed as she tried to give each little animal equal attention while they stumbled over each other to get closer. "What amazing little creatures. I had no idea goats could be so adorable."

She glanced up to where Dean stood leaning against the frame of the stall door. He gave a shrug in response to her comment, but she thought she saw the hint of a smile curving his lips. That hint was enough to create a wave of warmth within her.

She turned her attention back toward the kids. The one with caramel-colored markings had apparently lost interest in her and started wandering around the stall, while the other one kept stumbling over Courtney's lap as she sniffed at every fold in her skirt. It was not long before their mother gave a call and the two kids ran back to her side.

Courtney shifted to push back to her feet only to find Dean already at her side, offering his hand.

She looked up with a smile. The man had a few manners after all.

She put her hand in his and allowed him to haul her up, ignoring the disappointment she felt when he released her as soon as he could.

Leaving the goats behind, they walked down the center aisle of the barn.

"Would it be a terrible interference in ranch business if I visit the goats every now and then?" Courtney asked.

Dean slid her a narrow-eyed glance that told her

he heard every bit of the intentional insolence in her tone. "The goats aren't ranch business. They are one of Randall's harebrained ideas that became my responsibility. Visit them whenever you want."

She grinned. "Thank you."

They had reached the spot where he'd left his horse hitched outside the barn. He took up the reins and started leading the animal inside. Courtney wasn't sure if she should follow or if he expected her to head back to the house.

She decided to do as she pleased, so she remained where she was, watching him walk the horse away, noting the way his denim pants formed to his legs and buttocks with his long, easy strides and the way his cotton shirt—a faded red today—shifted over the muscles of his shoulders. She became lost in the rhythm of his movement, so confident and casual. So unabashedly masculine.

And so very different from the sedate, intentional way she'd been trained to move, with no excess exertion, no display of individuality, no hint of immodesty or emotion.

He stopped and turned to look over his shoulder. Courtney did her best to conceal her thoughts behind an indifferent facade, but for a moment, it seemed as though he knew everything she was thinking and feeling.

His expression tightened, his eyes narrowed, and the fan of crinkled lines formed at the corners.

Courtney held her breath. She didn't speak or look away, just waited for him to say whatever it was that had him turning back in the first place.

After what felt like forever, he said, "You wanna learn how to ride?"

"What? Horses?"

Her blush deepened. Of course he meant horses. What else could he mean? He probably thought her an idiot. She *felt* like an idiot. The man truly had a way of scrambling her brain.

She thought she saw a twitch to his lips as he gave a nod.

Being able to ride horseback would open up an entirely new world of independence and freedom. She could not pass it up despite a lingering note of fear. "Yes, I would love to."

"Come on then," he said, turning back to continue into the barn.

"Now?"

"I'll give you your first lesson on tack."

Excitement trickled through Courtney's limbs as she took another step forward in her new life of adventure. Though if she were being honest with herself, she wasn't exactly sure if the excitement came from the idea of learning to ride or from getting to spend more time with the man who'd be teaching her.

∞

Randall, Pilar, and Jimena joined them for dinner that night.

Dean was relieved and annoyed at the same time.

He was pretty sure that an intimate night alone with his wife was not a good idea. However, having three curious witnesses to the awkwardness of his unintentional marriage was not something he relished.

After visiting the newborn kids, he'd spent nearly an hour with Courtney in the barn, explaining the horse tack as he removed it before going through the instruments of proper grooming. She'd sat straight-spined and attentive on a stack of baled hay through the entire lesson, asking questions now and then, but otherwise just listening and taking in everything he did with those striking eyes of hers.

As soon as the lesson was over and she disappeared into the house, Dean struck out for the river. At its deepest, the water only reached his hips, but it was cold and effective for a man who needed to cool off in a hurry.

The most frustrating thing—and there were multiple frustrating things about the current situation—was that he couldn't even define what it was about her that got him so hot and bothered.

Take this afternoon, for instance. All they'd done was visit the kids and talk about horse tack.

Of course, there had been those moments when he'd had his hands on her body as he helped her down from his horse. He could still feel the way she'd fit against him, all soft, gentle curves and unexpected, barely banked fire.

But that shouldn't have been enough to get him into such a twisted state.

The woman affected him like no other female he'd ever encountered.

Even after several days away, the impact of her gaze and her ready smile had hit him like a bullet at close range, and his body couldn't help but respond. Just like that.

He had to figure out a way to control his reaction to her. Such a response served no purpose.

In fact, it was damned frustrating.

But now, surrounded by his extended family at the dinner table, a different kind of irritation took root as he watched the source of his discomfort talking and laughing so amiably with the others. In the days he'd been gone, she'd obviously developed a friendship with the other two women on the ranch. Pilar and Jimena seemed to genuinely like her, which fairly astounded Dean since he couldn't imagine what they possibly had in common.

And Randall, well…Randall was Randall. A consummate charmer with a boyish love of life that seemed to make anyone he came in contact with feel at ease. Dean used to envy his brother for his ability to fit into any social situation with nothing more than a grin and a fun-loving attitude. But then Dean realized that if they had both been such carefree rascals, the ranch might not have survived Augie's death.

"You gonna come down to the fire tomorrow night?"

The question, voiced by Randall and directed toward Courtney, had Dean lifting his head as he realized he'd lost track of the conversation.

"What fire?" she asked with a tilt of her head.

Randall glanced at Dean, a frown lowering his brow. "My brother didn't tell you?"

Courtney also turned to look at him with a sharply arched eyebrow that seemed to say, *Of course not. Your brother is a jackass who is determined to behave with only the worst of manners.*

Though it could have been just his conscience thinking that.

"Most of the boys are riding in from the range tomorrow for their monthly dose of R & R," Randall explained. "Whenever the bunkhouse is full, we have a bonfire out back. It gives everyone a chance to socialize and have a little fun."

"That sounds delightful."

"I'm not sure that's a great idea," Dean finally interjected, drawing all eyes to him.

"Just because you never join the festivities doesn't mean your bride ain't allowed."

Dean tossed his brother a swift glare. "I never said she wasn't allowed, but those things can get a little rowdy."

"I've attended a few of them myself," Pilar replied. "I simply head home before things start to get wild." She gave Courtney an encouraging smile. "I think you'd enjoy the party. Besides, it will give the men another woman to dance with, since I'm not very swift on my feet these days."

Dean's opinion was apparently not going to count much on this topic, but he doubted a lady from Boston, who had likely attended some of the finest dinner parties and balls to be had, would find much enjoyment in a bonfire attended by a bunch of rowdy ranch hands.

TWENTY-ONE

✦

DEAN SPENT THE ENTIRE NEXT DAY IN HIS OFFICE, leaving Courtney to her own devices once again. Thankfully, both Jimena and Pilar arrived at the house that morning to start preparations for the feast that would be made up for the men that night. There was corn to grind, vegetables to roast, meat to smoke, pan dulce to bake, and tamales to roll. Jimena had started a traditional mole poblano the day before and continued nursing the large pot of sauce.

Courtney was anxious to assist where she could, having already learned so much from Jimena in regard to cooking and appreciating the added benefit of being able to practice her Spanish. She had gotten to the point where she knew a great number of common verbs and nouns and a variety of descriptors. If she heard any words she still didn't know, she usually understood enough to get the gist of what was being said. And she truly loved the hours she spent in the kitchen. She had never realized how much camaraderie and respect could be experienced by joining others in a common task. Of course, the good-natured teasing and gentle guidance helped, as did the endless bouts of laughter. She couldn't even consider it work when it was so much fun.

Just after midday, the men started riding in.

At the sight of the first group, Jimena burst into a flurry of activity, issuing sharp orders to both Pilar and Courtney to get the food finished and prepped for serving down at the bunkhouse.

"These men are going to be hungry and tired," Jimena asserted in Spanish. "We must have a wealth of flavors to welcome them home."

"Mama believes everything can be made better with food," Pilar whispered in an amused aside to Courtney.

"That's because it can," her mother retorted from across the kitchen.

Courtney laughed as she rushed to complete the task had Jimena assigned to her.

By the time the sun touched the western horizon, more than twenty men had come in from the range. Their horses had been tended to and settled in with mounds of fresh hay, healthy grains, and cool water, while the men themselves had been fed near to bursting. Laughter and conversation resounded from the bunkhouse loud enough to be heard from the front porch of the main house.

Earlier, Courtney had brought a plate of food to Dean in his office. He had barely looked up from the paperwork and ledgers spread across his desk. Slightly annoyed by his lack of attention, and even more annoyed that it bothered her in the first place, she had decided not to go back to fetch his dishes. The man could carry them back to the house himself.

The remnants of the day of cooking had all been cleaned up, and Jimena had returned to the house beyond the pasture for the night. The two younger women were taking a moment to relax in the fresh air. As the long fingers of fading sunlight stretched across the yard, Courtney stood at the porch railing and had to forcibly keep herself from glancing toward the barn, wondering when Dean might make an appearance.

"Is it always like this when the men return?" she asked, hoping to distract herself.

"The first night, yes," Pilar replied from the rocker in the corner of the porch. "After tonight, some will settle down a bit while others will head into town for more entertainment. As much as they love being out on the range, coming home always feels a bit like a fiesta."

Courtney felt a stab of concern for her friend. Exhaustion was apparent in her deep breaths and her weary gaze. Though Pilar hadn't uttered a single word of complaint, Courtney had to suspect the woman's very large belly had caused some significant strain through the day.

Courtney was just about to suggest that Pilar go home to get some real rest when Randall came sauntering over from the bunkhouse and her friend's face lit up at the sight of him.

"Good evening, ladies," he said with a warm smile as he leapt over the porch railing to land right in front of his wife. He crouched down and took her hands in his to lift them both to his lips. "How is my loveliest of blossoms feeling tonight?"

"More like an overripe melon ready to burst on the vine than a flower," Pilar retorted, causing Randall to chuckle.

"Not much longer now, honey. Just a few more weeks, and we'll have a little one to snuggle."

Courtney observed the interaction with a smile, appreciating the love and optimism shared by the couple.

"And how has your day been, Mrs. Lawton?"

Courtney recognized Randall's teasing insistence on using her formal name exactly for what it was. The funny thing of it was that his determination to call her by a name she had never wanted managed to keep Courtney from taking the title too seriously. She credited Randall's unique brand of boyish mischief for keeping the situation in proper perspective.

Just because she was temporarily married to a man who barely seemed to tolerate her presence did not mean she had to pout or rail at the circumstances she had no immediate way out of.

"Courtney has been working beside us in the kitchen all day."

Randall's eyes widened as he rose to full height, though he remained standing at his wife's side. "Is that so?"

"Well, not all day," Courtney clarified. "I did take an hour to visit Snowball and Sunshine."

Randall lifted an eyebrow toward Pilar. "Who?"

"Nettie's new kids," Courtney replied. "It felt awkward continuing to call them the white one and the white one with spots, so I gave them names. I hope that's all right."

"I don't mind at all," Randall replied, but something in his tone reminded Courtney that he probably wasn't the Lawton she should be asking. Dean hadn't seemed too concerned with the idea of her visiting them, but she supposed naming a creature could potentially cross the line into interference.

"Well, the fire's been lit and the men are starting to head down. I thought I'd come over and see if you ladies were ready to join them." Randall glanced at his wife. "Unless you aren't feeling up to it?"

Pilar smiled and rose to her feet, placing on hand on the upper curve of her belly. "I'd like to go down for a little while, at least. It will be nice to see everyone again."

"All right. Mrs. Lawton?"

"I'll go if you stop calling me that," Courtney replied with a salty smile.

Randall laughed and gave her an unabashed wink. "I can't help it. It suits you, I think."

Courtney rolled her eyes.

"Besides," he added as they all stepped down from the porch and started across the yard toward the bunkhouse, "you should probably get used to it since that's who you'll be to all the men down at the fire."

Randall took Pilar's hand as they walked side by side. The comfortable display of their affection for each other was so different from what Courtney was used to back home. Holding hands so casually would have been considered practically scandalous.

She much preferred Montana's way of doing things. "I would rather just be Courtney," she said honestly.

Randall shook his head. "You're the boss's wife. They'll be affording you the respect Dean would expect of them."

Courtney figured Randall was right. She cast another glance toward the barn. Now that dusk had fallen, she could see the glow of light coming from the office window. Did the man intend to leave his office at all today?

"You mentioned last night that he does not join in with the men's revelry," Courtney said. "Why is that?"

"He used to enjoy a good party now and then, but it all changed when Granddad passed on and Dean took over. As boss, he has to keep a distance from the men so they continue to respect him."

"You don't feel the same way?"

"Naw. It's different for me. I'm just the foreman, and I spend most days working alongside them. Besides, I like people and I like parties way too much."

"Does your brother keep to himself out on the range as well?"

"For the most part. When he heads out, that is."

"That sounds rather lonely."

Randall gave a look she couldn't quite read. "It is."

The bonfire was taking place down near the river. Long wooden benches had been set up around the dancing flames, and more than a dozen men were already gathered around. Courtney had met many of them earlier when she'd helped Jimena serve their meal and was greeted warmly as room was made on a bench for the ladies to sit.

Then someone picked up a fiddle and started to play.

TWENTY-TWO

DEAN WATCHED HER FROM BENEATH THE SHADOWS OF a large spreading oak tree just beyond the reach of the firelight.

Her laughter was light—a musical sound—compared to the gruffer, often more bawdy chuckles and shouts of the men around her. At the moment, Buck was telling one of his stories. The old cowboy had a wealth of experience on the range and knew how to turn anything into a laughter-inducing anecdote. No one knew how much of his tales was even true, but the men sure as hell found them entertaining.

His wife appeared to as well, if her bright eyes and rapt expression were any indication.

Dean wasn't sure why he'd even come down to the river. He had no intention of joining the cowboys around their fire, but for some reason, knowing Courtney was there had compelled him to take a look, just to make sure she was doing all right.

He should have known she'd be fine.

The men knew enough to treat her properly, and

Randall wouldn't head home without escorting her back to the house first.

And then there was the fact that his bride seemed to face every new experience, even the more challenging ones, with good humor and an enviably positive expectation. She just didn't seem to consider the possibility that anything she did wouldn't go perfectly in her favor.

She apparently hadn't been exaggerating that day in town when she'd said she intended to make the most of a situation she hadn't chosen.

As the music changed to a lively dance tune, a young cowboy named Grant Wilde approached Courtney with a jaunty step. He gave a flourishing bow before he offered his hand. Though Dean couldn't hear what was said, it was obvious the man was asking his wife to dance.

Dean tensed as an unfamiliar sensation flew through his blood.

Courtney took the man's hand, and Grant immediately swept her off into a spinning, high-stepping cowboy waltz. The others clapped in time to the music and shouted their approval as the couple danced. Dean didn't like the sight of the cowboy's rough hand at her slim waist or the way her skirts swept around the other man's legs. But the smile on Courtney's face kept him from interfering.

He had no right to interfere anyway.

The thought shouldn't irk him so much.

It wasn't long before another cowboy stood up and cut in, taking his turn to spin Courtney around the fire. More men stood and partnered each other, a necessary practice when women were scarce and the urge to dance was too fierce to resist. Even Randall and Pilar took a few turns, though at a far more sedate pace.

One after another, the cowboys claimed his wife for a dance, until her face became flushed and laughter fell readily from her lips. By the end of the song, her hair had loosened and the curls that never seemed to stay tucked away for long softly framed her face.

She was beautiful. Full of life and laughter. Optimism and joy.

He doubted anything in the world could bring her down for long. Even her fierce temper cooled quickly enough when faced with her determination to find the bright side of any situation.

How would it feel to hold all that fire and delight in his arms? Would the darkness he sometimes felt pushing out from inside him overshadow her light? Would his regret crush her joy?

He clenched his hands into fists.

He shouldn't have come down to the fire. He was the boss. His men deserved to have their fun without him lurking around.

So did she.

The song came to an end with a round of applause, and Courtney was returned to her spot on one of the benches. Dean was about to turn and walk away when she glanced in his direction. Despite the distance and the dark of night, she must have seen him because she tilted her head and gave a little smile.

Dean felt like a match had been tossed on dried wood. Flames of desire and fear came to life. Need and denial.

He didn't want to feel so much from her smile, but there it was, in an instant.

As the fiddler began an old trail song that had the men joining their voices to sing the sad tale of a man who returned home from the War Between the States to find his sweetheart married to someone else, Courtney rose to her feet. She made her way around the gathered men and started heading in Dean's direction.

He stood stock-still, his breath tight, his body tense, and his eyes soaking up the sight of her. The firelight at her back threw her feminine silhouette into stark outline while keeping her features in darkness.

The closer she came, the higher the flames inside him rose. He struggled to tamp them down.

"I thought I saw you out here," she said as she came to stand beside where he leaned a shoulder against the trunk of the tree. Her voice was breathless from dancing. When she turned to glance back at the fire, he noted a light sheen of perspiration on her skin. Then she looked back up at him, tilting her head in question. "Have you come to join the others?"

Dean glanced past her to the gathered men. No one seemed to have noticed that the woman with fire in her hair had left them. He suspected the whiskey jugs being passed around were significantly lighter than when he'd first started observing. The men were headed toward a long and ruckus-filled evening. They deserved it.

"The men don't need me to spoil their fun," Dean replied.

Her answer was a quiet sigh.

They stood there without speaking. The moment

felt heavy with an atmosphere of unfulfilled expectation. He got the sense he'd disappointed her. He almost asked her if he had but was saved from uttering the embarrassing question when Randall and Pilar started heading toward them. His brother, at least, had noticed Courtney's absence from the fire.

"Didn't expect to see you down here," Randall noted as they reached the shadows of the oak.

Dean didn't reply. He didn't need to explain himself.

"It's getting late," Randall continued. "I'm gonna take Pilar home. Would you take over as escort for your wife?"

There was a hesitation, and Courtney quickly filled the odd silence. "That's all right, I can make it back to the house on my own."

"No," Dean interjected. "I'll take you."

Pilar stepped forward to embrace Courtney. She said something in Spanish that Dean didn't understand. Whatever it was, it made Courtney smile as she sent a fleeting glance in his direction.

Then they were alone again as Randall and Pilar disappeared into the stretching night.

Courtney observed the gathering around the fire. The men were getting boisterous in their celebration. "I suppose it is time for me to retire as well."

She was obviously reluctant to leave the festivities.

"It'd be best. The men are looking to let loose tonight."

She nodded, and they both turned to head up the path toward the house.

They walked in silence for a little while, then Dean asked, "Did you enjoy yourself?"

"I did," she replied emphatically. "So much. I have never been to a party like that before."

"You mean a bunch of rowdy cowboys passing whiskey around as they dance to the fiddle?"

She laughed. It was a soft sound. "Exactly. I don't think I have ever enjoyed dancing quite so much."

"When men work hard, they tend to play hard," Dean replied.

"It is too bad you chose not to join them."

"I'm the boss."

There was a pause before she asked, "And that means you are not allowed to have fun?"

Dean shook his head. "I've got more important things to worry about."

"Yes, I know."

Dean sent her a sideways glance at the hint of sharpness in her reply. He figured he imagined it when she continued in a softer tone, "It seems to me you could allow yourself some time to enjoy life every now and then while still successfully managing things. Randall probably wouldn't mind taking on a few more responsibilities. In fact, he might prefer to stay a little closer to home with the baby expected to arrive soon."

"That sounds an awful lot like interference in ranch business," he noted.

"Not at all," she argued with a sweet smile. "I am simply sharing my opinion."

He held back his amusement and gave a short grunt in reply as he watched his booted feet eating up the moonlit ground in front of him.

But her words had him thinking. It was an argument Randall himself might have made. A desire to stick closer to home would explain why his brother had been more adamant lately in asking for responsibilities beyond those of foreman, which took him out on the range more often than not.

Dean wasn't sure he could trust his brother to keep a firm hold on things. But he wouldn't know for sure unless he gave Randall a chance. If he did hand over some of the management duties to Randall, Dean wouldn't be left with so much to do. He might even find time to claim a little of that joy she was talking about.

It was not something he'd ever considered before.

Maybe he should.

Courtney came to a stop and reached out to place her hand on his forearm, bringing him to a halt as well. They had come around the bunkhouse, and the main house was just across the yard. He looked down at her face, all soft and pretty in the moonlight, though her expression was earnest.

"One idea I have come to embrace since leaving Boston is that life is too precious to dedicate entirely to duty and the expectations of others. We all deserve to feel fulfilled and happy in our lives. I cannot imagine how difficult it must have been for you to lose your fiancée, and I know the ranch means a great deal to you." She lowered her gaze to where her hand rested on his arm. After a moment, she let her hand drop to her side. Dean had preferred it where it was. She looked up at him again. The compassion in her eyes roped him in even as her smile knocked him off his feet. "And I know you don't like taking suggestions from other people, least of all me, but maybe you could just think about what I said."

A harsh wave of longing swept through him. The feeling crested with an emotional resistance he couldn't ignore.

Anne's death had hurt like hell. She'd possessed such an active, vibrant soul. For her to lose her life in a fall from her horse on land she'd ridden almost daily her entire life was senseless and tragic. It made no damn sense.

He mourned her still.

But he couldn't say her death had any influence on his choice to focus on duty and responsibility over all else.

No. He was pretty sure that seed had been planted long ago and had been part of the reason he and Anne had never gotten around to tying the knot.

Randall had been trying to get him to have more fun for years. Even when they were young, before Augie had died, and they'd head to town together for a little R & R, Dean would be chomping at the bit to return to the ranch. When exactly had the joy been sucked out of him?

A soft touch against the side of his face drew his attention back to the woman in front of him.

Her eyes reflected the light of the moon overhead as she rested her palm against his check. She searched his expression with a smile that was almost sad. "What is going on in that riotous mind of yours?"

Dean said nothing. There was nothing to say.

He couldn't explain it to himself, let alone to this woman who by all rights should be a complete stranger to him.

Yet she didn't feel like that. Not anymore. Maybe not even from the beginning.

There had always been something about her that tugged at his insides. He'd thought it was annoyance at first, and frustration, but he hadn't been annoyed by her in a long time, and the frustration he experienced in her presence was of a very specific kind. Yet that tug was still there—reaching deeper, pulling harder.

When she realized he wasn't going to answer, she allowed her fingers to caress the edge of his jaw as she slowly withdrew her touch.

Dean's entire body felt like a full-drawn bow as he gathered all the willpower he possessed to stand still and unmoved. But he *was* moved.

The flicker of her glance swept across his mouth before she released a listless little sigh and turned to start toward the house.

They crossed the yard in silence.

The light had been left on in the parlor, and the soft golden glow spilled gently from the window. As she approached the porch steps, her pace slowed and then stopped, as though she was reluctant to leave the dark quiet of night behind.

Dean followed suit, finding it far too easy to align himself with her movements.

"I don't think I'm quite ready for the night to end," she murmured. Looking up at him with a gentle curve to her lips, she asked, "Would you dance with me? Just once before we head inside?"

Dean hadn't noticed it before, but now he heard the gentle, distant melody of an old-fashioned waltz drifting up from the river. It was a slow and almost mournful tune, but it seemed to suit the current mood.

He shouldn't dance with her—place his hands on

her warm body and draw her toward him. Mainly because he wanted to way too much.

She took a step toward him. Tipping up her face, meeting his wary gaze, she smiled. "Come on. Just a few turns around the yard. When is the last time you danced?"

The last time he'd danced?

Years ago. So long ago he couldn't even recall when. "Please."

Her plea was soft and sweet, and he didn't want to refuse.

His stomach muscles drew tight as he reached out to take her hand in his. Her fingers were relaxed and her palm smooth against his calluses. She stood still as he slid his other hand around the curve of her waist. With gentle pressure, he urged her another step closer. She complied immediately, and he swept his hand up the narrow line of her back into proper position for the waltz as her free hand came up to rest on his shoulder.

They remained like that for a moment, their breaths mingling in the quiet space between them, while the moonlight cast a silver glow and the strains of the waltz filtered lazily from the distance.

Then Dean pressed his hand at her back and drew her into the dance. She followed gracefully through each step and turn. Her skirts flowed around his legs as his boots kicked up dirt from the yard. Though it had been a long time since he'd attempted a waltz and he had never been much of a dancer to start with, she made it easy, reacting instantly to the slightest press of his fingers against her back, seeming to anticipate what direction he'd take and staying with him even when he stumbled.

It felt natural to sweep her around the front yard at midnight, holding her gaze, neither of them speaking. So natural that he was able to stop thinking about every move and just enjoy the dance. They swirled in ever-widening circles, making use of the empty yard while he held her close in his arms. Close enough to soak up her warmth and vitality. Close enough to see the light of pleasure in her eyes. He waited to see that easy smile of hers widening her pretty lips, but her expression was oddly serious and thoughtful.

Now it was his turn to wonder what she was thinking. It was on the tip of his tongue to ask, but he remained silent, unwilling to break the magic of the moment.

Too soon, the music came to an end. The sweet, sad melody faded off into the night. Their movements slowed to a stop, but they didn't step away from each other.

Dean didn't want to let her go.

Maybe he was just caught up in the moonlight, the music, and the way the woman in his arms made him feel. The warmth of her body so close, but not touching—not in the way he wanted. Maybe it was the reflection of the stars in her eyes and the gentle glow of fire in her hair. The flush on her cheeks, her parted lips.

Maybe he was just so damn sick and tired of fighting the truth inside him. Maybe he wanted something sweet and beautiful for a change.

The desire to kiss her was overwhelming, as was the

urge to draw close enough to feel her heartbeat against his chest. For a moment, he stopped fighting it. His arm tightened around her back, curling inward until she pressed against him, the soft curves of her body fitting perfectly to his tense frame. She didn't resist, didn't pull away. She followed his direction so easily, just as when they'd danced. Her breath was quick and shallow, but he did not think it was from exertion.

It was anticipation…and he felt it too.

When her gaze darkened and dropped to his mouth and stayed there, Dean had to fight against every urge in his body not to take her lips with his. It took everything he had. He knew he should release her and walk away.

He just couldn't.

TWENTY-THREE

SHE WANTED HIM TO KISS HER WITH A LONGING THAT unfolded like a flower deep in her center.

There was nothing in her entire experience that quite compared with being turned about in the arms of this cowboy beneath the glow of a midnight moon. His hand at her back, guiding with steady strength, the brush of his thighs, the draw of his gaze. The minutes they spent turning about in the front yard felt like a dream.

And when the music came to an end, he didn't release her. Instead, he drew her closer. Closer to his heat, his sturdy strength.

But he did nothing more.

She wanted more. Her heart beat hard and swift with the yearning to take the moment further.

He wasn't going to kiss her. She knew it by the hard line of his lips and the tension in his jaw.

He wasn't going to kiss her, but she could kiss *him*.

She could be bold and fearless. She had to be. Because this longing inside her wasn't going to just go away. Most importantly of all, she didn't want it to.

With her hand still resting on his shoulder, she held his gaze as she rose up on her toes. Something intense flickered in his eyes, and she feared he'd pull away. He didn't, and her belly went wild with anticipation. A moment later, she pressed her mouth to his.

Such a simple act. But the sensation caused by the feel of his lips against hers shot like lightning through her blood. White-hot, electric, and devastating. Her fingers curled into the fabric of his shirt as she waited for his reaction.

Would he shove her away? She tensed for his rejection, quite certain it would break her into pieces.

Then a sound like thunder echoed from deep inside him before he released her hand to wrap both arms around her back. He tilted his head, shifted his lips in a glide of lovely friction over hers, and deepened the kiss.

Heat—delicious, melting heat—flowed through her muscles, softening her. She wrapped her arms around his neck, nearly dislodging his hat as she tried to get closer, hold him tighter, kiss him deeper.

The feel of his tongue sweeping along the seam of her lips released a gasp of surprise as her body was flooded with new sensations—exhilaration that reminded her of a summer storm gathering strength in a swirl of rising energy.

When his tongue slid past her parted lips to claim an intimate taste of her, she sighed her surrender. The velvet glide of his tongue against hers made her limbs weak though her blood rushed strong though her veins.

There was decadence in his kiss. There was also

a quiet strength, an almost reverent possession. She craved that possession. She wanted to feel as though she belonged to him, if only for that moment under the moon. She wanted to meld with him until her sole existence was about the feel of his arms encircling her, the heavy thud of his heartbeat, the hot, wet depth of his kiss.

She'd always dreamed a kiss could be like this, passionate to a point where nothing else mattered.

Never mind that it made no sense for her to want this man so badly. A man who had done everything to keep her at a distance despite the flashes of fire in his eyes that she hadn't been able to name until this moment. It did not matter that she intended to leave Lawton Ranch as soon as their marriage was dissolved.

All that mattered was how smooth and firm and perfect his lips felt as they caressed and shaped and drew on hers. And the way he tasted like rich bourbon and deep-buried need. And how he held her like he'd never let her go.

She could stand there kissing him for hours. She wanted to explore every flavor and texture of his mouth. She wanted to kiss his jawline, and the fan of lines at the corners of his eyes, and the side of his throat where his skin was salty and warm with his heavy pulse.

And then suddenly—with no warning at all—he released her. Tearing his mouth from hers with a harsh, smothered sound, he practically shoved himself away from her.

Courtney's eyes flew open to see the hard expression on his face as he took several steps back, leaving her standing alone and shaken. Where she had just been melting in his arms, she now stood on wobbly legs, confused and gasping for breath.

"Dean, I—"

"That was a mistake," he interrupted harshly. "I don't want a wife."

His words, though she'd heard them before, hurt all the more now, and she suspected she knew why.

"I understand," she replied softly, carefully, deliberately drawing her composure back around herself like an invisible but indestructible shield. She had never in her life been so grateful to her mother for teaching her how to hide the riot of longing and pain behind a stiff, imperturbable facade. "You still love her."

"It's not about Anne," he replied, his voice low and raw as he turned away from her. "This never had anything to do with her. It's about you."

Courtney's heart stopped. Oh. He didn't want *her*.

"I see." The acknowledgment hit deep, far deeper than she should have allowed him to touch her. "I am sorry I kissed you. It won't happen again. Good night, Mr. Lawton."

With as much dignity as she could manage while her legs still felt weak and her blood still thrummed through her veins, Courtney turned and walked up the porch steps. She made it through the front door without even the slightest temptation to turn around for another glimpse of him.

Just as the screen door closed behind her, he muttered an angry curse into the night. The expletive was quickly followed by the crunch of his boots on the gravel drive.

Courtney rushed up the stairs and raced down the hall to her bedroom. Without bothering to light a lamp, she went straight to her window just in time to see him heading toward the barn with a reckless stride. He disappeared inside a minute later.

She sat on the bench before the window for a long time after. Until her breath and heartbeat returned to normal and her skin no longer felt flushed and sensitive to the touch. Finally, she convinced herself to dress for bed.

After removing her dress and carefully laying it over the chair, she stripped down to nothing before slipping into the simple summer nightgown of billowing white cotton and eyelet lace that she had ordered from Mrs. Grainer. Courtney released her hair from the twisted bun and sat at the edge of her bed to brush through its length.

And all the while she thought of Dean.

She recalled the image he had made, a distant figure barely perceptible in the shadows beyond the fire. She had no idea how long he'd been standing there watching the festivities. At one point, she had just felt her gaze drawn out into the darkness and there he'd been. A silent and solitary figure.

Nothing could have stopped her from approaching him then.

When they'd started toward the house together, walking side by side in the darkness, he'd felt almost like a friend. She wasn't sure why she had decided to prod him as she did, urging him to shake free of his self-imposed reserve, beyond the fact that she had sensed something in him...something held back and bound. Everything he kept so carefully reined in needed to be set loose to breathe every now and then. She knew it because it was the same for her. She hadn't realized how much she'd denied of her true nature until she had left the confines of her Boston life behind.

Releasing the constant need to control her emotions—the good and the bad—had been liberating. Expressing her joy and delight only increased them.

She wanted him to feel that too.

Asking him to dance had been born of a simple desire to introduce him to something joyful. To distract him from thoughts of duty and responsibility and bring him back to the moment. She had not intended to kiss him, hadn't even really known she wanted to until the moment she did. And then it was all she wanted.

But it had been a mistake.

She shouldn't have given such strength to the feelings he inspired in her.

He had made it clear from the beginning how he felt. He might desire her as a man does a woman, but he didn't *want* her. She shouldn't have been surprised when he stopped the kiss the way he did.

Courtney Adams had always been confident of her attractiveness, her popularity, her perceived worth amongst Boston's social circles. But without the family name, the wealthy background, the props of her privileged existence—what did she have to offer?

Certainly nothing that would be of any value to a man like Dean. She was pampered and self-centered and had no discernable skills or particularly useful attributes.

And yet...he had opened up and revealed the depths of his passion if only for a few brief and stunning moments.

And it had been heavenly.

Finishing her hair with a few last frustrated tugs, she set the brush aside and climbed into bed. But the room was too hot and stifling to find any comfort or rest. She rose to open the window, then lay down again, only to agonize over every minute detail of her first real kiss. The tastes, the sounds, the sensations.

She twisted and turned in her sheets, finally casting them aside.

Though her body had returned to a normal rhythm after leaving Dean, something still simmered beneath the surface. Something had been awakened in his arms and would not go back to sleep.

The very faint sounds of music and occasional bursts of laughter drifted in through her open window. She expected the sounds to soothe her, but the heat of the night and the disturbing nature of her own thoughts kept her restless.

There was no help for it. She gave in to the call of the distant music and the draw of fresh, cooling night air. Not bothering to grab a wrap, she left her bedroom and went downstairs, seeking the relief to be found beneath the stars.

She stepped out the front door and crossed the porch to stand beside one of the posts. Then she tilted her gaze to the sky and breathed deeply. The cool summer night soothed but did not eliminate the restlessness she felt.

Wrapping an arm around the post, she leaned against it. She liked the feel of the wood against her cheek, the boards beneath her bare feet, the gentle night wind caressing her bare arms.

The sound of booted steps on gravel had her holding her breath as her stomach executed a swift dive. She glanced to the side just as Dean came around the house from the barn.

He nearly made it all the way to the front steps before he saw her. But when he did, he came to a swift and sudden halt.

His body was as tense as when they'd last stood out here an hour before. His jaw was tightly clenched, his hands were curled in fists, and the muscles that formed over his lean, masculine frame were taut and strained. She searched his expression for some indication of what he was thinking, but all she saw was frustration and a weariness that made her sad.

She hadn't come outside with any intention of looking for him, but as they stood face-to-face again, she acknowledged that she had hoped to see him.

It was a hope that felt foolish now that she stood in his presence.

She lowered her gaze and released the post, intending to go back inside and leave him to the night alone.

"Don't go." His voice—rough and low—touched her deep inside.

She looked up and was struck by how he stared at her, his focus intent. She became instantly breathless. A breeze kicked up and swept around her, lifting long tendrils of her hair. The air between them felt charged. *Alive.*

"I can't get you out of my head," he muttered in irritation. "No matter what I do."

Courtney didn't reply. She wasn't the slightest bit sorry for making him think of her. Not when she wasted so many hours thinking of him. Fair was fair.

She met his gaze with a bold confidence she did not completely feel. She'd committed herself to a liberated new life. She would not back down now that something she wanted so desperately was staring back at her.

He shook his head and lowered his chin just enough to cast his face in shadow. His next words barely carried to her on the night breeze. "I wanna take you to bed, Courtney, so bad it makes me ache. I tried to stay away. Tried not to think about you." His voice roughened. "I just can't shake it."

The words brought an instant image to mind of lying beside his large male body, moving her hands over his skin, looking into his eyes, kissing him.

Goodness, how she wanted to kiss him again. And more. "Then stop trying," she whispered in reply.

When he lifted his gaze again, what she saw there made her insides go warm and melty. Heat, hunger, and an intense desire to hold nothing back.

"I sure as hell hope you mean that." The gravel in his voice deepened.

Courtney acknowledged the scandalous path she was heading down. To want this man so intently—knowing there was no future, no true commitment between them—was the height of impropriety. But what did that matter? In her old life, such behavior would lead to abject ruin.

But this was her new life. *She* made the rules. *She* decided what was right and good for her.

And right now, it was Dean.

She nodded, her heart beating a wild and untamed rhythm. "I do."

"It's too damn much…" He didn't finish, and Courtney could see how he warred with the instinct to hold it all in. He still felt the need to fight it.

"It's okay to let go, Dean," she urged gently.

There was another moment of tense indecision, but then his expression shifted into something fierce and beautiful. It stopped her breath and flipped her world on its axis.

His boots ate up the ground in long strides as he approached. Courtney barely had a chance to blink before he ascended the steps and reached her side. He swept one arm around her waist, curving her body into his. His other hand dove beneath the fall of her hair to cradle the back of her head as he swooped down for a kiss.

And just like that, Courtney was lost.

The effect of his lips on hers was immediate and devastating. Her knees weakened, her belly flipped, and her heart took flight.

He swept his tongue past her teeth in swift possession, tasting and claiming. His need was fiery and strong and…*real*. And she loved it. His loss of control as he bent over her—his arm a solid band of muscle at her waist, pressing her hips to his, arching her spine—filled her with a delicious sense of power.

All that explosive fire and physical craving was for her.

Maybe he didn't want her for a wife. But he *did* want her.

A flutter of something unnameable swept through her, leaving her shaken and weak. Her yearning was raw and powerful. She wanted to crawl into him. She wanted to feel everything he held so tightly inside. All of his heat and passion, every ounce of wildness he could no longer contain.

She grasped his shoulders hard, soaking up his strength, drawing on his hunger to feed her own.

But far too soon, he pulled away.

Courtney made a sound in protest as his mouth left hers.

His response was a low and incoherent rumble that rose from his chest. Then he swept her up into his arms. The world spun in a kaleidoscope of anticipation and desire with Dean at the center, strong and wonderful. Holding her against his chest, he turned toward the house. With sure strides, he crossed the threshold and continued up the stairs to his bedroom.

TWENTY-FOUR

A LINE WAS ABOUT TO BE CROSSED. THERE WERE A hundred reasons to stop it, but Courtney could not bring herself to end the beautiful feeling of being in Dean's arms—of being desired so fiercely.

She wanted this. Despite all it signified and all it would change, she *chose* to claim this night with him.

He kicked his bedroom door shut behind them and headed straight for his bed. Without pause, he laid her on the soft, quilted blanket and lowered his body to cover hers. The weight of him—pressing down on her thighs, her hips, her belly—was intimate and unnerving. She'd never been so physically close to another, but the uncertainty this time was a heady thing.

He'd braced himself on his elbows, keeping his upper body lifted as he looked down at her. He did not kiss her as she expected—as she hoped. For a long moment, the only sound in the room was their unsteady breath as they stared at each other in the darkness.

Why didn't he kiss her? His earlier rejection echoed through her.

"Dean, are you sure you want this…" The sharp glint in his eyes became shadowed by a frown, and he tilted his head. "With me, I mean," she clarified, feeling a blush warm her face.

He brushed his fingers over her cheek and jaw. In a deep and intimate tone, he said, "I'm not sure of much anymore, but I know I want you more than I've wanted anything in a long time. I didn't want you to stir up so much inside me. But you do. And I'm tired of denying it." He took a long, steadying breath. His expression darkened as he said, "I should be asking if you want this with *me*. I've done wrong by you in more ways than one."

Courtney shook her head gently but remained silent beneath the distinct and lovely feeling of his roughened hands on her skin as he trailed his fingers down along the side of her throat.

"It's true," he asserted, his brows lowering over an earnest gaze. "An honorable man would resist the desire to take you to bed, knowing…" His voice roughened. "Courtney, I—"

"Don't want a wife," Courtney interrupted as her heart gave a sharp squeeze. "Yes, I know. And I ran away from Boston to avoid becoming a bride. We are totally unsuited to each other. This is not a real marriage." She sighed. The heavy breath lifted her chest, momentarily drawing his gaze to her breasts. "But here we are," she finished in a whisper.

"Here we are," he repeated, his voice thick as he traced his work-worn fingers along the crest of her collarbone, sending tingling goose bumps across her skin.

Deep down, Courtney understood that lying together wouldn't be enough to change the course they were on. He had his reasons for avoiding marriage. And she was still devoted to her goal of learning to live independently. They were not truly husband and wife.

She knew it.

But perhaps a tiny part of her wanted to imagine otherwise. The part of her that admired her husband's fortitude and his dedication to the ranch. That part that was drawn to his quiet loneliness and his stubborn determination not to show it.

She and Dean both knew how quickly and easily the best laid plans could be destroyed. Happiness was never guaranteed. But one could choose it when it came around in brief snatches and unexpected moments.

Like this one.

She knew what she *should* be thinking. And yet her feelings—the bright, joyful anticipation, the fearful uncertainty, the deep yearning—were all too clear.

She wanted this *anyway*. She wanted *him* anyway.

Lying there in Dean's bed, with only a few breathless inches between them while he did nothing more than caress her skin with light brushes of his roughened fingers, Courtney felt something shift inside her. It seemed as though the final constraints of her former life dropped away, like a cloak falling to the floor.

She was not defined by her past or her future. She could simply be Courtney, poised in this moment with her heart beating a frantic rhythm and her body flushed and tingling with physical yearning unlike anything she'd ever known.

She didn't know where her life would take her when the four weeks were up, had no idea what her future looked like.

But she had tonight. *This* moment with *this* man was all hers.

If she chose to take it.

Dean's fingers ceased drifting over her skin in the lengthening silence. He shifted his weight. "I'm sorry," he muttered, as he made to rise from the bed.

Courtney grasped his upper arms to stop him. "Please, don't be sorry," she pleaded softly, allowing the need inside her to become evident in her voice. She didn't want to shield her feelings from him. Not now. "I won't be."

He looked down at her with his expression tense and questioning.

Lifting one hand, she removed his hat and tossed it aside, not caring where it landed. Then she took his face in her hands—loving the rough texture of his jaw against her palms—and urged his mouth down to hers.

Though his body was tense, he accepted her direction and fit his lips perfectly over her mouth. The kiss sparked with desire and deeper need, but he held back, keeping the caress light and sweet.

Courtney wanted the level of passion they'd shared outside, but he seemed intent upon taking things slowly. She could not be sure if that was to allow *her* a chance to change her mind, or himself.

When he lifted his head, her gaze was steady as she met his. "This is my choice, Dean. What is yours?" she challenged gently.

There was another pause before he answered.

"I'm not like your fancy men out East. I don't have any refined manners or pretty words for you. I'm a cowboy. What you see is what you get."

"Thank goodness for that." She smiled as she slid her hands around the back of his neck. "It is you I want, Dean. Not practiced gestures and false flattery. I want your hands on my skin. Your lips touching mine. Your tongue…" she added haltingly as heat flared between them.

He swallowed hard, and something bright flashed deep in his eyes. "You want my hands on you, princess?" His voice rasped like velvet through her senses.

Courtney's breath caught, and her belly swirled.

Then he shifted his weight to the side while leaving one denim-clad leg draped across hers. Still propped on one elbow, he settled his other hand on her collarbone. His thumb rested gently over the pulse at the hollow of her throat while his fingers curved warmly over her shoulder. The weight and the roughness of his palm held a promise—an intention to be fulfilled. Courtney drew a slow inhale to still the dance of excitement inside her as she waited for what would come next.

He trained his focus on the movement of his hand as he slowly brushed his fingers over the curve of her shoulder, dragging the eyelet strap of her nightgown down as he went. When the edge of the cotton bodice caught over the swell of her breasts, he made a low sound that warmed the darkness.

As he shifted his attention to releasing the buttons running down the center of her nightgown, Courtney watched his face. She became mesmerized by the taut strength of his jaw, the masculine lines of his firmly curved upper lip, and the weight of his brow. He was so intent, so serious.

She wished desperately to see his smile.

But then he had loosened her bodice enough to pull one edge aside and bare a breast.

Courtney felt the moment acutely. It seemed significant that the area of her body now exposed and vulnerable to his view and his touch also held her heart.

Silent and reverent, he trailed the back of his fingers over her exposed skin—from the base of her throat, down over the upper slope of her breast, and then across the sensitive, peaked crest.

Shocking jolts of fire arced through her center when his knuckles gently passed across her nipple. Her belly quivered, and a gasp threatened to slip from her lips.

He turned his hand to ease his fingers in a soft caress that shaped the lower curve of her breast before trailing them back up along her sternum. He had been watching the path of his touch over her skin, but now he lifted his gaze to meets hers. Courtney drew a swift breath at the silent hunger shining in his eyes. Keeping his eyes locked on hers, he pulled the other strap off her shoulder and tugged the nightgown down to her hips.

Then he rolled atop her again, settling his large body low between her parted legs with his elbows braced against her hips as he lowered his head toward her naked abdomen. At the first feel of his warm breath wafting over her belly, Courtney tensed. A second later, it was the brush of his hair against the undercurve of her breasts and the breath-stealing sensation of his mouth on her navel.

She lifted her hands to gently grasp his head, loving the slide of his hair through her fingers as he rained soft, warm kisses across her belly. Courtney was melting, swirling, aching. The juncture between her thighs felt swollen. Her legs grew restless, and her spine arched beneath him.

With a heavy rumble in the back of his throat, he shifted higher, sliding his hands beneath her shoulder blades to lift her to his mouth.

The heat and glory of his lips closing over her breast sent a shock through her body. Who knew such decadence existed? Such exquisite torment. He twirled his tongue around the peak of her nipple, and she was lost. He lavished her with lush, velvety strokes of his tongue before drawing her flesh deep into his mouth. The he followed with a rough scrape of his teeth and playful flick of his tongue.

By the time he moved his attention to her other breast, she was balanced harshly on the edge of anticipation, not knowing if his next caress would be sharp and poignant or deep and languid. Lost in her own experience, drowning in the pleasure he wrought, she had no idea how long he showered her with such attention. But at one point she realized that she wanted to give some back to him. As much as she loved the feel of his mouth on her, she was eager for the feel of his skin beneath her lips.

She made a strangled sound in her throat in an attempt to speak. If he heard her, he ignored her as he drew the pliant flesh of her breast deep into his mouth once again. Her core swirled with fire, but she wanted more.

Gripping his head in her hands, she tried to lift him away, but he only drew harder on her breast. In a raw voice, she finally managed to utter one word. "Stop."

Twenty-Five

He lifted his head to meet her heavy-lidded gaze. The dark turmoil on his face went straight to her core.

"Just for a moment," she clarified. "I need to catch my breath."

He shook his head and lowered his lips to the hollow at the base of her throat, dropping a light kiss there. "I don't think I can," he murmured against her pulse.

"I want your skin on mine."

With a low-grumbled sound, he lifted himself from her sprawled form in a swift and sudden movement. Scooting to the edge of the bed, he swiftly released several buttons of his shirt. Just enough so he could reach over his shoulder and grasp a handful of the cotton to drag it off over his head. He tossed the shirt to the floor somewhere near his discarded hat before leaning forward to remove his boots and stockings.

He did it all in a hurry and likely had no idea how entranced she became with each removed item. How she stared in wonder and appreciation at the body he revealed. The hard, contoured lines, the strength and masculinity. The way the muscles in his back moved beneath his smooth skin as he rushed through the tasks.

As he stood to release the buttons on his denim pants, he turned to face Courtney on the bed.

The second he caught sight of her lying half-tangled in her nightgown, his hands stalled and a predatory spark ignited in his eyes. He stepped around to the foot of the bed and leaned forward to grasp the hem of her nightgown in his large fists.

Courtney held her breath as he pulled. The cotton complied easily with his command, sliding down past her hips. Then lower and lower, so slow, until it came free and was released to fall forgotten to the floor.

The look on his face was different from any she'd seen before as his gaze trailed slowly up the length of her body. She had never worried a great deal about how she looked beneath all the fine clothing she was accustomed to wearing.

But now she couldn't help but wonder if she was too tall and too slim. Were her breasts large enough? Where her hip bones too prominent? Her legs too long? Her feet too big?

Pride prevented her from trying to cover herself, so she lay still and nervous beneath his avid attention.

Finally, after what seemed like an age, he muttered, "You make my mouth go dry."

She accepted that as a good thing, and the corners of her mouth curled into a smile.

He saw the smile and seemed transfixed by it for a moment, his eyes sharp.

Then he lifted a knee onto the bed and crawled up along her body to lower himself onto her again. Sliding one hand through her hair to cradle the back of her skull, he pressed his other hand to the low curve of her back as he rolled to his side. She rolled with him, and he wrapped her in an embrace that crushed her breasts to his chest and arched her spine.

He paused then, with his head bowed close over hers and his breath escaping in swift puffs against her parted lips. The moment allowed her to feel every texture of his body against hers: the hot, hard contours of his chest covered by a dusting of crisp hair that teased and tantalized her sensitive nipples. The rough denim of his pants encasing long, muscled legs, one of which pressed high between her thighs.

The intimacy and power of the embrace as he held her to him—not under or over him, but tucked in close against him—caused her heart to race as her throat became oddly tight. Before she could analyze her reaction, he lowered his mouth to hers.

Dean kissed her as he had earlier, with expert pressure and a skillful slide of velvet friction, accented by teasing darts of his tongue that soon became deeper strokes that urged her to join in.

Craving the taste of him, she explored with her tongue and tugged on his lips with hers. Seeking more of the intricate experience, she began moving against him. Rubbing her breasts back and forth against his chest, bending her knee to slide her leg higher over his, and arching her back.

He responded with a heavy groan and lowered a hand to grasp her buttock. When he pulled her hips tight to his and she felt the hardness of his erection pressing against her belly, an unfamiliar sound rose from her throat: a plea made up of need and frustration.

The kiss changed then, becoming insistent and impatient with a harsh edge that sent tingling shocks through her body. The hand he had buried in her hair gave a gentle tug, positioning her mouth for the plunging possession of his tongue.

Courtney surrendered. She discovered she liked the rough desperation in the deep strokes of his tongue, the grinding of his lips against her teeth, and the firm grip of his hands on her body.

Dean Lawton was not a man of polish and pedigree.

He was a force of nature. Straightforward, honest, demanding, and raw. He was not a man who needed much in the world, but right now, he needed her.

Courtney wrapped her arms around his back, giving of herself with equal passion. His lean strength encircled her. It was a wonderful, heady sensation to be so close to someone, to be held so tightly and kissed so thoroughly. But she wanted more of him. She wanted everything.

Pulling back, she forced him to release her mouth, though he did not loosen his arms around her. His breath was heavy and swift. So was hers.

Their eyes met, and the fierce yearning in his gaze sent shivers of delicious anticipation through her blood. "I'm ready," she stated with breathless certainty.

He stared at her, silent and tense. His skin emanated heat and was coated in a fine sheen of sweat. "You sure?" His voice held a teasing threat, but she heard the underlying sincerity in his question.

Holding his gaze, she trailed her fingers down his back, following the hollow of his spine until she found the taut rise of his buttocks just above the loosened waistband of his pants. The corners of her mouth curled into a smile as she slipped her fingers beneath the denim, seeking the firm curve of his rear.

"Infinitely," she whispered.

His eyes darkened, and his arms tightened almost painfully around her. A low growl echoed from his chest as he gave a short thrust of his hips, tensing the muscles of his buttocks beneath her hand.

Then with a ragged breath, he released her and rolled to his back to shove his pants roughly past his hips before kicking free of them completely.

Now, it was her mouth that went dry. "Oh my God," she whispered in awe.

On the night before her wedding, her mother had explained what to expect in the marriage bed. Though Beverly Adams had mentioned nothing of the swirling heat or melting need Courtney had experienced so far in Dean's arms, she had haltingly described the act of consummation.

Courtney stared wide-eyed at the hard, male organ jutting out from Dean's groin and wondered how on earth such a thing could be possible. The brief glimpse she'd gotten of his manhood that day in the bath had not compared to the sight before her now.

Dean groaned and dropped his head back on the pillow, covering his eyes with his forearm. "I suppose you've never seen a man in a needful state before," he muttered.

"Nooooo," Courtney replied, drawing the word

out in her amazement. "I cannot say I have." She was unable to take her eyes off him, especially now that he wasn't looking back at her.

He was thicker and longer than she had expected, but once her initial surprise wore off and she had a chance to really see him, she had to admit that this was as beautifully designed as the rest of him.

She eased closer to him, pressing herself along his side. "I'm sorry. I was just surprised."

"Yeah, I got that." Lifting his arm from his eyes, he brought it down around behind her back, his hand falling to the curve of her hip. "I understand if you wanna stop."

"No," she responded instantly. "I definitely do not want to stop."

"Thank God." His relief was obvious as he rolled her up on top of him.

The full length of him was stretched out beneath her. His wide chest and taut abdomen, the muscled length of his legs, and the hard, hot, rigid length of his erection against her belly.

She drew a deep breath before letting it out slowly. "I'm not sure what to do next."

"Let me worry about that," he said.

Lifting his head, he caught her mouth with his and she was immediately drawn back into all the sensations he invoked. How did he do that so easily? One deep, consuming kiss, and her body went up in flames. One stroke of his tongue along hers, and her thoughts spun off into the ether, as did her inhibitions.

She couldn't stop moving over him, rubbing against him, delighting in the textures and the lovely friction.

And soon he was groaning into her mouth as he curved his hand around her leg and drew her knee up alongside his hip. When his hand skimmed up the back of her thigh, she tensed. As much as she wanted to feel his touch along her private flesh that ached so sweetly, it was unnerving to feel so vulnerable.

Sensing her reticence, he gently rolled them both until she was beneath him once again, her leg now hooked over his hip, his hand still wrapped around her thigh just below the curve of her buttock. The difference was that now, instead of feeling his hard length against her belly, she felt it there, between her legs.

He met her gaze, his expression tense and beautiful, as he gave a gentle roll of his hips.

She gasped and gripped his shoulders at the heady, silken glide of his flesh along her outer folds. Holding her leg high against his side, he repeated the motion. Her body responded with slick heat as she dropped her head back.

The feel of him there—the smooth, rigid intention, the delicious, aching promise—stoked the flames of passion burning inside her.

He gave another thrust along the entrance to her body and she moaned, her fingers digging into the muscles of his arms.

Lowering his head beside hers, he scattered light kisses along the crest of her shoulder as he shifted to ease his hand between their bodies. She held her breath while he explored past the patch of curls to glide his fingers over her swollen flesh. The first delicate stroke of his rough fingers had her senses spinning in a thousand directions. All at once she was hit with the scent of his skin, the taste of his sweat when she lifted her head to place an openmouthed kiss on his throat, the sound of their ragged breath, and the feel of him—his masculine weight covering her while his attentive fingers teased her with pleasures she had no idea existed.

"Jesus, Courtney, I want you so bad it hurts." His voice was gruff and heavy, as though the effort to speak was almost too much.

Courtney understood. She couldn't manage to form words necessary to make a response. Instead, she met his mouth with hers, open and hot. Her tongue sought his while she arched and twisted beneath him.

Accepting her silent urging, he eased a finger inside her. The intrusion felt strange and wonderful. He started to stroke a gentle rhythm, making her low belly tighten as her breath grew swift and shallow.

Kissing her deeply, he withdrew his finger to circle his slick fingertip over her clitoris. The rhythmic motion over the swollen collection of nerves coaxed delicious new sensations as her body drew taut beneath him.

With her breath catching in fitful gasps against his lips, he pressed two fingers into her. The gentle stretch and increased pressure nearly undid her, and she tucked her heated face into the curve of his throat, murmuring nonsense against his skin.

Then his fingers left her as he centered his hips between her thighs. The smooth head of his erection was poised against her core.

"Hold on to me," he muttered thickly.

Courtney opened her eyes to meet his beautifully

intent gaze and wrapped her arms around his neck. Then he started to press forward, parting her swollen flesh, slowly easing into her tense and wanting body.

"If it hurts too much, I'll stop."

"No," she gasped. "Don't stop."

Though the sensation of being stretched, filled, was singular and new, it was pleasurable in a way she hadn't expected. The intimacy of the act reached deep into her soul and wrapped around her heart. In his arms, she felt awakened. As his body took possession of hers, she claimed him as well, adjusting and softening to take him in.

When it seemed as though he couldn't go any further, he paused.

Courtney released the breath she hadn't realized she was holding. Keeping his eyes locked with hers, he kissed her, slowly and deeply. And he kept kissing her as he withdrew from her in a tantalizing glide of his hardness along her inner flesh. When he was poised once again at her entrance, he swept his tongue into her mouth, stoking her internal fire, increasing her breathless need.

Then another press forward, faster this time, more insistent, and when he reached the point where he couldn't go any further, he didn't stop. With a powerful thrust, he broke past the barrier of her virginity.

Courtney arched her neck at the sudden pain, breaking from his kiss with a harsh gasp.

He dropped kisses along her jaw and murmured soothing words until the initial discomfort began to fade, leaving behind a gentle burning that was not altogether unpleasant.

When she sought his mouth to kiss him back, he responded with a small movement of his hips, just a shallow, gentle rocking. The feeling inside was lovely and deep. He repeated the movement, and tiny points of pleasure sparked to life. Bending her knees, she lifted her legs around his hips.

With a heavy sound escaping his throat, he pulled himself almost completely free of her before pressing forward in a long, slow thrust that stopped her breath. The power of his full possession, the pleasure in her complete acceptance of him was overwhelming.

She wanted more.

With a tilt of her hips, she told him so.

He answered immediately. Withdrawing and reclaiming. Over and over until their bodies were slicked with sweat, and gasps and moans filled the room. Courtney clung to him, moved with him. She arched and tugged and drew from him. As the pleasure built higher, the need grew wider and deeper. Sensation was alive everywhere, but especially inside.

The tingling sparks became roaring flames that could no longer be contained. She could not stop the rigid tensing of her body, not even to catch her breath. In an instant, the pleasure burst free, taking over her body, her awareness, the entire universe in a dancing sweep of light and vibration.

Dean held her through the onslaught, keeping a steady pace of thrust and retreat that prolonged her pleasure through multiple waves of release.

Then, as the final wave crested, he tensed. His breath caught on a guttural moan, and his body pulsed within her.

TWENTY-SIX

Dean didn't think he'd ever be able to move again.

Or maybe he just didn't want to.

He'd never experienced anything like what he'd just felt with the woman lying beneath him.

He was probably crushing her, but he didn't have the strength yet to lift himself away from her warmth. And she didn't seem to mind, if the way her arms and legs were still wrapped around him gave any indication.

He was glad he'd been able to bring her pleasure.

No, more like downright thrilled. He had been worried about disappointing her, worried that her virginity would make it difficult for her to enjoy the experience. But there had been no way to miss the moment she reached her climax. All inhibition had been swept away. Pleasure was evident in every gorgeous line of her face, every gasp of her breath. Her reaction had been pure and unconstrained. It had been a stunning sight to behold.

A stunning sight that sent him flying over the edge himself.

After several deep inhalations, he gathered enough strength to drag himself to the empty space on the bed beside her. But that was all he managed. Collapsing facedown on the pillow, he left one arm flung wide across her midriff and one leg still slung over hers.

She sighed and turned her head toward him with a sleepy smile.

"Thank you," she murmured as her eyelids fell over her green gaze and her smile slid away on a slow breath.

For what? he wanted to ask, but his brain was too muddled to form the words out loud. He fell asleep before another thought could even take its place.

When Dean next opened his eyes, it was to discover that the sun was already high and bright in the sky. He rose from the bed in a rush and started to dress.

He hadn't slept past dawn since he was a kid.

What the hell could have knocked him out like that?

He froze in place, his hands gripping hard on the leather of one of his boots.

Shit.

He spun back to the bed.

Empty.

But the room still smelled like her. Sweet and fresh with a hint of something that made him think of fire in the night.

His body tightened in an instant, but he shoved aside the swift rise of lust. As much as he might have liked to, he didn't have time to indulge in the sensual memories of what had transpired in that bed the night before.

There was work to be done.

He finished dressing in a hurry. His hat had gotten kicked under the bed at some point, so it took him a minute longer than he wished to find the thing. Setting it on his head, he left his bedroom and went downstairs.

Jimena must have been cooking for a while already because the house smelled of sweet bread and cinnamon. He saw no sign of Courtney as he made his way to the kitchen, and with an odd clench of his gut, he figured she must have gone back to her own bedroom last night.

But then he recalled vague memories of her slim body curled up beside him through the night and her warm breath bathing his skin with the steady rhythm of sleep.

No, she'd stayed in his bed all night.

She must have slipped away in the early morning.

He stepped into the kitchen, hoping to grab a quick bite of whatever Jimena had made and take it to the barn with him. At the sight of Courtney bending over to reach inside the hot oven, he came to a sudden stop.

Her hair had been twisted into a bun at her nape, and she was dressed in a pale-yellow frock with white trim covered by one of Jimena's serviceable aprons.

He watched as she withdrew a pan from the oven, holding it carefully with a thick, quilted mitt. Setting it atop the stove, she bent forward to take a long sniff of the sweet-smelling bread.

"If that tastes half as good as it smells, Jimena's outdone herself."

She turned around with a startled jump, her eyes wide, the pan nearly going flying in the process. She righted the pan before she removed the mitt and pushed her hair back from her face. Then she turned to him again with flushed cheeks and a smile. "Good morning."

Though she hid it well, Dean could see her nervousness. It might have been so easy to detect because it matched his own.

Facing her this morning, after the intense night they'd shared felt strange and unexpected. Unexpected, because he wanted nothing more than to grasp her around the waist, toss her over his shoulder, and carry her right back upstairs to start it all over again.

"Actually," she continued, "I made the pan dulce this morning. Jimena mentioned yesterday that she would not be able to come to the house today."

Dean arched a brow. Jimena always came up to the main house when the bunkhouse was full.

"I hope that is all right," she added with a tilt of her head.

"Sure. It's fine."

"Would you like me to fry up some eggs for you? And there is a slab of bacon I can cook up—"

"No," he said curtly. "I'll just grab some bread and coffee before heading out."

"Oh." Her chin dropped a notch, but just for a second before it came right back up again. "I imagine you have work to get to."

Dean frowned. He could see her disappointment and felt a need to explain. "There's always work to do."

There was a pause before she replied, "Yes, of course." She turned back to the pan of sweet bread. "I will just wrap a few of these up for you. The coffee is hot. You can pour yourself a cup if you'd like."

He stood there for a moment watching as she moved about his kitchen.

Her dress was a near match to the yellow-painted walls, but Courtney Adams-Lawton was not the kind of woman who could ever be at risk of blending into her surroundings. Her natural vibrancy wouldn't allow it.

Dean had to force himself to look away.

After fetching a cup from the cupboard, he crossed to where the coffeepot sat on the stove. The brew was dark and fragrant, just how he liked it. He took a sip before turning to find Courtney waiting patiently behind him.

She had wrapped some of the sweet bread all neat and tidy in a napkin before setting it on a plate beside a small bowl holding a dollop of fresh cream.

How did she know he liked to spread the cream on his sweet bread?

Feeling a bit off-kilter, he accepted the plate with a short nod as his gaze flickered over her face. "Thank you. I guess I'll see you tonight then, at supper."

She smiled and gave a nod in return but didn't say anything.

Dean figured he was probably behaving all wrong, but he had no idea what else to do. It wasn't every morning that a man woke up after making love to a wife he shouldn't want.

Not that he regretted anything that had happened. It was just that he had no idea what came next, especially when all he wanted to do was grab the woman and kiss her deep and hard until she clung to him like she had the night before.

With a tightness in his belly, he left the kitchen through the back door. But he only made it a few paces before he turned and headed right back into that kitchen, not stopping until he reached her side. Setting the plate and his coffee down on the counter, he reached for her, curving his arm around her waist to turn her in to him as he lowered his head and planted a kiss hard on her lips.

He half expected her to shove him away.

She didn't.

With a low sound, she angled her body into him, draping her arms around his neck and dislodging his hat while she parted her lips to accept the wide sweep of his tongue.

Before he could convince himself to stay there in that kitchen all day, he released her, swept his hat up off the floor, grabbed his food and coffee, and strode back out the door. To keep himself heading toward the barn, he repeated a running list of all the things he needed to do that day.

He'd noticed some areas of the goat pen that needed reinforcing. If there was any weakness in the structure of their pen, the mischievous animals would find it and exploit it.

He had to process paychecks for his men. They needed their money for the next few days of R and R so they could head into town for some fun, so that should probably come first.

He needed to devise a way to catch whoever was responsible for the slaughtered cattle.

The thought had his stomach churning. He didn't want to believe the MacDonnells were capable of such violence. The old man had been one of Augie's closest friends. Dean and Randall had run around with Anne and her brother, Clinton, their entire childhood. They had been like family.

But death had a way of changing things.

If the MacDonnells blamed Dean for Anne's death in any way, they might feel justified in the ugly, vengeful behavior.

Hell, Dean wasn't sure it *wasn't* justified.

He'd been avoiding direct contact with them since Anne's funeral, keeping a distance whenever he spotted Clinton or his father in town. The idea of confronting them over this nearly made him sick.

But something had to be done before more cattle were killed.

∞

It was late morning by the time he made his way out to the goat pen.

It was just his luck that he'd finally managed to shove thoughts of Courtney into the farthest corners of his mind only to come upon her when he least expected to.

She sat on a hay bale while one kid tugged playfully at the hem of her skirts and the other hopped around on her lap. Her wide, sunny smile and quiet laughter as she teasingly admonished the young animals for their naughty behavior sent a shot of sharp regret straight through the longing inside him.

She looked so right sitting there in the sunlight. While he'd been doing all he could to avoid her, she'd managed to make herself at home on the ranch. She'd claimed the goats as her personal pets, found a place in his kitchen, made friends with his family, and even won over his ranch hands. What was next on her list of things to conquer?

He had a flashing vision of her riding on horseback across the wild open spaces of the Montana plains, and his stomach clenched with trepidation.

Anne had been the most accomplished rider and cattlewoman Dean had ever known. She'd grown up running wild all over Montana cattle land. If a simple riding accident could bring her down—a woman so confident and capable—how could a city lady like his bride possibly manage?

But the more he thought of it, the more he wanted to show Courtney the land he loved so much. He wanted her to ride beside him across the open range to see his herd grazing in the distance before heading back to the house at sunset.

Against his better judgment, his feet took him closer to her. She didn't notice his approach until he'd gone through the gate into the pen. Her smile was just a little bit shy but still so warm and joyful that he found himself speaking before he could stop himself. "Come on. I'm taking you for a ride."

Her eyes widened. "Do you mean on horseback?"

An altogether different kind of riding flashed hotly to mind before he chased it away. "You said you wanted to learn, right?"

"Of course, but I've only learned a little about tack

so far. I really don't know if I'm ready to get on one of the animals just yet."

Dean paused as the kid that had been tasting Courtney's skirts ran over to start bouncing around at his feet. He leaned down to scoop the little thing up in his arms where it couldn't do any damage to his boots. "Best way to learn is to get in the saddle."

She tilted her head back to look up at him. "I thought you had a lot of work to do today."

He heard the hint of challenge in her voice and shrugged. "I guess I could use a break."

The look she gave him was oddly disconcerting. But then she smiled. A big, bright, and beautiful smile that went through him like a blast of sunshine. "Then I'd love to go for a ride."

"Great," he said with a nod as he set the squirming kid back on the ground. "I'll get some horses ready while you change."

"Change?"

He swept an appreciative glance over her sunny-yellow dress. "I don't have a side saddle, so you'll need to wear something that allows you to ride astride."

"Of course." She rose to her feet. "I believe a split skirt was included with my order from Mrs. Grainer. I'll only be a few moments."

She rushed off toward the house, and Dean took a few minutes to check over the pen, deciding that the work could wait one more day before he headed into the barn to ready their mounts. He knew just the one to saddle for Courtney—a sweet, old paint mare with an easy gait and a steady, patient temperament.

Just over thirty minutes later, they stood in the

cool shadows of the barn as Courtney eyed the mare
with a dubious expression. She had dressed in a white
cotton shirt and a simple brown riding skirt. "How
do I know she won't decide to take off running when
I'm not ready?"

"Gwen won't do anything you don't want her to,"
Dean assured her.

"Gwen?"

"Short for Guinevere."

Her eyebrows shot up at that. "As in King Arthur
and Lancelot and the Knights of the Round Table?"

He should have known the fanciful name he'd
come up with so long ago would spark her interest.

Dean tugged on the mare's chest strap, making
sure the saddle was secure, even though he'd already
checked it twice. "It was a story my mother read to
us. Before she left."

There was a moment of silence before Courtney
asked quietly, "Do you miss her?"

"Nope."

"That's rather sad."

He looked at her over the top of the saddle where
she stood beside the paddock. "No, it's not. She made
her choice. There's been plenty of time to move on.
Besides, Randall and I had Augie."

"Your grandfather?"

Dean nodded as he adjusted the buckle on a stirrup.
"He took us in hand, gave us a home and a livelihood.
He taught us right from wrong and made sure we had
passable table manners."

"He sounds like a good man."

Dean noticed something odd in her tone. He

scanned her expression, but as expected, it gave nothing away. "What about your family?" he asked. "Do you miss them?"

She seemed to think through her answer. "My father holds an important position with the city council and on several other boards and was rarely home. If I added up all the time I spent in his company over my entire life, it would probably fit inside a day or two." She sighed as she reached out a tentative hand to stroke her mare's forelock. "My mother, on the other hand, has forever been at my elbow, making sure I knew exactly how to comport myself as a member of the Adams family. We had to keep up appearances, and I am afraid I was a challenging child. She must have been exhausted by the time I was presented to society, but it was her duty to ensure I was a success."

"And were you? A success?"

She lifted one shoulder in a half shrug. "Of course."

The reply was entirely without conceit. It also lacked any personal joy in the accomplishment.

"What about brothers and sisters?" he asked.

Her smile returned with that question. "Oh yes, I have several of those. Three sisters and two brothers to be exact. Unfortunately, they did not start coming along until several years after I was born. It would have been nice to have playmates when I was young. It's a great deal more fun visiting with the children than spending any significant time with my parents."

Dean could easily picture her running around playing tag across a huge green lawn or just sitting on the floor, reading a book with small children sprawled around.

"You want children of your own." He said the words almost to himself, not intending to say them out loud. But she heard him.

Her eyes sparkled as she replied, "I always imagined having children. At least I did when I'd thought I would be marrying Geoffrey." She glanced down. "But things change, I guess. Maybe someday," she finished optimistically.

Choosing not to dwell on such thoughts, Dean rushed through the rest of his instructions before he offered his linked hands for a leg up. As soon as her rear landed in the saddle, he could see the day was going to be more challenging than he'd thought. Dean was a bit surprised to find that she didn't take to riding as quickly and easily as she'd taken to everything else that had come her way since arriving at the ranch.

Her posture was way too stiff and unyielding, her boots were positioned too far in the stirrups, her hands were too tight on the reins, and her gaze was too jumpy. The only things going for her were her enthusiasm and optimism.

It was a start at least.

They kept to a slow and even walk, keeping close to the river that wound away from the homestead. Dean offered tips and adjustments along the way. But the city girl beside him just couldn't seem to relax enough to properly feel the movement of the horse beneath her.

"You've gotta find a sense of harmony with your horse. Move together, not against each other. Relax."

"I'm sorry. I am trying," she replied with a tight little glance before she tensed and tugged on the reins inadvertently as she reached to grasp the saddle horn. The abrupt movement caused Gwen to raise her head in protest.

"Do something for me," Dean said as an idea came to mind.

"What?" she asked without looking away from where her gaze was trained hard on a spot between her mount's ears. The strain in her voice was obvious.

"Loop the reins over the saddle horn."

The glance she sent flying in his direction was one of shock. "But then how will I direct her?"

"You're not going to. Gwen will stay at my side with no urging from you."

"What if she takes off?"

"She won't," he replied. "Trust me."

After a moment, Courtney did as he said. As soon as she let go of the reins, she immediately wrapped her hands around the saddle horn.

"Now, I want you to close your eyes."

"Not a chance, cowboy," she retorted so quickly Dean almost let loose with a laugh.

"Courtney," he said in a smooth, coaxing but firm tone. "You need to trust me."

Her spine tensed and her jaw tightened, but after a moment, she did as he asked and closed her eyes.

A second later, they flew open again.

"Keep them shut."

She made a sound of frustration and annoyance, but closed her eyes again. This time they stayed closed.

"Okay," he said. "Now all you gotta do is feel the movement of the horse beneath you."

"I assure you I can feel the movement quite well."

Dean smiled at her sassy reply. "I want you try to feel it not as something to resist or counteract, but as an extension of yourself."

"How on earth do I do that?"

"You start by relaxing. Soften your spine, princess. Release the muscles in your thighs until your legs are gently hugging the horse. Until you can feel her breath expand and contract."

He waited, watching as she tried to follow his instruction. After a while, her hands didn't grip the saddle horn so tightly, and her arms started to sway a bit with the movement of the mare. The position of her legs started to look more natural. Unsurprisingly, her spine was the last to release, but eventually it did.

"Good," he murmured once he saw that she had finally let go of her physical resistance. "Now, I want you to try to anticipate her next step, feel how it shifts your weight. How does it change the pressure of your feet in the stirrups, the way your hips roll in the saddle? Notice how your shoulders move in a balanced counteraction."

It took some time, but after a while, he started to see progress.

She must have realized it too, because her eyes opened and she turned to him with a beatific smile. "I'm riding!"

Dean swallowed hard when the joyful light in her eyes hit him square in the gut. "Yep. But now it's time to head back."

Her expression turned down in disappointment. "So soon?"

"Your rear end won't thank me if I keep you in that saddle too much longer."

Her blush as he commented on that particular part of her anatomy was a pretty sight, stirring a reaction he'd been trying to resist. His next words came through a throat that had gone suddenly dry. "Pick up your reins, and we'll turn around."

The ride back was more relaxed in regard to the riding, but less so in other ways. Despite his worry and anxiety over putting Courtney in the saddle, Dean realized he'd enjoyed the time away from the house. And away from his office.

Back at the barn, he helped her to the ground, feeling more than a little regret that she didn't hold fast to him like she'd done the other time he'd gotten her off a horse. Still, her smile was worth all the lustful tension flowing through him.

"Can we ride again tomorrow?" she asked.

Dean thought of what needed to be done the next day. "I don't know if I'll have the time." Though she smiled her acceptance, Dean could sense the disappointment she carefully concealed. "I'll see if Randall can manage a few things for me, maybe free up some time."

"Really?" Her wide-eyed, hopeful surprise made him feel like he'd just offered to hang the moon for her. And damn him if he didn't like the way that felt.

"We'll see. Go on up to the house. I imagine you'll want a bath after riding."

"Shouldn't I help you with the horses? Grooming and such?"

Normally, Dean would insist on it. Anyone learning

to ride needed to know how to properly care for their mount. But just now, he needed some time alone to sort through the mess she was making of his insides.

"I'll see to them this time," he replied.

She nodded, though he could see she would have preferred to stay.

He went straight to work unsaddling Gwen, making sure he was too busy to watch his wife walk away.

TWENTY-SEVEN

***

COURTNEY WAS SITTING ON THE FRONT PORCH WHEN she saw the dust cloud coming down the road.

It was late afternoon, and she was alone. Jimena was home with Pilar, who was not feeling well. And Dean had ridden off shortly after breakfast that morning.

His avoidance was frustrating.

After the riding lesson the day before, he had spent the rest of the afternoon into the evening working. He had stopped only once to pop into the kitchen just before suppertime to advise that he wouldn't be eating until much later and ask if she could just leave a covered plate on the counter for him.

Courtney had offered to bring his meal out to his office, but he'd brushed it off, stating that he wasn't hungry and he'd just eat later.

Later turned out to be well after Courtney had given up on reading in the parlor and retired to her bedroom for the night. Almost an hour after she had turned her bedroom lamp down, she'd finally heard him coming in the house. He'd headed straight to his bedroom.

When she woke in the morning to discover he had already left the house, she was not surprised. She'd tried to keep herself occupied, but for every hour that passed without him making an appearance, Courtney found herself reaching an even more distracting state of frustration.

Or was it a more frustrating state of distraction?

Either way…she missed him. After less than a day. It was ridiculous.

So, when she'd first seen the dust cloud approaching down the drive, she had felt relief. At least now she had something to get her mind off her stubborn husband. But relief was soon followed by a slight sense of trepidation as she wondered who might be coming to visit and why.

The homestead had quieted down again with so many of the hands enjoying their days off in town. At that moment, she was the only person around to greet the visitors.

Despite the niggle of uncertainty in her chest, the duties of a proper hostess were too well ingrained in Courtney for her not to show proper grace in greeting guests. Even uninvited ones.

She rose to her feet and walked to the railing as she discerned three riders approaching on horseback. Within a few more minutes, the men—cowboys by the look of them—entered the yard. One was older, perhaps near sixty, with faded gray hair, a bushy beard, and a thick, stocky frame. The other two were younger. And while one of them resembled the older gentleman enough to be his son, with dark-brown hair rather than gray and a solid-muscled frame, the other did not.

In fact, the father and son both wore smiles as they drew their horses to a stop at the hitching rail beside the porch, but the last man hung back and remained seated on his horse, as though he didn't really want to be calling on the Lawton Ranch at all. With his worn leather gloves and suntanned skin, he was clearly a man who spent a great deal of time on the range, so when he settled his gaze on Courtney with a hard and silent stare, she decided to excuse his ill manners.

She stepped around to the porch steps and turned her smile to the friendlier-looking cowboys as they dismounted and approached on foot. "Good afternoon, gentlemen."

"Hello, ma'am," the older man replied as he swept his hat off in his hand and gave a deep bow of his head.

"Ma'am," repeated his son. The younger man couldn't have been much older than Courtney. His brown hair was worn long and fell just past his shoulders. His features were handsome, and his brown eyes appeared open and friendly.

The one on horseback remained silent and scowling several paces away.

"If you are seeking Mr. Lawton, I am afraid he is not currently available to visitors. Unless you are here on an urgent matter?"

A look passed between the two before the older one took an almost hesitant step forward. "Though we'd like to see Dean, I'm not so sure he's interested in accepting a visit from us. We actually rode over today to meet you, Mrs. Lawton."

Courtney did not show any of the surprise she felt. People talk. It should have been expected that the news would have gotten around to some curious neighbors.

"Allow us to introduce ourselves. I am Horatio MacDonnell. This is my son, Clinton, and that there is our foreman, Gilbert Hayes. My ranch neighbors the Lawton place to the west. I was good friends with Dean's grandfather."

Good Lord, this was Anne's family.

"Yes, of course," Courtney replied. "Please, won't you come have a seat? I can fetch some lemonade."

"No, ma'am," Horatio replied with a smile. "We just heard Dean had gotten himself a bride, and we wanted to come by to offer our congratulations."

"That is very kind of you," Courtney replied, her stomach tightening over what she had to say next. If anyone deserved to know the full truth of how she had come to marry Dean, she imagined it was this family. "I am afraid my marriage to Mr. Lawton occurred under some rather unusual circumstances," she began carefully.

"I'd say," Clinton replied with a short laugh.

Horatio gave his son a warning look. "We were mighty surprised by the news, but we did hear some of how the union came about. Not that it's any of our business as I see it. I came here today to welcome you, Mrs. Lawton, and to express my hope that you'll decide to settle in for a more permanent stay."

Courtney wasn't sure just how much of her situation the MacDonnells understood, and she had no idea what Dean would want them to know. She hesitated in replying, though something told her these men (perhaps with the exception of the foreman) were offering honest felicitations.

"I am not sure yet what my future will hold, Mr. MacDonnell, but I appreciate your sentiment."

The older man took a step forward as he said rather haltingly, "If I may ask, Mrs. Lawton…I have no desire to offend or cause any emotional discomfort, but has Dean talked to you about my daughter, Anne?"

Courtney empathized with the gentleman's obvious struggle in bringing up the sensitive subject. Whatever he wished to say was likely important. She tried to put him at ease. "He did tell me that he and Anne had intended to marry."

Mr. MacDonnell nodded sadly. "The thing is, I understand Dean somehow blames himself for what happened. I tried to tell him that was ridiculous, but he didn't want to hear anything from me. He's been avoiding our family for nearly three years now."

"Stubborn ass," Clinton interjected.

Courtney agreed.

"I'd like to see the boy move on. I'm old enough to know how important it is to continue toward the future even as we mourn the losses of our past. I'll admit I'm hoping you might be that future for Dean. Even though he's shut us out of his life, he's still part of our family. I'd like to see him happy."

The sincerity in the older man's eyes squeezed Courtney's heart. She wished Dean were there to accept his wishes himself.

Unfortunately, if Dean was ever to find happiness, it was not likely to be with her.

"I will pass on your words, but I'm afraid there is little chance of a future between Dean and myself."

"Then he's a damn idiot," Clinton asserted.

Courtney smiled at him. "And please, though I never met your daughter, I hope your family will accept my condolences. From what I've heard of her, she was a unique and wonderful young woman."

Clinton gave a snorting laugh. "Unique is right, ain't it, Pa," he said with a clap on his father's back.

"That she was," the older man agreed with a wide grin. "No one could tell that girl anything. She lived by her own rules from the day she was born up until the moment she left this earth."

The foreman's horse suddenly sidestepped with impatience or nerves. The restless movement drew the other men's attention and had them shifting their feet.

"Well, it's time we headed back. Mrs. Lawton, it was a pleasure to meet you."

"And you," she replied in earnest. "Thank you for the visit."

Clinton stepped forward and offered his hand. Courtney returned the gesture, and he pressed a quick kiss to her knuckles. "I'll say it again. Dean would be twenty times more a fool than he has been the last few years if he lets you get away."

"Clinton, leave the woman alone," his father said in exasperation as he headed toward his horse.

Such flattery was nothing particularly new to Courtney, but the younger Mr. MacDonnell had a certain earnest affect to his delivery that was often absent from the gentlemen back in Boston.

"Thank you," she replied with a smile before the young man turned and vaulted onto his horse's back. Just as they turned their mounts to head back down the drive, another rider could be heard approaching.

This one came from the direction of the range, riding hard across the earth.

Tension thickened amongst the visitors as they watched Dean ride in.

"What are you doing here?" Dean's harsh words drew her attention to him as he pulled his horse up beside the porch. He was tense and angry as he directed his rude question at the MacDonnells.

"Hello, Dean," the older MacDonnell said in an even tone. "We stopped by to introduce ourselves to your wife. We were just about to be on our way."

Dean did not reply. He just sat stiffly atop his horse, the reins pinched in tight hands as his horse danced around in agitation.

Horatio MacDonnell met his gaze for a few long moments. The tension between them was thick and uncomfortable. The old man stared long enough at Dean that Courtney thought he might say something more, but then his son leaned forward and muttered, "Let's go, Pa."

Dean's expression remained hard and closed off as he watched the three men turn and head off down the road until all that was left was another dust cloud like the one that had heralded their arrival.

"What'd they say to you?"

Dean's sharp question had Courtney looking to him in surprise. Though his features hadn't softened one bit, there was something in his voice—buried beneath the tension and the anger. It sounded suspiciously like…fear.

"Just as Mr. MacDonnell said," she replied. "They introduced themselves and welcomed me to the area."

"Why the hell would they do that?" he muttered under his breath.

Dean's irritated and incredulous response—added to his inexplicably rude greeting of his former fiancée's family and heaped on top of her own insecurities about the man—rubbed harshly on her raw nerves.

"Why indeed?" she retorted. "Heaven forbid someone might have some neighborly manners and a desire to wish me well."

He snorted at that. "I want you to steer clear of anyone from the MacDonnells' place."

"Like you have?"

He settled his light-blue eyes on her. "I've good reason. They might seem nice and welcoming, but they've never forgiven me for what happened to Anne."

Courtney shook her head. "No, Dean. It's you who won't forgive yourself."

His expression hardened. "I'll say it one last time. Stay away from the MacDonnells."

Courtney's throat burned with the desire to argue with him about who she could or couldn't make friends with, his assumed right to dictate anything about her personal activities, and how he decided to show up just to order her around without explanation.

But the cold, hard look in his eyes held her back.

That, and the growing sense that even though they had spent a breath-stealing night in each other's arms, nothing had really changed between them.

She gave a shallow nod. "Of course, Mr. Lawton. I wouldn't dream of interfering."

Then she turned and reentered the house.

TWENTY-EIGHT

COURTNEY HAD BEEN LOOKING FORWARD TO HER FIRST opportunity to cook a full meal on her own. Pilar was still not feeling well, so Jimena had asked Courtney if she could manage supper without her. Excited and terrified about being in charge of an entire evening meal, Courtney worked hard preparing the roasted chicken, fresh vegetables from Jimena's garden, seasoned potatoes, and a creamy vanilla dessert Jimena had taught her to make the week before.

It was to be just the two of them for supper that night, and she had imagined Dean's appreciation and surprise when she brought everything out all steaming and savory-smelling and declared that she had done it all by herself.

Instead, he barely seemed to notice the food as he ate. He rarely looked at her across the table and didn't speak beyond perfunctory responses.

By the end of the meal, her tension and disappointment got the better of her.

"Are you honestly going to be angry with me for accepting your neighbors' good wishes?"

Dean looked up from his plate, a forkful of food halfway to his mouth. His expression was slightly confused. "What? I'm not angry."

Courtney folded her arms across her chest and leaned back in her chair. "Then why the silence?"

He lifted his brows and glanced back down at his plate. "The food is good. I'm eating."

She frowned. "So you are not angry about earlier?"

"No. You couldn't have known how things are between me and the MacDonnells."

She decided to step into the opening he had created. "Why did their visit upset you so much?"

He set his fork aside and pushed back from the table to sit straight and stiff in his chair. It was clear he did not want to answer, but when he looked across the table at her with the heavy scowl, she stared back expectantly. Patiently determined.

Finally, he sighed. "The MacDonnells and I haven't exactly been neighborly these last few years."

"Since Anne's death?"

His jaw clenched and his eyes darkened, but he nodded.

Courtney chose her next words carefully. She wanted to understand but had no intention of hurting Dean more than he had been already. "They said you blame yourself for what happened."

He looked down at his plate before he replied. "I do."

"Why?" she asked softly.

He took a ragged breath, and Courtney tensed for his refusal to talk about such a personal topic. Her heart ached for the obvious distress the discussion caused, but she felt compelled to understand. From everything she'd heard, Dean had taken his fiancée's death very hard. She wanted to know how much of that was still with him.

"Anne had ridden over to talk to me that day," he said in a harsh undertone. "She'd sent a note the night before saying she had something important to talk about. But that morning, something urgent came up involving the ranch… I honestly don't remember what it was anymore, only that it required I head into town right away. I decided the ranch's needs were more important than whatever Anne needed to discuss. I didn't even think twice about it. I just left, knowing she'd be coming over. When she realized I wasn't here, she took off toward town, thinking to head me off, I suppose. Along the way, something spooked her horse and she was thrown. Her neck was broken in the fall."

"That's terrible," Courtney whispered.

"If I'd been here—where I was supposed to be, where I'd been just about every other day of my life— she wouldn't have headed down that road that day, her horse wouldn't have been spooked, she wouldn't have been thrown against that boulder, and she'd be here today."

As his wife.

He did not say the last words, but he didn't have to. Courtney heard them anyway, echoing like a boom of thunder through her mind.

She shoved aside her personal feelings and reordered her thoughts. "It was an accident, Dean. You can't blame yourself for something that couldn't possibly have been predicted or prevented. And from what the MacDonnells said, they do not blame you either."

"Well, there's saying something, then there's feeling it." He lifted his gaze, and Courtney nearly flinched at the pain reflected there. "Do as I say on this, if nothing else. Steer clear of the MacDonnells."

She decided not to press the issue. Not now anyway.

She gave a nod, and after a moment, he picked up his fork again and went back to the business of eating, as though now that the matter was settled, he only wished to move past it. But she couldn't keep from watching him, thinking about all that he'd revealed and everything he had kept to himself.

After a little while, she came to realize just how much he appeared to like her cooking. He was quite voracious, in fact. "You truly are enjoying your meal, aren't you?" she asked with a bit of hopeful incredulity.

He gestured with his fork toward his plate. "It's really good."

She was more pleased than she'd expected to be by the acknowledgment of her success, as small and simple as it was.

"Why?" he asked as he paused to wipe his mouth with his napkin. "Did you make all this yourself?"

Courtney nodded, trying not to give away just how much his appreciation mattered to her. He wouldn't understand how the simple act of creating a successful meal felt like such a long stride forward from the woman she'd been. It wasn't that she was ashamed of how she'd lived before coming to Montana. It was just that she was pleased beyond measure to discover that she might possess a few hidden talents after all.

"I'm impressed," he said in that smooth way of his that always seemed to have a ridiculous effect on her body temperature.

"Thank you," she replied.

Seeing her smile, Dean narrowed his eyes and dropped his gaze to her mouth. "I wish you wouldn't do that," he muttered, his tone shifting into one that was disgruntled and rough.

Her smile slipped, and a frown tugged at her brows. "Do what?"

"When I see your lips curving all sweet and pretty like that, I start thinking things I shouldn't."

Courtney went still as her belly twisted and her breath became shallow. "What things?" she whispered.

He didn't reply.

The answer was clear in his eyes. He was thinking of what they had done together in his bed two nights ago.

And then she was too.

Her lips parted to draw a long, unsteady breath.

With a loud clearing of his throat, he stood. "We'd better get this cleaned up."

Courtney watched as he gathered his dishes and headed into the kitchen without looking back at her. She took a moment longer to gather herself before she rose and did the same. After a few trips back and forth, they had the table cleared. Without speaking, they started washing the dishes and getting things put away.

As they moved around the kitchen, they occasionally had brief moments of contact: a slight brush of shoulders, a fleeting touch of the hand, a bit of eye contact as Courtney passed clean dishes to him for stacking in the cupboard.

No words were spoken, but anticipation rose within her all the same. Her breath grew short, her skin tingled, and her body felt overly warm.

After washing and drying the last serving bowl, she handed it to him to put away. He took it wordlessly and returned it to its spot on the top shelf.

When he turned back to her and saw that there were no more dishes, he stilled and his eyes found hers.

The kitchen suddenly seemed too expansive. He stood only a step or two away, but to Courtney it felt like an insurmountable distance.

She released her breath on a heavy sigh, and his eyes narrowed at the sound as he bowed his head. "I need to go—" he began, glancing toward the kitchen door.

"No, you don't," Courtney interrupted gently. "Whatever work you have will keep until tomorrow." At some point during the last two days, she'd decided being patient and coy was going to get her nowhere with this man. "I want you to stay with me tonight."

"Courtney…" There was a thread of warning in his voice.

She ignored it. "Dean." She said his name on a quiet breath as she looked square into his resistant face. "Do you regret the night we spent together?" she asked quietly.

He opened his eyes and met her questioning gaze with a direct stare. "No."

"Yet you've been avoiding me, haven't you?"

"I had to," he replied, his eyes darkening dangerously. His voice was rough—a low, gravelly sound—and his handsome face showed everything he tried to hold back. It was in the heavy pull of his brow, the firm line of his mouth, and the taut muscles of his jaw.

He was so tense that Courtney had to fight the urge to soothe away his distress even as her own intensified. His rejection hurt. Deeply. And though she was willing to be bold, she couldn't bring herself to beg.

She wanted him to *choose* her. Willfully, intentionally.

As she chose him.

Turning away, she carefully folded the dish towel and set it beside the sink. She took her time with the task, hoping and dreading that he would just walk away and leave her to her personal yearning.

She tensed when she sensed him moving behind her, but when she expected him to continue from the kitchen, he stopped. His boots disturbed the fall of her skirts, making them brush against the backs of her legs. Then his arm brushed hers as he braced his hand on the counter beside her.

Courtney held her breath. Licks of fire ignited throughout her body. Though she was slowly melting inside, she remained still as stone, afraid he might back away again.

His warm breath fanned her nape, sending delicious little chills down her spine. She rolled her lips in between her teeth to keep from making a needful sound at the subtle, delightful pleasure of it. Then his chest came slowly, torturously into contact with her back, and his other hand came to rest on the curve of her hip.

Bowing his head beside hers, he murmured thickly, "I had to avoid you. I couldn't be near you without wanting to take you to bed again."

A small sound slipped from Courtney's throat. He responded by sliding his hand from her hip to splay against her low belly, drawing her back against him until her buttocks pressed intimately to his hardness. It was strange being able to feel him but not see him. Strange, and wonderfully wicked.

"I wanted to give you time. Time to decide if you want this," he explained, his words roughening with each syllable until his voice became a dark caress.

Courtney's fingers curled tightly into the dish towel, ruining the neat folds. She arched her spine, trying to press herself closer to him. "I want this," she muttered thickly.

He pressed his mouth to the side of her throat, touching her skin just briefly with his tongue. Her head fell back against his shoulder and her knees weakened, but she did not fear falling. He held her secure in his arms, his large body framing hers, supporting her as her muscles turned soft.

"You sure?" he asked. His voice was little more than a growl now.

Heat swirled around her frustration, transforming it into something far more intense and harder to control. "What do I have to say to get you to make love to me again?" she asked in a harsh whisper.

"That'll do it," he said as he turned her around with a swift motion to face him. Wrapping both arms around her waist, he hauled her against him and took her mouth.

She clung to him, pressing her body to his so she could feel all the barely controlled power in his frame. His lips moved intently over hers until she opened to the sweep of his tongue. When his mouth moved to the side of her throat, she held fast to his shoulders and dropped her head back.

"I've been going crazy thinking of the other night," he murmured against her flushed skin. "Thinking of all the things I didn't get to do to you. All the places on your body I didn't get to taste."

He had been thinking of her. Of this.

Pulling back, he took her face between his hands. Her eyelids fluttered open to see his handsome face. His eyes were intently focused on her. "Will you come upstairs with me? Now?"

"Yes." Her acquiescence came out on a long sigh.

Stepping back, he took her hand in his. With a gentle tug, he led her from the kitchen, down the hall, and up the stairs. Courtney followed, concentrating on each step to make sure her wobbly legs did not give out along the way.

He wasn't a soft man or a gentle man. And his moods were occasionally dark and often confusing, but there was something...something tender and sweet buried behind his hard outer shell. In allowing herself to get close to Dean and letting her heart lead her head, she risked a great deal. But weren't some experiences worth it, even when the outcome was completely uncertain?

She'd left Boston to push her herself to new limits and explore an unknown future.

For the time being, she was the bride of a man who wanted her. A man *she* wanted with every breath and beat of her heart. She could not truly be brave in this new life if she was not willing to take what she wanted despite what might come.

In a couple weeks, she and Dean were expected to part ways. But right now—for better or for worse—they were husband and wife.

When they entered his bedroom, he released her hand to close the door behind them before he lit the lamp on the bedside table.

The last time they had been in this room together, it had been in near darkness with the faint reach of moonlight from outside the only illumination.

Now, the room was cast in a golden glow as Dean turned to face her.

He was so handsome in the soft light.

Outside, under the stark sunlight, surrounded by rough lands and a homestead he loved, his strength of will and masculine appeal were fiercely apparent. The raw nature of his being was unapologetic in such a setting. He was larger than life, an immovable force.

But here, standing in his bedroom in the soft glow of the glass lamp, he was just a man. A man of inner strength and quiet desires, with a shadow of longing in his eyes as he stared at her from across the room.

"I should feel ashamed for wanting you so bad." His voice was hoarse and low as he spoke.

"Wanting me is shameful?" she asked.

"That's not what I meant," he replied in exasperation. "I don't have a way with words like some men." He took a ragged breath. "You asked if I regret what happened between us and the truth is…I don't regret a damn thing. I tried, but I can't. I just keep reliving every moment over and over. I can still feel the pulses in your body as you came apart in my arms. I've wanted you again every second since."

Courtney shivered, feeling a precursor to that pulse deep inside. It seemed to her that he had a rather powerful way with words. And those words were having a very specific effect on her body. But he wasn't finished.

"I tried to convince myself to stay away—"

"Please don't," she interrupted.

He fell silent, his expression closed. Then he replied in a soft, strong voice, "I won't."

His stride was slow but purposeful as he came toward her. Confident and wanting.

Stopping just within reach, he held her gaze as he lifted his hands to release the buttons running down the front of her dress. Though anticipation and desire swirled thick in the room, he displayed no impatience as he removed her dress and draped it over a nearby chair.

Then he took her hand and drew her forward to sit on the bed as he crouched in front of her, his denim-clad legs spread to each side of hers.

Courtney got just a glimpse of his face before he bowed his head to focus on untying her serviceable leather ankle boots. What she saw in his tense and angled features matched everything she was feeling. Anticipation. Yearning. And something deeper. An awareness. An acknowledgment of everything they were choosing in that moment.

After loosening her boots, he slipped them from her feet before he tugged off her stockings one at a time. Then he reached for the ends of the ribbon that cinched the bodice of her undergarment snug above her breasts. Holding her expectant gaze, he pulled on the ribbon until the garment gaped. From there, it took very little effort to slip the straps off her shoulders and down her arms, baring her breasts.

Dean stared at her for a few long moments, crouching before her, his hands braced on the mattress, bracketing her hips. His gaze was hungry. Everywhere he looked, her skin burned, and every second that passed made her more breathless as Courtney waited anxiously, desperately, for what he would do next.

She did not have to wait long.

Taking her hips in his broad hands, he urged her to stand in front of him. As she did so, the undergarment slipped to the floor, leaving Courtney standing naked before Dean's crouched form.

A low humming sound slipped from the back of his throat. The warmth of his breath fanned across her bared belly, and she trembled. Everything inside her caught and held.

With his shoulders strong and broad in front of her, he tipped his head back to meet her gaze. The soft glow of the lamp cast interesting shadows over his features, accenting the loneliness she'd only gotten glimpses of before. Needing to touch him, she brushed his hair off his forehead in a tender caress before sliding her fingers back through his hair.

His tongue darted out to wet his bottom lip.

Courtney's thighs tensed, and her hand stilled on the back of his head.

His next words came out in a husky whisper, "I wanna taste you. Say you'll let me."

Courtney nodded, expecting him to rise to his feet and take her in his arms for one of his soul-searing kisses.

But that is not what he did.

Not even close.

Still holding her gaze, his eyes ablaze, he leaned forward.

Completely stunned, Courtney watched as he pressed his nose to her soft curls and took a slow breath. Then she felt the glide of his tongue against the heated flesh between her thighs. The erotic caress shocked her with its wet, velvet heat.

She never could have imagined such a decadent act, let alone how it made her feel.

When his tongue extended for another languid stroke, her knees threatened to buckle, but he firmly gripped the back of her thighs, just below her buttocks, as he murmured heated words against her core. "Open for me."

She clumsily stepped her feet apart, and he muttered a word of appreciation she couldn't quite make out above the thundering pulse in her ears. As his mouth closed with sinful intent over the firm bud at the apex of her sex, she grasped his head and shamelessly held him to her.

The sound he made, somewhere between a hum and a moan, vibrated through her, making her gasp. He alternated between long strokes of his tongue against her folds, little flicks that teased her heightened nerves, and openmouthed sucking kisses that tightened every muscle in her body as he drew her into a pool of deep, swirling pleasure.

She felt worshiped by his mouth. Everything he did incited new and wonderful sensations. But it became too much. Her legs shook beneath her, and she murmured a soft plea.

He gave a few final devastating strokes of his tongue before rising to his feet. Standing at full height, he wrapped his arms around her naked body and hauled her in close against him as he put his mouth on hers.

The kiss was deep and musky with the taste of her body.

Courtney moaned before opening her lips to the hungry sweep of his tongue and wrapping her arms around his neck.

Her body, flushed and weak, felt every shifting texture of his clothing over the hard, male body beneath. She wanted him to be as naked as she was. She wanted to feel the smooth heat of his skin. Before she could pull away to tell him so, he tightened his arms around her. Without removing his mouth from hers, he lifted her off the floor and propelled them both back onto the bed.

TWENTY-NINE

NEED PULSED HOT AND DEMANDING THROUGH DEAN'S veins and echoed in his ears. He'd never known hunger like this before. He wanted to taste every inch of the woman beneath him, lick and bite her flesh, catch every sound she made in his mouth as he thrust into her body.

Instead, he drew back to look down at her flushed face.

Her hair had tumbled from the neat bun she had been wearing it in lately and spread in a tangled mess under her head. Her eyes were closed, and her thick lashes rested in half-moons against her skin, which had taken on a golden hue during her time on the ranch. He noted the freckles across her nose and the crest of her cheeks.

And her lips...

Desire flowed hot and unchecked through his blood.

Her lashes fluttered as she opened her eyes. Her gaze—deep and turbulent with longing—hit him hard in the gut.

Then she smiled.

And he just about lost it.

With a raw sound in the back of his throat, he lowered his head to brush his lips back and forth over hers. He wanted to learn the shape and texture of them, memorize those perfect lips so he could recall the feel of them after she was gone. He touched the curling corners with his tongue, tested the plush firmness of her bottom lip with the edge of his teeth, drew upon her sweet, breathy sighs.

It wasn't enough.

For her either.

Her hands tugged at his shoulders, fisting in his shirt as her hips rolled in a beckoning plea.

He knew he wouldn't last long once his bare skin touched her silken body. Her heat already burned through his clothes. Her need called to him.

He would have preferred to take things more slowly, but she started to release the buttons of his shirt herself as her mouth slid from his to press against the side of his throat. She sucked briefly on his skin before soothing it with her tongue.

Damn. She did things to him.

Pushing to his feet in a rush, he stood at the edge of the bed and swiftly removed his clothes.

Her lips were gently parted, and her eyes were bright with desire. She openly watched his every movement, and her skin grew more flushed with every item of clothing he discarded. When he returned to her, she took his face in her hands and drew his mouth down to hers before he had even lowered his body.

Why had he ever felt the need to resist her and this fire that burned so hot between them?

Because it won't last. Because she'll leave.

The thought was always there. Even when his head spun with scent of her skin, the sound, the heat, the demand of her desire. He tried not to think beyond the present moment, but deep down—especially when he was this close to her—he was far too aware of all the reasons their union was destined to be temporary.

Despite her occasional sass and strong opinions, she was a lady through and through. She wasn't a rancher's wife any more than his mother had been.

Even if he wanted her to stay, she wouldn't. Not for long anyway. Maybe just enough to make him miss her when she left.

A painful tightening squeezed his chest. To think of anything but her leaving was dangerous and stupid. It was far better not to think at all. So he kissed her. Deep and hard and long.

He covered her with his weight, pressing her into the mattress.

He slid his hands over her body, feeling every dip and curve, the soft fullness of her buttocks, the length of her legs, the smooth surface of her belly, and the gentle mounds of her breasts. He tasted her with kisses that roamed aimlessly over her skin and licks of his tongue that incited heavy moans and deep arches of her spine.

If all he had with her was a short time, he vowed to make the most of it by learning every bit of what pleased her. He'd just underestimated how much her pleasure would ignite his own.

When she finally gasped her plea—"Now, Dean…I

need you"—he was shaking in his efforts to keep from losing control.

Pushing back to kneel between her spread legs, he rested his hands on the tops of his thighs and allowed himself to appreciate the stunning picture she made. Her long legs were parted around his. Her arms were bent, and her hands rested on either side of her head, slender fingers curling gently toward her palms while her pert and lovely breasts rose and fell with her labored breath.

Unable to keep from touching her for long, he reached out to smooth his hands up the length of her thighs. When he circled his thumbs over the pale skin near her sex, she caught and held her breath. With the pad of one thumb, he explored the slick heat of her core in a gliding caress.

Her head tipped back, and her hands came down to grasp the bedsheets beneath her.

The heat of her body beckoned him, and he slid his thumb along her entrance again, pressing more firmly against her, coating his finger with her wetness. Then he circled the swollen bud nestled in her soft curls. And circled again. Locking his gaze on her face, he shifted his hand to gently pinch the taut nub between two fingers. In short motions, he massaged the sensitive flesh, alternating with slow thrusts of his fingers into her body.

As her breath quickened, so did his. As her neck strained and her head pressed back into the pillow, his chest tightened and his stomach trembled. And between his legs, his cock pulsed hard and full.

"Dean."

His name, gasped in a broken whisper of sexual need, pushed him to his limit. He grasped her hips in his hands and pulled her toward him until her buttocks rested atop his thighs and his erection was poised at her entrance.

With her eyes glistening and her lips parted, she watched and waited.

He liked seeing her like that, intent upon his next move, suspended in anticipation.

At the first gentle press of his body into hers, she moaned. Her eyes closed as she pressed her feet to the mattress, assisting in keeping her hips aligned with his. Lengthening her spine, she reached over her head to grab hold of the iron railings of his bed frame.

Dean stopped breathing.

His hands tightened on her hips. His body strained. Blood thundered through his veins, and something broke within him.

Holding her firmly in his hands, he plunged forward in a reckless act of possession. A small voice in his head warned that it was too much, too fast.

But the sound of deep pleasure that slid from her throat erased that thought.

She arched and tried to roll her hips, but he held her fast, setting his own pace. Long, hard strokes. Deep, penetrating thrusts.

It was not long before he felt her approaching the peak. She fluttered and clenched around him. Her breath caught in her throat. Then she opened her eyes and trapped him in the deep, swirling depths of her green gaze.

It was like a horse kick to the chest. With her body

pulsing around him, he became lost in her release. So lost that he barely noticed his own. They seemed as one. One moment. One climax. One deep, consuming fusion.

As the pleasure faded away, Dean was left shaken.

He slid from Courtney's warmth, lowering her hips to the mattress as he sat back on his heels, totally spent.

She gave a languorous stretch of her long, pale limbs, thrusting her breasts upward as she arched her spine.

Dean watched in renewed fascination, wondering how he could still feel the sharp spears of desire shooting through him while feeling completely sated and wrung dry. It was the nature of her sensuality, so expressive and honest.

It did him in.

It totally wrecked him.

He moved to the edge of the bed and strode to the washbasin. As he poured tepid water from a pitcher into the bowl and then soaked a cotton cloth, he froze with a disturbing realization.

Twice now, he had taken Courtney to his bed and released his seed inside her without any attempt to prevent pregnancy.

It would be the height of irresponsibility to bring a child into the mess of a situation he'd created. Their marriage wasn't real...or at least, it was only temporary.

What would Courtney do if a child came into the picture?

She'd expressed more than once that she wanted to

live independently. She wanted a new adventure, and she intended to seek it out.

Old wounds were tugged open as he recalled the day his mother left. Though Randall had been too young to know what was going on, Dean had been a mature seven-year-old. He had understood the choice his mother was making. He did not want to see Courtney facing a similar decision. He couldn't stand for another child to watch his mother walk away.

He didn't think he'd survive it.

"Dean?" Her soft, questioning voice came from the bed behind him, and Dean realized just how tense he'd become.

He had to force his fist to loosen around the cloth. Having squeezed all the water from it, he dunked it back into the bowl, wringing away the excess before turning back to face her.

Her expression was curious at first, but when she caught sight of his face, her fine-arched brows dipped in wary concern.

"What's wrong?" she asked.

"Nothing." He approached and extended the cloth to her. "You might wanna clean up a bit."

She held his gaze, but as soon as she took the cloth from his hand, he turned away.

He washed at the basin, keeping his back to the bed. He didn't dare watch as she passed the swath of cotton between her legs. Just the thought of it threatened to make him hard again, despite the emotion churning inside him.

"Do you know much about timing?" he asked without turning around.

There was a pause before she replied, "Timing? For what?"

He could hear her moving on the bed, her skin sliding against the sheets. He clenched his fists and locked himself into his current position to keep from turning around. "For a baby."

Everything stilled behind him. It got so quiet he swore he could hear her heart beating across the room. Slowly, he turned around.

She was standing on the opposite side of the bed—still naked, her red hair falling to her hips in a twisting, curling mass and her eyes round. "What?" she asked in a choked little voice.

"Pregnancy," he repeated, then gave a swift glance toward the bed. "We didn't take any precautions."

She'd followed his gaze to the rumpled sheets. Her attention remained pinned on the evidence of their recent activity. "Oh. I…ah…no, I don't, actually. My mother only covered the basics before my wedding day. She wasn't one to expound on such delicate topics."

Dean lowered his chin toward his chest. Everything inside him felt tight—his lungs, his stomach, every strand of muscle that wrapped around his bones. When he lifted his gaze again, it was to find that Courtney had replaced her shocked expression with one he was really starting to dislike. Her features were trained into a perfectly placid mask, revealing no emotion and certainly none of her thoughts.

She was thinking something, or she wouldn't have gone to the trouble of hiding it from him.

"Let's hope nothing comes of it," he said, his voice low. "But if it does, you'll need to tell me."

After a moment, she nodded. Then she turned in place and looked around on the floor, obviously searching for something.

When he saw the scrap of thin white cotton peeking out from under the edge of the bed, he stepped forward and swept it up. "Looking for this?"

She stopped and looked up. Seeing her undergarment in his hand, she squared her shoulders and started around the bed toward him.

Something in her proud, restrained bearing ignited his admiration. Though they were both naked as the day they were born and her hair was a wild mess, she still looked like a damned princess in that moment.

When she reached out for the undergarment, instead of handing it to her, he grasped her wrist and gave a tug, making her stumble forward into his arms. Her eyes narrowed at the tricky move, but she didn't pull away when he slid one arm around her to press his open hand to the low curve of her back. Her body was warm and damp with sweat, and her heart beat in a frantic rhythm against his chest.

"I pissed you off again," he said gruffly. His eyes fell to her mouth, which was pressed firmly closed. "You've probably figured this out, but I'm not good at talking to people, especially about anything important. I should have thought of the possibility of a baby, but I didn't. If something comes of it…" He paused. His teeth clenched as he fought back the image that rose in his mind of his child in her arms. "We'll figure it out. But we're gonna have to be more careful going forward."

One elegant russet eyebrow arched. "Going forward?"

The corner of his mouth tilted upward. "Aren't you the one who told me not to stay away?"

She gave a little nod. "I do recall something like that."

He lowered his head until his lips hovered just above hers. "If you wanna take it back, tell me now."

"I have no regrets, Dean," she murmured, the words barely audible as she slid her arms around his waist.

"Good," he replied before he lowered his mouth to hers.

No regrets. No staying away.

It had been stupid to try.

For better or for worse—for now, anyway—they were in this together.

And when it came time for her to leave, Dean would just have to find a way to deal with it.

THIRTY

Courtney opened her eyes slowly, fearing that the lovely dream she had been floating along in was about to be chased away by reality. But the dream *was* reality.

Dean lay beside her, sprawled on his back with one arm curled around her as she rested her head on his shoulder. She had one leg draped over his, and her hair had gotten twisted around his arm. His heartbeat was slow and steady beneath her hand, and the masculine scent of his skin was present in every breath she drew.

The sun was rising beyond the window in shades of orange and red, but she wasn't ready to leave the night behind and greet the day. The night had been too lovely…too wonderful and free and beautiful. If she had her way, they would remain there together indefinitely.

With a quiet sigh, she slowly rose to her elbow to tug her hair free, intending to scoot to the edge of the bed. But she didn't make it very far. Dean's arm tightened around her, and a low, rumbling sound of protest issued from his throat.

"Where're you going?" he asked, his voice sleepy

and rough. The sound of it traveled through her like a spark, reigniting the flames she thought had burned out the night before.

"It's morning," she murmured in reply. "We should be getting up."

He made another rumbling sound as he brought his other hand to her thigh, where it rested across his. The rough surface of his palm skimmed over her soft skin. "I say we stay right here."

Courtney's quiet laugh turned to a sigh as his hand came up to grasp the curve of her hip in a firm grip. "Don't you have work you need to get to?" she asked, feeling obligated to point out their responsibilities despite her desire to remain in his arms.

"I'd rather stay right here."

"All day?" She was unable to hide her surprise and delight at the thought.

His eyes opened a crack, and her breath halted at the light of his blue gaze peeking from between the fringe of his lashes. Despite his sleepy state, his eyes were bright and striking and so beautifully intense.

Rather than answering with words, he swept his hand up along her side, allowing his thumbs to brush purposely over the curve of her breast before he slid his hand beneath the fall of her hair to cup the back of her neck. With gentle but insistent strength, he drew her down. Her hair fell across his chest, and her breasts pressed firmly to his side as he brought her mouth to his.

His tongue swept across the seam of her lips. She opened on a sigh, and he took her breathy offering with a plunging, velvety stroke that elicited a husky moan.

Dean rolled over, pressing her into the mattress as he settled between her legs. She held her breath, anticipating his possession.

Lowering his head, he placed a soft and gentle kiss on her lips. For a silent moment, they looked into each other's eyes. Communicating without words. Then Courtney swept her hands down his back to grasp his firm buttocks, and he entered her in one sure, swift motion.

∞

Some time later, they eventually made their way downstairs, where they enjoyed some food that Jimena had made and left for them.

Courtney blushed at the thought that the older woman had been down in the kitchen while she and Dean had been enjoying their not-so-lazy morning abed. But the embarrassment didn't last beyond Dean asking if she wanted to take a bath with him.

Though they certainly got clean with all the soapy lather being smoothed across heated skin and the lovely, relaxing scalp massage Dean had given her as he'd worked the suds through her hair, the experience was unlike any bath Courtney had ever imagined and infinitely more pleasurable. She very nearly fell asleep nestled between Dean's legs, leaning back against the solid expanse of his chest.

But he wasn't in the mood to waste a single moment of the day.

As soon as they dried off, he suggested a ride.

It was sunny and warm with a bit of a breeze to

keep them cool, and they spent the next few hours riding through the beautiful Montana plains. Dean pointed out some of his favorite hideouts when he had been a kid: the swimming hole where he and Randall would meet Anne and her brother, Clinton, on the hottest days of summer, the makeshift racetrack where they'd competed to see who was the fastest rider, the cluster of boulders they'd used to practice roping.

Courtney loved it.

Not only because she could see by the warm curve of his mouth and the gentle slope of his brow just how much Dean was enjoying himself, but also because it was all so new to her. The sheer expanse of wilderness surrounding them astonished her. She had no idea a person could see so far without buildings to block the view. The sky was an infinite canopy of azure. The breeze smelled of sunshine, wildflowers, and sweetgrass.

It made her want to let down her hair and roll up her sleeves to feel the warmth of the sun on her skin.

So that is what she did.

Drawing her mare to a gentle stop, she looped the reins over the saddle horn and released the end of her braid.

Dean pulled up and twisted around in his saddle to watch her as she combed her fingers through her hair and then flipped the cuffs of her blouse back until her arms were exposed. She didn't notice the odd look on his face until she'd had finished and was able to nudge her horse forward again.

As her eyes met Dean's and she saw the quiet, simmering hunger in his gaze, the muscles of her thighs tensed. Her mare shuffle-stepped in confusion, and Courtney quickly grabbed hold of the saddle horn to steady herself, laughing gently at her momentary feeling of panic.

When she looked at Dean again, it was to find that the hunger had been replaced by a quiet, shadowed look of concern.

But then he turned around and urged his horse forward, continuing their ride.

⚮

"Dean? Dean, where the hell are you?"

Courtney stirred from a delicious slumber to the sound of Randall's shouts followed by a slamming of the front door.

She pushed her hair out of her eyes and sat up to see Dean already sitting on the edge of the bed. She glanced out the window and noted that the sky was already alight with the rising sun.

In the last few days, she and Dean had been indulging in more leisurely mornings. Though he hadn't taken a full day off from his duties as boss of the ranch, he had been making an effort to stick around for breakfast and had even managed to take her riding each afternoon. And their nights...their nights had been filled with the pleasure of each other.

"What is going on?" she asked, still half-asleep and confused by the shouting.

"I don't know," Dean mumbled as he rubbed his hands over his face.

"Dean! Get your ass out of bed," his brother called

up the stairs. "It happened again. Not long ago, and there are tracks."

"I'm coming!" Randall's last words had Dean jumping from the bed and scrambling to get dressed.

Courtney scooted to the edge of the bed to reach for her own clothes. "Do you know what he's talking about?"

"Nothing for you to worry about."

Courtney bit her tongue against further questions but kept dressing anyway. By the time Dean was thundering down the stairs, she was right behind him, still plaiting her hair into a braid down her back.

Randall was pacing in the entryway, and though his blue eyes flickered over the sight of the two of them descending the stairs together, both clearly having just risen from bed, he quickly turned his attention to Dean and gave his brother a hard-eyed stare that seemed to say far more than his next words revealed.

"The bastard got to the horses this time. Two in the pasture, along with several more cattle. Right by the damn homestead."

Courtney stood just beyond Dean's shoulder. She couldn't see his face, but she could see the way every muscle in his body drew taut with barely suppressed violence.

"There're tracks?"

"Yep, but a storm is coming, so they won't hold for long."

"Let's go."

Dean swept past his brother and out the door. Randall followed quickly on his heels.

Courtney rushed after both of them, only to stop

halfway through the door as Dean suddenly turned back around. His expression worried her. There was so much anger in his drawn features, but she also saw a weary kind of fear and sadness.

She stepped forward, not really thinking, just feeling a need to touch him, but his scowl darkened, stopping her approach. "You're going to Randall's for the day." He glanced at his brother. "I assume you told the women to stay inside."

"Damn right I did," Randall replied. "With a shotgun and instructions to shoot if anyone comes near."

Dean nodded, then looked back to Courtney. "You'll ride with us to Randall's and stay there until we return. Understand?"

Courtney nodded and held her tongue against the many questions spinning in her mind. Now was clearly not the time to press for information.

Less than thirty minutes later, thunder rolled fiercely in the distance as Courtney stood in Pilar's doorway, watching Dean and Randall ride off at a breakneck gallop. Once the men were out of sight, Pilar urged her to come inside before bolting the door behind her.

Jimena gave her a tight smile from the kitchen, where she was stirring something in a large pot on the stove.

"Come," Pilar said, "let's sit at the table. Have you eaten?"

Courtney shook her head. "No. We were still asleep when Randall came by. What is going on?"

"First we eat, then we'll talk. We will feel better once our bellies are full."

Courtney smiled at her friend. "You sound like your mother."

Pilar chuckled as she carefully lowered herself into a wooden chair at the kitchen table. Though Courtney knew it was still a couple weeks before Pilar expected to go into labor, the woman looked dreadfully uncomfortable. It amazed Courtney that she had never once heard the mother-to-be complain about the many physical tasks she still managed to accomplish every day. Back home, an expectant mother would have gone into confinement months ago, remaining in her bed to be kept comfortable until the baby arrived.

"Do you know what this is all about?" Courtney asked as they settled at the table, unable to wait for her questions to be answered.

A swift but telling glance passed between Jimena and Pilar before the younger woman spoke. "For some time now, someone has been attacking Lawton cattle. It started with just one animal found dead. Many months passed before the second attack." Pilar paused and pressed her hand against the side of her belly as she bowed her head for a moment. After a long breath, she continued, "There have been more than a half dozen incidents now, counting the one from last night. Each coming more swiftly upon the last."

An icy chill swept through Courtney. "That is terrifying. Do they know who is responsible?"

Pilar nodded and looked down at her hands where they rested on the scarred wooden tabletop. "They suspect the attacker is from the MacDonnells' ranch."

"What?" Courtney was stunned. The MacDonnells

had been so nice and welcoming to her the other day. She could not contemplate the idea that they might perpetrate violence upon the Lawtons' stock. Though the suspicion that they were involved certainly explained Dean's reaction to their visit. "Why would they do such a thing?"

Pilar turned her hands palm up and gave a shrug. Her eyes were sad as they met Courtney's.

And she knew.

It was connected to Anne's death.

Dean believed he was to blame for not being there to prevent the accident that took her life. Was he right in believing the MacDonnells blamed him as well?

The day they'd come to visit, they had claimed to hold no ill will. In fact, they had wished Dean well. Courtney had only seen sincerity and earnest sadness from both of the MacDonnells.

Not so for their foreman, however.

She recalled the man's cold silence as he hung back from the others during their visit. Could he be the culprit?

If the tracks left behind from this last attack led to the MacDonnells' place, Courtney could only hope Anne's family wasn't involved.

Glancing to the window, she noted how dark the sky was getting, though the day was just beginning. Thunder boomed loud and heavy in the distance.

The approaching storm was going to be wicked.

Jimena came to the table with two bowls of steaming, rich-smelling stew.

Pilar made a little sound in her throat and turned her head away. Jimena clucked her tongue and looked hard at her daughter. Concern drew heavy lines in the older woman's face as she ran her hand down Pilar's weary spine.

"How long?" she asked.

Pilar gave a short shake of her head.

Jimena pressed her hand to the flushed curve of her daughter's cheek, urging Pilar to look at her. The look that passed between the women was poignant and beautiful.

"It started before dawn. I didn't tell Randall because I wasn't sure what I was feeling. But there is no denying it now."

Jimena clucked her tongue again. "Eat, Daughter. You will need the strength. I pray for your husband's swift return and the safe arrival of your child."

Courtney clasped her hands and added her own silent plea to Jimena's prayer.

The rest of that day passed in a strange alteration of time. Moments seemed to last forever, while hours passed in a blink.

Though Pilar had been laboring already for several hours, the progress was slow and continued to be for several more. It was amazing to watch as Pilar's body and mind slowly accepted the increasing intensity of her pains. She walked when it felt good to do so, she sat in the rocking chair when she needed rest, she breathed deeply when she could and squeezed Courtney's hand in a death grip when she couldn't.

Jimena was all over the place—gathering bed linens and encouraging Pilar to drink water and keep eating in small bites when she wasn't feeling nauseated.

Courtney felt helpless and terribly ignorant. All she

could do was stay by her friend's side and complete any task Jimena gave her.

Throughout much of the day, wind whipped around the little house while thunder crashed loudly overhead and lightning split the sky with striking force. But the ferocity of the storm was barely acknowledged.

An even greater drama of life was unfolding within the walls of the small home.

THIRTY-ONE

"WE'VE GOTTA HOLE UP UNTIL THIS STORM PASSES," Randall shouted across the swirling wind. "The tracks will be washed away as soon as the rain hits, but we won't make it much longer without shelter."

He was right, but Dean resisted. So far, the tracks hadn't been leading toward the MacDonnells' ranch as they'd both expected. Instead, they'd headed out toward the open range. It was frustrating beyond measure. Dean just wanted to see this matter finished once and for all. No more death. No more violence.

"Come on, Dean. We'll ride over to the MacDonnells' place after the storm passes."

Dean had wanted the proof the tracks would have given him. But Randall was right. It was time to face Anne's family and hash out their grievance with him. And maybe come to terms with his grievance with himself.

Not to mention the fact that this last attack had been far too close to home. The killing of a man's horses was a serious offense. If he didn't put a stop to this now, there was no telling where the next attack would hit. And on whom.

He thought of Courtney as she had been that morning in his bed. All soft and warm and pliant in his arms.

Then he thought of Jimena and Pilar and the babe on the way.

His family had been threatened. The attacks were escalating.

But Randall was right. They weren't going to get anywhere once the full force of the storm hit. Finding shelter on the open range was not an easy task, but they made it to a group of large boulders where the cowboys would sometimes make camp. At least it provided a wall against the incoming elements and space where they could secure the horses. All they could do then was huddle in and wait out the storm.

It was another couple hours before he and Randall got back on their horses, and Dean's patience had worn down to nothing. They rode to the neighboring homestead in determined silence. By the time they thundered into the MacDonnells' yard, the late-afternoon sun was starting to peek through the parting clouds.

Horatio MacDonnell stepped out onto his front porch just as Dean and Randall drew in their horses.

Dean studied the older man's expression. He wasn't sure what he expected to see, but it certainly wasn't the calm curiosity and almost hopeful wariness he saw in the familiar brown eyes.

"Boys," Horatio said with a nod of greeting, "to what do I owe the pleasure of this visit? Though by the looks on your faces, I'm thinking this won't be pleasurable at all."

"We've had enough, MacDonnell," Randall blurted angrily.

Horatio's brows lifted. "Enough of what?"

"The attacks have gone too far. I don't know how you can feel justified in continuing the senseless killing, but no more."

As Randall went off in his usual, reckless manner, Dean watched the other man's reaction. There was genuine confusion, concern…and a total lack of guilt.

"What the hell is he talking about, Pa?" Clinton had come out to join his father on the porch.

A few years younger than Anne, Clinton had grown into a man in the time since Dean had last stood face-to-face with him.

"I'm not sure, Son."

"Don't give us that," Randall shouted. "It had to be you. All the incidents were near the border between our land and yours, and they didn't start until after…"

He didn't continue, glancing toward Dean.

Dean knew his brother expected him to support his accusations, but something didn't feel right.

From the very first slaughtered cow they'd found the day of Anne's funeral, he'd suspected the MacDonnells. It was the only thing that had seemed to make sense. The acts had clearly been perpetrated for no other reason than as a display of violence. No meat was ever taken; the cows were simply left to rot until they were found. The only thing that had come to mind was that Anne's family was striking out in their grief and anger.

Now, Dean wasn't so sure.

"Why don't you explain to us what happened," Horatio suggested, his tone even and sincere.

Dean finally spoke. "For the last three years, we've been experiencing attacks on our cattle. It started small, but each attack that followed has gotten worse. Last night, two horses in our western pasture were killed."

"And you thought we've been doing this?" Clinton's incredulous tone shifted quickly into anger. "Why the hell would we kill your livestock?"

Horatio bowed his head as he slowly shook it from side to side. "They thought we were getting revenge."

"For what?" Clinton shouted before his expression shifted abruptly to one of understanding. "Holy shit. Because of Anne?"

Neither Dean nor Randall replied.

It was obvious how wrong they'd been, and the realization filled Dean with renewed grief and regret. There had been a time when the two families had been so close. Anne's death and Dean's guilt had driven a deep wedge between them. Now he had to wonder if the wedge had nothing to do with Anne and everything to do with his own guilty conscience.

"What happened was a pure, inexplicable accident. We never blamed you, boy." Horatio's soft-spoken words cut through Dean like a knife glowing red from being set in the fire.

"Someone did," Randall pointed out.

The MacDonnells exchanged a swift glance.

"What is it?" Dean asked, his body tensing with the certainty that they knew something.

The older man sighed, heavily and deeply. His gaze,

as it fell on Dean, was almost apologetic. "Shortly after Anne died, we discovered that our foreman, Gilbert Hayes, had fancied himself in love with her. He came back from a night in town drunker than shit and went on and on about how they'd been in love and that, ah…" He paused, his expression tensing as though he regretted the next words he'd have to say. "He claimed she'd ridden to your place that day to let you know she and Hayes were planning on marrying."

Dean felt a familiar twist in his gut. He met the older man's gaze and gave a short nod. "She left me a note that day, breaking off our engagement. She said she preferred another man."

"You never told me that!" Randall exclaimed.

"After her death, it didn't matter," Dean replied stiffly.

"Hayes never spoke of it when he was sober. You wouldn't have known there was anything wrong at all. But when the man fell into a bottle of spirits, he'd go on and on about losing her right when he was about to have her forever." Horatio met Dean's hard gaze. "He blamed you. Claimed that if you had been home that day, she could have had her say and ended things with you. He's convinced that if she'd talked to you, her horse never would have spooked, and she wouldn't have been thrown against that rock."

Dean could understand. He believed the same thing, didn't he? If he'd just been home when she'd stopped by, the series of events that had led to her death would have been altered.

"Where is Hayes now?" Dean asked.

"We thought he'd been getting over things, but after meeting your bride, he went into a rage. This time he was sober. I had to pay him final wages and told him to leave the ranch. I'm sorry, Dean. If I'd known he might have been killing your cattle, I would've stopped it long ago. I just thought he was a grieving man. I took pity on him. I made a mistake."

Dean shook his head. "I should've talked to you about the attacks," he admitted regretfully.

"No point in looking back. If Hayes is still out there, we'll help you track him down."

"I'll get the horses," Clinton declared before he vaulted over the porch railing and took off at a lope toward the barn.

THIRTY-TWO

DEAN HAD NEVER BEEN SO WEARY IN ALL HIS LIFE. It was the kind of tired that went down to the marrow of a man's bones and made his heart ache and his head throb.

The four of them had ridden through the night, searching for signs of Hayes by the light of the moon and stars. Finally, as the soft rays of dawn started to spread across the horizon, Horatio convinced him to get home and rest. He offered to send some men over to patrol the borders of the Lawton homestead in case Hayes thought to get close again.

Dean was tempted to decline. He could protect his own.

But then he thought of the three women back home and Randall's unborn child. His pride wasn't worth their safety.

The MacDonnells turned toward their land, and Dean and Randall headed home as well.

They were quiet and solemn, bone tired and worried about when and where Hayes might strike next.

Dean didn't like the thought of Hayes going off the

deep end after meeting Courtney. The man might see their marriage as an added reason for revenge. Though the tracks from that morning had headed out onto the range, there had been plenty of time for Hayes to circle back.

It was all he could think about as they neared the homestead.

Thankfully, there was no sign of any disturbance as they approached Randall's house.

Both men tied their horses to the hitching post and went straight to the front door. The horses needed to be cared for, but first they both wanted to be assured that the women were safe.

They had to wait for the bolt to be drawn back, but as soon as it was, Randall rushed through the door. He barely made it over the threshold before he came to a sudden stop, a strange sound squeezing from his chest. Then he stumbled forward with a harshly muttered, "Holy hell."

Dean reached for the gun on his hip and stepped around Randall to see what the hell had his brother so startled.

A quick scan revealed no sign of trouble in the little home. Everything was as neat and cozy as always. Turning back, he finally noticed that Randall had gone straight to where Courtney stood just inside the door. He could see the red of her bowed head beyond his brother's shoulder as they both bent over something in her arms.

He stilled. Some of his alarm slid away as he started to suspect what had his brother so worked up.

"Where's Pilar? Is she…?" Randall asked.

"She is resting. Jimena is with her. Your wife is exhausted but lovely," Courtney replied.

"Thank God," Randall exclaimed before he spun in a rush of energy and went to check on his wife, leaving Courtney and Dean standing in the front room.

Damn, she looked good.

Her hair was twisted in a messy braid. She looked tired and soft. Her eyes were heavy with lack of sleep, and her mouth was curved in a gentle smile.

"Come meet your nephew."

A boy.

As he approached, he couldn't help but notice how it felt to see his wife cradling the swaddled little bundle as she rocked gently back and forth, her skirts swaying around her legs.

She was so serene. So sweet and calm and content.

She deserved a babe of her own.

The thought had his chest tightening so fiercely and swiftly that his breath totally left him. He shifted his attention to the baby in order to call it back.

All he could see within the folds of the blanket was a tiny face surrounded by a thick patch of black hair and one clenched fist.

Dean had no idea babies could be born with so much hair. In his opinion, which he'd keep to himself, the child wasn't the most beautiful thing he'd ever seen, but he supposed no one could expect much from someone who was less than a day old.

"Does he have a name?"

"Not yet. Pilar wanted to wait for Randall's return."

He reached out and swept the back of his finger against the soft curve of the baby's cheek. Though the little one had appeared to be sleeping, he immediately turned his head toward Dean's finger and opened his tiny mouth. He found his own fist instead and immediately started sucking on it. But apparently, it was not what he wanted, as his features scrunched up like an old man's and he let out a wailing cry.

Dean stepped back in alarm, his gaze lifting to Courtney's.

Her chuckle warmed his weary bones. "I think he might want his mother again. He has already proven to have a voracious appetite."

"Well, he's Randall's son," Dean replied.

"I will take him back to Pilar, then we can go home."

Dean nodded. "I'll go see to Randall's horse. Just come on out when you're ready."

She nodded and smiled. Bowing her head over the babe, she cooed soft, soothing words as she turned to take him to the bedroom.

Dean stood for a second and watched her go. The sound her voice had made as it formed the word *home* echoed through him like the drawn-out strains of a fiddle.

Cursing himself for being so softheaded, he went outside.

He took care of Randall's horse, making sure the animal had plenty of water and grain after working through the night. By the time he came back around to the front of the house, Courtney was already standing by his horse, running her hand along the gelding's neck as the horse rested his head on her shoulder.

Turning her head at his approach, she said, "Perhaps

we should walk back. I think he's far too tired to carry both of us."

Dean nodded his response, mostly because he couldn't speak just then.

Seeing the picture she made while comforting his horse in the early slant of morning and remembering the image of her with the babe that would forever be imprinted on his brain, he was struck by how different she looked now compared to when he'd seen her for the first time—all made up and fancy in her elegant white gown.

Her appearance this morning was miles away from what it had been that day, but when he thought of what had changed, he could only call up superficial things. The dress, the way she styled her hair, the setting.

He thought about her quick and ready smiles, her rarely shown but fierce little temper. The way she had forged ahead with the new experiences of life on a ranch—a life she'd never intended to live. How she reveled in new experiences and faced every challenge with an optimistic gaze.

Those things had been a part of her from the start and had carried her through what—by all rights—should have been a difficult and trying adjustment to circumstances.

He'd never been able to do that. He'd always needed the security of life unchanged, of predictability and the continuous necessity of work, day in and day out.

He admired her.

He'd never expected to.

By her example, he had started to see what he was missing by holding so rigidly to what he thought was expected of him. He was starting to realize that the expectation was no one else's but his own.

These heavy thoughts combined with the pervading fear of knowing Hayes was still out there somewhere and his complete physical exhaustion to weigh down his steps.

As though she sensed his weary distraction, and perhaps because she possessed some of the same, they walked the narrow lane around the pasture in companionable silence, their hands linked with interlaced fingers while he led his tired horse.

All Dean wanted to do was kick off his boots, crawl into bed, and hold his wife's warm body in his arms as they slept the day away. But as they rounded the last curve of the lane, Dean tensed at the sight of two riders coming down the road to his place.

His first thought was Hayes, but the man had probably worked alone in his quest for vengeance. And considering the foreman's prior behavior, Dean doubted the coward would ride right up to Dean's front door.

Still, the sight of the two strangers made his tired muscles tense.

Courtney—likely feeling the change in him—glanced at him in question, then followed his narrowed gaze.

Lifting her hand to shield her view from the sun, she asked, "Who is that?"

"Don't know."

They kept walking, but Dean released Courtney's hand so his would be free to draw his gun if need be.

Prior to Hayes's attacks, he never would have

been so quick to suspect strangers of bad intentions. Prior to Courtney, he hadn't had something so valuable to protect.

The two riders hadn't yet seen Dean and Courtney coming from the path beyond the barn. They rode casually up to the house, and both dismounted. One was a large man with gun on his left hip, handle grip forward. He looked rough and dangerous, even from a distance, as he surveyed their surroundings in swift, economical glances that told Dean the man was accustomed to seeing enemies lurking in shadows. He had the manner of a gunfighter, and Dean didn't like that one bit.

The other rider was significantly smaller in every way, practically the size of a boy. Short and slim, but exhibiting a spurt of barely controlled impatience as he leapt from his horse. He didn't even bother tying up the animal before heading for the front door of the house. Dean could have sworn he saw a long black braid swinging down the boy's back, but the distance and the angle of his view made him uncertain.

In the next moment, the big, dangerous-looking one spotted their approach. He stood facing them, all tense and watchful as he took in their appearance, then he visibly relaxed and said something to his friend. It was only a word or two, but it had the smaller one turning away from the house to start toward them with long, purposeful strides.

The dangerous one stayed where he was.

"Oh my goodness," Courtney gasped beside him.

Dean tensed. He had just decided the two probably weren't a threat, but shock was obvious in her whispered words.

"Alexandra?" she muttered under her breath before taking off at a run.

Now that she was closer, Dean could see that the small rider was clearly a woman dressed in men's clothing.

The two women reached each other and embraced. Both of them started talking at once, then laughed at each other and hugged again.

Dean reached them just as Courtney exclaimed, "My goodness, Alexandra, I did not recognize you at all. You used to tell Evie and me that you had lived a very different life out here, but I cannot say I expected you to be going about in breeches. And with a gun on your hip."

The other woman flashed vivid blue eyes at her friend in a teasing glance. "I barely recognized you either, but I cannot say I don't like the change. Montana seems to agree with you, Courtney Adams."

Courtney blushed and glanced aside at Dean. Her smile was a secretive little curl that twisted his gut in a delicious way and had him thinking things that weren't appropriate in front of company.

"Well, not Adams, I'm afraid." She linked her arm through Dean's and drew him forward. "May I introduce Mr. Dean Lawton, the owner of this ranch and my husband. Temporarily, that is."

Blue eyes bounced wildly back and forth between Courtney and Dean. "You're teasing me," the other woman insisted.

"Not at all," Courtney replied with a smile.

"Well, I'll be damned. But what exactly do you mean by temporary?"

THIRTY-THREE

COURTNEY COULD BARELY BELIEVE IT. ALEXANDRA was here. Along with her frightening ex-bounty-hunter of a husband. It felt so good to see her old friend again, but odd at the same time. It was such a strange mixing of past and present, but not in any way Courtney could have imagined.

The Alexandra Courtney had known back in Boston had been polished and tutored in all the ways of Boston's elite society. Alexandra's aunt had seen to it. Though Alexandra had often talked about her childhood in Montana, Courtney now suspected that she might have toned down the truth of how she'd been raised by her adventurous father.

One thing that was exactly as Courtney had expected was the relationship between Alexandra and her husband, Malcolm Kincaid. The man was as forbidding, hard, and frightening as any man Courtney had ever met—except when he looked at his wife. The love and respect in his eyes then could not be mistaken.

Courtney's heart warmed for her friend, even as it ached for herself.

Alexandra's arrival had put a bright light on the fact that her time with Dean was running short.

After an initial greeting, Dean excused himself to lead his exhausted mount to the barn. Watching him walk away, Courtney realized that she hadn't even asked how his night went—if he'd found whoever was responsible for the attacks on Lawton livestock.

Though Alexandra had a dozen questions after Courtney's announcement in the yard, Courtney insisted on waiting to explain everything until they were more comfortable.

Alexandra's husband excused himself, also claiming the need to see to their horses, and left the two women to settle in for a more private chat in the parlor.

"Your man is everything I imagined and more," Courtney declared as soon as they were alone.

"I know," Alexandra replied with a wide grin. "I am sorry it took us so long to get here. We weren't in Helena when your letter first arrived, but we headed out as soon as we could. I still cannot believe you left Geoffrey standing at the altar."

"It seems so long ago now, almost like it happened to a different woman. Like *I* was a different woman."

"From where I stand, it looks like that might be the truth of it," Alexandra replied, her blue eyes sharp and knowing. "You've gotta tell me how on earth you ended up married to a cattle rancher."

Courtney sighed. "Oh, it's such a strange story, I'm sure you won't believe it. I honestly did not know I was being married until well after it was done. The judge refused to grant an annulment until we tried out being husband and wife for four weeks. We've got another eight days to go."

"That's...that is, ah..."

"Unbelievable. I know. But it's true."

Alexandra leaned forward, her long black braid falling over her shoulder as she reached for Courtney's hand. "And how have you been faring here as a cowboy's bride?"

Courtney looked down, then gave a shrug before she met her friend's questioning, concerned gaze with a jaunty half smile. "I'd say I've managed pretty well. Better than I ever would have expected. I am learning to cook and speak Spanish, and Dean has been teaching me how to ride. I named two of the cutest baby goats you'll ever see. Oh, and I helped to deliver a baby just last night." She held her hands out to the side. "Which is why you found me in such a disheveled state. I'm afraid I haven't slept much except brief little naps while Pilar labored."

Alexandra stared at her in stunned silence.

When her friend's shock continued for several minutes, Courtney laughed. "What is it? You are looking at me as though I just grew an extra head."

"Did you? Is another brain controlling my friend right now? Because that might explain things."

"Oh, come on now," Courtney chided, her cheeks warming with a mixture of affronted pride and embarrassment. "I'm not so different. Perhaps I've just never had the opportunity to test myself. Maybe I've always had it in me to be a rancher's wife and just had to come out here to find out."

Alexandra's expression dimmed into a serious little frown. "You sound as though you wouldn't mind continuing on as such."

Courtney considered lying. She realized how such a confession would appear to her friend. But as their eyes met in the quiet of the little parlor, Courtney didn't want to keep the truth to herself any longer. "I want to stay," she whispered.

Alexandra blinked but did not look particularly surprised. "And your husband? What does he want?"

Courtney dropped her gaze. "Dean is...proud and strong and committed to his responsibilities and this ranch." She smiled softly. "He's fiercely loyal and brave and stubborn and far too serious most of the time, though that has started to change." She met Alexandra's gaze. "He also has no desire to take on the burden of a wife he never wanted, especially not a woman like me who grew up pampered and privileged with no particular skills."

"I think you are selling yourself short."

Courtney smiled. "No, I'm not. You know where I came from. I can host a grand party and shop like I was born to it. This place—Dean—deserves more than what I have to offer."

Alexandra frowned, looking like she still wanted to argue. "I'm sorry, Court. Does he know how you feel?"

She shook her head. Her throat was too tight to speak.

"What if you told him?"

Courtney looked at her friend in horror. "I could not handle that kind of rejection from him. And he would have to reject me. I am not the wife he wanted."

"Have you…been intimate?" Courtney's involuntary blush answered that question quickly enough, and Alexandra continued bluntly, "You might not be able to get an annulment."

"Then we will get a divorce," Courtney replied, doing her best to keep her heartbreak from showing in her voice, though she couldn't hold back the tears that filled her eyes. "One way or another, our marriage will end after next week."

"I'm so sorry," Alexandra murmured again.

Courtney gave her a watery smile. "At least I had him for a little while."

Alexandra stood and reached for Courtney's hands to bring her to her feet as well. "Why don't you go get some sleep? You look dead on your feet, and things might feel different after you've gotten some rest."

Courtney gave a weak little laugh. "I do feel like I could curl up right here on the parlor floor and sleep for hours."

"Go on then. Malcolm and I will still be here when you awake."

❦

Dean turned on his heel and headed straight back to the kitchen. He'd left his mud-caked boots outside the back door, and he shoved his feet back into them before heading to the barn in long, angry strides. The words he'd just heard battered at his heart like a blacksmith's hammer.

"You might not be able to get an annulment."

"Then we will get a divorce. One way or another, our marriage will end after next week."

Nothing good ever came from eavesdropping, even when it was unintentional, and as soon as he heard Courtney's firm declaration, he hadn't wanted to hear another word.

What had he expected? That she'd want to stay?

What an idiot he was.

He'd known from the start she didn't belong here.

He'd started to believe she might be different. That she might want to make a real go of things. That she might have grown fond of the ranch. Of him.

She might enjoy their marriage bed, but he had been stupid to think her feelings extended any deeper.

Idiot. That's what he was.

Storming into his office, he went straight for his grandfather's bourbon. He poured a shot into a glass and downed it in one quick swallow, then poured himself another.

"Mind if I join you for one of those?"

Dean looked up to see the gunfighter standing in his doorway.

"I was seeing to our horses," the man said with a jerk of his head back toward the barn. "You passed right by me."

Dean would have preferred to drink alone, but he had no idea how to get rid of the man. "Suit yourself," he finally said, reaching for another glass.

"Name's Malcolm Kincaid."

Dean had heard of him. A year ago or so, there had been a shoot-out over near Wolf Creek. Something about a corrupt land baron who had the law in his back pocket. From what Dean recalled, Kincaid was a bounty hunter who had seen justice meted out and freed a town from an oppressive tyrant in the process.

Not a gunfighter, but damn close.

Thinking of Kincaid's vocation recalled Dean to his current problem with Hayes. Perhaps a former bounty hunter could be of some assistance. He was afraid he was gonna need all the help he could get to see the matter finally resolved.

"Dean Lawton," he replied as he handed a glass of bourbon to the other man. "Have a seat."

THIRTY-FOUR

❦

BEFORE HEADING UPSTAIRS TO THE COMFORT OF HER bed, Courtney took a quick bath, marveling over the experience she'd had assisting Pilar with the birth of her son. She had never in her wildest imagining thought she might bear witness to such an event.

The euphoric joy and love in Pilar's eyes when she got her first look at her son had nearly stopped Courtney's heart. And immediately had her wondering what it might be like to have a child. A child with Dean.

The thought hadn't left her all night as she waited for his safe return. When he had walked into the house and seen her holding the baby, she could have sworn she saw the same longing she was feeling in his eyes.

But it had probably been her lack of sleep that allowed such wishful thinking. He'd made it clear from the start that there was no future for them.

Her limbs were heavy as she finished her bath and made her way up to her bedroom. She just needed a couple hours of sleep to restore herself. A couple hours and she wouldn't feel so lost and sad when she should be feeling ecstatic at being reunited with Alexandra.

Her gaze was cast downward in weariness as she entered her bedroom. Unfortunately, it kept her from noticing that someone else was already there.

As Gilbert Hayes, MacDonnell's foreman, stepped forward from behind her open door, Courtney sucked in a swift breath. Oddly, her first thought was one of confusion, but it didn't take long for fear to crowd that out. There could be no good reason for the man to be in her bedroom. Before she could force her breath out again in a scream, he grabbed hold of her and pressed a heavy, foul-smelling hand hard over her mouth and nose.

Her entire body froze in shock and terror. Her heart seemed to seize inside her, altering her perception of time. While her mind raced through the possible reasons he might have to attack her in such a manner, her gaze bounced around the room, seeking any means of getting away from him.

As though sensing her rising urge to fight, Hayes pulled her close in a punishing grip. He lowered his head until his face was within an inch of hers, and the crazy light in his eyes caused her to stiffen with another flash of terror. "If I can't have Anne, there's no way in hell he gets to keep you."

Courtney drew a breath through flared nostrils, then nearly choked on the stench emanating from him. She noticed smears and streaks of dark stains on his hands, arms, and clothing. Stains that looked an awful lot like dried blood. Her stomach lurched.

With a cry for help stuck behind the hand he had

mashed over her mouth, she twisted in his arms. Her exhaustion was gone in a burst of panic and fury. How dare this man sneak into her bedroom and assault her! She lashed out with jabbing elbows and kicking feet. She had no idea what he wanted with her, but she intended to fight him every step of the way.

She experienced a swift flash of satisfaction when her knee made contact with a vulnerable body part and he grunted in pain. But the man was strong and determined. His grip became even more punishing as he managed to turn her in his arms until her back was pressed to his chest, one of her arms was pinned to her side, and the prick of something sharp pressed into her side.

"Stop, or this knife sinks into your belly."

She was breathing hard through her nose from her physical exertions and realized with another forceful dose of horror that she didn't have enough strength or courage to fight against him and his knife. A knife that she suspected was already stained with the blood of Lawton livestock.

But the fact that he hadn't already killed her gave her some hope. She was alive, and she was conscious. She would think of something. She had to.

"Anne was gonna marry me. Didya know that?" he asked almost conversationally. "We were planning to head outta town that day. But she insisted on talking to Lawton first." His voice dropped to a feral growl. "He was supposed to be here."

Oh my God. Was Anne really going to end her engagement to Dean?

Whether it was true or not, the man holding a knife to Courtney's side certainly believed it.

"He took my bride, so I'm taking his," he said as he forced her toward the open door.

Courtney stumbled into the hallway, a choked whimper catching in her throat. She tried to resist his next shove—tried to shift her jaw to bite the hand covering her mouth—but it only caused him to tighten his grip, which sent the tip of his knife through the fabric of her dress. The sharp pain as the blade pierced her side urged her to comply.

Tears burned in her eyes.

He said he was taking her, not killing her. Not yet anyway. As long as she was alive, she had a chance. Dean was just out in the barn. And Alexandra's husband couldn't be too far away. Perhaps she would be able to get their attention once she was outside. But first she and Hayes had to get through the house.

Oh God, Alexandra!

She hoped her friend was safely away as well.

As the two of them made their way slowly down the stairs, the knife firm to her side, his hand harsh over her mouth, Courtney realized he would need to take his hand off her mouth at some point, especially if he intended to get her on a horse. Hopefully, he would need to shift his grip on the knife as well. That moment would likely be her one chance to scream and try to get away.

Just as they reached the bottom of the stairs, Alexandra stepped into the parlor doorway.

Courtney's stomach fell in a sickening dive. With her eyes, she tried to tell her friend to back away,

to let them pass, to stay out of the madman's reach.
But Alexandra's vivid blue gaze was trained hard and
unwaveringly on the man behind Courtney.

"Just where the hell do you think you're taking
my friend?"

He stopped at the threatening words, keeping
Courtney's body secure in front of him and the knife
firm at Courtney's side. Her eyes widened, and a
moan of fear rolled in her throat. What was Alexandra
doing? Sure, she had a gun on her hip, but it wasn't
drawn and Courtney was currently being used as a
pretty effective shield.

"I asked you a question," Alexandra stated, her tone
dropping.

"Stay back," Hayes warned. "I've got no issue with
you, but this one's mine."

"Wrong." Alexandra's reply was colder than anything Courtney had ever heard. "You're not stepping
one foot from this house."

Something in her friend's voice—the sheer confidence, most likely—bolstered Courtney's wavering
courage. She wasn't done fighting. While the two of
them focused on each other, Courtney surveyed the
hall. There had to be something she could use.

Hayes laughed, and the sound was grating, almost
maniacal. "And who's gonna stop me?" he asked
derisively as he shoved Courtney forward two more
steps. "You?"

Alexandra actually smiled. "That's the plan."

Courtney glanced toward the door. One more step,
and Hayes would have to make a quarter turn to get
around the table set in the entryway. It should briefly

open his left side to Alexandra's aim. That was their chance!

Courtney stared fiercely at her friend, willing her to see what she saw. As soon as Alexandra's gaze flickered toward her, Courtney looked hard toward the table. The moment of communication was a fraction of a second, but Courtney could see by the tilt of Alexandra's mouth as she returned her gaze to Hayes that she understood.

"You've got two seconds to let her go before I put a bullet in you. One." Hayes stepped and turned.

Courtney threw her weight hard to her right.

Alexandra drew her pistol and fired. "Two."

The knife at her side pressed hard for a split second, making Courtney gasp. Then it released completely as the man behind her fell back onto the stairs.

Alexandra stepped forward to grasp Courtney's arm and pull her roughly aside so she could keep the pistol trained on the man now groaning in pain as he held his bleeding shoulder.

"If you know what's good for you, you'll stay right where you are," Alexandra warned.

Courtney sucked in deep breaths and leaned back against the wall, her legs suddenly going weak and shaky. She stared at her friend in shock. "What an amazing shot, Alexandra. I've never seen anything so fast. You *must* teach me how to do that."

Alexandra gave a small chuckle but never took her eyes off the man bleeding on the stairs. "Cooking, riding, and now shooting? You might become a Western woman yet, Courtney *Lawton*."

The back door of the house flew open a second

before Dean appeared in the hallway with his gun drawn. He stopped at the sight of Courtney standing against the wall. Their eyes met for just a moment, and her heart squeezed tight at the fear she saw there before he glanced down at Hayes sprawled awkwardly at the bottom of the stairs.

"You son of a bitch," he growled as he approached the man with murder in his eyes. Grabbing the injured man by the front of his shirt, he holstered his gun and sent a fist flying straight into the man's face.

Kincaid swept through the front door. Seeing his wife with her pistol drawn and trained on the injured man, he reholstered his own gun.

Dean still leaned over Hayes, his fist drawn back to take another bone-crushing jab. "How dare you come into my home and threaten my wife!"

Hayes's features were tight with pain, but he still managed to twist them into a furious grimace. "You've got no right to go on about your life while Anne's lying dead in the ground. You deserve the same hell I've been through since you took her away from me."

Courtney watched as Dean struggled to retain control. Violence was just barely contained within his tense frame. She had no idea if anything Hayes believed was true, but it had to hurt Dean regardless to hear such things said about the women he'd intended to marry. She wanted to step forward, to somehow comfort and support him in that moment. But something in his posture told her not to interfere.

"Is this the man you were telling me about?" Kincaid asked from his wife's side.

Rather than answering, Dean directed his harshly growled words to Hayes. "Tell me why I shouldn't kill you right now."

Hayes's eyes were as flat as his voice as he replied, "Do it. End my hell."

Courtney held her breath. For a long moment, it looked like Dean's hand was creeping toward his holstered gun. Then his fingers curled tight into his palm, and a hard, swift punch had Hayes slumping to the stairs unconscious.

Dean released the man's shirt and stood over him. He stared at the foreman's prone form as though he wished the man would awaken so he could hit him again.

Alexandra reholstered her gun, and Kincaid stepped forward. "I'll take him to the sheriff. Will your neighbors offer statements on what they know of his criminal actions?"

Dean nodded, but he didn't turn around.

Courtney finally stepped forward to place her hand on Dean's shoulder. The tension running through his body was like lightning trapped in a bottle—explosive and frightening. She could sense his desire to shrug off her touch, though he didn't move.

She dropped her hand back to her side.

"Let's get him tied to the saddle while he's still unconscious," Kincaid said as he stepped forward.

Both men hefted Hayes between them and dragged him outside.

Alexandra turned to Courtney, concern in her eyes. "Are you all right, Court?"

Courtney nodded, took a deep breath, then nodded again. "I'm fine. Surprisingly." She gave a little laugh, realizing it was true. In thinking of everything she'd gone through in the last twenty-four hours, she probably should have been close to hysterical. But she wasn't. She really was fine.

Dean and Malcolm had Hayes in custody. She hadn't been hurt beyond a brief prick of Hayes's knife and had actually assisted in her own rescue. She might even be a bit better than fine.

She gave Alexandra a smile. "I imagine you'd like to go help your husband."

"I should get a horse readied so they can tie him to the saddle before he comes around."

"Go ahead. I'm all right."

Alexandra sent her an earnest look before walking away. "You did good, Court."

Courtney agreed. Once she was alone, she took a moment to acknowledge how much she'd changed over the last weeks. The old Courtney would never have even considered fighting back against a man with a weapon. She liked the woman she'd become. She hoped, when this was all over, that she wouldn't lose that at least.

By the time Hayes started to come around, he was secured to the saddle, with his hands tied tight behind him and one ankle tied to the stirrup, ensuring that if he tried anything stupid, he'd likely get dragged to his death.

Courtney watched the proceedings from the porch. Though she tried to keep the circumstances in perspective, Dean's demeanor worried her. She wasn't sure what she expected of him, considering everything, but she had hoped at least to glean something of what he was feeling from his expression or his familiar gaze. But he seemed to do everything he could to keep from looking at her.

And she did what she could to not interfere.

"I've gotta let my brother know Hayes has been caught. Then I'll fetch the MacDonnells and meet you in town," Dean stated once Kincaid and his prisoner were ready to go.

Kincaid nodded and gave his wife a quick kiss before mounting his horse and heading down the road, leading Hayes's mount on a short rope.

Courtney got the sense Alexandra would have ridden with her husband into town but chose to stay back with her instead. She slid Courtney a pointed look as she walked up the porch steps and passed by to enter the house, leaving Courtney and Dean alone outside.

Dean turned to head toward the barn, still avoiding looking at Courtney.

Her chest tightened with the need to assure herself he was all right.

"Dean." His name held a note of desperation she couldn't hold back. It brought him to a stop, and he turned to look at her full-on for the first time since he'd charged into the house.

Their eyes met, and for a moment, Courtney expected him to glance away again and keep walking. Thankfully, he didn't.

With a fierce set to his jaw and an unreadable gleam in his eyes, he vaulted up onto the porch and gathered Courtney into his arms. The relief of his rough embrace—his warmth and strength—soothed the last of her shaken nerves. She wrapped her arms around his middle and breathed him in.

Bowing his head, he buried his face against her neck and held her tight. "I'm sorry," he muttered gruffly.

"No. Dean, you couldn't have known the man would be hiding in my bedroom," Courtney argued quietly.

His body gave a hard jerk. "I should have checked the house. I shouldn't have left you alone. I wasn't thinking."

"It's all right. He's been caught. He will pay for his crimes."

"You could've been killed." He lifted his head, and Courtney met his hard gaze.

"But I wasn't. I am fine, I swear it."

Dean made a low sound and dropped his mouth to hers.

Courtney poured absolutely everything into that kiss—all that she was and everything she wanted to be. She allowed herself to feel in that moment as if she were truly Dean's wife. Not just for now, but for always.

But in the back of her mind, she knew it wasn't enough.

THIRTY-FIVE

Not much later, as Courtney watched Dean ride away, she experienced an odd mixture of hope and fear. His reaction to finding her in danger suggested that he might actually feel something for her that went beyond physical desire. He'd worried for her safety, he'd rushed into the house prepared to fight to protect her, and he'd just kissed her as though he were afraid to ever let her go again.

But he did let her go, and before he turned his horse toward Randall's and then the MacDonnells' place, she saw a haunted look in his eyes that made her muscles tense and her skin pebble with a chill.

Once she and Alexandra finished washing Hayes's blood from the stairs, Alexandra insisted that Courtney claim some much-needed rest. Unable to enter her bedroom without smelling the stench Hayes had left behind, she lay down in Dean's bed instead and was asleep in seconds.

When she woke up a few hours later, she found Alexandra in the kitchen surrounded by the very welcome aroma of coffee.

"Mmm…I really hope there is some of that left for me."

Alexandra laughed. "Of course. Have a seat."

"Has anyone come back from town?"

"Not yet. Sometimes the paperwork can take a little time." Her blue eyes met Courtney's with steady assurance. "They'll be back."

Courtney nodded, accepting that as truth, though she yearned for Dean's presence. Something just hadn't felt right when he'd left, and her nap had done nothing to dispel the disquiet inside her.

Once the two women were seated at the table with their steaming coffee in hand, Alexandra drew something from the pocket of her breeches. "I didn't have a chance to tell you earlier, but yours was not the only letter awaiting our return to Helena, I'm afraid."

She placed a sealed envelope on the table and slid it toward Courtney. The envelope was made of the finest paper, and the address was written in a sure and elegant hand. The handwriting had become familiar to Courtney over the years and only recently had been infinitely burned into her mind in words of love, desire, and devotion intended for someone else.

It was from Geoffrey.

Courtney hesitated.

It wasn't that she feared what he might have to say to her. The explanation she had hastily provided in her letter to him after leaving Boston had been honest and true. Being left at the altar had no doubt been an excruciatingly public humiliation. She could understand if he decided not to forgive her for having made the impulsive decision to flee that day.

Her reluctance was because she wasn't sure she wished to reconnect with a past that now seemed to have existed so long ago. A few weeks could never be considered a lifetime, but it sure felt like it to Courtney.

Still, she and Geoffrey had been friends of a sort for a long time. She was worried about how he might have fared after her departure.

Especially now that she understood how it must have felt for his true love to be out of reach. *Especially* now that she had fallen in love as well…with someone who had been very clear about not wanting her.

The acknowledgment of how deeply she'd fallen for Dean slid through her like the ring of a bell. Beautiful and pure but startling.

Yes, she had fallen in love with Dean. And the situation was as hopeless as Geoffrey's had been.

With a deep breath, she picked up the letter and slipped her fingers along the seam of the envelope to withdraw the sheet of paper from inside. She had to read through it twice because the first time around her eyes teared up and she was pretty sure she'd missed some of what he'd written through her blurred vision.

Alexandra reached out to cover one of Courtney's hands with hers. "Is everything all right? What does he say?"

"He extends a heartfelt apology and expresses his undying gratitude."

Her friend blinked, her eyes going wide with surprise. "Gratitude? Really?"

"Yes. He says he understands why I left and that he is sorry for being so deceitful, but that he really had not seen any other way. He hadn't intended to fall in love with anyone, especially not a woman his family would never consider to be an appropriate match. He hadn't set out to hurt me and thought I understood our marriage would not be based on deep feelings. It had never occurred to him that I might hope for something more."

Alexandra gave a quiet snort.

"He goes on to say that by not going through with the wedding and showing the courage to seek my happiness elsewhere, I inspired him to do the same. He and his true love have eloped."

Alexandra gasped. Even though she had spent her childhood in the wild territories of the West, she had grown to adulthood with Courtney in Boston and knew well the rules by which Geoffrey's society played. Alexandra had caused a scandal herself by running away from Boston shortly after becoming engaged to a prominent member of their society. She understood as well as Courtney did how unheard of it was for a man of Geoffrey's social standing to marry someone so far outside their social circle.

Yet he'd done it.

Because Courtney had inspired him.

She was both saddened and thrilled by the news. Her jilted fiancé had managed to claim his happily-ever-after while she found herself about to say goodbye to hers.

As though sensing Courtney's conflicted feelings, Alexandra gave her hand another squeeze. "I'm sorry, Courtney. That must be…difficult to read."

Courtney shook her head and flashed a smile. "No. Not at all. I am very happy for him, and I will write back to tell him so."

Alexandra smiled in return. "Well, in that case, do you have something with which we can offer a toast to the lovely couple?"

Enjoying the mischievous gleam in her friend's eye, Courtney replied, "There is some bourbon in the parlor."

"Perfect."

The next hours were spent catching up and reminiscing with Alexandra. It was the best way to distract Courtney from worrying about Dean. With Jimena planning on staying close to home over the next few days to help Pilar, it was just the two of them in the house. They talked about their days at school and their time together in Boston's social whirl before Alexandra had left. The only thing that would have made the time more perfect was if their friend and Alexandra's cousin, Evie, had been present. The three of them had been inseparable, and it just did not feel the same without her.

But Evie was back in Boston, preparing for her own grand wedding, which was to take place in just a couple weeks.

While Courtney was thrilled for the opportunity to reconnect with her friend, she couldn't help but notice how different it felt. Better. And the changes she saw in Alexandra were nothing short of stunning. Her friend had obviously concealed a great deal about her true nature while being groomed for a future amongst the Boston elite.

It was clear that this woman before her, wearing breeches and a ready smile, was the true Alexandra. Her time in Boston had put polish on the wild girl she had been, but it hadn't erased that wildness entirely.

Courtney wondered if the changes she'd felt in herself since coming to Montana were only a similar facade. She had learned so much in the time she'd been at the Lawton Ranch. About herself as a person, what she was capable of, and most importantly, what she wanted for her future. She had left Boston in search of adventure and independence.

She had found both on a Montana cattle ranch.

She could never go back to the many restraints that existed in her old life. She enjoyed the freedom of thought and behavior she had experienced out here. She loved the sense of confidence and self-expression she'd gained. All those things that had been suppressed for so long, though they had always been inside her, stirring and desperate for release.

As the day slid toward night, she strained to catch the first sound of hoofbeats signaling Dean's return from town. It had been late morning when he and Malcolm had left the homestead. She expected them back by nightfall at least. But as the sun fell closer and closer to the horizon, she began to worry.

Keeping supper warm and ready to be served, Courtney and Alexandra went out onto the front porch to await the return of their men. They were quiet in the gathering darkness.

It was not long before the sound of riders approaching brought both women to their feet.

The men rode up to the house first. Courtney's chest tightened at the weariness apparent in Dean's posture and expression.

"How did it go?" Alexandra asked.

Kincaid gave a sharp nod. "No problems."

"Supper has been kept warm," Courtney said. "I imagine you are both hungry."

"We'll be in after we see to the horses," Dean replied. His tone was flat and distant.

Rather than bringing everything to the dining room, the four of them gathered in the kitchen to eat. Kincaid explained that Hayes was being held in jail to await trial. Horatio and Clinton MacDonnell had both come forward to repeat what Hayes had told them after meeting Courtney. Hayes denied none of it, claiming he had a right to Dean's bride since Dean had taken his.

It was all very disturbing. Courtney shivered to think what might have happened if Hayes hadn't been stopped. She watched Dean while Kincaid filled them in about what to expect going forward. She was only half listening. There was something in Dean's demeanor that bothered her. It was more than his typical moodiness and more than exhaustion.

Once again, he was reluctant to look at her, even as she willed it with everything in her. His eyes fell on her only once or twice before he shifted them away as quickly as possible. As though he didn't want to see her thoughts—or perhaps, more, didn't want her to see his.

After the meal was finished and cleaned up, the Kincaids excused themselves and went up to the bedroom that had been prepared for them earlier, leaving Courtney and Dean alone in the kitchen.

"You must be tired," she said softly.

"You too, I reckon," he said gruffly, keeping his gaze trained toward the floor.

"I got a little sleep earlier," she replied. "Are you all right, Dean?"

He looked up then. For a moment, his light eyes sparked with emotion before it was carefully banked behind a stern expression. "Fine. I'm gonna wash up before heading to bed. No reason for you to stay up."

The words were simple enough, but Courtney felt something layered in with their meaning. Something unsettling. He was putting distance between them.

Because of Alexandra's arrival? Was he already preparing for her to leave?

"Go on," he said as he turned his back to her and headed to the bathing room.

The click of the door closing between them echoed through her.

Numbly, she went about turning down the lights, leaving only what Dean would need to make his way upstairs. Once in the upper hallway, she paused outside his bedroom door.

She wasn't ready for their marriage to end. They still had eight days together before the annulment. Courtney was not going to waste them.

Instead of continuing down the hall to her own bedroom, which she suspected was what Dean had intended that she do, she entered his room. Closing the door gently behind her, she didn't bother lighting the lamp before she shed her clothes and slipped between the sheets of his bed.

He might have decided not admit it, but she had no issue with acknowledging her need for him. Not just in a sexual sense, but in every way. She needed to feel him close, to have his warmth and strength and quiet, awkward reluctance open up to her. At least here in this room there had been times when he'd allowed all that was between them to drop away. He'd revealed his desire and his loneliness and longing, and he'd allowed her to fulfill them as he'd fulfilled so many of her secret dreams.

She was still awake when he came upstairs and knew the exact moment when he noticed her lying in his bed. His breath halted, and he froze in place. She couldn't see him beyond the shadowed outline he made in the darkened room, but she knew some silent battle waged within him.

She held her breath, curled up on her side, waiting for his decision. Would he stay or find somewhere else to sleep?

After what seemed like a painful eternity, he continued across the room and sat down on the other side of the bed to remove his boots. The rest of his clothing followed swiftly after, and then she felt the mattress dip as he lay down behind her. Another breath and he reached for her. He wrapped his arm around her middle and drew her back against his bare chest, curling her into his body as his breath fanned over her bare shoulder.

A moment later, he was asleep.

Courtney remained awake for little while longer, soaking in the security of his embrace and matching her breath to his. As cherished and protected as she felt, the tight ache of dread would not leave her.

THIRTY-SIX

DEAN AWOKE WITH HIS WIFE CURLED AGAINST HIM, naked and so damn soft. He was hard in an instant.

He shouldn't have lain down beside her last night. But he had been so tired, his weariness going deeper than any he'd ever known, down to his bones, to his heart and soul. And he'd needed her. Her closeness. Her comfort.

But it had been a mistake. A selfish move.

Because he'd known what the morning would bring.

Acknowledging his weakness, knowing the honorable thing would be to sneak from the room and leave her be, he still slid his hand over the curve of her naked hip and down the length of her thigh.

The sleepy sigh she breathed fed his hunger and helped to drown out the grumbles of his conscience.

She knew their union would end. She'd said it herself just the day before, with as much conviction as he'd ever heard in her voice. If things ended sooner than she'd expected, it would likely only make her happy. She would be free to move on with her life and finally leave the place she'd never intended to make her home.

As soon as she was gone, he'd figure out how to find some peace.

That, or he'd just do what he'd always done. He'd keep working—from sunup to sundown—and maybe eventually he wouldn't ache for her smile and yearn for her laughter or her gentle, heated touch.

Awake now, she turned in his arms to face him in the golden glow of early morning.

Her eyes were only half-open and sleepy. She arched into him as she slid her leg up over his and brought her hand to the side of his face.

Though he pressed his palm to the small of her back, holding her to him so she could feel his erection against her belly, he did not speak and did not try to take her mouth in a kiss, even though her plush lips beckoned him.

He waited, somehow convincing himself that if she kissed him, if she made that move toward him, then somehow he might be absolved of selfish intentions.

It was a lie he chose to believe.

She stroked her fingers over the rough stubble that spread along his jaw, then used her thumb to trace the firm press of his lips.

Her eyes met his, and her lips parted while she took a breath. She seemed about to say something but apparently changed her mind.

Dean partly wished she'd spoken and was partly relieved she hadn't.

Then, with that familiar, lovely curl forming at the corners of her lips, she brought her mouth to his. Her kiss was quiet and sweet. It was an awakening and the whisper of a secret. He parted his lips to take that secret whisper for his own and met her tongue with his in a velvet touch.

She rose over him, and he rolled to his back while the riotous length of her hair fell around them like a veil of intimacy, shielding their kiss from the light of the morning sun and the rest of the world. Her breasts flattened on his chest, and her heartbeat shuddered through him. Or was that his heart beating so hard and fast?

With one hand, he gripped the curve of her buttock, holding her hips to his while he throbbed beneath her. His other hand slid up beneath the tangle of her hair to cup the back of her head as he adjusted the fit of their mouths to deepen the kiss.

She moaned softly, breathlessly. Her tongue sought his, and her body shifted like silk over him.

He took over in a burst of energy, rolling her beneath him. Her legs parted to allow for the weight of his hips, and her arms encircled him in a ready embrace as her spine arched toward him, seeking.

When he paused to look down at her, feeling another stab of regret for what would never be, she returned his serious gaze with a warm and sensual smile.

When he didn't smile back, her expression tensed and her gaze grew wary. Her eyes darkened, reflecting the understanding of their inevitable parting, though she didn't yet know just how soon that end would come.

Dean's chest tightened. Unable to find any words appropriate for such a moment, he followed the dictates of his body instead. With a roll of his hips, he slid his aching erection along the seam of her heated sex.

Her eyelashes swept over her gaze, and her lips parted. She slid her hands up the muscles of his back until she could curl her hands over his shoulders. Dropping her head back, she tipped her hips in encouragement.

Another roll of his hips, another glide of slick flesh, and another breathless, needful moan. The sound was the sweetest, deepest torture. It twisted through him like a silken rope, tying him in knots, ensnaring him despite himself.

Finally, when the teasing caresses became too much, Dean slid his hand beneath her hips, holding her steady as he angled his erection to enter her.

Courtney held his gaze as her breath stopped in anticipation of his possession.

He took her in a slow, measured stroke. He was desperate to feel every bit of progress in minute detail, savoring the way she claimed him even as he claimed her. All he knew was her heat surrounding him—her gentle possession, her self-assured generosity, and the commanding pull of her gaze.

He was lost.

With a ragged breath, he dropped his head to press his mouth to the side of her throat, where her pulse thrummed steady and sure. He kissed a trail up to her ear, nipping sharply at her earlobe while starting a purposeful rhythm with his hips.

She held him tight, meeting every thrust as her need steadily increased. Dean sensed her frustration. He loved the way her fingernails bit into his skin and her body urged his to a faster, harder pace. Despite her insistent demands, Dean maintained a relentless, building rhythm.

Finally, she succumbed to her passion, and with a low sound echoing from her chest, she shoved at his shoulders until he slipped from her body and fell back on the bed. Rising over him, she pressed her hands to his chest and straddled his hips.

Dean reached for her breasts, his hands covering their modest weight, his palms circling over their peaks. She gasped and arched, letting her head fall back so the curling ends of her hair brushed the tops of his thighs and her hot, wet folds pressed to his cock. His hips gave an involuntary buck and he groaned, deep and long.

The movement and the sound drew her attention, and she looked down at him from her commanding position. Holding his gaze, she took him in hand, holding him as she lifted her hips, then lowered herself onto him.

The sight of her taking him into her body nearly wrecked him. He ground his teeth against the rush of release, amazingly holding it at bay. And once she had him fully sheathed, she leaned forward with a sweet and wicked little smile. She pressed a kiss to his lips and rocked her hips.

The shifting of his body in hers was deep and decadent. Dean released her breasts to grab hold of her hips—not to guide her, but to anchor himself to her as his control began to fracture. He was determined to stay there with her to the very end.

But she seemed equally determined to make that difficult.

Every deep roll of her hips, combined with the sliding friction of her breasts against his chest, sent ripples of pleasure down to his toes. Her lips pressed warm kisses along his throat, interspersed with fiery licks and nips of her teeth.

When she finally rose up again, sitting tall and proud and beautiful, Dean was stunned by the sight of her. Her skin was golden in the morning sun, and her tangled mass of hair fell like fire around her shoulders and down her back. Pressing her palms flat on his abdomen, she moved—lifting her hips along his length until just the tip remained inside her before lowering again in a powerful act of claiming.

He gave himself over to her. Holding on, letting go.

His jaw ached with the effort to hold back his release as she moved faster and faster. Her eyes were tightly closed. Her body bucked and rocked in a demanding rhythm. Her breath became short and swift. She was so close.

Dean smoothed his hands up her thighs and slid his thumbs over the slick folds where her body surrounded his. A slow moan slid from her lips before getting caught in midbreath when he circled one thumb over her swollen bud.

Her eyes opened, heavy lidded and dark with passion. Holding her gaze, he circled and stroked until panting gasps slid from between her parted lips.

Then her body tensed sharply and her back bowed as she ground herself down on him hard.

Feeling the pulsing contractions deep inside her, Dean finally released the reins on his control. Grasping her hips in his hands, he rocked her against him in one, two short strokes before he lifted her off him just as his pleasure burst free and he pumped his seed across his belly.

She lowered herself to his side, resting her head on his shoulder as she tucked her face into the curve of his throat. He felt her body softening as the last echoing shudders receded.

It took a few minutes before Dean felt he could move again. He wiped away the evidence of his release before taking Courtney in his arms. For a moment, at least, he simply wanted to hold her, feel her breath and her heartbeat, soak up her warmth and womanly softness.

After a little while, she lifted her head to press a sweet kiss to his lips.

"Good morning," she murmured.

Dean's throat closed up. He had to say the words that would send her way from him. Now. Before he lost what nerve he still had. "I convinced Judge Wilkerson to file paperwork for a divorce."

She stiffened. All sensuality was gone from her gaze in an instant. "Excuse me?"

"In town yesterday," he explained. "It took some talking, but Wilkerson agreed to end the marriage ahead of his deadline."

Dean let his arms fall from around her, and she immediately pushed to a seated position beside him.

"I don't understand."

"Now that the Kincaids are here, I figured you'd want to head out."

"I...I didn't realize it would be so easy."

It wasn't.

Dean clenched his teeth. "Like I said before, Wilkerson's word is law."

She stared at him in silence—her expression entirely inscrutable—for a few long moments. Long enough for Dean to tense up.

"How very efficient of you," she finally replied. Her cool tone chilled him from the inside.

What had he expected? A passionate declaration? Some indication that she might have changed her mind?

No. He didn't want those things. He wasn't sure he'd believe them. She wasn't for him, no matter how badly he wished otherwise.

She'd said it herself yesterday. *The marriage had to end one way or another.*

Recalling the sound of those words in her unwavering voice had him firming his resolve. "I didn't see any point in delaying things."

"I see," she said as she turned and rose from the bed. "I don't suppose today is too soon for me to leave?"

Dean hesitated. He had to force himself not to rub the center of his chest where a hard knot had formed to press against his heart and lungs. "If that's what you want. The divorce papers can be sent to you for signing."

She said nothing to that, just started pulling on her underthings and then her dress before she used her fingers to comb through her hair. All the while, she kept her face averted.

"We knew this couldn't last," he mumbled, the tension inside him growing.

"Right." Her tone was clipped. "And you never wanted a wife."

He hadn't wanted a wife and never expected to want Courtney. But he did.

Still, none of that mattered if she didn't want him back. "You'll be free again to live the independent life you wanted," he replied.

Independence.

Really? Is that what she had been after?

The word sounded hollow as it bounced around in the turmoil of Courtney's mind.

Truer words came swiftly to mind: fulfillment, confidence, happiness, love.

The last had her throat closing up, and she bit hard on her bottom lip to distract from the pain spreading inside her.

"I must gather my things," she said in what she told herself was a steady voice. The voice of a woman with the strength to make her own choices and go after what she wanted.

Even though it was a lie.

She wanted Dean. She wanted a life with him. A real marriage.

But she was too afraid to say it out loud. Not now that he had the power to crush her with his rejection.

Refusing to turn back to see Dean lying naked in the bed where they'd just made love for the last time, she slipped out into the hall before she could say anything she'd regret.

If she told him her true feelings, he would have to tell her his. And everything he'd done or said from their first meeting on the boardwalk had made it clear that all he wanted was to get back to the life he'd had before her.

He wouldn't want to hurt her, but if she confessed her feelings and asked for a chance at a true marriage, that is exactly what he'd have to do. Because he didn't want her. He had never wanted her.

God, she was such a fool to let her heart get so tangled up in him.

Once in her own bedroom, she gathered a change of clothes. The house was quiet, suggesting that the Kincaids were still abed, but she likely only had a short time to wash up and put herself back to rights before the house became active.

She paused in front of her window, where she'd sat so many times gazing out over the unfamiliar landscape. It was not so unfamiliar anymore. The morning sun bathed everything in golden light, but she couldn't see past her reflection in the glass. Though her image was faint, Courtney could easily see the shadow of heartbreak in her eyes and the trembling of her lips.

Seeing her own despair brought on a rush of deeper emotion. She made a momentary effort to hide what she was feeling, to tuck it away as her mother had taught her.

But the mask no longer fit.

With a rush of courage, she allowed herself to feel it all. The pain and sadness. But also the newfound strength and courage. Intentionally acknowledging everything inside her brought a sense of calm and purpose.

She would get through this.

It wasn't so long ago that she'd left behind the

only life she'd ever known. She could certainly leave Lawton Ranch with some semblance of dignity.

Even though the two events were nothing alike.

She hadn't loved Geoffrey when she'd fled the church on her wedding day. She had simply been disappointed by the loss of an imaginary future. This time, she had to walk away from a man she loved with all her heart.

She had come out west to discover herself and to challenge herself. She'd done both, and she was proud of what she'd learned in the last few weeks.

It had never been her choice to become the bride of a cowboy, but if given the chance to do it all again, she'd choose Dean over and over.

Dean, however, would always choose his duty to the ranch.

There was nothing she could do about that. The only choice left to her was to move on.

THIRTY-SEVEN

Dean paused beneath the hot summer sun to drag in some deep breaths before he walked over to get a quick drink from the bucket of water he'd set by one of the arena fence posts. He'd been working all day with a new gelding they'd acquired, readying the horse for the vigorous requirements of life on the range, and they both deserved a short break.

The hard work and the mid-August heat compounded to a miserable degree, but Dean welcomed the physical discomfort and mental stress. It kept him from thinking of other things.

From wanting other things.

It had been three weeks since Courtney had ridden away with the Kincaids. Things should have returned to normal by now, but that was not the case.

Jimena had started coming back to the house to cook, but Randall had been doing more and more of the work Dean used to do. Dean allowed it because he knew his brother wanted to stay close to Pilar and little Emilio, but the truth was that Randall was doing a fine job with the administrative tasks. That allowed Dean to spend more time out on horseback, which was the only time he felt he could breathe.

He glanced back at the house and immediately thought of the last time he'd seen her.

After that morning in his bedroom, he'd dressed and gone out to the barn. He hadn't known what to say to her when everything inside him was resisting the truth he hadn't been able to deny.

As he suspected, she hadn't wasted any time in getting ready to leave. He'd hung back, out of sight, while the three of them mounted their horses. Courtney was on Gwen, the mare she'd come to favor during their lessons. He would have gifted the horse to her if he'd had the courage to talk to her. But she'd ended up sending the horse back, only needing it to get to town, where she must have purchased or rented another horse to get her the rest of the way to Helena.

He'd thought watching her ride away that day was the hardest thing he'd ever had to do.

He'd been dead wrong.

Every day since had gotten worse. Just getting up in the morning had become a form of torture. Everywhere he went on the ranch that had been his home and pride from the time he'd been a small boy seemed to be missing something vital.

Her.

Plain and simple, the place was missing Courtney.

He was pathetic. Pathetic and stupid.

Realizing it was too hot to continue working the gelding, he took the horse back to the barn for a good brushing, some water, and well-earned grain.

As he strode back across the yard toward his empty

house, he heard the approach of a horse and rider. He knew without turning around who it was. He was almost shocked it had taken this long for Randall to insert his nose into Dean's business.

Not bothering to stop, Dean continued his long stride. He made it to the house just as Randall pulled his horse up to the hitching rail out front.

"Hiya, Brother. You look like you've just been dragged behind a horse."

Dean ascended the steps up to the porch, craving the bit of shade it provided, before he turned back to Randall. "I was working the gelding."

"It's hotter than blazes out here."

"Which is why I stopped," Dean replied curtly. "Now, have you got something important to say, or did you just ride over to annoy me?"

Randall grinned. "You do know how I love to annoy you, Big Brother."

Dean gave a rough snort but didn't reply. Randall wouldn't go anywhere until he'd said his piece. The sooner he got to it, the sooner it'd be over.

But the other man didn't seem to be in much of a hurry.

Randall swung down from his horse and strode over to take a seat on the porch steps. "The jury found Hayes guilty. He's to be hung."

Dean felt a small jolt of pity for the man who'd loved Anne so much he'd felt compelled to exact revenge for her death. But then he recalled how Hayes had tried to take Courtney, and all sympathy passed.

"Pilar and Emilio are doing well, if you were wondering. That boy is one good eater."

Dean *had* been wondering and he was happy for his brother and his family, but Randall likely knew that. His brother was far more astute than he often let on.

"You know," Randall said, turning to glance at Dean, "you could come around to visit sometime."

"I know."

"Or maybe we should all come by for supper one night like we used to. Maybe tonight."

"Tonight isn't good."

"You can't hole up over here forever."

"I ain't holed up. I've just got work to do."

"Bullshit."

Dean gave his brother a hard look and waited. Randall didn't disappoint.

"When the hell are you gonna go after her and bring her back?"

Every muscle in Dean's body tensed. He'd thought he was prepared for this conversation. He wasn't. He could barely think of her without feeling like he was falling apart. How the hell was he gonna talk about her? "I'm not."

"Then you're even dumber than I thought. And too damn proud and stubborn for your own good."

Dean clenched his teeth and glanced out over the yard toward the road. He couldn't think of how many times he'd looked down that road over the last few weeks. He wasn't sure if he was looking for signs of someone coming, or if he was imagining himself leaving.

"She didn't want to stay," he finally replied.

"Bullshit."

Dean looked at his brother, anger rushing through him. "If she'd wanted to stay, then why didn't she? She came from finer things, Randall, just like Mother."

Randall shoved to his feet, his expression one of exasperation. "You've gotta be kidding me. Courtney is nothing like Mother."

"How would you know? You don't even remember her."

Randall paused at that, and the two brothers stared hard at each other. Finally, the younger man glanced down before replying, "And I'm damn glad for it too. I wish you'd find a way to forget. Mother's leaving has been a yoke around your neck for way too long." He stepped up to Dean, his blue eyes hard and serious. "Now you listen to me good, Big Brother, because I figure I'll only say this once. Dad died, and our mother left. It happened. It's over. Granddad made sure you knew how to take care of this ranch, and you've been doing a fine job of it. But you've run your personal life like shit."

Dean started to turn away. He didn't need to listen to this. But Randall caught his arm in a fierce grip. Dean glared at him, but his brother was determined. If Dean didn't want to send a fist into Randall's face, he'd have to stand there and hear him out. He ground his teeth and waited for Randall to continue.

"You never loved Anne, and that's the truth."

A growl rumbled in Dean's chest as his hands formed into fists.

"It's true," Randal insisted with a stiff jaw. "You didn't love her like you should have to marry her. She was like a sister to both of us. You only wanted to marry her because that's what Granddad wanted and because it was convenient. And she knew it."

Dean jerked his arm out of Randall's grip and turned away. Years of guilt and anger and fury over the unfairness of life and death pushed through his veins, making him feel like he was on fire.

It was true. All of it.

He strode to the far end of the porch. He considered leaping over the rail and walking away. Away from Randall, the ranch, and all the mistakes he'd made since becoming his own man.

"It was different with Courtney, wasn't it?"

Randall's quiet words hit Dean harder than shouting could have.

Because that was true as well.

Everything had been different with Courtney. Life had been different. Better. He had been better. Content. Challenged. Fulfilled.

And now he felt...broken. Lost and half a man.

"Doesn't matter," he muttered as he gripped the porch railing in both hands, his grip so tight he could feel splinters jabbing into his palms.

"Of course it does, you dumbass. Go after her."

Dean turned to face his brother. The fear was too much to keep hidden. "What if she doesn't feel the same? What if she doesn't come back? What if she only stays for a while before she decides this life isn't for her and she walks away?"

He'd been devastated—wrecked—the day his mother chose a life of comfort over her sons. Even Anne had chosen someone other than him.

What if he asked Courtney to choose him and she couldn't?

"Yeah, maybe that could happen. Bad things happen all the time. But if you don't even try, you'll never get the chance to see the *good* that could happen too. What if she loves you and comes back to stay forever?" Randall countered. "Be bold, Brother. Isn't she worth the risk?"

His brother's words hit Dean square in the chest, shocking him with the sudden clarity they invoked.

He'd never been a man to take risks. He'd always preferred to maintain the status quo, especially if he had something to lose.

But where did that get him?

Sure, he could stay here—miserable and empty—believing she didn't want him. Or he could go out and try to convince her otherwise.

Even if she broke his heart in two, it couldn't be much worse than how he felt right now, missing her, longing for her, loving her. And if she didn't love him back...if she couldn't fathom living out her days as his wife...well, he'd deal with that as it came.

At least he'd know for sure.

THIRTY-EIGHT

COURTNEY STOOD ALONG THE WALL OF THE GRAND ballroom housing the elaborate yet intimate party gathered to belatedly celebrate the unexpected marriage of Mr. Geoffrey Cabot and the former Miss Margaret Flaherty. The elopement of the young couple had come as a shock to just about everyone in Boston's highest social circles, causing a scandal that wasn't likely to blow over for some time to come.

But Geoffrey didn't seem to care.

Courtney's former fiancé displayed an attitude that appeared to embrace a new sense of rebellion and independence. In that vein, he had thrown a grand ball, inviting all of his family's connections and his wife's family to partake of the revelry.

Courtney had written to Geoffrey shortly after reaching Helena, providing her congratulations on his wedding and assuring him of her continued friendship. When he wrote back within a week to advise her of his plan to introduce his bride to Boston society and asked if she would be willing to attend the event as his friend, she'd accepted.

It was not an easy decision, but Courtney felt it was a necessary one. Not only to show her support for a lifelong friend, but also to face her family and accept responsibility for whatever consequences had befallen them after she'd fled the city all those weeks ago. She owed it to her parents and younger siblings to try to make amends for her hasty actions on the day of her wedding.

Her reunion with her parents had gone mostly as she expected. Tense, distant, reproachful. They hadn't been interested in hearing of her experiences out west, and she wasn't particularly inclined toward sharing. In not so many words, they'd stated that they would allow her to stay with them until the spectacle of Geoffrey's wedding had passed, but that Boston would not be welcoming her back on a permanent basis.

She had burned that bridge to the ground with her impulsive decision to run away.

That was fine by Courtney. She had no plan to stay in Boston for long.

After leaving Lawton Ranch, she had settled for a brief stay with Alexandra at her father's spread outside Helena. But she'd realized quickly that she couldn't remain there for long. Even the Kincaids were only visiting for the summer and would be off again on another trek across the territories by fall, this time heading south to Colorado. According to Alexandra, they eventually planned to settle down somewhere. Malcolm had been offered a couple of sheriff positions over the last year, but for now they were enjoying an extended honeymoon of exploration and adventure.

Courtney's skills with a needle had improved while

she'd assisted Pilar with the baby's clothes, and she hoped to find a shop in Helena willing to pay her for the skill. It would be a start, at least, toward her goal of living more independently.

Helena was a beautiful, growing town, nestled at the base of the awe-inspiring Rocky Mountain range. There were shops and restaurants and a theater. If it lacked the grand prairie vistas Courtney had recently grown accustomed to, at least it was still in Montana… even if it was almost a hundred miles from where she'd left her heart.

She was surprised to learn that her parents had decided to attend Geoffrey's party as well, but she soon realized what a buzz he'd created in town by so openly rebelling against the social conventions so many of them adhered to like a lifeline. He'd become a novelty, and no one wanted to miss out on the spectacle of the year—even if they all stood about with pinched faces and disapproving gazes.

Courtney found it rather amusing from her current position along the wall. She had been watching everything with an odd sense of displacement and wondered how she'd ever felt at home amongst the quietly reserved members of Geoffrey's set. She much preferred the more relaxed and open nature of the bride's people, who weren't afraid to show their joy in celebration of a true love match.

Courtney almost felt a desire to join them, but she did not want to draw any unnecessary attention to herself. After all, she was the prior fiancée who had jilted the groom not too long ago. Though all outward focus was on the newlyweds, nothing could stop the covert glances from sliding Courtney's way. Curious, sneering, and judgmental.

It was all she could do not to smile in response to their narrow views.

She had discovered how little such opinions mattered. They did not know how it felt to ride through the wide-open Montana prairie with the summer breeze carrying the scent of wildflowers and the sky so big and beautiful above.

She didn't belong here in these tight, elegant spaces with these self-contained people who rarely knew what it was to live to the fullest. Though she was dressed again in a corset and layers of silks and lace, with her hair done up in elaborate fashion, underneath it all, she longed for the freedom and comfort of a simple cotton frock.

The only thing that might have made this visit more tolerable would have been Evie. But her friend had recently married and was off on her honeymoon to New York City. Courtney wished she had been able to attend her old friend's wedding, but her presence had not been welcomed by the groom's family. Though Evie's last letter had despaired of not having her two closest friends at such an auspicious moment in her life, she had never been one to willfully dispute the dictates of her family or society.

Courtney considered staying in Boston until her friend returned, so they could have a more private reunion, but she already longed to be back in Montana.

She longed for far more than that, but at least she'd be able to breathe again.

The musicians started a waltz, and Geoffrey led his

smiling bride to the dance floor. The couple gazed at each other as though the rest of the world had disappeared, and Courtney realized that neither of them cared one little bit whether their marriage was accepted by all these people. They would be happy regardless.

She truly wished them well.

Looking around, she wondered how long she would have to stay. Perhaps only another moment more. She'd paid her respects and displayed her support to the bride and groom; surely no one would expect her to stay and dance the night away. Her mother and father would feel it necessary to stay the required length of time dictated by proper manners, but she did not have to abide by such conventions.

Not anymore.

As she debated whether she should let her parents know she was leaving, she noticed something odd. A twitter of awkward curiosity was spreading through the room as people stopped in midconversation to twist around for a better look at the main entrance.

Whispers wondering at the identity of a late-arriving gentleman drifted within Courtney's hearing. Now would be the perfect time to slip away, while so much attention was directed toward this newcomer.

More whispers swirled.

Not from Boston.

Not from anywhere around here.

Clearly from that wild land to the far west.

Courtney tensed with a rush of yearning. Obviously, whoever they were talking about wouldn't be Dean, but it didn't stop her from picturing just that.

She smiled at the thought of her husband (and she

still thought of him as such, even though she'd signed the divorce papers before leaving Montana), dressed in dusty denim and scuffed boots with his shirtsleeves rolled up and his hat tipped forward to shield his face from the glaring gas lighting.

Her plans for a discreet exit stalled when she saw Geoffrey and his bride making their way through the crowd, presumably to greet the mysterious guest. People shifted in their wake, attempting to gain a better view.

Whoever the gentleman was, Courtney hoped he enjoyed all the attention he was gathering because it didn't appear that the stir of his appearance was going to die down.

A moment later, the press near the entrance opened up to reveal the sight of the newly wedded couple heading straight toward Courtney. Beside them, dressed in a fine charcoal-gray suit with a black vest over a snow-white shirt and a brand-new black cowboy hat, strode Dean.

Courtney's breath stopped. Her heart stopped. Time and the rotation of the earth stopped as she watched Dean Lawton walk toward her across the ballroom, as elegant as any gentleman she'd ever seen and a hundred times more handsome than he had a right to be.

She noted the tension in his face. His spine was stiff and straight, preventing his usual purposeful swagger, and he kept his eyes focused on her as though he wished he could make the rest of the room disappear. She had never seen him so uncomfortable and out of his element.

Though she soaked up the sight of him like a woman starving, she made no move to meet them. Her legs were far too weak to manage anything beyond a locking of knees to keep herself upright.

Why was he here?

Had there been an issue with the divorce filing?

She couldn't imagine any other reason why he would bother to travel all the way to Boston, let alone walk into a crowded ballroom for what appeared to be the sole purpose of seeking her out.

As the trio reached her, Geoffrey spoke with a noted look of concern in his eyes. "This gentleman says he would like to speak with you. If you wish, I will have him escorted off the premises immediately."

Only then did Courtney see that two large servants had followed them across the room and stood back a few steps, awaiting further instruction.

"No," she replied quickly. "It is all right."

"He claims to be your husband," Geoffrey added in a lowered tone, a note of shock and disbelief in his voice.

Courtney's gaze flickered to Dean's face, but his expression was unreadable. Looking back to her old friend, she replied, "There is no need for concern. Please feel free to return to your other guests."

After passing a long glance over Dean, Geoffrey stepped back and slipped his arm around his bride's waist. "Remember, you are among friends," he assured Courtney before turning away.

And then it was just the two of then standing along the wall.

Though Courtney suspected they were still objects

of countless curious stares, she had no problem ignoring them all.

Dean stepped closer but did not reach out to touch her. She tried not to think about how badly she wanted him to, but it was impossible. His presence ignited the air around her. He lowered his chin and sent his warm gaze over her in a sweeping, hungry glance.

Heat and confusion consumed her. She could have hid all she was thinking and feeling behind that old familiar mask. But she preferred to live more honestly these days. Needing to say something, she asked, "Is there an issue with the divorce? I signed the papers and sent them back to Judge Wilkerson."

"The divorce went through without a hitch," he replied, the words heavy and rough.

"Then why are you here?"

"Why are *you* here?" he asked in return, bringing his chin up just enough to gaze at her from beneath a heavy brow.

Her stomach tightened. "My, ah, former fiancé has married. I am here to offer my support."

Never taking his eyes off her, he asked quietly, "And who is here to support you?"

He had noticed her wallflower status. She tilted her mouth into a slight smile, feeling no shame in her changed circumstances. "I have discovered that I am quite capable of supporting myself."

He gave a short nod. "Yes, you are. You always have been."

There was pride in his voice, and the warmth of it traveled down Courtney's spine, softening her posture. She tipped her head. "You haven't answered my question, Dean. What brought you all the way across the country?"

"You."

One word, spoken in perfect confidence.

A light flickered inside her. A light she quickly tried to dampen before it brightened to full hope. He did not mean what her heart heard.

With a subtle jerk of his chin, he asked, "Dance with me?"

Courtney hadn't even realized the musicians had started up again and were playing a waltz. She looked at Dean, her eyes wide with the surprise she couldn't manage to hide just then. "Now? Here?" she sputtered.

His lips twitched. "Here and now, princess."

He offered his hand and waited.

Without conscious direction, she laid her palm in his. She'd never relied on proper thought when it came to Dean Lawton. Instinct seemed to come to the fore instead, and right now, everything in her yearned to be in his arms.

Though some of the guests still watched them with open curiosity, many others had decided to get on with the party, and the dance floor was starting to fill up again with swirling couples.

Dean led her to the edge of the dancers and turned to take up the proper position. The feel of his large, capable hand at her back nearly made Courtney sigh, but she still somehow retained enough control to hold it back. Laying her hand on his shoulder, she reveled in the way her other hand was held so securely in his.

When, after a few moments, he didn't move to start the dance, she lifted a brow in question.

His expression was stern while his eyes reflected more than the light overhead. "I should've danced with you around the bonfire that night." His hand on her back tensed, drawing her an inch closer. "I should have kissed you under the stars every chance I got." Another inch closer. "I should've brought you flowers every day and taken you for fancy dinners in town." Another inch.

Courtney's skirts swept against his legs. Her lifted, corseted breasts were a breath away from his chest, and her lungs felt tight within the confining stays. But she didn't protest or resist his improper direction. She was too lost in the movement of his mouth as he murmured the soft words that went straight through her center and made her skin tingle.

"I shouldn't have let you go, Courtney."

Drawing her body flush against his, he stepped into the waltz with a grand, sweeping stride that pulled a gasp from her lips. There was no chance to reestablish the proper distance between them. It was all she could do to hold on and surrender to his lead. Though it was not quite the vigorous, animated dancing she'd enjoyed with the Lawton ranch hands, Dean's style of waltzing was still far more robust than what the Boston elite was accustomed to. In a word, it was perfect.

So she ignored the disapproving looks flying by in her peripheral vision and kept her gaze locked on Dean's face. His handsome, proud, resistant, wonderful face.

Except that he didn't appear so resistant tonight. Certainly not in that moment as his eyes traveled freely over her, pausing over every detail until he reached her mouth. And there he stopped. His eyes sparkled with a familiar light, making Courtney's knees weak.

"Why are you here, Dean?" she asked again.

The question caused a slight stiffening in his body, just a bit across the shoulders, but it transferred down his arms and passed through to her, where their palms were matched, and his hand pressed to her back in what seemed to be an involuntary attempt at holding her tighter.

"Is there someplace we can go to get away from all these people?"

"There is a small parlor through that door," she said with a nod toward the back of the ballroom. "But it might be occupied."

"I'll make it work," he muttered as he abruptly shifted his hold on her to start walking her directly across the room toward the door in question.

The stares were revived by the rude intersection through the still-active dancers.

"We could have gone around everyone or waited until the dance was over," Courtney noted with a curl to her lips.

"I don't wanna wait any longer," he said, casting her a look from stormy, blue eyes. "I've already waited all my life."

THIRTY-NINE

Dean didn't even try to take a more measured stride when what he really wanted to do was toss Courtney over his shoulder and bolt into the private room so he could lock everyone out but the two of them.

Judging by all the stares he'd gotten since arriving at the fancy mansion, he figured he'd broken at least a dozen etiquette rules already. He didn't care much, other than hating having everyone's eyes on him, but these were Courtney's people, and she might not take too kindly to such a crude display.

As they stepped into the little parlor, it was to find two couples seated in conversation. They looked up at Dean and Courtney's sudden appearance. Their voices trailed off and their eyes went wide as Dean continued into the room with purposeful steps, sweeping Courtney along beside him.

"Pardon the intrusion, folks," he said with a nod. "Might I ask you to leave the room for a bit? I'd like a private word with the lady."

He thought he heard Courtney make a small sound,

but he didn't shift his gaze from those he was talking to, silently urging them to their feet.

The room's current occupants glanced at one another curiously, none of them making an immediate move to depart. One of the gentlemen looked outright mutinous, while the others simply appeared too shocked and confused by the request to respond.

"Look," Dean said, growing impatient. "I haven't seen my wife in over a month. I'm sure you can understand how we'd like a moment alone."

One of the ladies finally tapped her companion's arm and gave him a look. They rose to their feet, and the other couple followed suit.

"Of course," the lady said with a gracious nod before turning to Courtney. "You will let us know this time if you decide to leave town, dear?"

"Yes, Mother," Courtney replied.

Dean's entire body froze. He glanced at the lady leading the group from the room and noticed belatedly the slight resemblance to his wife in her slim form and graceful movements. The gentleman who followed her, however, sent him a striking, green-eyed glare similar to those Dean had received from Courtney in the early days of their marriage. The other couple kept their gazes trained forward as they passed. Dean didn't move until he heard the click of the door shutting behind him.

"I suppose that wasn't well done of me," he admitted.

"On the contrary, it was perfect," Courtney replied. "I swear, I have never seen my mother at a loss for words. It was a pure delight."

The laughter in her voice warmed him from the inside.

Damn, how he'd missed her.

Turning toward her, he resisted the urge to pull her into his arms. Being so close to her again, seeing the light in her eyes and the curve of her lips, breathing in her soft, female scent—it made him tremble with everything going on inside him. The hope and fear, the joy and reckless desire.

He wanted to tumble her down onto the nearest sofa and show her how badly he'd missed her. But he had some things he needed to say first, and if he touched her as he wanted to, he'd never get the words out.

"I've been a jackass, Courtney," he stated bluntly. Her eyes widened at the declaration, but she didn't refute the statement. "From the very start."

He swept his hat off his head, belatedly realizing he probably should have removed it when he'd first entered the party. Tossing his hat to the sofa beside him, he shoved his hand back through his hair. After a ragged breath, he charged forward.

"When we were first married, we agreed to part ways as soon as possible."

She stiffened. "Yes, I recall," she replied, and in her tone he heard the same sadness and regret that echoed inside him.

"I was certain that a fine city lady like you wouldn't last out the day, let alone four weeks, without a load of complaints."

She tilted her head at a proud angle. "I think I managed all right."

Dean took an impulsive step toward her. "More than all right. You're an amazing woman, Courtney

Lawton. I've never known anyone to take such rotten circumstances and turn them to your favor. No matter what challenge was in front of you, you faced it with a smile and forged ahead bravely."

"Do not get me wrong, I adore hearing you extol my virtues," she said with a rueful smile, "but why are you saying this now? You filed for divorce, Dean. You didn't want me."

He saw the hurt in her eyes and made a silent vow to sweep it away forever.

"I did want you, Courtney. I swear on everything I hold dear, I wanted you."

A furrow formed between her brows, breaking up the smooth planes of her face. "Then why didn't you tell me?"

Dean dropped his gaze. "That day your friend arrived"—he paused to lift his eyes back to hers—"I heard you telling her that one way or another, you wanted our marriage to end."

"No," Courtney said urgently, stepping toward him. "I *expected* it to end. I didn't want it to, but everything you'd ever said to me made me believe it was what *you* wanted. And then you convinced Wilkerson to allow the divorce. What was I to think?"

"That I'm a damn fool."

Dean sighed, heavily and deeply, as he brought his hands to her trim waist and finally drew her in against him. He was encouraged when she didn't resist; rather, she seemed to melt against him in the most wonderful way. "From the moment I met you," he continued roughly, "I convinced myself you were too much like my mother. She didn't stay. She'd tried, but as soon as things got too tough, she took off, leaving me and Randall without a backward glance. She chose a comfortable life over us. Even Anne didn't choose me in the end. I couldn't fathom that you would."

Courtney opened her mouth to reply, but he shook his head. "Naw, let me finish." He took a deep breath to try to expel the pressure that been building inside him for way too long. "I told myself you'd leave me like they had. I needed to believe it. It was the only thing keeping me from begging you to stay. Because somewhere along the way, I fell so deep in love with you that I didn't seem to know up from down anymore. I figured that in getting that divorce, I was saving myself from heartbreak." He sighed, and his lips tilted with self-deprecation. "But my heart broke anyway the day you rode away."

She laid her hand softly against the side of his face and whispered his name. "Dean."

Doubling his arms around her waist, he looked into her shining eyes. "I'm so sorry I chased you away."

She sighed, sliding her hand up the back of his neck. "I'm just glad you're here now. I missed you, Dean. Terribly," she whispered as she rose onto her toes to press a kiss to the corner of his mouth.

The sweet female scent of her surrounded him, fanning those flames deep inside where his love for her burned unheeded.

With a shaky breath, he stepped back, fully releasing her to lower himself to one knee. Pulling out the ring that was burning a hole through his breast pocket, he lifted it toward her.

"Courtney Adams Lawton, will you do me the

greatest honor of my life and allow me to love you for the rest of my days? We can make a home here in Boston, if that's what you want. Randall will get the hang of things at the ranch eventually. He's been doing fine enough so far. I just can't imagine going on another day without you." He dragged in a harsh breath. "You have a choice this time. Won't you choose me and say you'll be my bride?"

She glanced at the ring, then back to his face. Her silence caused sweat to bead beneath the snug fit of his collar. Emotion swirled in her gaze. The hope and love he saw there was humbling.

"You would give up the ranch for me?" she asked in a quiet whisper.

Dean answered readily. "If that's what it takes."

She gently grasped his face in her hands, urging him to his feet. When she spoke, her voice was husky with emotion. "I would never want you to do that. You belong in Montana, riding across the prairie under that big, blue sky." Her lips tilted upward. "And so do I. The ranch is my home too. I may have signed those divorce papers, but I never stopped being your wife, Dean. I love you, and I want nothing more than to marry you. Again," she added with a smile.

Relief and so much more flooded through him as he took her hand to slide the ring onto her slim finger. Then he swept her up in his arms and kissed her full and hard on the mouth before spinning her around in a whirl of silk and lace.

Her laughter filled the room and every lonely, shadowed space that might have been left inside him.